TROUBLE IN THE RUINS

BOOK THREE OF
THE STONES OF GILGAL

TROUBLE
IN THE RUINS

BOOK THREE OF
THE STONES OF GILGAL

C. L. SMITH

MOUNTAIN VIEW PRESS

Published by Mountain View Press, www.mountainviewpress.com, Toll Free (855) 946-2555.

Mountain View Press is honored to present this title in partnership with the author. The views expressed or implied in this work are those of the author. Mountain View Press provides our imprint seal representing design excellence, creative content and high quality production.

Other scripture quotations, unless otherwise noted, are taken from *The Holy Bible, New International Version*®, *NIV*® Copyright ©1973, 1978, 1984, 2011 by Biblica, Inc.® Used by permission. All rights reserved worldwide.

Scriptures marked WEB are taken from THE WORLD ENGLISH BIBLE (WEB): WORLD ENGLISH BIBLE, public domain.

Scripture quotations marked (GNT) are from the Good News Translation—Second Edition © 1992 by American Bible Society. Used by Permission.

ISBN 13: 978-1-68314-860-9
ePub ISBN: 978-1-68314-861-6
Kindle ISBN: 978-1-68314-862-3
Library of Congress Catalog Card Number: 2019902438

DEDICATION

To my brothers—a priceless gift of belonging and family roots

To Jim, the close companion of my childhood who passed away in 1994. Before a word of the Stones of Gilgal saga was written, Jim gave me a book on the culture of ancient Canaan and encouraged me make my story idea a reality.

To Gary and John, two previously unknown brothers who were adopted out at birth. In an astonishing and delightful twist to my life story, they discovered me and each other in 2017. Although each man is a unique and wonderful person, I frequently catch glimpses of Jim, my mother, and a favorite aunt in their expressions and gestures. My cup overflows with brotherly love.

CONTENTS

ACKNOWLEDGMENTS

I want to begin by thanking the many friends and readers who have encouraged my writing. I feel honored and honestly humbled. The accolades of friends might be expected, but a number of perfect strangers made the effort to find my contact information, then followed through with an enthusiastic call or note. One such note read: "How you could make a story that is thousands of years old come alive is beyond me. The people were drawn with such realism they seemed like neighbors or family." Those words touched a chord in me. My characters seem more like another set of children than fictional creations. Some days I can hardly wait to get my fingers on my keyboard to see what they will do next.

I want to thank the publishing team at Mountain View Press (Redemption Press). The talented Marcus Park sets the mood for *Trouble in the Ruins* with another fabulous cover painting. Graphic designer, Zac Calbert, updated the close-up insert for the map, hand-drawn for my first book by Marjorie Moran. My sister-in-law, Heather Smith, organized and formatted my list of characters. These competent behind-the-scenes people helped transform my manuscript into a beautiful book. Thank you all.

Above all, I am thankful for the loving assistance and insistence of my own family during this entire writing venture—especially my husband Eden, the greatest encourager of my life. Since finding my "new brothers," I have thought a lot about the importance of family and realize more than ever how Eden's love and stability over the years have helped repair the damage caused by my fractured birth family.

Thank you, also to my children Eden III, Melissa, Melinda, Michelle and their families. You mean the world to me. Not only are they each making a positive difference in the world, but their critiques and encouragements have improved each of my books.

Trouble in the Ruins is a book about belonging, the bonds connecting members of a community who live and worship together. It's about friends helping each other face troubles of all kinds, and outsiders struggling to find belonging. Fortunately, Rahab the Canaanite refugee did not have to face her post-rescue transition into a foreign culture alone. The ancient text does not tell us anything about her parents and siblings, but they must have been remarkable people—the only family in Jericho who didn't cling to the prevailing fear and hatred of Israel, the only family willing to humbly accept the demonstrated superiority of Israel's God.

As I write of family and belonging, I feel a pang of sorrow for those reading this from a place of loss or abandonment. There are no easy answers for the pain and loneliness in our world, but I can tell you with absolute certainty that God is immeasurably wiser and more compassionate than any human being. His ways are higher than our ways. His desire is to make you (and others influenced by your story) "mature and complete, not lacking anything" (James 1:2–4).

> *Sing to God, sing in praise of his name,*
> *extol him who rides on the clouds;*
> *rejoice before him—his name is the LORD.*
> *A father to the fatherless, a defender of widows,*
> *is God in his holy dwelling.*
> *God sets the lonely in families,*
> *he leads out the prisoners with singing;*
> *but the rebellious live in a sun-scorched land.*
> *(Psalms 68:4–6)*

PROLOGUE

I will make the Valley of Achor
a Door of Hope.
My people will respond to me there
with singing and dancing
as they did on the day when I led them out of Egypt.
—Hosea 2:15, author paraphrase

Abihail

Abihail caught Acsah's eyes over a rumbling river of wool. This was a childhood dream come true. Herding sheep. Together. She and her dearest childhood friend, feet solidly on the Promised Land. And the crossing of the Jordan could not have been more glorious. Like the stories of the Red Sea crossing after her parents left Egypt. Abihail hummed the melody of Miriam's victory song while scores of little hooves pounded the triumphant rhythm into Canaan soil.

Who among the gods is like you, Yahweh?
Who is like you—
Majestic in holiness,
awesome in glory,
working wonders?[1]

It was an old song, but everything else was new. It was Abib. The first month of a new year. A new start. A new land. She breathed in the earthy-sweet fragrance of freshly cut wood and smiled at the memory of her husband working side by side with Caleb, building a sturdy new enclosure for their combined flocks. Like father and son. For as long as she could remember, she and Acsah had been as close as sisters. Now, Acsah's father embraced her and Eliab as family. New family . . .

1

Did she dare hope? New family in both directions. That would be the best *new* of all. New life in her womb. She had not told anyone yet. Not even Eliab. And even now she pushed the dream aside, choosing to enjoy the solid realities of the day. Even Yahweh's covenant with Israel was beginning anew after the forty-year training in the wilderness. The men were newly dedicated to the covenant by circumcision this very day. And on the fourteenth day of Abib, Israel would celebrate Passover for the first time since Sinai. The annual cycle of feasts beginning anew.

She began singing Miriam's song aloud.

> *The people of Canaan will melt away.*
> *Terror and dread will fall on them—*
> Baa . . . baa

Abihail laughed at the throaty obbligato. Old song, new embellishment. Even the sheep were excited about their new home.

> *By the power of your arm*
> *they will be as still as a stone—*
> Baa . . . baa
> *until your people pass by, LORD,*
> Baa . . . baa
> *until the people you redeemed pass by.*
> Baa baa, baa baa

"Hey, hey, Naggai," Acsah crooned to the fat ewe waddling into the sheep pen. "I expected you to be coming in with twins this evening."

"Naggai?" Abihail's attention snapped back to the task at hand. "How did I miss the signs? Her udder is definitely filling. In here, old girl, where we can check on you." She diverted the pregnant ewe from the larger enclosure to the birthing pen adjoined to the side.

"Don't worry about getting up, Acsah. Get your rest tonight. I will come back to check on them by myself. All three of these old girls have done this before."

"I don't think so. How could I sleep knowing Naggai might have unexpected trouble? The possibility of losing our childhood playmate just when she arrived at the pastures of her dreams would give me Promised Land nightmares."

Abihail giggled. "I wonder if *she* remembers our Promised Land dramas."

Acsah caught her eyes with intense scrutiny. "In all our dramatic plots and plans of Canaan, we never even dreamed of such productivity, did we?"

Did Acsah just scan my abdomen in search of a bump? "All these new lambs?" she asked innocently.

"And kids and calves," Acsah added with an enigmatic smile. "It is as if the grass or the air in this valley breeds fertility." The quick lift of her brows said more than her next words. "I suspect we'll see a bumper crop of human babies in the next few months too."

"Flocks and herds *and* people benefit when they follow the Shepherd of Israel," Abihail responded quickly. She launched into the victory song again.

> *In your unfailing love you will lead—*
> Baa!
> *the people you have redeemed.*
> Baa! Baa, baa, baa!
> *In your strength—*
> Baa, baa!

"Hodevah! How can I sing?" she scolded with a laugh. "You are off key and not keeping time."

> Baa! Baa! Baa!

Acsah bit her lip as the plaintive bleating continued. "My father chose Hodevah's yearling for the Passover feast. She is still looking for him."

Abihail lovingly patted the grieving mother as she followed the others into the fold. They had been blessed with half a dozen newborns in the one day since crossing the river, but that did not make losing one sheep any easier. Hannah, the next ewe, nosed through the gate with an adorable, hours-old lambkin following close behind. Abihail reached out, brushing Hannah's wooly back just as the gangly little one broke line. Before she could think to react, Acsah hooked the lamb with her toe, aborting the exuberant leap for freedom.

"Quick footwork!" Abihail scooped the lamb up in her arms and nuzzled the fuzzy head with her nose. "You are too cute, little girl. We refuse to lose you to the wolves of Canaan." She released the lamb at the threshold of the fold, and this time the little one scrambled between her mother's legs, disappearing beneath the jostling wooly mass. "I am so glad most of our sheep waited to give birth on this side of the river. We were able to enjoy the glory of the miracle instead of watching for and arresting scores of breakaways like that during the crossing."

Acsah exaggerated a yawn. "Now it's sheep instead of sleep. Three birthings last night and a string of sleepless nights to come." She ran her eyes down Abihail's abdomen. "But when *you* are ready to deliver . . . I will not bemoan any lack of sleep."

A blush crept hotly from Abihail's neck to her crown. With all her being, she hoped it was true, but she was not ready to voice a hope that might end in disappointment. "I know I have missed my cycles in the women's purification tent ever since I was so sick during the plague," she mumbled. "It doesn't necessarily mean . . ."

Acsah tilted her head and looked at Abihail from the corner of her eye. "Being fruitful and multiplying is in the air here. Don't be surprised if it's twins."

"Don't—" Abihail started to protest.

Acsah's lips stretched in a self-satisfied smile. "And I will come to check on you day or night as needed."

Abihail nudged the last ewe inside the protective palisade. She could not express how desperately she wanted Acsah's prediction to be true. Summoning faith and hope, she shut the sheepfold door with all her strength. The booming crash shook the enclosure, shushing the bleating flock into total silence.

"Oh dear," she whispered, wincing as she slid the lock bar into place. "I hope they won't be too terrified to sleep."

Acsah touched her arm. "Listen."

Abihail leaned into the unnatural hush. It wasn't just their flock silenced. There was no soft lowing and bleating of any neighboring flocks or herds. Not even the sound of birds. She scrunched her face in an exaggerated expression of regret. "I even stopped the evening bird chorus."

"I said *listen*, not blame yourself for the silence. Listen to the rushing sound." Acsah paused again with her eyes focused far away. "It may only be the wind in the trees . . ."

"But it sounds like the Jordan," Abihail breathed. She pictured the *Zor*, the dense thickets of the ravine, mostly submerged by the raging torrent. She could hear the surging water biting at rocks along the margin, pulling up trees and driving them like battering rams against the riverbanks.

Acsah laughed out loud. "God's timing is never what we expect."

"Timing?" Abihail looked at her sideways. *If this conversation was heading toward the topic of childbearing again, she needed to deflect it.* "You mean Caleb and Eliab getting this sheepfold finished before the circumcision?"

"No, silly. We're talking about the river. No one in his right mind would have dared a crossing now—but Joshua did."

"True." Abihail paused thoughtfully. "The victory over Sihon and Og came in such a blaze of glory that we all expected an immediate, victorious march into the Promised Land."

"That timing would have made sense. But one crisis after another . . ." Acsah began ticking them off on her fingers. "The rebellion. The plague. The Midianite War. The death of Moses . . . and then the rain. Not until the flood rose and fords were impassable did God say, *Go*. And Uncle Joshua was listening. He commanded the priests to carry the ark into the middle of the river." She held up a hand, signaling *Halt*, ending her narrative with great drama. "The waters surged and roared in protest, but they obeyed the command of Joshua."

"Joshua *is* amazing. How many men would have had the faith to believe they heard God right as Joshua did?"

"I would never tell my father this, but as much as I admire the heroic spy story of my father and Joshua from forty years ago, Joshua seemed to me a poor substitute for Moses. I don't think any Israelite felt confident about following him across the Jordan into alien territory."

"We were like lost children," Abihail agreed.

"But the miracle changed everything." Acsah's eyes danced with the bold announcement. "A hesitant assistant no longer, Joshua shot into the dark skies of our despair like a comet, the word of the Lord in his mouth as powerful as Moses' rod. We follow a mighty conqueror."

The force of Acsah's words shot through Abihail like lightning, melting and fusing every unstable sand particle of her life into faith as rock-solid as the new gilgal. Taking a deep breath of sweet Canaan air, she lifted one arm, pointing prophetically toward the Valley of Acacias east of the Jordan. "You terrors of the past, your shadows no longer touch us." She pivoted toward the west. "O Canaan, we fear nothing you can throw in our path."

Suddenly a withering, demon-like laugh cackled across the stillness of the evening.

"Only a night bird," Acsah whispered.

"A night bird," Abihail agreed. An icy finger of fear traced down her spine just the same. She clutched Acsah's hand, not letting go until, running and stumbling through the gathering darkness, they arrived safely back at camp.

CHAPTER ONE

PREPARATIONS

Pallu of Gibeon

ow-slung rays of sunlight beamed across the open-air forum, pitching forlorn shadows of empty stone benches across the pavement. Pallu remained
on his seat on the dais along with his three companions. The assembly had ended.
The senate disbanded. Only he and his companions remained. Through many
years, many crises, they had served together as the high elders of the Federation
of Gibeon, but never had this fellowship of four faced anything like this.

Pallu listened to the thunder of scores of donkey hooves pounding away in every
direction, retreating into the distance, fading until they were indistinguishable from
the leafy rustlings of the breeze. "We should follow," he said softly. Or perhaps he only
thought the words for no one answered. No one moved.

In less than an hour, the sun would drop behind the coastal mountains. Although
his own house here in Gibeon was not far, Pallu's companions faced journeys an
hour or more in three different directions through forest and rough terrain—Ibzan
to Kiriath-Baal, Likhi to Beeroth, and Meshullam to Kephirah.

Gibeon and her sister cities crowned the hilltops of central Canaan. Four
glorious cities, well-nourished by springs and bejeweled with pools of water. They
were surrounded by fine forests of cedar and oak, teeming with deer and other wild
game. Fruitful orchards and gardens covered the slopes close to their cities, but it was
the terraced vineyards, luxuriant with grapes year after year, that ensured the great

wealth of the Federation through its wine trade. And, because the Federation had long ago cast off the notion that rule by kings was a desirable state, there was no greedy monarch to impoverish the populace with his extravagant whims. Justice prevailed, more often than not, as the people governed themselves through their assembly of elders. Most importantly, although wars frequently broke out between the scrappy kings surrounding them, peace reigned in Gibeon. The fine combined army of the Federation, undefeated for as long as anyone could remember, was highly respected.

This long senate session had been emotionally draining. But in the end, the assembly voted unanimously against war. Gibeon would seek to negotiate a covenant of peace with Israel and do all in its power to convince the other kings to join them. Couriers with news of their decision were already racing to each of the power centers of Canaan—northward to Hazor, southward to Jebus, and down the eastern slope to Jericho.

But would the kings of Canaan swallow their pride and do the only sane thing? Pallu sighed a deep shuddering breath. Not Nahari. The message was certainly not needed to inform that deranged monarch of the invasion. The Israelites occupied the valley not five miles from the famed walls of Jericho. Prior to the crossing, those ill-equipped desert dwellers defeated every ally King Nahari had on the other side of the river. Then they defeated the floods of the Jordan. A king would be insane to believe he could stand up to them and be victorious. But Nahari was not known for his sanity.

A sense of dread rose in the depths of Pallu's heart. Everything he knew and loved would change if they went to war. "We must not let Nahari start a war with . . ." *The God of Israel,* he started to add, but his mouth was so dry the words refused to slide from his tongue. Fear beyond any he had known in battle rose from deep within, but he willed it back with an audible groan.

Ibzan, the eldest and highest of the high elders, looked at Pallu sharply as if reading his thoughts. "There is absolutely no other explanation for such an extraordinary crossing. It had to be the act of a powerful god."

"A powerful god who promised to give the land of Canaan to the descendants of Jacob," Likhi snapped. "Our land!"

"But their land before it was ours," Meshullam countered, wagging the forefinger of his plump right hand. "It was the inheritance of the descendants of Shem until wrested from them by Canaan's armies."

Ibzan nodded his agreement. "The four-hundred-year-old prophecy given to Abraham. Judgment will fall on Canaan for its overwhelming violence—just as it did on Sodom."

Grief contorted Meshullam's pleasant face. "Will war be our fate in the end?

What say you, Pallu?"

"It will if one of our kings attacks first."

"Exactly the point," Likhi barked. "Too many hot heads and egomaniacs. War is inevitable."

"But our federation has Pallu." Ibzan's right hand clapped the muscles of his shoulder approvingly. "My dear commander, your arguments today were brilliant. The gods blessed you with great wisdom."

Pallu snorted a half laugh. "How fortunate that wisdom attended me *today* rather than at some gathering of lesser importance."

Meshullam chuckled warmly. "Wise words are never rare on your lips, my friend. Every man in Gibeon knows that." The beaming smile was brief, then the round, soft face grew serious once more. "The kings of Canaan will be more difficult to convince, I fear."

"If only we knew the intentions of these people." Ibzan tugged at his whiskers.

"No matter what Israel does next. No matter how powerful the god who brought them here—Jericho will not tolerate their presence," Likhi said brusquely. "Nahari will attack."

"Then I don't see how the rest of us will avoid getting tangled up in it," Meshullam added with a sigh.

"It was difficult enough to quell arguments for a preemptive strike among the younger members of our own assembly this morning," Ibzan said somberly. "A stranger would not have guessed that we are normally negotiators."

"Our spies have seen nothing since the ceremony with the river rocks, erecting that *gilgal* to commemorate the crossing." Meshullam's round eyes brightened with a hopeful gleam. "Since then, Israel has been curiously quiet."

"Surely they intend to claim the inheritance promised to their ancestor, Abraham." Likhi snapped. "Why else would thousands of men of war cross over as a vanguard for the rest of Israel, leaving their women and children alone in the conquered lands across the river?"

"Indeed. Livestock also left behind." Pallu slumped in his chair. The thought was like a fist slamming into his gut. "*Why* would they leave family and wealth unprotected east of the river, unless they plan on war? A war they expect to be sudden and short." He exhaled loudly as if to expel the discouraging thought.

"What if Nahari decides to attack and asks for our aid?" There was a quaver in Meshullam's voice.

"Nahari would never humble himself to do that," Likhi growled.

Pallu leaped from his chair and began pacing. "If he does, we must summarily reject his proposal. A needless attack, a response driven by panic, will certainly bring about our undoing just as it brought the mighty empire of Egypt to her knees forty years ago. We must not let that happen."

The first Gibeonite messenger pressed down the steep, rough road to Jericho all through the night with his urgent message. Dawn was just touching the clouds with rosy fingers of hope when he arrived. The gates were still barred. No sentries in sight.

"Ha-loo," he called loudly.

A crow pecking at a decaying head fastened high beside the gate cawed irritably and flapped off to observe from a nearby palm.

"Ha-loo," he called a second time. "Official message from the Federation of Gibeon."

"It does not matter who you are," a sullen voice from above announced. "We have direct orders from King Nahari. These gates open for no man."

The messenger sighed wearily. There would be no food, no drink, no rest before he made his return trip. "Please deliver Gibeon's message to the king," he called, craning his neck upward.

A movement on the high bridge overhanging the entire span of the gatehouse caught his eye. A lone sentry thirty feet above him, began nocking an arrow menacingly as he peered over the parapet. The courier noted three massacre holes in the floor of the overhead bridge. Picturing a rain of boiling water, fiery coals, or rocks pouring from the one directly over his head, he determined to deliver his message quickly and leave.

"Kindly inform his majesty, King Nahari: The Federation is quite aware of the danger he faces, but we urge restraint. Our elders plan to approach Israel with a proposal of peace within the next few days. War with these people will surely end in disaster for all Canaan."

"We will crush Israel—and we will choose the time," the sentry growled. "Our walls are solid, our supplies sufficient for a long siege, and our gates will hold against any foe."

Two archers pushed their way past the first sentry, aiming their arrows directly at his chest. "We do not need the advice of the cowardly senators of Gibeon," one proclaimed in an official tone.

"Be gone if you value your life," the other snarled. He loosed a warning shot over the messenger's shoulder and quickly pulled a new arrow from his quiver.

The courier dodged to one side, retreating prudently. If he began the long trek up the road toward Gibeon now, he would reach Ai and Luz by late afternoon. Surely one of those towns would join the ranks of reason. Surely, he would find at least one rational king who would welcome Gibeon's warning.

He thought perhaps he had when he was invited to rest on a stone bench within the gatehouse of the small fortress at Ai. When the humorless sentry returned from King Birsha and they exchanged curt diplomatic bows, his hopes rose higher.

"The king himself will see the messenger from Gibeon," the man reported. With a terse "Follow me" and a nod to certain of his companions, he wheeled and left the well-guarded gate. As the courier scurried behind, the tramping of heavy war sandals surrounded him, a unit of four dour guards marching in lockstep beside and behind.

The courier felt more like a prisoner than an emissary from a friendly neighboring nation as the entourage led him through streets bustling with more soldiers. They led him past a marketplace at city center, emptied of commerce and transformed into a bivouac of foot soldiers. Without a word or friendly glance, the guards brought him to a tower at the center of the fortress.

There were no sentries surrounding the doorway to the stark stone structure, but the courier noted a row of openings below the roofline that could be used in the same way as the massacre holes above Jericho's gate. He imagined the king's guards peering down from that high vantage point right now. They would have an excellent view of the ground below in every direction while suffering little risk of being shot by an arrow.

The courier was fairly certain he saw faces watching him now. He tensed as the lead guard rapped twice on the massive oak door with the butt of his spear, half expecting a lethal rock to drop on him. With no spoken response from the interior, no answering raps, the lock bar rattled and chains clanked. The door swung open as if without hands. Two more guards materialized out of the shadows and joined the grim patrol prodding the courier on with their spears. They passed quickly through the thick-beamed portal into the dim interior of the tower, not hesitating until they reached an expanse bathed in the pale light of a high window. The attending guards forced the man from Gibeon to stop ten paces from the throne.

What do they think I have come to do? he wondered as they formed human walls locking him in place, beside and behind. He masked his apprehension with a deep bow before the warrior-king. Six more fierce-faced bodyguards stood behind King Birsha's throne. A tall, thin dignitary robed in black, presumably the king's right-hand man, his *yad rashi*, hovered close to the throne. The king hardly seemed to notice the messenger's arrival, but the hawk-like eyes of the yad never left his.

The messenger of Gibeon waited to be acknowledged, his eyes flicking nervously between the predatory stare of the yad and the king who continued to regard his surroundings absently. The courier stretched his head forward, looking down the line of guards walling him in place on his left and then his right, attempting to catch their eyes and signal openness and honesty. No one made a move to welcome him or signal him to begin.

The long period of silence grew increasingly awkward. At last, he hailed the king with another deep bow. "Your Majesty, forgive me if I address your throne in breach of protocol. I have waited in respect to deliver an important message from Gibeon . . ."

The flat affect of the king did not change until the messenger added, "Regarding Israel."

Instantly, King Birsha's face twisted with fury. "Israel! ISRAEL!" he screeched. He bolted from his throne and began pacing like a leopard trapped in a pit. "How could those people defeat a *river*? Who does that?" The monarch pulled off his helmet-crown and raked his fingers through sweat-matted hair. His lips slavered as he glared at the courier, eyes deranged with hate.

The courier chose his words carefully. "Your Majesty, you command a stout little fortress, a very important post in central Canaan. Gibeon believes that the wisest strategy at this time is to wait. Be prepared, of course, but do not initiate war. Perhaps Israel will be content to remain in the Jordan Valley."

The king did not speak as he paced. Perhaps he was listening. The courier continued. "Spies sent by the senate of Gibeon have been watching Israel closely. They have reported nothing that appears to be preparation for war. We urge restraint. Wait to see what they will do next. Gibeon will send a delegation to them within the next few days proposing a treaty of peace for central Canaan."

The king groaned and slumped into his royal seat. "Why does Jericho not drive them back across the river?"

"May I be so bold as to point out," the messenger ventured hesitantly, "that the arrival of these people has been to our benefit so far. The terrorizing raids of King Og and his Rephaim giants will never trouble us again. No longer must we fear attacks by the rapacious Sihon of Hezbon. You know his intention was always to absorb our kingdoms into his empire."

The king's face had gone blank again. "How are we to eat?" he whimpered. "These foreigners will seize the barley and wheat harvests from the river valley that we depend on."

The courier made several attempts to drive home the point of his message, but the distraught monarch could not seem to comprehend it. Pitiful, shapeless sounds formed in his royal throat and tried to escape, but intelligent dialogue no longer seemed possible.

The flowing black garments of the king's yad rashi rustled as he swooped from his place by the throne. "The king is unwell." Looking down his long, curved nose from an uncomfortably close range, he fixed the messenger's eyes with protective fierceness. "It is best that you leave now."

Deeply discouraged, the courier left Ai and trudged up the dreary road toward Gibeon. He would not bother seeking an audience with the king of Luz. The road led sharply upward through a steep, rough canyon, but he did not slacken his pace. It was mid-afternoon, he guessed, from the length of the shadows and he still had another five hours to go before he reached home.

Not a shadow nor scuffle of sandals whispered a warning. The rough hands of the mysterious assailant pulled him into a headlock, and the blade that pierced his back was cold as ice.

"Jericho? Or Ai?" he croaked as everything around him went black.

The second courier raced up the spiny backbone of the southern ridge from Gibeon to Jebus, to the palace of Adoni-Zedek, undisputed leader of the southern kings. He too was escorted into the presence of an agitated monarch who cut him off before he could state his purpose.

"You lean toward the wrong side, Gibeonites. Hearts of women. Mired in weakness. You have the best army in the region, yet you fight with your mouths. Diplomacy and covenants. The kingdoms of Canaan must unite in strength. We must fight, not prattle like girls. I will crush that nest of hornets before they swarm over our hills with their deadly sting. I will launch firebrands into their midst. Flaming arrows into the heart of Israel. And we will utterly consume their camp with fire."

"With all due respect, Your Majesty, that sort of attack is what our senate believes will precipitate a war we cannot win. No one has prevailed against their powerful God."

"The key is to strike first. If we wait for them to come up against us, we will die."

"Our spies are watching the foreigners closely, and the Gibeonite council meets often to keep abreast of their activities. We urge you to wait and see what they will do."

"Gibeonites are traitors in the land. You have a powerful army, yet you would stand idly by while Israel picks off the kingdoms of Canaan one by one."

"But there has been no attack on this side of the river. They are making no preparations for war at this time. Restraint, my lord, restraint!"

"We will give you this much restraint; if Israel attacks even one city, we will retaliate immediately," Adoni-Zedek howled in rage.

A confident smirk stretched his wide mouth. "We will be prepared." Turning to his yad, he began issuing orders maniacally. "Pack up my household immediately. Inform all my top aides. Inform the army. We are moving to the stronghold of Adullam. Send for Koz. The high priest must go immediately to negotiate with Libni. If that over-sized white grub will not crawl out to defend Canaan at our side, let him remain in the deep chambers. But Adullam is *our* stronghold, not his. We will not disturb his lair, but we must establish emergency headquarters in the great hall and the upper rooms now."

The king stopped abruptly, catching his breath, his eyes switching from side to side as if searching his mind for other needful preparations. He cast a quick glance at the messenger. "And you," he snapped, addressing him as if suddenly remembering that he was there. "Let the senate of Gibeon know that we are moved into Adullam. We will have none of your proposed treaty. Our cause is right, and right will prevail."

King Jabin of Hazor smirked at the third Gibeonite courier the entire time he was delivering his message. When the messenger finished, the smirk dissolved into a look of bored disdain. "I am not particularly concerned about a ragtag army of foot soldiers," he said smoothly. "They are no match for my war chariots."

The messenger stared at the king incredulously. "Those ragtag foot soldiers recently defeated the powerful, well-trained army of King Sihon."

"Yes. I know." The king twiddled his thumb back and forth on his jeweled scepter. "Perhaps I should have loaned Sihon a few of my choice chariot units. I will not lend them to that arrogant fool, Zedek. Impossible to fight with chariots in the hills and ravines of the south anyway. I expect Israel will defeat Jericho and all the southern kings. Not a bad outcome, I say. Then Hazor will reap the glory of annihilating the invaders. I will annex southern Canaan as well as the lands of Sihon and Og across the Jordan. I foresee a glorious new empire of Hazor."

He stared at the ceiling for a moment as if expecting applause, then locked eyes with the courier. "No, I will not attack first. I will lure Israel into coming to me."

"Sir, may I remind you of the fate of Egypt and of Midian, to say nothing of King Sihon and King Og, whose lands you now covet."

The king's brow furrowed. "Why Og could not defeat such a puny foe is beyond me."

The messenger tried again to make King Jabin understand. "The kings of this region respect you. Alert your allies, but, exercise caution. We beg you. Can you not see that war against Israel is futile? The fate of northern Canaan lies in your hands."

King Jabin sat quietly for a long, tense moment. At last, he looked up, his decision final. "Guard, escort this man from the throne room."

Othniel

Othniel shuffled along the path toward the bold, lion-emblazoned banner waving high above the tents of Judah. The sun was warm on his hair and face, the open air unbelievably refreshing after two days of confinement. If he held his robe away from his body and walked slowly, there was little discomfort—and when he did feel the burning of his tender wound, he reminded himself of his dedication to the covenant. Caleb's request for him to run this errand while he was still in recovery from the circumcision surprised him, but obedience proved his uncle's wisdom once again. He could not remember feeling so alive.

"Shalom, Othniel. Good to see you." Salmon's mother continued her work under the dancing shadow of the Lion of Judah, the words drifting over her back along with the sound of the grindstone. It was unusual for Abijah not to turn and welcome him face to face. He could only guess she had noticed his strange gait and politely averted her gaze. Unlike her daughter. Nothing escaped the keen eyes of Salmon's little sister, Ada. The pert little face unashamedly appraised every faltering step of his approach.

Othniel adjusted his carriage self-consciously. "Salmon inside?" he asked casually.

"Where else?" Ada tossed her head and rolled her eyes. "Today is the twelfth of Abib. Day two of your recovery. Humph. My brother is always telling us how *wise* Othniel is."

"Shush, child," Abijah scolded.

"Well, why would a *wise* man have to ask where Salmon would be today?"

"He's being polite, young lady, and you are not."

Othniel laughed. "*I'm* here, Ada. So, we can't simply assume . . ."

Salmon's mother turned and gestured toward the doorway. "Go on inside, Othniel. All this lying around healing gives my son more time for cogitating than is good for a man."

Othniel smirked as he brushed the tent flap aside. *The general consensus has it that walking around while healing isn't good for a man either.* He grunted at the searing pain as he bent down to pass through the doorway, and Ada's giggle followed him into the tent.

Salmon lay motionless in the semidarkness, eyes closed, a carefully constructed blanket canopy covering his nakedness. Othniel eased himself down on a pallet beside the bed. Not a muscle twitch acknowledged his presence.

"Shalom, friend," he said quietly.

Salmon's eyes opened, black and starkly hollow. "My little sister doesn't give us men much sympathy, does she?" he mumbled.

"She should. You look absolutely terrible."

A hint of a smile pulled at one side of Salmon's mouth. "There have been a lot of days since Abba died when I have felt useless as a child trying to fill a man's place. Now when we need to be preparing for our first feast in the Promised Land, I *am* totally useless."

"And sinking into a pool of self-pity."

Salmon forced a half smile. "I'm a boy missing my Abba more than ever."

In the long period of silence that followed, Othniel watched the dark swirls of anguish twist Salmon's features and felt again the sting of his own loss. "The fangs of a snake, an unfeeling reptile, killed my father," he said after a while, "but yours was murdered by the hands of his Israelite brothers. I can't even imagine how difficult that is to deal with."

"If only he could be here to tell the Passover story. He lived it. I barely can remember any of the details."

"Actually, that is the reason I limped over here. Caleb would be pleased if your family joined ours for the feast."

Salmon's eyes brightened. "That would be a blessing not only to me but to *Ima* as well. Tell Caleb she will bring a large basket of flat bread. The rasping of the grindstone has hardly stopped since we got our camp set up. One would think she was planning to bake up enough bread for an army."

"Your mother's way of dealing with the grief." Othniel chuckled. "We'll have to tell Joshua in case there is an impending campaign and the army needs a good supply of bread." He watched the shadows playing on the tent walls. "Such losses are not easy for anyone. I don't know what I would have done without Uncle Caleb. He has been like a father to Seraiah and me since our father died."

"What is wrong with me? So many have lost their fathers." Salmon rolled over on his side, wincing at the movement. Othniel had to lean in to hear the words muffled into the pillow. "Why is it so hard for me to put on my father's sandals and walk like a man?"

Othniel shook his hair back over his shoulders, giving himself a moment to think through his response. "Every story is different. Even with Uncle Caleb's wisdom and advice, it isn't easy for me to know what to do. And I am not the prince of a whole tribe."

"My father almost made it here to the land of Canaan . . ." Salmon pushed up on his elbows to engage Othniel face to face. "Every day for the past two months, I have had to beg Yahweh to take away my anger against the men who ended his life. Not only my father, those Simeonites nearly brought an end to all our people. How long do they think we would survive without the covenant protection of Yahweh?"

Othniel raised his eyebrows in agreement. Not just Simeon. It was still incomprehensible to him how quickly the leadership of all the tribes abandoned the covenant and joined the rebellion.

Salmon looked into his eyes searching for answers Othniel was quite certain did not exist. "In some ways I can understand how Zimri was snared by the idea of becoming king, co-ruler with Cozbi. But did he really think he was the answer to the dreams of a Midianite princess? That she had no other goal than being his lover?" His eyes flashed darkly as the questions gushed forth. "The unfaithfulness of the elders of Simeon is harder to understand. Why were they so eager to become the leading tribe of Israel? What benefit do they think Judah reaps from that responsibility?"

Othniel didn't reply.

"There I go again. Anger and grief are like weights dragging me down into dark waters. Like the day Jathniel and I nearly drowned. No . . . Worse than that . . . When the flood of the Jordan pulled us under, there was a muddy, murky surface to struggle toward. This is different. I am underwater with no place of light or breath to swim toward."

"Well, there is now," Othniel said. "The Passover feast is the light this week. When it seems like you're drowning, swim toward the light. I'll be there, brother, and we'll inhale deep draughts of life-giving air—together."

"You can be certain I will listen to Caleb's story very, very closely, knowing I'll be expected to tell it next year." There was a long pause before he spoke again.

"Everyone in our generation needs to hear the story again from someone who lived it. We have Moses' writings, but we must not let the living force of the story be lost. I will organize storytelling convocations that include every family of Judah before Passover next year."

Othniel flashed an approving smile. "I think you wear Prince Nashon's sandals quite well." He took a deep breath and pushed to his feet but could not hold back a soft moan. He hunched over, crippled by the searing pain of the movement.

"You're a true friend," Salmon replied. "But don't expect me to swim toward that light before Passover eve. My groin groaning will stay right here." He flashed his teasing, lopsided grin. "I'll send Ada over to help your mother search for bitter herbs."

"Thanks, but I'm pretty sure Acsah has that covered."

King Nahari

The sound of brass-reinforced war sandals rang out against the stone pavers of the throne room. Shinab responded to the summons with admirable speed, but as King Nahari watched the loose, gangling gait carrying his captain toward the throne, he felt a deep pang of remorse. The king truly missed the solid tread of Ahuzzath. He appraised the splotchy, pimpled countenance of his new captain with mild revulsion. Somehow even the fearsome spiked helmet looked silly on his new captain and those clopping footsteps evoked the image of a donkey. *But it can't be undone. The change had to be made. Ahuzzath failed.* The king suppressed all lingering regrets. *Shinab is shrewd and faithful. If only he had the experience of the head decomposing beside the city gates.*

The irritation rising from these conflicted thoughts erupted in a question while the young man was still bowing in reverential obeisance. "Captain Shinab, what do you advise regarding these invaders?"

"It is not mine to have opinions," Shinab answered meekly. "I merely await orders."

"You will have opinions if I ask for them."

Shinab looked up with a start. He searched Nahari's face silently for a moment. Then his eyes narrowed, surprisingly cold for one so young. "The invaders are vermin—vermin to be exterminated. Our forces can easily overtake their camp. Only say the word."

"And their god?"

"That is the concern of the priests."

"Get up, Shinab. How am I to respect a captain who remains groveling on the floor while we discuss an enemy as powerful as Israel?"

"As you wish, m'lord," the gangly youth mumbled, scrambling awkwardly to his feet.

"My priests ask for more sacrifices. Always more sacrifices." Nahari drummed his fingers on the carved cedar arms of his throne. "After these desert rats poured into King Sihon's valley and eliminated every inhabitant of Heshbon, my priests bid me sacrifice bulls. When they defeated King Og, it was more bulls. When Balak summoned Balaam to curse them, more bulls. When Jacob defeated Midian, yet more."

Shinab sniffed in contempt. "And now that the vermin crossed the floodwaters and made their nest in our own valley. Let me guess, more bulls."

"No. Now that I've all but depleted my cattle barns of sires for new calves, they say that only the blood of infants will stir our Lady Asherah. All the firstborn males under the age of two. The pride of every mother in Jericho, including my wives. The thought of giving up my little princes revolts me—but . . ."

He pinned Shinab's eyes with what he hoped was an intimidating look. "What do you think? Wait for help from Asherah or attack?"

"Their apparent power must be deceit," Shinab answered with an icy calmness. "They are the children of Jacob the Deceiver." He returned the king's glare with the unblinking gaze of a serpent. "Do not attack until we discover their weakness. While we wait, we must strengthen the defenses of our city. Assign the sharpest eyes to the watchtowers. Rotate the best of our archers and spearmen on the wall day and night. Maintain a full guard at the gate through the night watches." The specific details gushed from the young man's mouth with no hesitation. It seemed he had carefully considered every contingency. "But we are *Jericho*," he concluded triumphantly. "We will not remain cowering within these walls forever. When the time is right, we will attack and destroy."

There was a semblance of ancient wisdom in Shinab's words. And power—in sharp contrast to the words of the priests. The king's confidence was renewed. "Let it be so," he said.

CHAPTER TWO

PASSOVER

Caleb

Caleb swallowed the last bite of roasted lamb and tossed the shank bone on the platter. The bread basket and bowls were empty. The wine cups drained. All that remained of the Passover feast was a heap of clean-picked bones. Licking the savory grease from his fingers and wiping his mouth on his sleeve, the old warrior gazed contentedly at the boisterous circle—his children and his children's children. The tent canopy his sons erected for this feast was large enough to accommodate them all, bringing the entire clan together tonight in exceptional harmony. Caleb was as happy as he could remember.

Acsah's eyes sparkled as she leaned close. "Forty years since you experienced this," she whispered and nestled her head into the curve of his shoulder.

"Forty years," he repeated, patting her hand. What a wonder she was, this child of his old age. His only daughter. All she knew of Egypt were the stories, yet how often her thoughts ran close to his. How did she know the memories of the last Passover filled his head at this very moment? Could she understand the thrill of the first anniversary of Passover?

He had been a much younger man then, a father with but two young sons. Over the year spent at Mount Sinai, the euphoria of their newfound freedom morphed into hopes and dreams of a glorious new life in the Promised Land. No longer slaves, they were learning to live as free men and women. No. More than live. They were

19

learning to *thrive* as a nation governed by Yahweh's law of love.

As that first year of freedom drew to a close, the people completed construction of the tabernacle as a dwelling place for their God. They set it up on the first day of Abib dedicating each part with great ceremony according to the precise instructions given by Yahweh. As they finished the dedication, the magnificent cloud began to rumble as it did on the day God spoke the Ten Commandments. Great peals of thunder sounded, and flashes of lightning crackled over the peak of Sinai. The cloud crept down the mountain, filled the inner compartments of the sanctuary with fiery glory, then shot high into the sky with towering cumulous glory—Yahweh signaling his intention to travel to the Promised Land with his people.

On the fourteenth of Abib they celebrated the first Passover. Everyone expected to enjoy the next feast, *Shavuot*, the Feast of Weeks, fifty days later in Canaan. They began the seven-week count as they packed up their camp and followed the cloud toward the Promised Land. But long before the count neared completion, the people failed miserably, and God sent them into the wilderness for faith training. That festival never happened.

Tonight, the cycle of feasts was beginning anew. *Only for the children though,* Caleb reminded himself. *The corpses of an entire generation sleep in graves scattered in the trackless wilderness. My friends, my parents, my brothers, and all three of my wives—everyone who celebrated the first Passover at Sinai.* "Gone," he groaned softly.

"What?" Acsah sat up so she could search his face.

His granddaughter Rebekah twisted around on her father's lap to stare. And his son, Naam, across the room, stopped chatting with Othniel. Both young men gave him quizzical looks. "What is gone, Father?"

Well, that *word certainly sounded a discordant note amid this happy chatter.* Caleb cleared his throat dramatically. "Every person who left Egypt with me the night the Death Angel passed over our homes. My entire family is gone, except you children. Lack of faith has dream-crushing consequences."

Tears of compassion gleamed in Rebekah's eyes, and Caleb regretted his mournful explanation. The Passover story must begin with faith and hope. He caught the child's eyes with a smile and winked. "We must not be sad for what might have been. Grandpa's generation, the Exodus generation, found significance in teaching their children to live in covenant with Yahweh. You are the Gilgal generation. The shame of failure is rolled away, and tonight, we celebrate a new beginning."

Almost like a sneeze that could not be contained, a hymn of blessing shot from his mouth. "How blessed are all who have learned to trust Yahweh." The baritone notes blared startlingly loud to every corner of the large pavilion and any remaining chatter ceased.

Rebekah laughed. "Sing it again, Grandpa."

He did, and his heart brimmed with joy as one voice after another joined the familiar song.

> *How blessed are all who have learned to trust Yahweh.*
> *How blessed are those who walk in his ways.*
> *In joy you will eat the fruit of your labor,*
> *And all will be well with you.*[2]

Caleb chortled inwardly as the room reverberated with enthusiastic singing. *My family thinks I planned this as part of the proceedings. Well and good if it begins a most excellent tradition.* As the happy melody flowed, he gathered his thoughts. He must tell the story well. All the faces glowing in the lamplight around him tonight were either born during the Wanderings or left Egypt as very young children. *Passover is not their story, but it must become so. It is the birth story of our people. I must tell it and retell it. Make it theirs. Tell it every year until I die—my parting gift to future generations.*

As the last notes of the song hung in the air, he leaned forward like a runner impatient for the signal to begin the race. "Never forget, my children. Never forget to celebrate Passover. We must remember the day Yahweh led our people out of bondage."

"Was the first feast as much fun as this one, Grandpa?" Mushi asked thoughtfully

"The anniversary celebration was very joyful like this feast, my child, but the actual Passover was not a celebration. It was a terrifying night—and a glorious night. Our last night in Egypt." Caleb could feel the expectancy growing in the room and switched to his deeply resonate storytelling voice.[3]

"Before even one plague had fallen, Moses and Aaron went before Pharaoh with only a shepherd's staff and a command from God. 'I come as ambassador of Yahweh, God of Israel and Ruler of Heaven and Earth. This is his message to Pharaoh, king of Egypt—Let my people go. They must hold a festival to me in the desert.'

"'Who is Yahweh?' Pharaoh sneered. 'Show me a miracle that will make me believe in him.'

"At a glance from Moses, Aaron threw his staff to the floor. It fell clattering on the stone steps at Pharaoh's feet—and suddenly raised its flared hood, no longer a wooden staff, but a living cobra. As the staff-snake drew its body into a thick coil, Pharaoh's priests instinctively recoiled. But the symbol of the rearing cobra encircled the ruler's crown. His faith in the power of Wadjet to protect him and all the land of Egypt never wavered.

"'Show these sheepherders who rules Egypt,' he commanded.

His sorcerer-priests obeyed, tossing their own staffs on the polished pavement between Aaron's threatening cobra and their Pharaoh. One by one, each finely-crafted staff also became a serpent.

"'Ha,' cried Pharaoh. 'Who is Yahweh? Why should I obey him and let Israel go?'

"But Yahweh had not finished. Slowly, Aaron's serpent-staff slithered toward the magician's snakes. It swallowed one, and then another. When all had disappeared down its gullet, the cobra coiled around and began inching toward the priestly sorcerers. The superiority of Aaron's staff was clear. If his serpent was merely a terrifying illusion—their counter illusions had vanished. If an actual serpent, they were now bereft of solid staffs for defense—and it seemed quite probable that the remaining cobra was not an illusion. As one, the priests fled the room. But the monarch wearing the cobra crown sat unmoved between his bodyguards. While the echo of priestly sandals pattered out of the palace, Moses seized the cobra by its tail, and the serpent became Aaron's ruggedly-twisted wooden staff again.

"The room grew deadly silent as Moses returned the staff to his brother. He fixed Pharaoh with a burning look. 'This is what Yahweh says—Israel is my firstborn son, and I tell you, let my son go that he may worship me.'

"'Remove these men from my throne room,' Pharaoh bellowed.

"Long after the guards hustled the two Hebrews out of the palace, Moses' final words hung in the air. 'If you refuse to let Israel go, your firstborn son will die.'

"The next morning, Moses met Pharaoh at the river. And the power of Yahweh began to defeat Pharaoh's gods, beginning with the lifeblood of the land—the Nile itself. Nine times the fist of Yahweh fell heavy on the land of Egypt, and nine times Pharaoh shook his tiny fist back at Yahweh, his heart growing harder with each new disaster.

"The first three plagues—the bloody waters, the frogs, and the gnats—afflicted everyone who dwelled in the land. But the seven last plagues did not touch the people of God. By the end of the eighth plague, every Egyptian, including Pharaoh, had suffered biting flies, boils, and battering hail. The livestock were decimated, and the crops stripped bare by locusts. The ninth plague—three days of thick darkness, burning the eyes and searing the lungs—proved Yahweh's superiority over Ra, the sun god. But for every plague, Pharaoh and his advisors found another cause, another explanation for the calamity. Pharaoh refused to listen to Yahweh. He refused to let Israel go.

"There was but one deity left, Pharaoh himself, born of the gods to be god on earth. The first warning given to Pharaoh by the Lord of Heaven and Earth was about to become the final blow in this battle of the gods. The destroying angel would pass through the land in the dark of night, taking the firstborn of both man and beast. Yahweh would rescue his firstborn, but Pharaoh would lose his.

"All who believed Yahweh's instructions found a way of escape through the blood of a lamb. The Death Angel would pass over their blood-slathered doorways—and that is how Passover got its name. As Israel made preparations, slaying their lambs and painting their portals with blood, bands of Egyptians came, watching, scoffing, and jeering. All day Moses raced through the land of Goshen with tears, urging the doubting ones to believe, until finally, as darkness fell, every Israelite home closed blood-framed doors on the sounds of Egyptian mockery.

"After my father slaughtered the lamb as required, he handed the bowl of drained blood to his youngest son—Othniel's father."

Caleb paused, letting his eyes rest on his nephew Othniel. The family-warm memory of those preparations brought a smile to his face. Caleb winked at the young man. *Kenaz . . . my favorite brother.*

That brief moment of attention, every eye in the room turned on him, brought a flush to Othniel's face. He turned his face up toward the hangings forming the ceiling of the pavilion and shook his hair back over his shoulders. Caleb coughed, drawing attention away from Othniel's odd way of hiding his discomfort and pulling it back to the narrative. He dropped the formal intonations. This part of the story was personal.

"With the entire family watching, my father and I dipped branches of hyssop in the blood and slathered the doorway of our house. I can still see my young brother's hands trembling as he held the bowl, worrying that a spill could be deadly to the family. But he did not spill it, and the lamb provided abundantly more than we actually needed. We painted and repainted the crimson stain on post and lintel again and again until the drips formed a spreading puddle on the threshold. When we finished, my father roasted the lamb while my mother baked the unleavened bread. My aunts helped my mother with the baking and prepared bitter herbs while my brothers and I helped my uncles load the wagons and corral the herds close to the house ready for travel.

"All the while we worked, I brooded over the possibility of deaths in our family. My father was the firstborn of his mother. My eldest brother was the firstborn of his mother, and I was the firstborn of my mother. I was father of a firstborn son—as were three of my brothers. Seven lives in our one household hung by the fragile thread of faith in the blood framing our door.

"All Egypt must have smelled the thousands of lambs roasting that evening. A surprising number fled to our blood-marked homes with their firstborn sons. Many shared that first Passover meal with us and then followed us out of Egypt. One young Egyptian mother with two children arrived at our doorstep during the final hour of preparation, begging us to let them come in. She retreated to a corner, too afraid or too shy to offer her help. As we came in and out of the house engaged in our busy tasks, she did not lift her head, but the eyes of her children, round and dark with fear, watched our every move. When the sun set and we closed the door to share the Passover meal exactly as God had commanded, my father insisted that she and her sons join us.

"As the lamb with flat bread and bitter herbs was distributed, foreigner and family formed one circle. Flanked by my parents, the three Egyptians became a connecting arc, an essential part of who we were that night—God's promise to Abraham—that through him all nations would be blessed. Remember that promise as we claim our inheritance. We dare not form alliances with unbelievers, but we need never fear embracing those who reach out to us in faith."

Caleb withdrew into his memories for a moment, aware that his family sat in bewildered silence. The thought he had just thrown out to them was incomprehensible. How was it possible for Israel to wipe out the memory of the evil nations of Canaan as Moses commanded and yet be a blessing to all nations? Caleb himself could not answer that question. He resumed the tale.

"That first Passover was a night of fear rather than festival. We were all dressed for travel. Wearing our cloaks. Even holding our walking sticks. The bundles we would hand carry were stowed right behind us. We ate the lamb and bread and herbs in total silence. Ate in haste without even sitting down, for we had no idea how soon we would leave. When we finished eating, we all looked to Father. But he merely nodded back with a vague and uncertain expression. We had reached the end of the instructions.

"Our family remained clasping hands, connected to one other as well as the three Egyptians. Waiting. Trusting that the destroying angel would see the blood and pass over the house. After a while, my mother scooped up the empty platters, scrubbed them free of grease with handfuls of sand, and packed them into the bundle of cooking utensils behind her. Still we waited.

"Although I was thirty-nine years old on that first Passover and a father myself, my mother reached out to hold me, her firstborn. I can still see the fear flickering in her eyes. My own dear wife, clutched you to her breast, Iru, and I could not help wondering which of the children clinging to the Egyptian mother was her firstborn. With heartbeats of fear throbbing in our ears, we continued to wait."

Caleb slipped back into his formal storytelling mode as he finished the tale.

"In the darkest hour of the night, the air became heavy. We felt the arrival of the death force even before we heard its sound. Like a howling wind, now moaning sorrowfully, now shrieking dreadfully, it swirled about the houses of Goshen then moved on. Wails and cries of grief from the homes unprotected by blood marked the wake of its passing through the Egyptian settlements.

"The Death Angel took the firstborn of the land of Egypt without discrimination—powerful courtiers or simple gardeners, rich or poor, grandfathers or infants—even the heir of the royal throne. Pitiful animal cries rising from the stables mingled with human keening as the firstborn of all the cattle, oxen, asses, and horses fell cold and still.

"Pharaoh threw off his crown, defeated at last. Clutching his lifeless son in his arms, he called for Moses and Aaron. 'Up! Leave my land—you and every Israelite. Take your flocks and your herds and worship the Lord Yahweh as you asked.' He fell to his knees, sobbing, 'And bless me also.'

"Moses sternly demanded repayment for all the years of forced labor. At Pharaoh's command, grieving Egyptian families pressed gold, jewels, fine linen—whatever treasure they possessed—into the hands of their former slaves, begging them to leave immediately. 'Otherwise,' they said, 'we will all be dead.'

"Thus, our people left Egypt with much of the wealth of that great civilization. Like a gentle shepherd, Yahweh led his firstborn out of bondage. The unrelenting blows of his rod had finally defeated the predator."

Othniel

A cloak of silence fell over the room when the story finished. The golden lamplight accentuated a network of wrinkles crisscrossing Caleb's leathery cheeks. But even at age eighty, his eyes were not dull with age. They glittered with life and experience. The wild, white hair and beard signified wisdom . . . innumerable challenges met and overcome . . . battles fought and won.

Othniel had no words for his admiration. He had no words to express how deeply the power of the Passover story resonated in his heart, nor for the feelings of belonging welling up inside him. Throughout the meal, Othniel tried to understand each symbolic food item and memorize every wise and wonderful answer to the children's countless questions. He knew of no other leader so strong in the home as well as on the field of battle.

Othniel could feel his mother relaxed and comfortable beside him. As Kenaz's widow, he knew she was grateful for Caleb's support. He scanned the family circle—the manly faces of the old warrior's sons, bearded and strong in the flickering light, the gentle faces of their wives, and the earnest, sparkling eyes of the little ones. *Do they have any idea how privileged they are to be part of this family?* Salmon's eyes shining with excitement throughout the tale left no doubt of his feelings. Another face, he knew, would be glowing with adoration, a face more noble in intelligence and beauty than all the rest of Caleb's large, bustling family. But he could not risk another look in her direction.

During a pleasant conversation with one of Caleb's sons, Othniel took advantage of his position directly across from Acsah and dared a lingering look at his cousin. Her head was resting on her father's shoulder. Cascading ribbons of sleek, obsidian hair framed a face that appeared in more dreams than Othniel would care to admit. Her remarkable eyes, curtained by thick, black lashes, were focused on her hands as she languidly interlaced and released her fingers. Suddenly, a question shattered the magical moment. "What is gone, Father?" and Acsah trapped him with one overpowering glance. His breath caught in his throat, and he tossed his hair back in a desperate attempt to escape her glittering green eyes, but he could not control the flush spreading hotly over his cheeks.

To his relief, Caleb began a hymn of praise. "How blessed are all who trust in Yahweh." Othniel tried to join the song but found himself choking on the words while the brilliant clarity of Acsah's voice soared above the others, dancing with his heart, twirling and diving—the sound of purest joy.

All evening, Othniel burned with the desire to lead like Caleb. Along with the challenge of leadership, the longing for a family of his own boiled through his veins. He could not imagine himself with anyone other than Acsah, but that song proclaimed reality. Acsah was a songbird in flight. He was a crow in a field of dry stubble. She was the spirit of Miriam, dancing victory with her tambourine. He was a mute rock, fixed and dull on the shore of the Red Sea. He did not risk another glance in her direction as Caleb recounted the Passover story.

Now as the festival drew to a close and Caleb pronounced a blessing over his family, Othniel sat befuddled in a churning brew of hope and despair. Oh to be as heroic in the war against evil as Caleb—his uncle had not faltered even when facing giants. But how could he stand up to God's enemies if he could not even meet the eyes of Caleb's daughter? As the clan prepared to disperse, he mumbled his thanks to Caleb and was the first to leave.

Ignoring the call of his friend, Salmon, Othniel rushed back to the tent he shared with his mother and younger brother. He pressed back any unwarranted notions about Acsah's beauty as he snuggled into the warmth of his bed. *Rehearse the Passover narrative while it is fresh in your mind,* he told himself pragmatically. Before he got to the end of the staff-serpent competition between Moses and the Egyptian magicians, he was fast asleep.

Suddenly, a wild rolling of the earth jarred him to consciousness. He lay panting on his pillow. The images of a heady dream lingered in his head—a dream in which he led the entire army of Israel into battle as high commander. The ground beneath him quit trembling, but he did not. *What was it that shook me so deeply?* Not the earthquake. He had experienced several since Israel settled in the Jordan Valley. He could not explain the sense of impending doom, a feeling he was heading for a shaking, shattering confrontation with a malevolent force unlike anything he had ever imagined. He stared into the darkness. Much as he wished the dream shattered by this quake to be true, deep in his heart he knew its fading fragments were an illusion. *I am no high commander. I am little more than a boy, a pitifully untrained, ill-equipped soldier totally unprepared for whatever lies ahead.*

As Othniel lay sorting out his thoughts, he felt the ground shake even more violently. It did not seem that he had fallen asleep again, but with blinding clarity, the vision of a vault in a deep underground cavern filled his head. There, as the intensity of the earthquake increased, he watched a huge white form emerge. The stony pavement buckled under his feet as he clambered out of the depths of the cave. Chunks of falling limestone clattered onto the ground around the pale-skinned giant as he straightened himself to a terrifying height. When he lifted his face to the sky, white hair swung about his head like a ragged, battle-worn banner and his eyes glinted in the moonlight, red as smoldering coals.

The giant shook his fist as if answering a challenge. "You have summoned me to war at last, Yahweh," he bellowed. "I have been waiting for this battle for forty years, waiting to utterly crush your pitiful followers. I will scrub all knowledge of Yahweh from the earth."

Othniel stared into the darkness. Caleb told of seeing such a giant while spying out southern Canaan with Joshua forty years before. He was the king of the great walled city of Kiriath-Arba, the king of the Anakim who unnerved ten of Israel's spies—the ten who shattered the faith of all Israel, sparking the rebellion that resulted in the Wanderings.

But why had this vision or dream come to him? More importantly, where did it come from? Was it happening now? Was it a warning from God of things to come? Or was it a delusion designed by demonic forces to terrify him?

Othniel's younger brother, Seraiah, slept soundly in the bed beside his, and he could hear his mother snoring lightly in her room on the far side of the dividing curtain. The earthquake had not disturbed their sleep. He did not wish to disturb it either. Shrugging off a light wool blanket and peeling his sweat-drenched tunic away from his skin, he rose, pushed through the tent flap and staggered into the moonlight.

The beauty of the full Passover moon straight overhead seemed cold and aloof tonight, its light all but obscuring the star stories he loved so well. He could identify only one star. The red star glittering just above the black silhouette of the hills and trees—the lurid heart of the Scorpion. On the ridge above camp, the arms of the oaks flailed in a wild pagan dance with winds sweeping down the western hills into the warm Jordan Valley. Gusts from the strongholds of Canaan were blowing an alien chill into Gilgal.

"What *is* this place?" he whispered. *We have called it the Land of Promise all our lives. Tonight it feels like the very epicenter of evil.* Chilled by the damp clothing against his skin, Othniel pulled his cloak tighter, determined to face the darkness in spite of cold or fear. For the first time, he understood the terror that caused Israel to rebel instead of entering Canaan. Unlike them, he fought the fear. He squeezed his eyes closed and pictured the Gilgal. He remembered the feel of *his* rock, the rock of Judah, solid and cool under his fingers.

"The river stones are real," he said aloud. "The power of Yahweh brought us across the Jordan. This land is Jacob's inheritance, promised to his descendants."

Othniel looked toward the sky again. The star patterns were still too dim to trace, but he knew them by heart. He pictured the Woman representing Israel, bound by chains. But she did not need to fear the Sea Monster lurking on the southern horizon because the Strong Deliverer was already striding across the sky to rescue her. The thought filled him with courage. The forces of evil would threaten—the Serpent, the Dragon, the Sea Monster, or the Scorpion. But each of those terrifying images was countered by a sign of victory—the Roaring Lion, the Charging Bull, the Serpent Wrestler, the Warrior aiming his Arrow straight at Scorpion's heart, and, of course, the Redeemer Prince coming to rescue his bride. Night after night, the stars declared Yahweh's message. Israel did not face evil alone. God would provide a deliverer. It was the message of Passover.

Libni, King of the Anakim

The cold light of a full moon bathed the empty streets of Jebus in silver. It was a beautiful city, the crown of Mount Zion, the noblest of all the royal cities of Canaan. But if someone were awake on this warm spring night, he might catch a glimpse of an ashen movement stealing in and out of the black shadows, tall as the tightly-packed houses. The white shadow was barely visible in darkness, but when the pale flesh caught the moonlight and reflected it back to the night sky, the creature burst forth, huge and terrible. Libni, king of the Anakim, stalked the city. He had broken the necks of the guards and removed the barred gate as if it were a child's toy. Now he slipped through the dark streets, scanning the flat rooftops, peeking through doorways and high open windows, scrutinizing family after family as they slept.

A few inhabitants yet remained in this city who would have recognized Libni. To most he was only a legend parents told naughty children to motivate better behavior. In truth, the ancient Anakim giants had withdrawn from the political maneuverings of Canaan long ago, and few had seen their king in four decades. But tonight, Lord Baal summoned this one out of his long seclusion.

"You pathetic creatures think you sleep secure," the king muttered over yet another family slumbering on the flat rooftop of their home with scrawny, imperfect children. "It is not peace that roams the streets of ancient Salem tonight. In the morning, the inhabitants of this city will know they dwell in Jebus, the Threshing Floor. Here all threats to the power of Canaan's gods will be mercilessly trodden underfoot."

In ancient times this city was known as Salem. Peace. But Baal did not leave it in peace as long as its priest-king, Melchi-Zedek and his subjects exalted only Yahweh. When the ancient priest died, Lord Baal overthrew the peace-loving inhabitants of Salem. He gave victory to the Jebusites, who drove all descendants of Shem from the city and renamed it Jebus, Trodden. The name was a salute to the expansive threshing floor just outside the city walls, as well as to their ancestor, the third son of Canaan. The name was most fitting, for Baal threshed out the followers of Yahweh, winnowing out the last of them by withholding his rain and driving the family of Jacob to Egypt.

For centuries, no one following Yahweh remained in the land at all. No one, that is, until four days ago when the children of Jacob crossed the Jordan—crossed it at flood season, swarming into Canaan to reclaim their ancient inheritance. War was on the horizon. This time, the gods would free the land of Canaan from the influence of Yahweh forever.

At the end of a long street, Libni stopped at the sight of what looked to be twins, a boy and a girl, sleeping under a rooftop canopy beside their parents. Both were flawless children. It suddenly occurred to him that he did not know whether the war goddess had an appetite for a male child tonight or a female. "O Baal, show me which sacrifice will please our Lady Asherah and ensure a victorious ending to the Great War."

Libni snatched up both beautiful children, working in such stealth that the residents of Jebus, even the sleeping parents, would not know of their loss until they awoke at daybreak. Rapidly leaving Jebus behind, the pale-skinned warrior-king sped down the terraced gardens and fields illuminated by Asherah's glorious moonlight. He carried his small victims, bound and gagged, one tossed over each shoulder like bags of wheat, and ran with long, loping strides into the forests of central Canaan, neither pausing nor slowing his pace until he reached the woodlands of Kiriath-Baal.

The deed filled every fiber of his limbs with ferocious strength, and suddenly he was ravenously hungry. Following a trail into the forest, his eyes darted from side to side with a hunter's cunning, watching for freshly uprooted vegetation, sniffing the air for the smell of damp earth. As soon as he noted signs indicating the route of wild pigs, he stopped and dropped the children like piles of baggage beside the trail.

The look of horror in the children's eyes and their muffled expressions of fear amused him. "You know of me, do you not, my pretty little ones? King Libni, the giant who haunts your nightmares. Did you think I was a myth, a story designed to frighten little children into obedience?" He chuckled as he shook his head close to theirs, his long white hair flying wildly about his huge head, his eyes squinting with an intentional look of malice. "Is this the face of a myth? Cry out now for your parents. Call out for your relatives and neighbors. Appeal to the gods," he exclaimed as he ripped off the gags. "Ha!" He could detect the foulness of his own breath billowing over the captives along with his laughter. He needed to cleanse his palate with fresh, warm blood.

As soon as the gags fell, the children shrieked and screamed in terror. "Yes. Yes. Call for help," he grunted approvingly. "If it comes—I give you my word—I will return you to your family."

Without saying any more, he hid himself, crouching down in the dense shrubbery nearby to wait. An hour crawled by, and the children's loud cries and hoarse pleadings dwindled to whimpers. Still not a single beast had emerged from hiding. The forest was unusually quiet. Rising to his gargantuan height, Libni scowled at the cowering creatures beside the path, unmoved by their tear-streaked faces, even blaming them for their unproductive screams. "Worthless children. Where is my blood feast?" he growled. "Now I must do this the hard way, and I may not be near to protect you."

The children did not so much as whimper while Libni circled the area, alternately beating the brush and then listening for telltale grunts. Suddenly, in a blurred rush, a huge dark form crashed out of the bushes in front of him, rushing his captives. Although the charging animal was fast, Libni was faster. Leaping onto the back of the huge boar just before it reached the youngsters, he pulled back on the tusks with his bare hands. He flipped the ponderous beast heavily onto its back, containing the squealing fury with his powerful arms and legs while he bit through the large vein in its neck, slurping the warm blood noisily until the animal sagged and gave up the struggle.

"The animal's power is mine," King Libni cried, glancing triumphantly at the children. As he ripped the quivering carcass in two by its hind legs and began feeding on raw organs and muscle, he watched the children from the corners of his eyes, taking perverse pleasure in the disgust and horror expressed on their faces. He smacked his lips loudly and grinned at them. He knew very well the fear instilled by the sight of a bloodstained mouth, dark in contrast to milk-white skin. He remembered all too well how it chilled him through when he was a lad.

His grandfather, the legendary white-skinned, red-eyed King Arba, ruled Canaan with an iron hand from his royal city for a hundred years. Though the child Libni knew his own small, white body matched that of his grandfather's, he cringed in visceral helplessness and dread at the sight of the old Anakim king, mouth dripping with blood, sucking the power from some wild beast, as Libni was now.

Most terrible was the night when Arba used him as bait on Asherah's night. His father *gave* his sister and him to the old man knowing that one would not come back. Little did his father know that neither of his children would return to him. The gods selected the daughter to be the offering, and Libni lived. He was forced to watch Arba bind the beloved companion of his childhood on the altar and her screaming terror in the sacrificial flames of Lady Asherah. Nothing was ever the same again. He never left his grandfather's side after that night, never saw his mother or father again, and never forgot the horror of it.

The old king's final act before he died was to order the deaths of Libni's father and his uncles and all their families, unexpectedly placing the crown on the head of the only grandson who resembled him. Thus at seventeen years of age, Libni began his reign as king of the Anakim in the city named for his grandfather, Kiriath-Arba. It was to that city that twelve spies from the tribes of Israel came forty years ago when he was but twenty.

The descendants of Jacob were a wretched nation of slaves recently escaped from Egypt. They quickly lost their first skirmish with the kings of southern Canaan, but everyone suspected the defeat was a ruse—a trick to draw out all the kings of Canaan. How else could they explain such an easy defeat of the army whose God devastated Egypt and drowned Pharaoh's army in the Red Sea? At the advice of his priest, Libni placed a puppet king, a Canaanite, on his throne in Kiriath-Arba, and retreated to the labyrinthine chambers underlying Adullam. There he remained, awaiting a great confrontation. But the Israelites disappeared into the desert. For forty years now he had been waiting in his dark vault in the bowels of Adullam with forays out only to feed. For forty years he waited, his loathing for the Sons of Jacob seething and distilling to pure hate.

When Libni had eaten his fill, he unbound the boy and pressed a crimson print on the child's forehead with a bloodied thumb. "My son, Asherah sent a boar, not a sow. The sex of the beast determined your fate. He is your substitute. Run back to your home."

The boy stared at him in frozen terror.

"Go, go," the giant ordered gruffly. "See how the sky is beginning to lighten on the rim of the eastern hills. Keep the rising sun before you and you cannot miss Jebus. The gods will see you safely home."

The boy stood, staggering stiffly for a step or two, then without a backward glance, sped away through the trees. The king caressed the top of the girl child's head gently. "Do not believe any horrible stories that have been spread abroad by my enemies. I am Protector of Canaan, appointed by Lord Baal. You do not need to fear me."

The child did not answer. She watched her brother until he disappeared. A tear slid down her cheek.

"Do not worry. He will make it home safe and sound."

"But the night is dark and howly with wild beasts. They will tear him to pieces."

"Nonsense. The wolves and jackals do but howl their admiration for the goddess of the night. Lo, Asherah's moon yet gleams over the western hills. Trust her to light the way for your brother until sunup."

"Please take me home. I am afraid to go alone as he does."

"Ah, do not fear. I will not turn you loose in the dark like the boy. I promise. The sun will greet you, released on the fields close to your home. My own hands will set you gently on the ground near Jebus. Do you believe me?"

The girl's eyes narrowed with suspicion. "Why did you snatch us from our beds?"

"An enemy wishes to steal the land of Canaan from its people. They would kill your family and burn your house down. Our worship of Asherah at dawn will empower her to help us destroy them. You have an important role to play. What do you think of that?"

She looked at him with great seriousness as she thought about all he had said.

"Don't look so glum." Making a silly face, Libni flicked his tongue in and out in rapid succession. It had been split at the tip like a reptile.

"You are a silly giant lizard," she giggled.

"Silly and gentle," he said in almost a whisper. "Do not fear me. This will be the crowning night of your life. But we must move quickly to reach the high place before dawn. Would you like to ride on my shoulder?"

"Will you untie these ropes?"

"Yes, my pretty child," he answered, freeing her hands and feet and hoisting her onto his right shoulder. "Ride your king. Ride unbound to Asherah's altar."

Just after sunup, Koz, the high priest of Jebus, scraped the girl's smoldering ashes from the altar stones at the high place of Kiriath-Baal. As Libni and a group of five kings from southern Canaan watched in silence, the priest mumbled an incantation over the ashy remains of the burnt offering, then covered the container and presented it ceremoniously to the towering son of Anak. The giant gnashed his teeth and raised a milk-white face to the sky. The dawn light flashed on blood-red eyes flaming with malevolent fire. "For you, my lady Asherah."

Taking the pot in his huge hands, he grunted his approval of the ceremony. Then, one by one, he met the eyes of the southern kings—Adoni-Zedek of Jebus, Hoham of Kiriath-Arba, Piram of Jarmuth, Japhia of Lachish, and Debir, king of Eglon—cruel-eyed, loyal kings all. Not one would hesitate to butcher his family if they showed any inclination to worship a god other than the ancient deities of Canaan. The craven Nahari of Jericho had not responded to Libni's summons. He trusted in the defense of his stone walls. The elders of the Federation of Gibeon refused to come. The cowards trusted that they could negotiate an acceptable treaty. Jabin of Hazor and his cohorts in the north trusted their iron chariots. Fools. But these five were enough. Joined with the Anakim, they would rid the earth of the Sons of Jacob forever.

"For centuries, Salem stood in opposition to Baal," King Libni cried. "In that city Yahweh was exalted rather than the gods of rain and harvest, the gods of earth and sky. His presence there suppressed the power of the Canaanite gods. My blood boils at the thought of Abraham, the ancestor of these hated invaders, arriving in this land, ignoring all other Canaanite kings, but bringing offerings to Salem, repeatedly bringing offerings, sheep grown fat on the fertile soil of Baal's land. Once he brought the spoils of war to Melchi-Zedek—with not a sandal-lace given to honor Lady Asherah though *she* is Canaan's goddess of love and war. But Asherah and Baal did not ignore this affront. Within a century, the seed of Abraham had been driven from the land."

King Libni's voice was husky as he began to relate his own experience with the descendants of Abraham. "Forty years have passed since the children of Jacob threatened our southern border. After they were driven back, I withdrew to the cave of Adullam to perfect my war plans. Too late, I realized they were not coming back anytime soon. Over the years my subjects scattered. Word trickled back to me that Sheshai and Talmai had developed high renown as military heroes for the kings of Eshtaol and Gath. Their brother, Ahiman, went north to Beth-Shean. I heard reports of others who joined in battles here and there for brief moments of fame. The majority of the Anakim settled in solitary lairs in the cave-ridden hills as I did. The glory days of my people passed. With their king in seclusion, the sons of Anak have been all but forgotten.

"That is changing. Our Lord Baal calls us all to war. My scattered Anakim brothers have heard the call. They are gathering. Pledge yourselves to join us in these desperate times. The enemy is at the door, threatening to shred the very fabric of Canaan beyond repair, but we will stop them."

As soon as the five kings had pledged their lives and their armies to join his coalition, Libni carried the lovely little pottery jar of ashes to the fields south of Jebus. True to his word, he set the girl free near her home in the bright morning light, the ashes of her sacrifice scattered in devotion to Asherah. Farmers in their fields trembled at the sight of the white giant and word spread that Anakim were abroad in the land again. But Libni returned to the depths of Adullam to await his next assignment from the gods.

CHAPTER THREE

WALLS

Joshua[4]

L ong before dawn on the day following Passover, a wolf-like shadow slipped through the palm groves surrounding Jericho, prowling close to its rocky foundations. The formidable weight of its walls crushed all sense of hope, but Joshua had a promise. He set his feet solidly on the path around the city, praying as he walked. *Do you see your servant, Lord? I am circling this city. I did not cower before the walls of Canaanite cities forty years ago. I will not cower before them now. I believe your promise—"I will give you every place where you set your foot . . . As I was with Moses, so I will be with you. I will never leave you nor forsake you."*[5] *Jericho guards all roads into the highlands of our inheritance. Will she try to prevent our travel to Mount Ebal and Mount Gerizim as instructed by Moses?*

With his circuit more than half complete, Joshua stopped near the gates. *Are we to wait until they attack us? Are we to attack? I need to know what to do. Tell me and I will do it.* As he prayed, he scanned the pale blocks of buttressing beside the gate. Higher, higher, they rose into the dark sky. Suddenly, the hair on the back of his neck prickled as hollow eyes met his. His blood ran cold. Silent as a shadow, he crept deeper into the blackness cast by the dense palm grove. Standing still as a rock, he tried to make sense of what he saw. *Only the remains of a dismembered, decomposing head. A skull. A warning from the king of Jericho.*

Joshua lifted his chin defiantly, addressing the dark forms of the trees around him in a whisper softer than breath. "I do not fear this city."

But the words froze on his lips as he realized that the shadow directly in front of him moved. The shape was a man, not a tree. Pale starlight glinted off the tall warrior's heavy bronze helmet and breastplate. An unsheathed blade gleamed in one hand, a bronze and leather-clad shield in the other.

"Who goes there?" Joshua barked. His hands involuntarily balled into fists.

The warrior loomed closer—almost seemed to drift toward him—but did not answer.

Joshua grabbed the hilt of his own sword in a fierce gesture. "Are you for us . . . or for our enemies?" Fear cracked his voice mid-sentence, and Joshua knew he had lost any hope of mental superiority.

The reply was gentle, authoritative. "As commander of the army of Yahweh I come. Take off your sandals. The place where you are standing is holy."

The burning bush. God's words to Moses. I know who this is. Joshua crumpled to the ground. He stretched out face down on the bare earth. "What message does my Lord have for his servant?" he asked.

There was no answer. In the protracted silence, Joshua realized he had been given a command. He sat up and pulled his feet close, fumbling to unlace his sandals. As soon as he finished, the warrior effortlessly lifted him to his feet as one would pick up a cast-off cloak. He turned and pointed toward Jericho with his sword. "Do not be dismayed by these fortifications. Jericho will not prevail. I have given you the city."

Joshua nodded. "What must I do?"

"Sound the shofar in camp at daybreak, on this the first day of the Feast of Unleavened Bread. Summon all Israel to watch as Eleazar waves the first cutting of the barley before me."

"We are already set to do that."

"Tell the people that the firstfruits are mine alone. It is I who gives the harvest. Following the presentation of the wave sheaf, you may harvest and freely enjoy the remainder of your crop. Just so, Jericho is mine. You may take no plunder from this city, but of every other city given into your hand, you may plunder freely."

"But, Lord, you must tell me how to breech these walls."

"After the ceremony of the wave sheaf at dawn, lead the army to Jericho. Circle the city one time in silence."

"In silence. One time. What more?"

"The warriors of the eastern tribes will lead the ark of the covenant. Assign seven priests to march directly before the ark carrying ram's horn trumpets. The armed warriors of all the other tribes will follow in the usual formation."

"The priests sounding their horns?"

"Only when you assemble the army in camp and again when the circuit is complete. Walk in silence. No horn blasts. No battle cries. No idle chatter."

"When we complete the circuit, then what?"

"Return to camp. Repeat this for six days during the Feast of Unleavened Bread." Joshua nodded. "Six days. Then?"

The commander's eyes bored into Joshua's, but the old warrior was not afraid to return the gaze. An infusion of energy flowed through him as the heavenly warrior spoke again. "On the seventh day, I will give the city into your hands. Go out at dawn and march around it in silence as before. But continue for seven circuits. Instruct the priests to blow a single blast of their shofars at the end of each circuit. When the seventh is complete, have the priests sound a long and mighty blast. Tell every man to join in a loud shout when they hear the ram's horns, and the walls of the city will collapse. Only the home of Rahab and her family will remain. Instruct my army to go up over the rubble of those walls, every man straight in from every side. You must utterly destroy Jericho. Burn the city as an offering to your God. Warn my people severely to take no captives, no plunder. Devote the city and all in it to me. Spare only the faithful Rahab and her family."

Filled with fear and wonder, Joshua did exactly as he was told. And when the warriors returned from circling Jericho, he commanded them to march to the barley fields and begin gathering grain. Earlier that morning, as the soldiers went out to march around the city for the first time, their wives and children gathered manna as usual. No one, not even Joshua, knew that manna would never fall again.

King Nahari

Naked, except for fantastic swirls of purple and black paint covering his body from ankles to neck, King Nahari staggered to his feet and dropped his bloodied scepter. His head throbbed violently as he descended the stairway leading from the high altar. He was exhausted. He wanted nothing more than to sleep, but the questions throbbing in his head could not be ignored. He stopped at the bottom step, staring blankly at the statue of Asherah. *Did she drive back that . . . that . . . siege or attack or whatever it was. That silent circling of Jericho yesterday morning?*

Asherah's moon was one day past full strength. It would shrink to complete darkness in two weeks' time. The king couldn't shake the nagging worry that Asherah's power was waning as well. Just when they needed her. He fell to his knees before the image, lifting his eyes to hers. *What hope do you offer us? Will you destroy Israel now? Will they return?*

The hard face of the Queen of Heaven gazed unfeelingly over his head. He dropped his eyes to the golden breasts glimmering in the flickering light of hundreds of olive oil votives. Asherah was supposed to nourish her worshippers, not plunder them.

"O Goddess of Jericho, we depend on you," he prayed aloud. "We have given you scores of bulls and rams in recent weeks. We have given our firstborn children. Tonight, we have offered the fairest virgins of the city. Are you satisfied, goddess of blood? Had you lifted your arm in our defense weeks ago, we could have sung your praise in celebration of the harvest. Do you see our reapers cowering inside these walls? No harvest. No lusty festival. No promise of continuing fertility. Instead, this night of terror. This mad bloodlust."

The king cringed at a soft shuffling behind him. The maddening swarm of priests. Not what he needed at the moment, but a flash of purple at the edge of his vision alerted him that his chamberlain was with them. He turned slowly as the man slipped his favorite embroidered robe around him, and the retinue of priests bowed low—disgustingly obsequious.

"The power of Baal possessed you tonight, O king!"

"Surely these sacrifices aroused Our Lady to fight for her city."

"O great Nahari, your name will be a legend in Canaan."

The king glared at the fawning swarm, fighting the urge to swat them like flies. "What of Israel?" he growled.

"Nothing, my lord."

"Not a sign of them, O king."

"Israel will not dare come near our city again."

Nahari sneered at them. "Oh really? Shall we throw open the gates today? Shall we send out the reapers to harvest the barley? Shall we begin to plow and plant the summer crops?"

The high priest coughed. "You must believe. Our goddess will not fail us now." He bobbed his head in a nervous bow toward the image.

The younger priests smirked their agreement. "Twenty-four virgins. Royal loins and scepter. No king could do more to win Asherah's favor."

An old priest, with a shiny, bald head and watery eyes, gazed at his king in awe. "The last girl died on the altar at the exact moment the moon slipped from view. A powerful omen."

"As seed dies to produce the harvest, her sacrifice will birth great victory," the high priest intoned.

"Was her blood of greater value to the gods than all the others?" Nahari shrieked.

This priestly prattling was stealing his sanity. He squeezed his eyes closed against the pulsing in the center of his forehead, but the pounding of his own blood pushed images of all the recent sacrifices into sharp focus behind his eyelids. *Blood, blood, and more blood.*

"What about the blood of all our infants? Did Asherah not see their crimson plea flowing down the temple steps. Did she watch their precious blood mingle with the filth of the marketplace gutters. The lives of my little princes excreted out of Jericho with the city waste? For what? What about all the bulls we sacrificed at her altar? *Where is she?* Where is Baal?"

"But Israel did not attack, my lord. She circled only once, and she has not returned."

The king blinked. "But what does that mean?"

The high priest laid his hand on Nahari's shoulder. "The sacrifice of the children secured Asherah's protection. It weakened the power of Israel so she dared not attack. But the worship this past night will bring about their complete defeat. The temple guards are posting the sacrificed virgins along the top of the wall as we speak. Their flaming bodies will usher in an era of peace and safety."

The king shook free of the priestly clutch. He had lived with the man's lies too long to believe he really knew how to manipulate the gods.

"Do not undo this power by your doubts, my king. The ancient writings have spo—"

The distant wail of ram's horns cut off the old man's protracted speech. He reeled back from the sound, cringing in confusion as Shinab sprinted through the portico with an urgent shout.

"They are back, my lord!" The young captain offered a quick military salute to the king and continued bellowing the news. "Marching around the city just as they did yesterday."

The king did not remain in the temple to hear more. He shoved his way through the bevy of priests and rushed to the top of the wall just as the twenty-four human torches burst into flame. The back of his mind registered the moaning, the final shrieks of those who still lived, but he could not look away from this frightening army circling his city. Thousands of feet, marching, marching, marching. Despair twisted everything inside him. The ominous tramping drove whatever power had been released by Jericho's virgins into the dirt.

Nahari was aware that Shinab and the priests gathered behind him on the wall, but he did not acknowledge them. Finally, a unison blast of ram's horns broke the interminable sound of trudging feet. Like a perfectly choreographed dance line, the armed vanguard peeled away from the circuitous path, pulling the entire train along behind. The army of Israel left Jericho for the second time without attacking and headed north to their camp in total silence.

"What *is* this?" The king's voice was hoarse with fatigue and desperation.

"Surely the shield of Asherah confuses them each time they come to attack," the high priest answered in a shrill prophetic voice. "She stills their battle cry and demolishes their assault plans."

"Does this look like confusion to you?"

"It doesn't matter," Shinab snorted, "What kind of threat can they pose? Look at them—mismatched armor, a hodgepodge of weapons, priests with ram's horns instead of trumpets, and . . ." He laughed derisively. "A box shrouded in blue cloth for a god."

"Fool!" the king snapped. "Have you forgotten Egypt? The Red Sea? When the Israelite army is on the march, nothing can stop them." Spittle flew from his mouth as he said the words, but he didn't care. "That *box*, as you call it, just stopped a river at the peak of spring flooding. And that mismatched, hodgepodge army just marched across the dry bed of the Jordan into Canaan."

"But, my lord, who remembers a time when Jericho was even attacked, let alone defeated?"

"Unless Asherah awakes, there will be both attack and defeat. Did we not watch King Sihon, King Og, and the Midianite Five topple like ten pins on the other side of the Jordan? But this is not sport. It is the end of our civilization."

Two deep creases formed between Shinab's eyes. "Perhaps we should send out messengers to Moab or to the kings of Canaan for help."

"Would that I had formed alliances when I had the chance. It is too late now."

"Do not let pride prevent you from trying. We can send messengers out as soon as it is dark."

Nahari watched the dust of Israel's rearguard disappear where the road entered the thick vegetation. "Make it happen," he said quietly. "Also, order the engineers to inspect all fortifications. We must not allow the enemy to breach these walls."

Salmon

The altar fire, blazing brilliantly in the wan predawn light, crackled and licked at the slaughtered ram. For the third morning in a row, Salmon stood in full armor, marshaled with his battalion, ready to march. He was proud to stand under the lion banner of Judah and serve under the command of Caleb, but he knew military prowess would not bring down the well-fortified city of Jericho.

For the third morning in a row, Eleazar reminded the people of that very truth. Carrying a ram's-horn shofar in his hands, Eleazar left the altar and strode to the tabernacle with a double column of priests marching behind. The first six priests, also carrying horns, lined up as a ceremonial guard on either side of the entrance while Eleazar led the remaining four into the Holy of Holies. As soon as Eleazar emerged from the interior, the seven priests announced the appearing of the ark of the covenant. Seven ram's horns in unison. Hooooohooooooo. The blast was long and loud, continuing as they escorted the ark through the courtyard past the great bronze laver to the flaming altar.

The sacred chest itself was shrouded from human eyes by a covering of blue linen, but the glory light hovering above it announced a divine Presence. With slow and steady steps, the final four priests of the procession bore the weight of the ark on their shoulders by long gilded carrying poles. Even priests did not dare touch the holy symbol of Yahweh. Eleazar stopped beside the altar and raised his arms in blessing while the remaining six shofar-bearing priests marched on to the courtyard entrance, once more falling into honor guard formation, three on each side, flanking the colorfully-curtained gates.

"May Yahweh, God of heaven and earth, bless you today," Eleazar proclaimed in a loud voice. "You are the army of the Most High. You have this honor not because you are invincible, but because you choose to live in covenant with the Invincible One—the God of your fathers: Abraham, Isaac, and Jacob. He does not accompany you in this march around Jericho because you physically follow the ark, but because you follow his commands and march out in faith.

"When you faced the flooded Jordan, you did not have the power to defeat the storm god. But Yahweh, your God, did. You obeyed his command. You followed the ark of the covenant into the flood by faith, defying the power of Baal. You crossed the river on dry ground. Just so, Yahweh, your God, will go with you and give you victory when you are assailed by hostile armies. Trust his goodness and obey his commands. He is faithful to the faithful."

Defeating Jericho is just as impossible as stopping the Jordan. Salmon nodded agreement. How well he understood that impossibility. Less than one turning of the moon had passed since he and Jathniel explored the city and its surrounding lands. Joshua's naïve spies. They were the first Israelites to view the daunting height of those walls up close. First to get an idea of the brutality and numbers of the enemy troops. Feeling very small and alone, he and Jathniel walked through Jericho's imposing gates, buttressed on both sides by massive gate houses. They saw the arms stockpiled there, more than enough to supply an army twice the size of Joshua's. Together they gauged the thickness of the walls. Then, as captives held at the North Wall Inn, they got a close-up view of rooms built into the space between the inner and outer walls. They assessed the dimensions of the city and its fortifications from the top of that wall before Rahab hid them beneath a pile of stinking, soggy flax.

Once Eleazar's blessing was complete, not another word was spoken. With great dignity, the high priest, still carrying the shofar, strode through the courtyard entrance. At the same time the army began to move. First the vanguard, followed by the ceremonial guard of seven with their horns leading the ark of the covenant, and finally, all remaining divisions as rearguard.

Salmon felt a twinge of dread as Caleb raised his sword to signal the tribe of Judah to fall in behind the ark. It wasn't dread of the enemy, but of the march itself. His movements would be stiff and uncomfortable at first, easing as they marched. Each day a little easier than the day before. He could hardly complain. Nearly every man in every division was in the same stage of healing. All but Caleb and Joshua, as well as Eleazar and his brother Ithamar, the two priests shouldering the golden poles at the front of the ark—four old men who had been circumcised forty-one years earlier after the Red Sea crossing. Salmon smiled grimly. No, there was no way this invalid army could conquer the city of Jericho.

Somewhere between the tabernacle and the city, the clouds billowing in the eastern sky broke into the full rosy glory of dawn. By the time Salmon and the division of Judah began the march through the palm groves on the eastern side of the city, its formidable walls were awash in brilliant sunlight. For the third morning in a row, Salmon's chest clutched at the sight of crimson draperies pulled closed across a very familiar window high on the north wall. Memories of his days of spying had begun to slip into a strange, hazy reality. Hiding under piles of flax. Slithering down the rope from Rahab's window. Cowering in the cave listening to the echoing voices of their pursuers. Those scenes were like a campfire story. Someone else's story from a faraway time, a faraway place. Salmon snorted. *A time best forgotten. A place best avoided.*

To an unwitting observer, the drapery cord hanging from the window would seem to be the result of carelessness, fallen out of place when the scarlet draperies were pulled. It was the agreed-upon sign between Rahab and the spies, but viewing it now from the march around the city, it reminded him of a long drip of blood oozing ominously from the windowsill. Blood that could easily have been *his* or Jathniel's . . . or Rahab's.

The flood of intense emotion stirred by the thought of her astonished him. Not that her image hadn't risen in his mind over the past two weeks . . . often. The exquisite perfection of Rahab's face was permanently seared into his memory by the fires of fear and deliverance. This definitely was not someone else's campfire story. His life and destiny were knit together forever with that Canaanite girl and the family still trapped in the nightmare of Jericho.

Faithfulness to the faithful, he repeated to himself. Remarkable faith and, he had to admit, remarkable beauty.

Rahab

The blare of ram's horns, hoarse and distant, shattered Rahab's dreams. A rustling and scrabbling rushed by her bed. Sandals pattering. Skirts swishing up the ladder. She rubbed the remnants of drowsy confusion from her eyes as her mother and sisters-in-law disappeared through the trapdoor. She recognized now the excited voices of her nieces and nephews and the deeper voices of her father and brothers, mingling and echoing down from the open trapdoor in her ceiling. *The fourth circling—and I am the only one not yet on the roof.*

Rahab leaped out of bed, pulling on her cloak, flying up the ladder and onto the roof just as the Israelite vanguard began to fill the pathway in silent circuit along the north wall. In contrast to the ominous tramping on the road below, the children giggled and shrieked in a game of tag around the bundles of cured flax. The adults watched silently. This was not a time for the faint of heart. She drew in a deep breath to steel her faith and suppress a sense of dread.

Even in broad daylight, the streets of Jericho had become a living nightmare. Foot soldiers massed by the gates, thousands of spear-throwers and archers perched on the ramparts, heavily armed patrols swarmed through every quarter—and the blackened remains of the virgin sacrifices stretched upward to the realm of the immortals in a ghastly plea for help. Compared to that visible reality, one promise quickly spoken by two Israelites—enemy spies, no less—seemed a flimsy lifeline.

The king had ordered all citizens to store water in every empty jar they had, enough to survive a long siege. Her parents grumbled about Nahari's insanity. The well at city center had not failed in a thousand years. Now, with fear prowling the streets, sure to grip her in its cold clutches if she ventured out, she was glad for the king's edict. Her family could get by without going to the well for weeks if they rationed carefully.

Her brothers, Helek and Zetham, long settled in homes of their own and prosperous in their careers as merchants, understood that this Israelite horde was unlike any threat Jericho had faced before. But, unlike the rest of the city, they were not paralyzed by fear. As soon as they learned of her league with the spies, they grasped the odd hope she offered and moved their families to the inn. And now for the fourth day they huddled together on the rooftop as the thunder of thousands of feet shuddered up through the normally solid walls of Jericho.

"Maybe today," Grandmother Shua said in hushed awe.

One of Rahab's sisters-in-law moaned softly. The other's face twitched in obvious trepidation. These two women had not grown up with the stories of Israel's God laying waste to the power of Egypt. Rahab had, but could find no comforting words for them. If only her faith could be as joyful and confident as Grandmother's.

Shua seemed to understand. Without a word, she pulled all three women into one embrace as if they were children. "Don't be afraid. I've lived long enough to know when to be afraid and when not to."

Tell me how, Grandmother. These righteous people may spare us as promised. But will they allow us to make their camp our home? Tell me how to banish forebodings of aimless wandering. Of being aliens wherever we go. "I wish I knew how to not be afraid," she whispered.

"I'm not afraid," Keziah sniffed, "but I don't see how circling a city will accomplish anything. This war strategy is just plain strange."

Rahab looked at her mother in astonishment. She really didn't seem to be afraid, but over the years she had lost the dream of belonging to Israel. "Yahweh *is* a strange God, Mother. When I was small, you and Grandmother both told me the stories of his power. A God unlike all others."

"What do I care about gods and their power? I just want to be safe and happy with my family around me. Whether here in Jericho or somewhere else, it makes no difference to me."

Grandmother gently unwrapped her arms from the three young women and pointed toward the blue-shrouded chest carried by priests in white linen. "That is what makes all the difference."

"What is it?" Curiosity seemed to drive away Naarah's fear.

Jerusha's eyes opened wide. "Is that their god?"

"Not their god. Yahweh, the God of Israel, is beyond imagining. No image could represent him."

"Well, what is it?" Jerusha asked. "How do they get that light to hover over it?"

"That is a glimmer of Yahweh's character. He lives in covenant with Israel and that chest contains the terms of the covenant, his law."

"A covenant? Like an alliance between kings?"

"Yes. Much like a royal blood covenant of trust and loyalty that cannot be broken."

"I cannot fathom trusting any of our scheming, capricious gods to keep a covenant—even if we could persuade one to enter such a relationship."

"How do you know all this, Grandmother?"

Shua shrugged enigmatically. "Rahab is not the only one who entertained Israelite spies."

"Really? You?"

"It's a long story. I will tell you about it while we eat breakfast."

Rahab smiled. Her sisters-in-law had always considered Shua a strange old lady.

Now they looked at her with new appreciation, and Rahab felt closer to her brother's families than ever. Family. One family. That is what her mother wanted. That is what they were here and now. And this crisis made it happen.

A high-pitched shriek behind the adults overpowered the sound of tramping feet. Instantly, Jerusha seized her eldest son by a handful of his tunic as he ran past, stopping him from following his cousin in a great leap onto Grandfather's neatly piled prize crop of flax. "No, you don't. Those bundles are scutched and heckled, ready for market."

"But, Ima. It's no fun being stuck in the inn day after day."

Jerusha's tone was adamant. "We women worked hard to finish those delicate fibers. The best crop in years. Bored children will *not* be spoiling them."

"No need to stop their fun." Jokshan grinned. "I do not know exactly how it will happen, but Jericho's day of doom has come. The victors will either carry off all our possessions or destroy them. I do not expect to sell the flax this year. Let the children play."

King Nahari

It was the fifth day. The Israelites were circling again. The king stormed into the temple and howled at the image of Asherah. "Your priests have demanded our gold, our jewels, and fine garments. We sacrificed our best bulls. We sacrificed our firstborn and Jericho's most beautiful virgins. What more?"

He threw himself down at Asherah's feet. "Your priests deceive me. I will give them nothing more unless you give me an undeniable sign of your favor."

"She *is* showing her favor, my lord," the high priest intoned from behind him. "She has not allowed an assault on our city. Even now she holds back Israel's attacks so they only circle once in silence. Soon our gracious goddess will reward us with deliverance."

The king scrambled to his knees and swirled around. He caught his high priest by the ankle. "Asherah speaks to *me* now. Seven is the number of Israel's God. If they come back, if they circle the city again, my soldiers will round up seven priests, starting with the youngest. They will be the next sacrifice to our *gracious* goddess." He snorted, nostrils flaring with the fury of a bull. "I'm done with waiting. I will see seven priests sacrificed every day until Israel is driven away. Pour out your most powerful prayers—if indeed you have any power at all. Your lives depend on it."

Acsah

By the time the men tramped out of camp on the sixth morning of the Jericho circuits, Acsah was already laboring over a dye vat with Abihail and the sisters rescued by her father during the Midianite War. Abihail was abnormally quiet, her forehead creased with worry over this strange war. Acsah stopped stirring and tried to cheer Abihail with a teasing look. "If a woman were in charge of the military, we would be finishing the circuit and heading home for breakfast by now."

Abihail laughed. "Acsah, there is not another girl in Israel who speaks as brashly as you."

Acsah shrugged. "Words weakly spoken might just as well not be spoken at all."

Abihail rolled her eyes, then leaned close to the little girls to be certain they heard her. "Learn from Acsah's excellent domestic skills but model your speech after gentler women of Israel. It will most likely keep you out of grave trouble."

Acsah smiled as she lifted a ladleful of the steaming berry and water mixture and let it dribble slowly back into the pot. One could dwell on horrors that might happen or look with humor on brighter possibilities. In this case, the latter won. Abihail's forehead was smooth and she was smiling.

Hogluh and Hodesh hopped and wiggled around her, piping like baby chicks. "How can we help? What can we do?"

Acsah chuckled. In such a few weeks, these Midianite refugees had become as much a part of her as her arms or legs. She would be crippled if she lost them now. The work they managed to accomplish was truly helpful, but she treasured their childish prattle most of all. They made her laugh, and when she was tempted to worry during this time of war, they kept her mind occupied with happier things.

"Can we put the wool in now? Can we stir?"

"I'm not certain you are old enough to work around a boiling cauldron. Why don't you help Abi get the wool from the saltwater bath?"

"But we want to see how the color works."

Abihail's sweet nature could not let the little girls be disappointed for even a moment. "Don't worry. You won't be restricted to the saltwater. You'll get to help with the dyeing. Just be sure to obey every command instantly."

Hogluh and Hodesh nodded solemnly.

"Now, see the two empty baskets over there? If you girls would each grab one and bring them to me, I will load them up. Then you can watch Acsah drop the yarn into the pot."

Acsah strained out a few remaining seeds and skins with a gourd ladle drilled full of small holes. She gave a final stir. "God didn't give us red sheep, but I think we will have red wool by the end of the day."

Abihail piled dripping skeins of creamy white yarn into Hogluh's basket. "Maybe now she will tell us what she is going to use the wool for."

"You are as bothersome as the little ones, Abi. Just enjoy the process today." Acsah eased pieces of wet wool from Hogluh's basket into the dye vat. "I will tell you about my project only if the color is successful." She attempted to sound as mysterious as possible.

Hogluh watched the wool bob to the surface, already the pink of spring blossoms. "Oh Acsah, it *is* successful," she cried. "Look how pretty it is."

Hodesh ran to them with her batch of wool and stood on tiptoe beside her sister to get a better look, steadying herself by pulling on Acsah's skirt. "When can I put mine in?"

Acsah nudged the curly-headed tyke back. "Help her balance, Abi. My skirts will not hold her up if she starts to fall." Only when Abihail had stabilized the child, did Acsah proceed. "Now we are ready. Lift your basket higher. Hold it carefully. I will drop the skeins in gently so there is no splash."

Hogluh's eyes sparkled with excitement. "Our sheep in the desert were black so our dresses have always been dark brown. Will you make red dresses for us?"

"Not with this yarn. I have an idea for a *big* project. I will need all this wool and more. But . . . perhaps we can use a little of this red for an embroidered border on the neck of the dresses you have."

Hodesh bounced on her toes. "I would love that."

Acsah gave the girl an affectionate squeeze. "You certainly deserve beautiful new dresses. If you had not become so quick with your spindles, we would not have enough finished yarn for my surprise."

Abihail watched the color deepen as Acsah stirred. "Please tell us what your project is."

"Not yet. It must remain my secret, chiefly because I don't want to raise hopes in vain."

"Then I will come back every day to help with the weaving."

"We want to help too," Hodesh chirped. "Even a simple rug woven from red wool would be lovely."

"But she is planning something much bigger than a rug," Hogluh reminded her.

Abihail frowned slightly at the rich, purple-red color. "This color is beautiful, but it is also the color of blood. Are you worried about Caleb when he goes off each day to circle Jericho?"

"If I start to worry, I remind myself how Yahweh stopped the Jordan for us. How can we hesitate to follow him anywhere after that? The hard part is watching Abba go off each day without *me*. I would give anything to see God at work when they conquer that city."

"Not me. I want to remain safe in our camp, and I want Eliab right here beside me. I am so relieved every time he returns home to me, woundless and whole."

Acsah looked thoughtful for a moment. "It is amazing that the soldiers on Jericho's walls only watch—not an arrow shot, not a spear thrown, not a stone cast." She chortled. "The only wounds our men have suffered so far in Canaan have been inflicted by our own flint knives."

"Don't remind me of that. I hated seeing Eliab so miserable. What if Jericho had attacked us immediately after the circumcision? Our men could hardly move. Eliab confessed that the first day of marching around the city was very uncomfortable, but each successive day helps him regain more and more strength and ease of movement."

"The Lord's plans are always the best plans."

Abihail's brow crinkled again. "I wonder what will happen tomorrow when the walls fall."

"We don't have to wonder. We know," Acsah said confidently. "We know that Yahweh has given us the city."

"But does that mean we will not lose any of our warriors?"

"That we don't know. We simply have to trust God and enjoy our men every day they are with us. As I have said before, our people should fear the enemy within more than the enemy without."

Hodesh looked at Acsah with wide, black eyes. "Are there Canaanites within? Within camp?"

"No, my little one, I mean the enemy that speaks inside your head and tries to steal your heart away from Yahweh."

"No enemy could ever steal me away from Yahweh. He brought us here to you and Master Caleb."

"Yes, Hodesh, I believe he did." Acsah continued stirring the yarn slowly. Suddenly, she stopped. "Hush! Do you hear it?"

The distant blare of the priest's horns signaled the completion of the sixth circuit of Jericho.

King Nahari

The king woke to anxious murmuring around his bed, blurry shapes moving about in the semidarkness. As he tried to orient himself, the horror of recent images raced through his mind—*earthquakes, Israel crossing the dry bed of the Jordan, silent marchers circling Jericho. Blood flowing down the steps of the temple—bulls, infants, virgins, and then yesterday . . . seven priests. Were these the ghosts of those sacrifices?* He repressed the thought and sat up. Throwing his feet over the side of the bed, Nahari growled at the whispering gray shapes. "Who dares enter this chamber while the king sleeps?"

"It is only your loyal priests and physicians, my lord."

"I did not call for priests—and why physicians? Am I ill? I don't remember being ill."

"Afflicted with a bit of hysteria last night, O my king. We hope to cure it."

Nahari hated the nasal whine of the high priest's voice. "You cringing cowards. You didn't like last night's sacrifices because something is finally affecting you."

"Be calm now, most valiant lord. Lie down and rest."

"What are you up to?" the king asked sharply, peering intently at the shadows. "Why is it so dark in here? Let me see your faces."

The shadowy figures backed away from the royal bed, leaving only the king's bodyguard close at hand. "Open the draperies," the high priest's voice commanded.

The heavily armed guard left the bedside, reaching the window in two strides. Nahari stopped him with a snarl. "I give the commands here."

Before the man could completely turn to receive other orders, the king added sullenly, "Open the draperies."

Dawn light, too brilliant, too red, flooded the room and Nahari clapped both hands over his eyes. Dimly, he overheard the high priest calling for the royal wine steward. By the time the king's eyes had adjusted to the light, his steward entered carrying his favorite silver chalice.

"Test," the priest said.

The steward held the cup close to his lips and hesitated.

"Test, I said. His highness needs this mixture and must feel confident it is safe."

The priest seized the cup the moment the man had taken the obligatory sip. He held it out to the king. "On my orders, the royal apothecary has added a potion to the wine to strengthen your body and sooth your mind."

Nahari ignored him. He leaped up and ran to the window. "Listen!"

From beyond the city wall came the dreaded sound of thousands of feet pounding the earth. "What are they doing? They set up no siege. They bring no ladders to scale the walls. No battering rams to breach them. They prowl around the city like a lion sniffing his prey—and then retreat to their lair without so much as a roar. How much longer will they do this? An attack would be a relief."

"O my lord, do not say that."

An insect-like buzz arose from the priests around the perimeter of the room as the high priest slipped to the king's side and extended his hand again with the royal cup. "You must remain calm and clearheaded, Your Majesty. Drink this."

The king shoved the cup away, splashing blood-red droplets on the pristine white of the high priest's robe. "Where is Shinab?" he shrieked. "Summon my captain."

The priest ignored him and continued in a soothing drone, "Your people are near panic. Jericho needs a composed and levelheaded ruler to restore confidence in our strong walls and in our Lady Asherah's protection. I am trying to help you."

King Nahari opened his mouth to reply, then stopped when clopping footsteps echoed from the hallway outside the room. "Shinab? Is that you?" he called.

The priests eyed each other nervously.

The young captain stopped in the doorway, obviously surprised to see a crowd gathered in the king's bedchamber at daybreak. He addressed the king hesitantly from where he stood. "They are circling again. The seventh day."

"Seven . . .? Seven?" Nahari stared at him, aghast. Only vaguely did he notice that his steward, suddenly pale and wiping large beads of sweat from his forehead, staggered out of the room on the arm of a priest.

"What is your command, Your Majesty?" Shinab asked quietly.

"Command . . .?" King Nahari looked from Shinab to the high priest. "I must clear my head."

The king seized the cup from the high priest's hand. As he quaffed a long draft, the grinning, bobbing faces of the priests pressed toward him from every corner of the room.

"Out!" he shouted, spewing droplets of red wine on Shinab's leather breastplate. "Get these charlatans out of my chamber."

The high priest shooed the priests toward the doorway with a wave of his arm. "Calm yourself, Your Majesty," he murmured in soothing tones. "Finish your wine. You must have a clear head, as you yourself said."

The king drained the cup and, not seeing his steward, returned the bronze vessel to the high priest's hands. He smacked his lips against a tingling numbness.

"Your orders, sire?"

"This is day seven. We must strike back. I will go to the wall myself to direct," he said decisively. "Our slingers will afflict that rabble with a hail of rocks. When the army of Israel begins to scatter in disarray, we will send down a rain of arrows. I want three battalions of spearmen followed by three battalions of swordsmen massed at the gates ready to pursue and destroy the last of those marchers. We will attack and demolish everyone in that camp of cowards."

"O very wise! Very bold, my lord!" The covey of priests in the doorway bowed and tossed oily smiles at the king. "Asherah will grant certain victory."

"Why are you still here?" Nahari's irritated glare drove them back a few steps. He turned back to his captain. "Shinab, set this up with orders for all troops to wait for my command. Call for the yad to meet me here in my chambers." He paused a moment and looked his captain full in the face. A wild, unnatural glint flashed in Shinab's cold eyes as Nahari added, "Capture that chest if you possibly can. It must be the secret of their power. I want it for Jericho."

"It will be done, my king," Shinab answered with a smart salute and left the room.

"Where is my steward? I must dress." King Nahari looked around in confusion.

"He was suddenly unwell, your majesty." The high priest called for an understeward familiar with the king's wardrobe.

"Get my best robe," Nahari barked as soon as the man appeared. "The one from Babylonia. Whether I meet the captain of Israel defeated under my foot, or finally surrender this city to him as victor, I will do it in dignity."

The high priest stepped forward. "Do not utter words of possible defeat. Words have power."

"Get out, all of you. Back to your temple, you lying, greedy vultures. And quit your circling. I am no corpse."

While the bevy of priests jostled and shoved one another in their haste to exit, Nahari held out his arms. The steward pulled an intricately embroidered coat over his linen tunic, and then belted the robe snugly to his waist with a leather girdle studded with amethyst and turquoise.

"Your breastplate and helmet, my lord?"

"No," he answered, feeling flushed. "This war is beyond such armor. The battle is drawing to a close . . . one way or another. Bring my crown."

Other servants oiled his hair and beard, crimping neat curls into place. King Nahari inspected their work in a bronze mirror. His face looked unusually pale in contrast to the deep purple of the robe. Or maybe it wasn't. Maybe it was the mirror. His reflection was unacceptably blurred this morning. "See that this mirror gets a good polish today. The image is not clear. Where is my yad? Tell him to meet me on the wall at the top of the palace stairs."

He placed the crown on his head himself. It felt strangely heavy, but he lifted his chin proudly, and headed out to face . . . to face . . . well, whatever this day was going to bring.

At the doorway, he nearly collided with a soldier rushing toward the royal quarters. "Captain Shinab sent me, my lord. The horns of the Israelites sounded the end of their circuit, but they did not retreat. They are circling a second time."

Nahari dashed out of the palace and up the stairs. He seemed to float as he reached the top of the city wall. *Perhaps it was the sudden activity so early in the morning. But maybe it was the high priest's potion.* He paused to catch his breath and stood swaying slightly as he gawked at the enemy. The army of Israel circled his city in total silence save for the sound of their feet just as they had for six days. Frowning down on the miserably equipped battalions, Nahari caught the eyes of the warrior who led Israel with his upraised sword.

The king saluted. "You are not worthy of being my enemy, dog," he muttered. "But how convenient for you to continue marching today so I can carry out my plan. Your feet have harassed me long enough—" He pressed his hands against his temples. The footsteps pounded in his skull. The measured thud of thousands of feet thundered through his head. *My troops will stop those feet today,* he assured himself.

As the seven priests with ram's horns passed directly below him, the king stared at the covered chest of Yahweh. Just above it, a light hovered—its glow eerily luminescent even in the brilliant light of the morning. *Strange,* he thought. *How can there be a shining brighter than sunlight . . .?*

The rest of the landscape grew darker and darker in comparison. Nahari's bodyguard quickly grabbed his arm. "Forgive me, my king. I dare touch your royal person only because you wobbled." Nahari could see him only through murky shadows.

By the time the king's head cleared, the dreadful tramping was accompanied by the low, monotonous chanting of his own priests. Nahari sat up, nearly crashing heads with the physician-priest who hovered over him. The chant ceased and a shaky voice from somewhere nearby whispered, "You brought him back from the dead."

The high priest hissed, "Silence, you fool. You know the king merely collapsed. Let him rest here until he has enough strength to resume command."

Nahari winced at the searing pain that drove through his skull. "What happened? Did I pass out?" he asked. Black spots floated before his eyes as the physician-priest's face came in and out of focus.

The royal physician bent down and placed a hand on the king's forehead. "The clammy coldness has abated."

"You needed calming, m'lord," the high priest answered, kneeling beside the physician-priest.

"What did you do to me?" Nahari raged. He stretched out his hands to throttle the annoying voice of the old man forever. The high priest easily dodged out of reach, while the king fell back on the stone pavers, exhausted by the effort and shaken by his state of weakness.

"We prepared a potion so you could rest—not foolishly race up the stairway to the top of the wall," the physician sniffed.

The high priest nodded. "It should have been stronger. We did not intend for you to awake for a long, long time."

"What of Israel's army?" the king mumbled. "Send for Shinab."

"I am here, my master. The slingers and archers on the wall are ready. The attack force you ordered waits at the gate. We need only your command."

"Could you not execute the plan without me, you fool—seeing that I was indisposed?" Anger energized him in spite of his weakness and he sat up.

"But m'lord, our first concern was for you, and we . . . had some time . . . the Israelites continue marching."

The king struggled to sit up again. He could see that the sun was already past zenith. "What hour is it? How long have those desert vermin been circling my city?"

"It is the seventh hour, Your Majesty. They are nearly finished with the seventh circuit."

"Seven? Does anyone else understand the significance of the number seven to the God of Israel?" The rush of fear twisting in the pit of King Nahari's stomach was followed quickly by incredulous rage. "I have been on this wall in a drugged sleep for five rounds by our enemy? Shinab, why did you not proceed with our counterattack?"

"The orders were to wait for your command, sir."

All at once the pounding feet stopped and enemy ram's horns sounded a long sonorous blast.

"Shall I call for the attack to begin now?" Shinab shouted.

"Why does this blaring last so long?" the high priest's reedy, nasal voice quavered. He pressed his hands over his ears to block the unremitting sound. "Why don't they stop?"

As if the gods had heard, the deafening blast stopped with shocking suddenness, but that brief moment of complete silence was more terrifying yet. Then thousands of voices echoed against the hills from every direction, building to a great crescendo, reverberating through the streets of Jericho. "For the Lord and for Joshua. Give way, O walls."

As the king struggled to his hands and knees, the solid stones began to vibrate beneath him. Small cracks grew and split into gaping chasms. With a shriek, the high priest slid into a void that opened between himself and the king. Shinab leaped the gap and pulled Nahari to his feet. "We can make it, master. The stairs are right over there."

"Too late," the king cried as the entire wall heaved, tottered, and collapsed toward the center of the city.

CHAPTER FOUR

ESCAPE FROM JERICHO

Salmon[6]

R am's horns shattered the stillness, and every nerve in Salmon's body sizzled with energy. It shivered up from the soles of his feet and awe seized his voice.

"For the Lord and for Joshua!" he shouted.

Ten thousand voices merged with his in a thundering roar of faith. "For the Lord and for Joshua! Give way, O walls!"

The ground trembled beneath his feet. The earth rumbled and rolled. Fracture lines shot up from the foundations. Parapets split and splintered. Buttressing cracked. The renowned walls of Jericho toppled and crashed into the city they were built to defend—an eggshell crushed by the hand of Yahweh.

Through the dust and din, Salmon could hear Joshua's howling commands and the short, quick blasts of the seven priest's horns blowing in unison, directing the first companies into the city from all four sides simultaneously. But Salmon and his friend Jathniel of Ephraim remained in place, muscles tensed, awaiting their special orders. Joshua had placed them with the troops covering the north side of the city rather than with their own tribes.

Neither of them knew the men charging toward the rubble, nor those who remained standing guard in the line beside them. But they knew each other in ways they had never known anyone else in their entire lives. They both knew the fear of skulking through a city as enemy spies, the panic of being trapped, and the euphoria of escape.

Jathniel tipped his head toward the wall and looked up. Enveloped by a cloud of dust rising from the debris, a single section of the wall stood strong, the red cord in the window clearly marking it as the home of the Canaanite girl who saved their lives. He lifted his brows as he caught Salmon's eyes. The two of them understood the faithfulness of their powerful God in a way others could not.

"Salmon. Jathniel." Joshua loped toward the two of them. "Time to keep your promise. Go get Rahab and her family."

Salmon immediately broke formation, sprinting toward the upright section of the wall, and Jathniel ran beside him, matching stride for stride.

"A different sprint than on our night of escape, eh?" Jathniel shouted, his heavy eyebrows dancing, a distinctive habit that often made Salmon laugh. Right now, he was laughing more at the irony than at the silly mannerism.

"I could never have imagined us racing *into* Jericho."

He slowed his pace. Racing where exactly? How were they to get to the inn door? The first wave of soldiers had long been swallowed up by a swirling wall of dust nearly as high as the formerly impregnable walls. It would be wise to determine the best pathway *before* entering that choking cloud. He came to a full stop, scanning the wreckage on either side of the inn.

As if a signal had passed between them, Jathniel halted at his side.

"What do you think?" Salmon asked him.

Jathniel's face was lifted toward the window of their escape, his eyebrows knotted in a serious frown. "That's the sign." A barely detectable tremor twitched his chin.

"I mean, which is the best route in?"

"I thought we would need that sign to find her home again." Jathniel continued staring at the cord in the window. "The shattering force passed right over the inn."

Passed over. As soon as Salmon heard the words, the heavy linen draperies seemed to flame brighter, an outrageous flush of red completely framing the pale faces peering from the window. No longer the North Wall Inn—this was a home slathered in blood as a sign for the angel of death to pass over—the saving Passover of the tenth and most dreadful of the plagues of Egypt.

"Rahab's Passover," he whispered.

"Passover?" Jathniel's eyebrows arched high. "We need to be expediting her *Exodus*. Come on. There seems to be a decent pathway east of the inn."

Rahab

"Quickly now, children. One at a time. Women go next." Rahab could remember the way her father's authoritative commands induced a sense of order, but she was not certain if she clambered down the ladder with her sisters-in-law or with her nieces and nephews. She wasn't even sure which group she fit in. Dazed and confused, she complied with her father's nudgings toward the window. The window and the red cord. *Where was the brave woman who placed that sign there? Surely not this shaking child with the pounding heart.*

She had pictured countless variations of this story—her escape from Jericho—but none of them came close to this reality: the city of her birth, the city of her suffering, literally collapsing around her. One moment she stood with her family on the roof of the inn, watching the silent tramping of Israel's armies. The next, an ear-splitting blast of seven ram's horns brought the marchers to a stop. The deafening shout, "Give way, O walls," hung for a moment in the clear morning air, then Jericho roared in protest, spewing a choking cloud of dust into the air.

Rahab could not hear her own scream as a sea of crashing and grinding masonry dropped away, leaving her family shrieking and scrambling for footing on a lone tottering island. Only Jokshan seemed to have his wits about him. "Children first! Children first!" he shouted at the squirming mass clawing at the trapdoor. "Quickly now, children. One at a time. Women go next." His confident directives soothed the family hysteria and they obeyed, filing down the ladder one after another.

The heavy draperies of the red room muffled distant screams and shouts, but not the loud throbbing of her own blood. Rahab rubbed her temples and was drawing in deep calming breaths when . . . a resounding thud reverberated through the walls and floor.

"It's the inn crashing down now!" a nephew shouted.

A niece whimpered. "We're going to die."

"Hush, hush," her mother soothed.

"It was our door," Grandmother Shua whispered. "It's *them*."

"The door!" Mother cried, seizing her husband's arm. "Why didn't you lock it, Jokshan?"

"Lock it? Against what, Keziah? What just happened to the walls?"

"Ooooh," Jerusha moaned and slumped into her husband's arms.

"Trust the promise," Helek murmured. "Trust the promise . . ."

The voices wafted to Rahab like a fog of fears from another world, like the incomprehensible voices of the busy inn drifting into the dark room of her childhood when she woke with night terrors. Then the racing footsteps crossing the dining hall below trapped her in the living nightmares of her past. *Helpless and alone, waiting, listening as heavy footsteps came for her, dreading the horror about to burst through the door—Uncle Thahash looming over her with his rod, battering and threatening until she submitted to his authority. One of the mauling, slobbering drunks who paid a high price in silver or gold to buy time with her. Ahuzzath leering, raping her with his eyes when he no longer had access to her body. The king's guards shackling her in the total darkness of the king's dungeon.* Rahab shuddered as the pounding footsteps started up the stairwell, coming for her. *Again.* Her mind went numb.

"There, there, child. It's *them.*" Grandmother said the word with warmth, reaching out to comfort her. Rahab's body was cold, but much as she wanted comfort, she could not yield to her grandmother's embrace.

"Them?" she repeated mechanically.

Shua cupped Rahab's face and lifted it so she could look into her eyes. "The spies promised to return. I know it's them. We are saved."

"Maybe not," her mother snapped. "Just as easily, a desperate man from the streets."

Not one desperate man, Mother. There are at least two. But you are right. It could be thugs from the street. Or the king's guard returning to drag us all to prison. They know where to find us.

"Let's go!" An urgent shout sounded from the stairwell. "Let's go! Let's go!"

The words mingled with the muddle in Rahab's mind. Then a second voice cut through the fog. "Rahab!"

Not just any voice. Undeniably Salmon's voice.

"Rahab, gather your family. Time to leave Jericho."

She stared at the scarlet-draped window. *I did not think to get another rope.*

Jathniel burst into the room, still shouting, "Let's go. Let's go."

Rahab looked around. *I don't understand. The family is gathered already, but how shall we leave?*

"Quickly. Follow us." Jathniel's strident tone roused her brother Helek to action. Rahab watched him herd his wife and children toward the door.

She watched Salmon race to the window and snatch the red cord. He thrust it into her hand. "Carry this," he said. "All Israel knows about the sign." Then as quickly as he appeared, he charged out the door, his final command echoing over his shoulder. "Stay together. Jericho runs amok."

As if in a trance, Rahab watched her brother Zetham's family filing from the room. Her parents followed. Then Jathniel reached for Grandmother Shua's arm.

"Let me help you, my good woman."

"I've been waiting for this day for forty years, young man. I am quite capable of fleeing a crumbling city on my own."

Jathniel shrugged and followed Grandmother. "Bring up the rear, Rahab," he ordered. He tossed one last urgent look her direction as he disappeared, but Rahab remained in the center of the room clutching the red cord. Her fingers twitched in search of a comforting tune on imaginary harp strings.

"Rahab, where are you?"

The sharp edge in Keziah's voice jarred her out of her bewildered state. She looked around. The room was empty, but she could hear the family footsteps slapping down the stairwell and across the stone floor of the main-level dining hall below. "Coming, Mother."

"*Stay together.*" That's what Salmon said. "*Stay together. Jericho runs amok.*" The floor trembled under her feet. *I must hurry after my family, but . . .*

Her mind suddenly cleared. A quick glance around the room told her the one thing she could not leave behind was missing. Focused on finding it, she dashed out of the room and down the corridor to Grandmother's room at the end of the hall. The opposite direction from the spies and her family. But she would hurry. She would catch up.

"Rahab!" Keziah called again. "Rahab, we are waiting at the door. Where are you?"

"Sorry, Mother, I *am* coming," she answered breathlessly. She scanned the dark recesses of the tiny chamber as she finished her sentence, "—but not without *it.*"

"Rahab! Hurry, Rahab." The childish piping of her nieces and nephews now accompanied her mother's cries.

"Come on, Rahab! We can't wait forever."

"Hurry!"

The sound of panic was growing stronger in the family voices. And she knew her answer had been too soft. Bracing herself in the doorframe as a rolling aftershock shuddered through the inn again, she took a deep breath and called out in her loudest voice. "I am on my . . ."

"Rahab, come now!"

Her final word was completely swallowed by the thunderous summons from her father.

She sighed. She was quite certain no one heard her over her father, and she was also certain her precious instrument was not on the upper floor of the inn. She rushed out the door toward the stairway.

For the past week—a bizarre week, with Israel's silent tramping around the city each day and tension building in the streets—she had played her harp often to calm herself . . . to calm the children. In truth, to calm the whole family. *Now—how could it be? In the precise moment she needed to grab the thing and run, she had no idea where it was.* She raced down the steps, her every step barraged by the family's increasingly frantic cries.

Then, as she emerged from the stairwell, sudden silence smothered the voices. A dozen sets of accusing eyes met hers. They were all clustered in the antechamber close to the door between their Israelite rescuers. Salmon's hand was already on the latch. *How would she ever convince them to wait while she searched the lower level?*

She smiled feebly with a glance that swept from Salmon, across her family's anxious faces, to Jathniel and back again to Salmon. She hoped her expression reflected the penitence she felt.

Salmon acknowledged her with a curt nod. His mouth was tight.

"I'm sorry I . . ." Her apology was swallowed up in a renewed frenzy of complaint.

"What were you *doing*, Rahab?"

"We don't want to leave you."

"Can't you feel the inn shaking?"

"Stay with us now, daughter," her father's voice rumbled over the babble.

Rahab hesitated at the foot of the stairs, and Salmon caught her eyes. As the recriminations flew, one side of his lips pulled up in a charming, crooked smile that communicated *None of you has any idea what is out there.* Without losing contact with her eyes, he pushed the door ajar and a deafening roar from the street strangled all remaining cries.

"Thank you. Now that I have your attention," he shouted over the bedlam. "Stay together. May the God of Israel be our shield." He gripped the hilt of his sword and plunged into the chaos of the street.

"Stay close this time, Rahab," Jathniel repeated. He followed Grandmother Shua and the last straggling children out into the street. And the doorway was empty.

Rahab stared at the scene framed by the familiar portal of her own door. It could not have been more alien. The palatial homes across from the inn had split open. Their fine furnishings lay splintered and crushed under blocks of fallen masonry while gaping holes marred the bright frescoes of interior walls. Up and down the street, citizens milled about, dazed and distressed. But more shocking than any of the rubble or confusion on the streets was the incredible void. Where massive walls had once towered protectively around the perimeter of the city, there was only a stark panorama of hills and sky blurred by rising billows of dust.

Then the door swung shut. Rahab needed to follow, but she couldn't. Not yet.

With a desperate prayer for help, she resumed the search. *Yahweh God, surely you understand. The songs of Canaan will remain in this room, but my harp is my soul.* She stared hard into the semidarkness. The instrument was not on the platform, nor around its edges. *Help me, God of Israel. From this day and forever, all my songs will be for you. I will teach my children and my children's children to sing your praise.*

As if in immediate answer to her prayer, the door behind her swooshed open. A flash of light rushed in catching the sheen of polished wood against the far wall near the kitchen—but Rahab froze. Her heart trapped between the joy of discovering her harp and the terror of who just discovered *her.*

"What are you *thinking?*"

Before she could identify the voice or the silhouette darkening the doorway, it lunged for her, seizing her upper arm fiercely, shouting as grit from the ceiling sifted over them. "Do you want to die in here? We must go now."

Salmon. Her fear vaporized. She read concern in that sweet face, not anger. "Please . . . I was searching for something."

"What if the rest of the north wall comes down? What if the inn implodes?" He stepped toward the doorway, attempting to drag her along with him. "Let's go."

Rahab ignored his demand, planted her feet solidly and twisted to break free of his grip. "Please. I know where it is now."

Salmon maintained his hold on her arm, but stopped and drew in a long, slow breath. He adopted a calm reasoning tone. "I can't force you to live, but I swore I would bring you safely out of Jericho if you hung this in the window." He relaxed his grip and reached out to touch the red cord still clenched in her hands. "Let me fulfill my vow."

Rahab glanced at the cracked ceiling. She would not ask because Salmon would never understand. With a burst of strength, she broke away, rushed across the room, and seized her precious instrument. "I cannot leave this."

Salmon exhaled and ran his hand through his hair. "I don't suppose you know about Lot's wife."

"Immortalized in salt," she said quickly. A smile twitched at the corners of her mouth. "Don't be angry,"

She wriggled out of her cloak, bundling the instrument as tenderly as one would swaddle an infant as she returned to him. For a fleeting moment, she thought she detected a look of admiration as he watched her cross the room. Then he motioned toward the door with a quick jerk of his head. "My task is to get the two of us out of the city. Alive. You are not supposed to bring anything."

His stern tone did not frighten her when so much kindness radiated from his eyes. "My harp and I are one," she said matter-of-factly and finished binding the bundle securely with the red cord.

Salmon shrugged helplessly and opened the door. "Let's stay together this time." He gripped her upper arm again leading her into the street, while Rahab clutched the most precious thing she owned tightly to her breast.

Once outside, the rush and confusion threatened to pull them apart. The sanity of Jericho's inhabitants had been shattered with their walls. Cries of the injured and dying mingled with curses. Market baskets and goods lay cast off and crushed underfoot. People living close to the crumbled walls raked through the debris for precious things, oblivious to bloodied neighbors and family members partially trapped or struggling to crawl from the rubble. A few citizens hovered in broken doorways, staring blankly at the crush and confusion while others, armed with spears or war clubs, plunged into the thick of it, lashing out at anyone in their path.

Salmon and Rahab had not taken ten paces into the crowd when warm, sticky wetness splattered across the back of her head and shoulders. She turned just in time to see a mop of gray hair split open like a melon, revealing a pulsing mass of brains and blood. She recognized the man with the severed skull as one of the inn's regular patrons. He slumped to the ground and a wild-eyed priest wielding an ax, blinked at Rahab. "I know you, sweet singer," he muttered. "But not him. I think he was an Israelite."

"God help us," Salmon breathed as he pulled her through the chaos.

Progress was slow and, at times, they were forced backward. Although Rahab was sorry she had been the cause of delay, she was not at all sorry she had searched for and found her harp. Slowly, lovingly, her fingertips caressed the familiar carvings under the layers of her cloak and comfort flowed into her. She cast her eyes down, simply following where Salmon led, blocking out the jostling crowds and the angry epithets against Israel and Yahweh their destroyer God. A praise melody began to form in her mind and flow, phrase by phrase, from her lips in counterpoint to the curses.

I will rejoice for Yahweh is my God.
He has saved me by His powerful hand.

"Slaughter every Israelite you find!"

He leads me out to a safe place;
He delivers me from evil.

"Drive them back to the desert."

My God can split the waters . . .

"Is that disgusting rat over there an Israelite?"

My God can raze a city . . .

"Crush all vermin creeping over our walls."

No force can hold back his mighty hand.

"Death to them all!"

My God is mighty to save.

"Death! Death!"

"Keep singing," Salmon whispered as he shouldered a path through the rabble. "Apparently these madmen know you. When they catch a little of your beautiful voice, they step back. Listen. They are warning their comrades not to hurt the singer from the North Wall Inn."

Rahab puffed out a half laugh. "Little do they guess the topic of my song or who it is that accompanies me."

"Your gift is our shield."

She cringed. Salmon would never say that if he knew her shame. Her gift had definitely not shielded her in the past, but his words gave her the perfect ending to her song.

When foundations crumble and madness reigns
Yahweh alone is my strength and shield.

The words were a prayer, not merely a wish.

Achor[7]

Israel's immolation brigade swarmed over the broken walls into Jericho led by a vanguard of swordsmen sentries. Their orders were to burn the entire city to the ground. No plunder. No captives. Nothing was to be salvaged but precious metals for the tabernacle. The command was as clear as it was drastic.

Achor was energized by the staggering demonstration of Yahweh's power he just witnessed. Proud to be part of the platoon from Judah, he and his eldest son, Jamin, charged down the mountain of tumbled blocks into the uproar, adding the smoke of their torches to the miasma of rising dust. As they skirted a jumbled pile of crushed masonry blocking entrance to the street, a weak voice called out, "Help me." At the same time, a colorful flash of purple registered on the edge of Achor's field of vision.

"Stop, Jamin." Achor turned aside and peered into a cove formed by two fallen pillars. "What have we here?"

He could just make out five twisted bodies sprawled within the darkness of the shelter. The central figure was dressed in the brilliant purple that first snared Achor's attention. He thrust his torch back into the shadows for a better look and gasped. The richly-garbed man clutched a crown.

"Look Jamin," he whispered. "We found the king."

He heard the sharp intake of breath as his son bent down beside him. "Look at that fabulous robe!" Jamin breathed.

The wide leather belt cinching the king's waist winked and blinked in the flickering torchlight with a multitude of jeweled eyes. At the neck and from mid-thigh down, the rich purple cloth was embroidered with alternating rows of gold and scarlet. Achor had never dreamed of such an exquisite garment. Wonder and reverence welled up within him and rose from his lips as a prayer. "Only may Yahweh allow me to find another as fine as this in one of the cities where we *can* take plunder."

Jamin did not respond directly to his father's words. "One of these Canaanites called out. Someone is still alive here. Our job is to ensure no survivors escape."

"And that all their belongings burn," Achor mumbled. He kicked at the body of a young, pimply-faced guard close to his feet. "Up now!"

The man did not move.

Handing his torch to Jamin, Achor ducked his head low, stepping over the dead soldier and entering the small cove. The three bodies swathed in priestly garments were as unresponsive as the guard, but when Achor's toe nudged the fallen monarch, the corpse wheezed. Prominent, hooded eyes snapped open, staring deep into his.

"He's alive," Achor croaked. He stumbled and fell backward over the dead guard. "The king is alive!"

"For the moment," Jamin replied flatly, drawing his sword.

Achor lay sprawled on his back close to the dying king. Lifting his head and shoulders in a scramble for dignity, he propped himself up by his elbows and found himself looking directly into menacing black eyes.

"Help. Me." The injured king repeated the words emphatically, one at a time. No longer a plea of desperation. It was a whispered command from someone clearly accustomed to obedience.

Achor could only stare at the Canaanite king in horror.

When there was no answer from either Israelite, the king struggled to a sitting position. He winced with the pain of his effort, taking short, rapid breaths to restore his strength. The dark eyes never ceased drilling into Achor's with disdainful authority. Achor grew increasingly uncomfortable, all too aware that he, of the conquering army, was still on his back, draped over a crumpled dead body. He should not be looking up at the defeated foe. He pushed himself to a crouching squat, eye level with the king, and addressed his son.

"Time to set this cove aflame, Jamin. We should catch up with our brigade."

"Wait," the man commanded. "I am King Nahari of Jericho." He held up the crown, trapping Achor's eyes as he toyed with the bejeweled symbol of his power. "This spot was the antechamber of my palace, but all is worthless to me now. Take this crown and help me escape."

Jamin stooped down and pushed the torches into the dim shelter. The piece in the king's hands glittered in the fiery light, but Jamin didn't give it a second look. "What use have we of a crown?" He knocked it to the pavement with the butt of one torch. "We are but simple Israelites."

King Nahari's eyes swam momentarily with desperation. Then he turned hopeful eyes to Achor. "I heard your words of admiration when your eyes first fell on this purple robe." He thumped his purple-swathed chest in a noisy pat. "It was given to me by the king of Babylonia. A gift when I took his youngest daughter as my wife. I am loath to give it up, but help me and it is yours."

"You and your city are beyond help. Everything will burn."

Nahari's fingers fumbled at the jeweled girdle around his waist. Amethysts, rubies, and turquoise stones glittered and gleamed as he unfastened it and tossed it toward Achor.

Achor's mouth went dry. He picked up the wide belt, seized by the urge to hide the thing under his own clothes and run. As the king began pulling the magnificent purple garment over his shoulders and head, he squeezed his eyes closed and steeled himself against the thought. He laid the belt on the broken floor between them. "I cannot take this."

Nahari ignored the words. A wave of his hand drew attention to his thin undergarment. "You can see that under the royal trappings, I too am but a simple man in a tunic." He turned one of the inside-out purple sleeves right again, panting with the effort as he continued. "I perceive that you are a rare man, as I am myself. One who appreciates fine things. Take it. There is no finer garment in all Canaan. It is said to bestow mystical powers of authority on its wearer." He met Achor's eyes boldly and hissed his last words with utter contempt. "Only a fool would let it burn."

"*You* are a fool if you think we would help you just to gain such a thing," Achor snapped. "No Israelite would dare wear clothing from Jericho."

The king seemed to sense a crack in Achor's resolve despite the emphatic words. He turned to Jamin with a confidential tone. "I have a small treasury back here. Wedges of gold. Bags of silver. My robe for the elder. Silver and gold for you. Take as much as you can carry," he coaxed. "Only help me. Surely the gods will reward your kindness."

"Such an act would be treason against our God and our people," Achor answered, firmly repulsing the pull of his own desire. "Ignite this den of temptation, my son."

"Wait, Father."

Jamin thrust both torches firmly into a crevice and fixed the king with a hard look. "Give me the robe. You may wear my outer cloak as a disguise and walk with us until we get outside the city. Then you will be on your own."

"Agreed," the king promised. "I will flee across the desert to Babylonia. I swear, I will never stir up revenge against your people nor join with anyone who dares attack Israel."

Jamin held the robe out to Achor. "Conceal this beneath your cloak, Father. We will keep it hidden until Israel has taken other cities and is permitted to carry off the plunder from them. Who could ever know it came from Jericho?"

Achor stood motionless. "Yahweh will know."

"The question is . . ." Jamin sneered, "will he care? We can sacrifice something of equal value to him later." He dangled the robe in front of his father. "This garment suits you. Clothing acquired in another city will burn as brightly in sacrifice to Yahweh. This or another, what is a robe to God?"

Jamin picked up the belt, pressing it along with the royal robe into his father's hands and then leaned over the king in a threatening pose. "Where is your silver and gold? Show me. I will not give you my cloak as disguise until I see it."

"My steward stocked it close at hand. We thought to escape the city this very night. Too late—" the king choked on his words.

Achor felt a twinge of pity for the man. "We will help you make that escape. Show my son your trove."

The king scrambled over the bodies of the three priests, kicking at their corpses angrily. "These charlatans deceived me. Burn them. Burn their filthy bodies." He crawled farther back into the cove until Achor could see only the white undergarment covering Nahari's back parts and the soles of his sandals. The king's voice echoed back from the depths of darkness as he scrabbled in the ruins. "Oh, that I could have torn them to pieces with my own hands while they lived. I could have fled. But they urged me to sacrifice more and more of the treasures of Jericho. To what end? Your people could not be stopped."

Tossing more complaints than rock, Nahari worked at clearing the rubble. "Long before its walls fell, Jericho had been plundered by its own priests. They depleted my treasury. Emptied my stables. Forced me to watch as they slaughtered Jericho's infants. Even my own flesh and blood . . . Can one of you help me here?"

Jamin ducked past his father and rolled aside a large chunk of broken masonry blocking a splintered door, then helped the monarch pull it open. The king hardly paused in his rant. "We sacrificed Jericho's fairest virgins on Asherah's altar. To what end? While my priests clamored for more and more, my gods remained silent." He pushed two heavy bags toward Jamin. "Here. Two hundred shekels of silver."

Jamin picked up one of the bags, opening it to verify the contents as the king continued rooting around in the blackness of his storage vault. "Take this wedge of pure gold. Can you carry more? I fear not. I have not the strength to carry but a few silver coins myself."

He lifted the gleaming metal, holding it up to Achor. "I will flee to Babylonia a pauper. But *my* fate is preferable to that of my subjects. Not one will escape our own conniving priests and the hand of Yahweh."

As Achor took the heavy wedge from the king, a quiver of delight passed through him. "It must weigh fifty shekels," he murmured approvingly.

He lifted his eyes just in time to see Jamin bring a massive block down on the king's head. The rock crashed into the rubble and King Nahari slumped to the ground, never knowing he had been deceived yet again.

Jamin rolled his eyes at the look of horror on his father's face. "With that crimped hair and beard, there is no way he could have posed as an Israelite. We could not have gotten him through the cordon surrounding the city—even if we really had wanted to help him."

Rahab

Rahab continued singing as Salmon shouldered a path through the crowd-clogged street. Their progress seemed to be in inches, but she found herself strangely calm when she closed her eyes against the violent clamor and concentrated on her song.

> *My God can split the waters,*
> *my God can raze a city.*
> *No force can hold back his mighty—*

Suddenly, a flash flood of pandemonium rushed at them from every street and alley. People who had been fleeing from the wall reversed direction and surged toward the standing section of the inn. Like the forceful backwash of a mighty wave, these panicked citizens slammed Rahab and Salmon back toward the inn. Salmon struggled to hold the ground they had gained but could not. Rahab clung fiercely to her harp. As they fought against the tide, she saw flickers of firelight bobbing and flashing through the dust and confusion.

Rivers of fire began to flow into Jericho from every direction. Soldiers with torches poured over the broken sections of the wall. Fire-bearers streaming into the streets, homes and shops crackling and blazing in their wake.

"We're too late," Salmon groaned. "The immolation brigades. My people. Not yours." For the first time, he looked really frightened. "Their assignment is to make this place a burnt offering to Yahweh."

Frenzied crowds shoved and joggled, forcing Rahab and Salmon back, step by step toward the inn. One misstep and the surging mob would overwhelm them, submerge them. One slip and the rabble would trample them—and never know or care. Salmon looked at her with great sorrow. "You saved my life, Rahab, but I am no longer certain I can save yours."

As the press forced yet another backward step, Rahab's heel struck hard against stone. She would have tripped over backward if Salmon had not held her upright. She glanced behind her. They were pinned against the steps of the inn where they started. "My house!" she cried.

"Forget your hous-s-s-se," a woman with flowing white hair hissed in her face. "I have served Asherah all my life, but she turned her back on Jericho today. The God of Israel defeated Asherah's city." She pointed toward the missing wall with a gnarled finger, then lifted her face to the sky and shrieked, "We are finish-sh-sh-sh-shed."

Salmon desperately searched the seething chaos around them for a way of escape and then shook his head hopelessly. "The window in the red room is the only escape route I can think of." He fingered the red cord tied around her harp bundle and a weak half smile touched his lips. "You don't happen to have another rope handy, do you?"

Rahab could not return the smile. Her arms hurt where the sharp corners of her harp pressed into the flesh, but she could not loosen her hold on it even now. Guilt and fear roiled in her stomach. She was the cause of their predicament. She should have escaped with her family. She should have left her beloved harp behind even if it left her a half-person. If she did not make it out of Jericho, she could only blame herself. Yet Salmon would die with her.

"Salmon, I—"

"Don't be afraid. God will deliver us." Salmon's eyes did not show the confidence of his words, but he manufactured another smile. "Remember the words to your song—'*No force can hold back His mighty hand.*'"

Then like a wisp of spray on thundering surf, Rahab detected a different call over the roaring crowds. Command rather than chaos. Salmon heard it too. He tilted his head uncertainly in the direction of the sound.

The voice wailed again. "Ru-u-u-u-u-nnnnnn!" This time Rahab clearly understood the word. "Hah! If only we *could* run."

Salmon lifted his eyebrows as if in response to a joke, but the rest of his features were a mask of hopelessness.

"Ru-u-u-u-u-nnnnnn," the voice called again over the babble, louder and more insistent with the repetition. "Get ba-a-a-a-a-ack. The North Wall Inn is coming down."

"Wait," Rahab whispered. She seized Salmon as if she needed to hold him in place and strained toward the sound.

"Ru-u-u-u-u-nnnnnn! Flee the north wall and the inn."

"It's my brother," she cried, pulling excitedly on Salmon's arm. "It's Helek!"

"Helek? Your family should be out of the city by now."

"Perhaps they should, but he's here. I know his voice."

"You'll be cru-u-u-u-ushed! Flee the falling inn."

"Why would . . .?" Salmon stopped.

Rahab stared in amazement. A woman here, a man there pulled back. A space began opening around them, slowly at first, then, as comprehension of Helek's message exploded through the crowd, people fled the inn and the north wall. In a crazed frenzy, they turned toward the central market, plunging into smoky lanes, even through tunnels of flame between burning houses and shops.

Salmon stepped into the open street, searching for the best way over the broken wall, when a loud cackle gave away Helek's location. Perched on a large tumbled block atop the debris to the west of the inn, Rahab's brother grinned down. "Come up this way," he called, leaping down, block by block. He stopped on the lowest chunk of masonry, his smile positively impish. "What took you so long?"

"We couldn't move—" Rahab's voice broke. She was beyond playful banter.

"I could see what delayed you," Helek confessed. He extended his hand and gently pulled her up to his rocky platform. "I shouldn't tease."

Rahab's knees buckled and she collapsed into the strength of her brother's arms. "I have never been so glad to see you." She gripped his neck tightly with her free arm, clutching her harp with the other and made no effort to hold back her sobs.

"Do you think I could leave my little sister behind?" Helek brushed away trickles of tears with his thumbs. "My problem was getting back to you. So . . ." He caught Salmon's eyes with a rascally grin. "I redirected the crowds a little. Truth be told . . . I lied. The inn and its section of the north wall actually seem to be quite solid still." He snorted a short laugh.

"Let's go then," Salmon said curtly. He bounded up to the stony platform where Rahab and Helek stood and brushed past, mumbling, "Enough delay for one day."

Rahab watched him forge into billows of dust and clouds of pitiful groaning. For the first time, she really looked at the mountain of rubble and found a greater horror than the bedlam of the streets. The broken bodies of the regiments patrolling the wall were jumbled into the collapsed fortifications. Moans and muffled curses of the dying rose all around them, even beneath their feet as she and her brother began picking their way over and around the crumpled masonry.

The dust cloud hung heavily around them, mingled now with a rain of powdery ash from the fires. The collapse of everything familiar had not seemed as devastating when Salmon was guiding her with a solid hand. Rahab coughed and wrapped her veil across her lower face. Tightening her grip on the harp bundle to stave off a feeling of emptiness, she reached for Helek's arm. She closed her eyes, trying to lose herself in a song, but it was impossible to grope blindly through this rubble. Worse, the song had vanished. A wave of panic rose with the realization she could not recall a single word. The sooner she got out of this place the better. She released her brother's arm, scuttling as rapidly as possible up the rough face of a sizable block. She slipped and scraped her knee.

Helek laughed. "Looks like you are over your lingering at last, dear sister."

She rolled her eyes. "I just want to get out of here."

Helek motioned up the slope with his eyes. "Not sure about him."

Salmon stood not far above them, head downcast, shoulders hunched. The rescue was taking an obvious toll on him. "We're coming," Rahab called. "No need to wait."

Salmon didn't move.

"Go on ahead, Salmon. I'll help my—"

Rahab heard Helek's sharp intake of breath and stopped abruptly beside him. Even for those hardened in the forge of Jericho, the bloodied arm and head of a young girl protruding from the debris just in front of Salmon's left foot was a gruesome sight. The child's other arm, ripped from the shoulder lay nearby, its fingers reaching pitifully back for her. Her legs and torso were crushed beneath a massive block.

"Jericho eats its young," Rahab snarled, surprised at the visceral rage she felt.

Salmon glanced at her blankly, then returned his gaze to the child.

He has no idea. No comprehension of what life in Jericho was like. "I do pity the poor child," she mumbled apologetically. "I don't know why I said that so harshly."

"That was what you lived," Helek responded quietly. "Jericho's children were not safe from the ravenous appetites of those who should protect them. From fathers and uncles to cousins and brothers. From the king down to the common drunk in the streets. The men of Jericho took what they wanted, when they wanted to feed twisted urges for pleasure, power, or wealth."

Helek's outburst revealed as much suppressed rage as her own. Once during their childhood, grasping vaguely what was happening to her, Helek attacked Uncle Thahash. When Uncle locked him in the dark wine cellar for three days with no food, Helek never criticized or spoke of her sessions in the Red Room again. "This wall was built to defend our citizens, yet we find this girl chewed up in its jaws." His eyes flashed. "That is the way of Jericho, as my sister well knows."

Salmon was so focused on the girl, he did not seem to hear. "She looks to be the age of my little sister," he whispered. A sheen of tears welled up in eyes already red-rimmed and watery from the irritating smoke.

Salmon's words were so softly spoken, Rahab barely heard him over the clamor and confusion from the burning city, but the little ears heard. The girl's eyes fluttered wide. "Israelite dog," she hissed. "I pray the gods that you die a death tenfold worse than mine."

He stooped down beside the child, his expressive eyes registering the sting of her words. "I would not choose this for you, little one." But she was past hearing. Her eyes stared into the sky, fixed and empty.

Salmon was unlike any man Rahab had ever known. Her father and brothers were compassionate men. Rare in Jericho. They often expressed sympathy for friends or close kin, but she had never heard anyone express such concern for an enemy. "Baby cobras are still cobras," she said, stepping over a gaping split in the fallen fortifications.

She flashed a smug smile at Salmon and Helek. "It is my turn to urge *you* to hurry from this nightmare."

Helek grinned and nudged Salmon forward. "Go on. I'm right behind you."

Then, quick as a striking serpent, a hand flicked out of the rift in the rubble and seized Rahab's ankle. A second hand snatched her skirts, and before Salmon or Helek could react, the hairy arms dragged her down into a shadowy chasm.

Rahab shrieked and clutched at the tumbled blocks around her. The last thing she saw as she fought the unrelenting pull into the darkness was her harp sailing through the air. It tumbled and clattered into the rubble and came to rest in a nest of rocks—still tied up with the brilliant scarlet cord. The sting of her loss hurt more than the sharp edges of broken masonry scraping against her knees and arms. And even as she lost the struggle and crashed into the black pit, she felt an irrational satisfaction knowing that the harp wore her protecting cloak.

A tangled black beard and bloodshot eyes loomed out of the darkness inches from her face and all thought of the harp vanished.

"Helek! Sal—" A hard, calloused hand clapped over her mouth.

"Hush, hush, honey lips."

"Geh-off-mm-me," Rahab mumbled, kicking and twisting to free herself.

The beast reeked of strong drink, but he had the strength of an ox. "Look what the gods sent," he cackled gleefully, pressing her to the cold stone floor. "Don't I know you?" He pinned her down with a knee on her chest, studying her face.

Sand and debris rained down from the opening in the ceiling as someone kicked and wriggled, lowering himself through the opening. "Stop!" The command was loud and emphatic. "Off her, crazy man!"

Helek!

The drunk looked up startled and confused. "What? Crazy? It's the gods who are crazy. I prayed for deliverance, but Asherah sent *her*."

Helek lunged at the man, jerking him away from Rahab in a quick cross-armed maneuver.

As she scrambled free of her assailant, the man seized Helek's leg with a wrenching twist, bringing him to his knees. In a blinding, snarling fury, the sinewy creature flew at her brother's throat, shrieking, "She is mine!"

"Helek!" Rahab shrieked and hurled herself against the man to throw him off balance, but the drunk had her brother firmly by the neck. He grappled against the choking grip, thrashing and flailing to free himself, but the man's knuckles only whitened, tightening in a throttling death grip.

Rahab pulled at the constricting hands, determined to peel them away, but the struggle knocked her to the floor. In helpless dismay, she saw her brother writhing, twisting, and kicking. He could only produce desperate, meaningless gurgles, but his eyes briefly caught hers, pleading for her to get out of the cave.

No way, my brother.

She looked about frantically for a rock she could use as a weapon. Finding none, she seized the drunk's matted hair, yanking back with rage-infused strength, slamming his head against a protrusion of rock jutting from the wall. "Die, you piece of filth!" she screamed. The man cursed but did not loosen the stranglehold on her brother. Helek went limp and slumped to the floor as Salmon swooshed into a straddle over the two men in a shower of pattering gravel and sand.

"Release him," he commanded with resolute determination, the command backed by the whisper of metal on leather as he unsheathed his sword. The man blinked in confusion at the blade pointing ominously at his chest and released his deadly grip. Then with animal instincts and lightning speed, the man sprang back, one hand whipping out, grabbing Rahab and throwing her to the ground between his feet. A bronze dagger flashed in the semidarkness.

"You can't have her, either of you!" the drunk snarled, crouching over Rahab like a leopard over his kill.

"No one *has* her," Salmon muttered through clenched teeth. "With us, she is safe and that means free."

A growling deep in the man's throat exploded and he flew at Salmon with a beastly screech. "M-i-i-i-i-ine!"

Rahab scrambled backward as Salmon's blade flashed bright in the gloomy half-light and caught his assailant midair. The momentum of the man's leap doubled the thrust of the sword, and the point burst through his back in a fine crimson spray. Salmon crumpled under the falling weight and the two thudded heavily to the floor.

Flopping and twitching in a final convulsion, the drunk's grip on the dagger failed. Rahab snatched the weapon as it clattered to the pavement in front of her. She clutched it tightly, drawing it back, ready to thrust if the man moved. She was vaguely aware of her brother sputtering and coughing beside her and Salmon thrashing his way out from under the body, but she could not take her eyes off her assailant lest he show any sign of life.

As soon as Salmon extricated himself, he rolled on his side toward her. "It is over. You can put down the knife now." His tone was gentle and calming as he stretched out his hand encouragingly. "You are a brave woman. A loyal sister . . ."

Rahab glanced numbly at the dagger and let it clatter to the floor.

Salmon nodded and staggered to his feet. Although he felt weak and shaken from his own struggle, he reached out to Helek. "Can you get up?"

"Barely," Helek whispered, gagging, hacking, and gasping for breath as Salmon helped him to his feet.

"I need you to get your sister out of here," Salmon announced calmly. "Can you manage it?"

Helek coughed and continued rubbing at his throat.

"We can do it," Rahab answered, gently nudging her brother directly below the opening she had fallen through. She stared up. The patch of light was beyond her reach. "How?"

"On my shoulder," Salmon answered, dropping to one knee before she could finish. "Then you can help Helek from above."

Rahab glanced at her attacker, lying in a pool of dark blood with Salmon's blade still protruding from his back as if pointing the way out. She did not need to be told twice. She stepped lightly onto Salmon's shoulder, stretching for rocky handholds, pulling herself up as Helek and Salmon stood in a hissing rain of sand and gravel, pushing her feet from below.

Her whole body tingled with life and a sense of freedom as she scrambled out of that black pit into the light. There was still dust and smoke hanging thick over the rubble. But she was free to run, and there was nothing she wanted to do more. Run far, far from that foul den of death and far from the choking atmosphere of Jericho. But Helek and Salmon were still trapped in that dark cavity. Without another thought about herself, she dropped to her knees beside the gap in the rubble, guiding her brother's hands to the solid holds she had found. With her guidance from above and Salmon assisting from below, it did not take long for Helek to scrabble up and out.

"Let's go," he gasped.

Rahab did not recognize the hoarse, rasping voice. His eyes darted around warily as he stood, hunched in a crouch stance, ready to fight or sprint away.

"We will," she clucked comfortingly. An irrational sense of peace flooded through her. "All three of us together." She pulled him down beside her and called into the dead man's lair. "Salmon! Reach for Helek's hands."

"Don't wait here for me." Salmon's words rose up from the shadows. "I need to retrieve my sword."

Rahab bent over and peered into the darkness.

Salmon had been staring at the drunk's corpse, but he seemed to sense her looking at him and lifted his face toward her. He didn't smile. "Go. Get to a point where you can see the Israelite security line and wait for me there. I'll catch up as quickly as I can."

The orders were given in an imperative tone impossible to disregard.

CHAPTER FIVE

TROUBLE

Salmon

Extract it, Salmon told himself.

He stared at the sword protruding through the back of the corpse, vaguely aware that his assailant's knife, a finely-crafted bonze blade with a handle of bone, lay nearby. But that weapon was easy to ignore. The command was indelibly etched in his mind. *Do not take any of the treasures of Jericho for yourself.* His father's sword was another matter. Fine Egyptian craftsmanship salvaged from the shores of the Red Sea after it closed over Pharaoh's army—a filament of faith connecting him to his father.

He hunched down, carefully reaching under the dead man, feeling for the hilt of the sword. Lifting and pushing, his fingers searched until they wrapped tightly around the familiar grip. Holding his breath, he gave a sharp pull. The body jerked toward him and one limp arm cuffed his foot. An eye peeked out at him from under a mound of greasy hair.

Salmon leaped back, letting the body slump against the stony floor.

He is as dead as the rocks around him, he told himself firmly. *He moves only when I move him.* The truth didn't really help. The sword had not budged, and he still had to retrieve it from a dead body. It simply was not going to be pleasant. Taking in another deep breath, he conjured up enough courage to push the corpse over on its side. He placed one foot solidly on the man's flank to hold him in place.

"I mean no disrespect," he mumbled, "but I'll be needing this." He bent down again, gripped the weapon, and gingerly rocked the corpse back and forth. His lip curled in revulsion as flaccid arms and legs flopped against the rocks. This tugging extraction was far more disturbing than the fatal thrust.

When the blade broke free at last, Salmon stared at the clots and smears of crimson on its gleaming surface. He wanted nothing more than to get out of this pit of death, but he could not sheath a weapon covered in gore. He began wiping and rubbing it with the corner of the man's garment, the words of Moses ringing in his head—*The life of a creature is in the blood.*[8] Even this foul blood represented a life created by God.

As soon as the blade was cleaned and sheathed, Salmon took a running leap, found solid handholds, and pulled himself out of the pit. Rahab and her brother were nowhere in sight and nothing of the colorful city remained. Only rubble, flames, and the black billows belched up by the inferno. A gray world shrouded now in silence, the final cries of the dying licked from the ruins by smacking tongues of fire. He was scanning the deserted wreckage for the best route out of the ruins when a splash of red winked at him.

There, not a stone's throw away, nestled flagrantly bright in the soot-gray rubble, he recognized the scarlet drapery cord. Rahab's pale cloak not only protected her harp but camouflaged it. He would never have noticed the bundle but for that cord. Before Salmon could even consider whether it was safe or sensible or right, he went back to retrieve it, lifting it tenderly from the jagged-edged debris. He tucked it under one arm and smiled. *Rahab said she and the instrument were one. She called it her soul.* He could only imagine her joy when he returned it. Clambering from block to block, intent on catching up with her and her brother, he passed the dead man's lair.

"Please, Lord, no more trouble."

Trouble . . . trouble . . . trouble.

The word reverberated in his head, stirring up echoes of Joshua's warning words. *Every treasure within these walls is devoted to Yahweh.*

Trouble! Trouble!

Salmon hesitated. Perhaps he should leave the harp and not tell Rahab he had seen it. Then a melody took wing, rising from the brutal remains of their ordeal and soaring over the rubble of Jericho like Noah's dove of hope and peace.

I will rejoice for Yahweh is my God.
He has saved me by his powerful hand.
He leads me out to a safe place;
he delivers me from evil.

That song. A Canaanite woman expressing faith as great or greater than any he had witnessed in Israel. Using *this* instrument. And she risked her life to save it.

No plunder . . . No relic of Jericho . . . Destroy all . . .

But it is tied up with the red cord, which Joshua specifically instructed we bring as we fled the city . . .

Joshua!

Salmon heaved an audible sigh of relief. He did not need to make the final decision. He would return the harp to Rahab but notify Joshua. With the liberating joy of a settled decision, he began humming Rahab's melody.

My God can raze a city . . .

A gravelly scuffle sounded behind him.

No force can hold back his mighty hand . . .

A second gravelly step, followed by a scraping and scratching.

Salmon froze.

These were not solid steps, but . . . dragging . . . someone barely alive pulling himself over the debris. Perhaps chains dragged by an unknown villain escaped from Nahari's dungeon. Or was it . . .? The hair on the back of his neck stood up. The body wasn't yet cold when he extracted his sword. *Could that miserable creature still be alive?*

He moved quickly behind blocks of rubble large enough to hide him, not daring to resume Rahab's song of hope as a trail for whoever . . . whatever followed him. The scraping steps . . . the clinking . . . continued following with a ghastly rhythm. He imagined the bronze dagger striking stone. *Why didn't I toss it beyond reach?*

Quietly as possible, he slipped through a narrow passageway between two blocks of broken masonry, chiding himself for not simply looking back. Another clunking step, closer now. The raspy scraping. A metallic clink.

Calm yourself, Salmon. The man is dead. And even if he were only injured, there is no way he could climb out of that pit. Listen. That is not the clinking of a dagger striking rock. Your imagination is running wild.

He finally forced himself to step from his cover to look.

Hah! The joke is on you, Salmon. Just two straggling Israelites. Achor, a leader in Judah, and his son Jamin.

Salmon stopped to watch the younger man wrestle a large wedge of gold over the rubble, hoisting it to a rocky plane above him and then pushing it across the flat surface. Obviously, they had been assigned to carry precious metals back to the temple treasury, the only spoils of war allowed. Jamin's father followed, carrying two bulging bags joined by a rope slung over his shoulders. *Jewelry? Silver coins?* Each time Achor stepped up behind his son, the bags struck each other with a solid metallic clink. Salmon stifled a laugh at his own runaway imagination. Not at all the sound of a bronze dagger striking stone.

Salmon watched the silver-haired man, sword drawn, ready to protect the tabernacle treasure, and felt an odd connection. He saw his own fears, both rational and irrational, reflected in those furtive glances over one shoulder and then the other, eyes narrowed and dark with dread, constantly scanning the rubble for the enemy. He understood all too well the feelings this city could produce inside a man. Their eyes met. "Shalom, Elder Achor. Let me help you."

Jamin's head jerked up. "Tend to your own tasks. We'll tend to ours."

"Respect, Jamin," Achor responded under his breath.

Salmon ignored Jamin's rudeness. "Perhaps I could join you as guard since we are exiting the city together."

The father-son duo climbed one step closer. *Clunk, scrape, clink.* Jamin's averted eyes and firmly set jaws declared his desire to be left alone, but Achor was clearly suffering from the effort and tension. The harp tucked under Salmon's arm was awkward, but at least it wasn't heavy like that gleaming wedge of gold or the awkward bags of coins. Surely, as prince of Judah, he should at least guard the temple metals.

Salmon slipped one arm under the bands of the red cord and slung the bundle onto his back. By the time he lashed it securely with his belt, Jamin was shoving the golden wedge across a block just below him.

Salmon drew his sword and offered his help a second time. "Sheath your weapon, Elder," he said. "I will help escort the Lord's treasure."

"That is a kind offer, Prince Salmon. Do you think escort is necessary?" Achor's tone was polite, but he did not meet Salmon's eyes.

Jamin looked at him coldly. "Have you had to fight off any enemies in this deserted rubble?"

"Actually, yes. Just minutes ago. But only one. I doubt many survived the collapse of these walls."

"We thought we were the last Israelites leaving," Achor mumbled.

"There cannot be many more." Salmon gestured at the flames and black smoke roaring in the heart of the city.

"What are *you* bringing from Jericho?" Jamin asked, eyeing the harp. There was a hint of accusation in his tone.

Salmon blushed. "I was assigned to bring Rahab the harlot and her family from the city. This belongs to her."

"The woman who rescued you spies, eh? I heard she was a beauty." He looked around. "I don't see her . . . or her family."

"As I said, we encountered one assailant, and I stayed back to be certain he was dead and . . . then I had to clean my sword. Rahab and her brother wait for me ahead . . . somewhere."

"If it is as you say, then you neglect your duty by stopping to help those who have not asked for it—and do not want it."

Jamin lifted the gleaming metallic wedge and slammed it down on the flat surface of the rock where Salmon was standing. He skipped back to save his toes. "If you would truly like to be helpful, step aside."

Achor shot a disapproving glance at his son but did not say anything.

Jamin is right, Salmon thought. *My duty is not with these two.*

He leaped to a higher rock. Within a few bounds, he left the two unhappy men with their *clunk, scrape, clink* behind.

He found Helek and Rahab waiting just below the crest of the broken wall. The upright section of their old home towered behind them, the high window framed with vibrant red draperies. The color of blood and death. The color of Passover faithfulness.

The rubble dropped sharply down to a fierce line of soldiers guarding the base of the ruins. The sight of his fellow Israelites should have been a comforting sight, but as far as Salmon could see in either direction, there was only an unbroken line of strangers, the division of Dan, not Judah. Every man with sword drawn, each one assigned to watch for escapees from Jericho. Salmon sighed. One more obstacle in Rahab's exodus. He clambered down chunks of broken masonry to the brother and sister, wishing he could open a path like Moses. But this wasn't the Red Sea. It was the army cordon set by Joshua and he didn't have a rod like Moses, only a voice.

He planted his feet, cupped his hands around his mouth, and shouted. "Hear me, men of Israel. I am Salmon. Son of Nashon. Prince of Judah. Charged by Joshua to bring Rahab of Jericho and her family out of the city."

Not one of the grim-faced men so much as blinked as they lifted their swords. The sound of dozens of bronze blades slicing the air spoke for them.

"Salmon?" Helek gestured toward his rescuer. "Prince of Judah?"

Rahab's eyes were dark with uncertainty and fear.

This should not be happening. I made a promise . . . She trusted me . . . We had a sign.

The sign! His fingers fumbled as he hurried to unlash the harp bundle from his back. He snatched the red cord in one hand as soon as he worked it free and held it out. "The sign!" he called. "The red cord."

There was no response from the cordon below.

He thrust the harp bundle toward Rahab, its wrapping of soft gray fabric falling away to reveal the polished wood. "Yours." *So much for a meaningful presentation.* He wondered vaguely if Rahab's startled gasp expressed joy at seeing the harp or fear she would drop it.

"This was the sign," he called out, waving the cord even higher and more vigorously with both hands. "The sign marking the home of the one who saved Israel's spies. Rahab saved Jathniel of Ephraim and me."

There was a movement of uncertainty, a barely perceptible scuffle in the line of soldiers, but the hoped-for pathway did not open. Salmon wracked his brain for information that might convince the soldiers. "Look. The North Wall Inn still stands. Yahweh our God honored our promise to Rahab. He preserved her family. Here she is—the faithful Rahab and her brother Helek." He waved the cord again. "This is the sign of the promise."

A silver head appeared at the point of disturbance in the cordon and an authoritative voice bellowed, "Lower your swords. Let them pass." And the wall of swords lowered so quickly it was difficult to tell which came first, the action or the command.

Joshua strode into the open space between his troops and the ruins of the wall. "This is indeed Salmon of Judah."

Salmon waved the red cord again in a salute of gratitude.

"I am relieved to see you at last," the commander said warmly as Salmon led the Jericho refugees off the rubble. "Jathniel was most anxious about your safety. He asked to return to Jericho to find you. But I deemed it best not to risk another good man."

"It is quite likely he would not have found us, sir. We ran into some trouble." He closed his eyes as he added, "I had to kill a man with my sword to rescue Rahab from a pit. It is a great relief to be out of Jericho at last."

Salmon took a last look at the ruins. Achor and Jamin were picking their way through the debris with their load of precious metals. One last soldier was quickly overtaking the slow-moving father and son.

"Over here," Joshua called to the stragglers, then returned his attention back to Salmon and his charges. "I am most interested in hearing about your trouble, but first take the refugees to camp." His eyes swept over Rahab and Helek. "Your family should be well settled by now."

"The delay was entirely my fault." Rahab shyly looked up into Joshua's face. "I would not leave until I located my harp."

"I . . . was . . ." Salmon stammered. He should have insisted that Rahab leave the thing at the inn. More to the point, he should not have retrieved it from the rubble. Joshua had made it very clear that the treasures of the city were for Yahweh alone.

The commander's eyes registered amused surprise more than anger. He chuckled aloud, grinning at Rahab as one does a small child. Oblivious to all but the harp cradled in her arms, Rahab had just brushed a large ashy flake from her nose leaving a black streak across her face. It was not the first. The billowing smoke had been raining ash over everything close to the city.

"Get your charges back to camp as quickly as you can. You will all want to wash before the sun sets this evening." Joshua was still grinning. "It sounds as if you will need corpse contamination rituals, but for now let's deal with soot contamination."

"We found the king of Jericho," a gasping voice interrupted. Despite his wheezings from the effort of carrying heavy bags of coins, Achor was eager to deliver his news.

Jamin dropped the gold wedge at Joshua's feet. He took a deep breath and rolled his shoulders to loosen the tight muscles. "Jericho's king is dead. We instructed two sentries to carry his body to the city gates while we redeemed this treasure . . . for the tabernacle."

"You identified the king positively?"

"Positively." Jamin stretched his frame tall and looked Joshua in the eyes. "The man told us his name was King Nahari . . . and this was definitely his." He tossed his head proudly in a gesture calling attention to the crown his father was untying from his belt. "We brought it to you as evidence that he had not escaped."

Joshua took the crown from Achor and turned it in his hands thoughtfully. "We will hang this on the tree beside the king's body, burying it all beside the gate under a memorial of stones at sundown. Take the other treasures back to camp as instructed," he said. "Then join the other soldiers east of camp for purification. You did well to find and identify the king before he died."

"More than merely find him," Jamin asserted. "I killed him myself with a chunk of masonry from his own palace. Without touching the corpse. And I was able to summon sentries to retrieve the body without becoming contaminated myself." He laughed, obviously proud of his own cleverness. "I did not touch dead flesh. I won't be needing those purification rituals."

"I will," Salmon muttered. A skipping palpitation fluttered in his chest at the memory of the gore he had to wipe from his sword. The metallic smell of blood still hung hauntingly over him. *I need those rituals. I want purification.*

Joshua gave Salmon a look of sympathy and waved him off. "Go. Lead your charges back to camp."

The human barricade broke to let them pass and Salmon led Rahab and Helek through, glad to put distance between himself and Jamin's boastful words.

"Stay alert, my boys," Joshua was saying to the men of the cordon as Salmon started down the road, setting a pace designed to keep well ahead of Achor and Jamin with their cumbersome load. "Continue to watch for survivors trying to escape with our fire brigades. Ask for family, clan, and tribal identification. If you are uncertain, bind and hold until . . ." Horn blasts and criers passing on Joshua's commands drowned out the last of his words.

"I need to find my family." Helek interjected abruptly beside him. "My wife must be near hysteria by now. I told her I would be right back."

Before Salmon could respond, Helek jogged down the road, disappearing where it bent into the lush tropical undergrowth. His final words trailed over the oleanders along with a half-muffled laugh. "I will leave my headstrong sister with you."

Ada

Ada's tummy knotted as she studied the tight faces around her. Jathniel's eyebrows were definitely drooping. That was not a good sign. They were not that way when he led the refugees into their temporary camp earlier. He came back almost giddy, shouting, "Jericho's massive walls were nothing. What can stand when Yahweh shakes a city?"

"Where is Salmon? Where is my brother?" she kept asking him until he broke from his story. But he only patted her head condescendingly.

"Don't worry, little one. Your brother will be here any minute."

With only a wink, he returned to his story of ram's horns and roaring voices. "Give way, O walls." His silly eyebrows danced along every phrase describing a city crumbling into a heap of rubble. "Every block in those massive walls fell flat—except for the home of Rahab the harlot. Like a watchtower in a field, only the North Wall Inn remained standing."

"But you and Salmon went in together, right?" Ada tried to picture it. "What happened? Why are *you* here, but not Salmon?"

Jathniel glanced at her, barely pausing as he told of scrambling up piles of broken blocks, finding a path through the debris to the inn door. "We raced inside and found Rahab's family waiting for us upstairs by the window with the red cord. Exactly as we had agreed."

"Both of you together?" Ada could not understand why Jathniel was so unconcerned. "Where is my brother?"

"Salmon led the way when we left the inn." He wiggled his eyebrows up and down at her. "The problem as usual was a woman." He laughed at his joke. "Specifically, Rahab. We hadn't gone far when Grandmother Shua pointed out that Rahab wasn't with us. Your brother insisted on being the one who went back for her. Don't worry, little one, Salmon will be along soon."

"Maybe they got caught by enemy soldiers."

"Look. I had no trouble at all getting eleven people out of that mess. The people of Jericho were so stunned that no one seemed to notice us."

Ada was far from reassured, but a crowd pressed around Jathniel. He told the story again and again, paying no more attention to her.

She wandered to the road and sat waiting and watching patiently, but still he didn't come. She was fighting back tears when the Jericho refugees gathered around her. First the old one, the grandmother, cupped her chin gently and lifted her face. "Don't worry a bit. My grandson Helek went back to help too. If Jathniel could get the rest of us out of the city so quickly, they should be here any minute. How hard can it be for two grown men to get one stubborn young woman out safely?"

One girl, about the same size as Ada, slipped up shyly, and stood half hidden by the grandmother's skirts. "Rahab was lagging all morning," she said softly. Ada couldn't tell if she said the words to the grandmother or to her.

"You don't even know what lagging means, you little mouse," an older boy jeered.

"I do so, Jared. Mother said Rahab was lagging when the rest of us came downstairs and she didn't. And she said Rahab was lagging again when we got out in the streets and Salmon had to go back for her. Lagging means she wasn't keeping up with us."

"You are exactly right, Atarah," the grandmother answered, "but Rahab wouldn't distress us without a good reason. She must have remembered something important she needed to do."

"What could have been so important?" a dignified man with gray hair and beard asked. "We waited to leave the inn until she was right there with us at the door." Ada guessed it was the innkeeper, the father of Rahab the harlot.

"*I* told her to stay with us," the man's wife snapped. "*You* told her to stay with us. Both of the spies told her to stay with us. If she had, she would be safe and Helek would not have had to go back."

The entire refugee family began to offer opinions all at once.

The littlest one tugged on Ada's arm. Her high voice chirped confidently over the voices arguing back and forth. "Helek is my abba. If he is with them, they will be safe."

The innkeeper patted his granddaughter on the head. "That is true, Azuba." He smiled kindly at Ada. "Your brother is a brave young man, and so is our son Helek. They will be here with Rahab any minute now."

His wife's voice was tight with frustration. She shook her finger in her husband's face. "Your daughter's antics today put both her and Helek in needless danger . . ."

"As well as Salmon," the father added quickly with a sideways glance at Ada.

The woman seemed to see Ada for the first time. "As well as your brother," she repeated. Her smile seemed strained.

The grandmother wrapped an arm around Ada's shoulder. "The God who got *us* out of there will get them out safely too."

Now the rest of the children pressed close, reassuring Ada too. "Don't be afraid." The tallest boy appointed himself spokesman. "Helek is my father. He knows the best routes around and through Jericho better than you know the lines in your palm."

"Jared is right," another added. "Uncle Helek will get Auntie Rahab and your brother out. Just wait and see." The other children nodded their agreement.

Ada wanted to believe them. She tried hard to believe them, but more time passed. Maybe an hour. No one was saying those things now. And there was no sign of her brother.

She filled twelve washbasins with water. She helped distribute food. She helped her mother bring cushions to make the refugees comfortable. Now as the women gathered the empty platters, she noted their worried expressions. She caught similar worried glances pass from face to face among Rahab's family members, but the most disturbing face of all was Jathniel's. She had never seen his eyebrows droop before.

"Ada, take these platters back to our tent," her mother commanded. Her face was definitely worried too.

"But Mother, I want to watch . . . Can't they wait until . . ."

"Take them now."

"Please . . . can I come back after?"

Her mother's face relaxed with a weak smile. "Of course, Ada. See if you can be back before Salmon arrives."

Salmon

Salmon stopped to look back. "Let's go, Rahab." He sighed. She was twenty paces behind and seemed not to hear as she ran her hands over the harp, checking for damage. He couldn't help mumbling under his breath as he went back for her. "Helek is not the only one with family close to hysteria over our absence."

Weary as he was, he made every effort to sound authoritative. "We need to go *now*, Rahab. You can check that in camp."

Rahab continued inspecting the intricately carved lion and twining vines decorating the frame of her instrument, as heedless of his words as of the shower of gray flakes sifting onto her hair and shoulders. She was a stunning woman— even here like this. The delicate bow of her lips, tightened with determination, the perfectly arched brows, plowing a tiny furrow in the smooth perfection of her forehead, the apple of her cheeks, blushed by health beneath those ashy smudges. His chest locked at such close proximity to extraordinary beauty . . . foreign beauty. The differences between the two of them and their worlds shivered through him in an unfamiliar surge of attraction and danger.

"There are only a few scrapes," she said. "A bit of carving broken . . . here . . . but nothing that will affect its song."

"I can . . . uh . . . try to . . . repair it," Salmon stammered. He struggled at a long, jagged breath. "I mean . . . I enjoy working with wood."

"You have done more than enough, Salmon. You managed to get my harp and me out of that city . . ." She looked up through her lashes with a forlorn little laugh. "Both of us with only minimal damage."

He returned the laugh, though clearly reading pain in her eyes.

Rahab tenderly wrapped her cloak around the harp again and clutched it close like an infant. The inn that had been the center of her old life towered above the smoking rubble behind her, a sign of divine deliverance—but her old life in that place had definitely left scars.

"Let's put some distance between us and Jericho," he said gently.

As he turned back toward camp, Salmon noticed Achor and Jamin staggering down the path. He was relieved to see them stop and lay down their burdens of precious metals for a rest. He took Rahab's arm, starting off at a swift pace, but Rahab's first steps on the path toward her new life wobbled. He wrapped an arm around her waist to steady her, and the touch shot through him like fire, a spasm of pleasure so intense it frightened him. Neither of them spoke, but Salmon felt her relax into his guidance, leaning against him for strength. Willing the erratic thudding of his heart to steadiness, he focused on the road ahead.

He knew the path well. Seven times he had followed it from Gilgal to Jericho and for the seventh time he was returning home. Every turn through the palm grove, every bend and constriction after it disappeared into the dense shrubbery was indelibly fixed in his memory. *Did that seventh daybreak march really take place just a few hours ago? The silent tramping, the ram's horns, the victory shouts.* He pictured the breathless moment when the walls cracked and fell. *Had it actually happened just this morning?*

In this moment, walking beside Rahab along a long sweeping curve through the palms, sandals crunching in tandem, the road, the city, the long day, all seemed strangely unreal. The luxuriant beauty of these dense, spring-fed thickets, air fragrant with mint and oleander, was a world apart from the bedlam in the city streets and the acrid smell of burning. Everything faded until there was nothing else. Only the closeness of Rahab on this garden-bordered path. It was as though everything good and bad in his entire life had brought him to this moment and had given him the noblest of causes—protecting this girl from any further danger or pain.

Suddenly, Joshua's face loomed from the shadows. The old commander's eyes flared with indignation. His instructions echoed loud and clear. *Do not be snared by the women of Jericho. Do not be enticed by any of their treasures. Everything in the city is to be destroyed. The Lord has made that very clear to me.*

Panic doused the enchanted moment. Salmon's arm fell limp at his side. The orders were to escort this family to the safety of camp. Nothing more. He imagined Joshua growling at him, *"You were enticed by this woman's beauty. You have disobeyed the Lord."*

He imagined his feeble excuses. *I intended to obey your orders, but she said the harp was part of her soul.* Salmon's head was spinning. *Am I weak like the men who worshipped at Mount Peor? Or has this foreign woman bewitched me?*

"We are almost to the camp," he said flatly. His voice sounded as empty and hollow as he felt inside. "We will have to talk to Joshua about that harp." He pushed ahead, stifling any lingering desire to be close to her.

Rahab's musical humming followed him but stopped abruptly when the thick vegetation fringing both sides of the road opened to the plain of Gilgal. "Your camp," she gasped. "I had no idea!"

Her excitement rattled Salmon's carefully constructed barricade. Framed by the shaded branches of oleander, myrtle, and palm, sunlit tent rows marched into the haze toward the distant mountains of the north nearly filling the plain from the river to the western slopes. He had to admit it was impressive.

"It is so vast and so ordered." Rahab slipped to his side, her eyes wide and full of wonder.

Salmon forced himself to remain detached. "I had an opposite reaction to Jericho," he responded flatly. "So vast—but so chaotic. So invincible—and so evil."

A smile touched the corners of her perfectly-shaped mouth. "One would expect more order in a permanent city and less in a camp of desert wanderers."

Salmon gestured indifferently at the neat rows, avoiding contact with her eyes. "Well, after forty years practice pulling up stakes and then pitching tents again in each new location, we have developed a system."

She laughed. "I would not have guessed that you were forty years old."

"Me? Forty?" Forgetting his resolve not to be snared by her beauty, he whipped around to make sense of her statement.

She shrugged innocently and blinked. "Forty years of practice . . .?" she prompted, raising her eyebrows. Her lips curved into a wry smile.

"Oh . . ." Salmon fought to stay disengaged. "My people have had forty years of practice setting up camp."

Rahab laughed. "I wish you could see your own expression." Her face grew serious, and she turned again toward the camp. "I don't know how I can jest on a day like this. I have dreamed of being free from Jericho all my life. Now I wonder if I will ever really feel at home anywhere else. The city is gone, but will I ever feel safe?"

"You have a home with our people. A new and better home," Salmon reassured her. "And you are safe and free of all that evil forever." *How could he not try to comfort her? Israelites were supposed to show kindness to strangers, weren't they? That was the Law of Moses. This whole situation was so confusing.*

"How can I feel safe and at home when I have no idea how or where my family is to live."

Like a flash of lightning, the thought struck Salmon. He had no idea where she was supposed to live either. Then, like resounding thunder following the flash, the solution to everything roared into his head. *Acsah! Check with Acsah. What had come over him? Rahab's courage had saved his life, but she was not an Israelite. She was not even a virtuous woman. Acsah was a woman of virtue, intelligence,* and *beauty. Moreover, Acsah would know where to take Rahab.*

"Where is your tent in all this vast array?" Rahab's voice intruded from somewhere beyond the thunder.

How had he forgotten Acsah? He must find her. He needed to find her. She would set his feet on solid ground again.

"Where is your tent?" Rahab asked again. She brushed his arm lightly.

Salmon shrugged from her touch and pointed toward the flag hanging high from its standard straight before them. "There, in Judah." There was no movement in the smoke-hazy air. The banner hung in drooping folds as if Judah's lion hid, ashamed of its prince. Salmon's voice sank. "That is the banner of my tribe. Most days, the great lion, the symbol of Judah, looks as if he is leaping across the field."

"The lion of Judah . . ." Rahab's eyes sparkled with wonder. "I want to learn everything about your people."

Salmon was numb. Utterly weary and detached. Beyond joy or sorrow. He just rescued a family of strangers out of a city of strangers, even killed a stranger in the process. Now he the prince of Judah was a stranger in Judah. It was as if he emerged from this mission an alien.

"Come," he said flatly. "I will introduce you to Acsah, a young woman of Israel well worth knowing. She can tell you anything you want to know about our people. I'm certain she will also know where your family is to stay."

"I would like nothing better."

Without checking to see if she followed, he stumbled toward camp thinking of Jathniel and the others already resting. Just a little longer and his task would be complete as well. The ordered tent rows impelled him forward. Every stride, one step closer to home.

CHAPTER SIX

UNCLEAN

Salmon

Rahab skipped to catch up as Salmon strode onto the sun-bright plain. "How will we find my family in all this?" she asked, matching pace at his side.

My question exactly. I don't even know where to find my own family . . . or Acsah on a day like this.

Suddenly, a flurry of movement burst from the tent rows of Judah. Hair swinging, tunic flapping, and a spray of sand flying from her feet, Salmon's little sister sprinted from the shadows. Dashing down the center of the road, eyes trained on the ground in front of her and totally oblivious to anyone standing in her path, Ada's pounding sandals gobbled up the distance between them.

"Oh!" Rahab hopped off the path. "She's going to crash right into us."

"My sister," Salmon said, rolling his eyes. "Whoa, Ada. Watch where you are going."

Ada stopped abruptly just in front of him, staring open-mouthed. Trails cut by rivulets of tears ran through the dust on her cheeks. She looked from Salmon to Rahab and back to him again. "Where . . .?" Her voice was high-pitched, barely audible. "Have you been?"

"A better question might be, where on earth are you going?"

"Jathniel thought you were right behind him." A fresh flood of tears overflowed onto her cheeks. "But you weren't. I thought you were trapped in the city, and Jathniel said it's burning."

"Hey, hey, Ada. Don't cry," Salmon soothed. He held up one hand in a blocking motion as she reached out to him. "Careful. I have touched death. I must go through purification before I hold you again." He dropped to one knee in front of her. "My dear little sister, were you coming to rescue me?"

"I . . . I . . . didn't know . . . wha . . . wha . . . what I could do." The words were fragmented by sobs and noisy gulps for air.

"So you would just run blindly into a city suffering the judgment of God?" Salmon felt tears collecting in his own eyes as he rose to his feet. "Where is Jathniel? . . . And where are the refugees from Jericho?"

Ada's emotional storm passed as quickly as it had begun. "Over there," she chirped, pointing past the grazing flocks and herds to a dark line of trees at the base of the ridge. "I will tell everyone you are safe."

Before he could answer, she raced away, her gleeful shouts echoing back. "Salmon is coming. Salmon is coming. Salmon is coming with the harlot from Jericho."

Salmon cringed. When he had come home from spying and told the rescue story to his family, it had not seemed inappropriate to tell of the harlot of Jericho who saved them, but it was not the same with Rahab standing beside him. The protective instincts he felt earlier welled up again—but this time in a more rational way. It was just and right to treat her with respect and kindness. She was a courageous woman—in spite of her past.

Rahab either chose to ignore the childish shouts or hadn't heard them. "I can't see any tents over there," she said, squinting at the shadows with one hand shading her eyes.

"Before we go there . . ." Salmon looked into her eyes with intentional compassion. "You need to understand that according to our law we are unclean, corpse contaminated.⁹ You and I both. Don't touch anyone."

She nodded imperceptibly, and he encouraged her with an upbeat grin. "Now, let's see if we can help you rejoin your family without touching them." Without warning, she struck out running across the meadow in the direction Ada had gone.

Salmon trailed behind, his head swirling with images of safety and belonging from his childhood. Following Moses and the cloud wherever God led. The cloud itself a comfort, shading by day, warming at night. Days on the march with Acsah and other friends who preferred trekking at the head of the long, dusty line of travelers right behind Moses. His place with the royal family of Judah. Rahab's life had been immeasurably different from his.

And, just that quickly, those happy memories turned to smoke. The man who brought laughter and joy to the most mundane scenes of his childhood was dead. His father, murdered by the privileged people of Yahweh while Rahab's father survived the violent city of Jericho. Salmon tightened his fist and pounded it lightly against his chest to ease the clutching sense of loss. *No logic or reason can predict where evil will strike.*

He caught up to Rahab near the area designated for the refugees. "So many people," she murmured, scanning the bustle around the lean-tos. "I don't see my family."

Whether from kindness or curiosity, it seemed as if all the women of Israel had come to help. Salmon chuckled. "You left wealth and comfort behind, but—at least this afternoon—you have more than enough servants."

"There. My parents," she cried and rushed into the whirl of activity.

Salmon caught up with Rahab at the first lean-to in a row of five where the innkeeper and his wife lounged in the shade of the small canopy. Up close, the lodgings were an embarrassment. Old goat hides stretched over poles. Flimsy makeshift dwellings. *This . . . for Rahab's family? It wasn't right.*

"I'm sorry," he mumbled apologetically to Jokshan and Keziah. "Not exactly the comfort of the North Wall Inn."

"We left Jericho behind," Rahab and her father responded in duet.

"With no regrets," Rahab added.

"But you deserve more for what you did."

"Really? What I did?" Rahab stared at him with incredulity. "A flax pile on our roof where you hid under the beating sun? Three nights in a cave while you were hunted by King Nahari's dogs?"

Salmon shrugged. "You saved our lives."

Jokshan gestured toward the nearby bluffs. "I told my daughter to ask you and Jathniel to show us your cave. It obviously served you well."

Salmon laughed. "It is hard to imagine worse conditions than these rude dwellings, but I can assure you—they are a step up from that dark, damp cave." For the first time, he was glad he had authority to correct a wrong. "I am prince of Judah. I will see to better accommodations if you decide to stay with Israel rather than move away."

A flicker of distress crossed Rahab's eyes. "Where else would we go, Salmon?" Her voice caught, and she looked away quickly.

"We are grateful for any shelter you can give us," Jokshan affirmed.

Salmon noted the families of Rahab's brothers reclining comfortably on rugs and cushions. Clean faces, hands, and feet showed that the washbasins stacked beside the tent had served their purpose already. The bevy of women still bustled about, pressing food on refugees who only picked at it halfheartedly. Several of the children had already fallen asleep.

"Your tent will be apart from the others for a week," Salmon whispered to Rahab. "Don't forget. We can't touch anyone or let them touch us. We are unclean."

"Unclean. . ." Rahab echoed vacantly.

Suddenly, Ada broke out of the milling crowd with Jathniel in tow. "Look! My brother and the harlot are here at last."

"Ada—"

"What happened?" Jathniel interrupted. "I thought you were right behind me." His heavy brows frowned in consternation. "I told Ada that you were and then you didn't come."

"You might have gone back to help," Ada pouted. "My brother could have been killed there all by himself."

"But he wasn't." Jathniel wiggled his eyebrows at her childish impudence.

Salmon rolled his eyes. "I see that my little sister's charms have snagged you already."

"She is *adorable*," Rahab whispered. "And she obviously adores you."

"As I adore her. But, adorable? Sometimes, yes. But often not."

Ada ran to a woman heading toward the refugee tents with a stack of blankets. "Salmon is back with the harlot that saved my brother." She tugged on her sleeve. "See. There she is." Without waiting for a response, she raced back.

"Her name is Rahab," Salmon whispered sharply.

"Her name is Rahab," Ada called. "Come meet her."

Jathniel engaged Rahab with a friendly lift of his brows in a deft attempt to cover the awkward moment. "You and Salmon did give us a bit of a scare when you took so long getting back."

"One delay after another." Salmon sighed.

"Didn't Helek tell you what happened?" Rahab asked with alarm.

"Helek?" Jathniel looked both directions. "Where is Helek?"

"You don't know?" Rahab looked from Jathniel to Salmon. "He rushed ahead of us to let Jerusha and the children know he was all right. You didn't see him?"

"Stay calm," her father replied. "Mother and I saw him briefly, but he wasn't here long. One of the women asked if he had touched death. They have very detailed laws about that." He shook his head. "Last I saw, Helek was trying to explain to a hysterical wife why he needed to stay down by the river where the soldiers are quarantined."

"I don't see why he has to be separated from us. These are not our laws," Keziah sniffed.

Salmon looked at Rahab's mother in wonder. Purification was a normal part of camp life. How else could mortals live so close to the incandescent presence of immortality? War merely added another layer to the basic need; but apparently, the concept was incomprehensible to this family.

"Whatever your rules, Helek and I will both comply," Rahab said firmly. "I am unclean too."

"What?" Keziah looked at her sharply. "What happened to you?"

"Mother, look at me!" Rahab brushed at the dried spatters of brown-red blood on her dress. "Everyone had gone berserk, rushing about, swinging clubs and swords. Salmon and I couldn't move. We were trapped. Didn't Helek tell you? Without him, we might not have made it out."

"He told us." Jokshan met her eyes with a calming nod. "I think all Mother heard was that Helek had to endure quarantine."

"Here's the short version," Salmon added with a nod to Rahab's mother. "A drunk trapped Rahab in a cave deep in the rubble. When Helek tried to help, the drunk seized his throat, nearly strangling him—until I leaped in to rescue them both, skewering the man with his own sword."

Jathniel's eyebrows hopped along each word; then he stopped with a big grin. "You will be the one telling campfire stories about the Jericho rescue, my friend, not me."

Salmon took a deep breath. "I never thought getting Rahab out would be such a nightmare."

Rahab looked at him with a feeble smile, then down at her harp. "I made it more difficult than it needed to be."

"But . . ." Salmon's eyes followed hers to the harp. "It needed to be."

"Acsah! Acsah!" Ada called excitedly.

Salmon laughed to himself. *My little sister should have been the spy. While I was distracted with this conversation, her sharp little eyes picked out the very person I have been watching for.*

"Acsah," Ada shouted again. "Come meet the harlot who saved Salmon."

"Ada," Salmon hissed in an exasperated whisper. "I want you to address her properly. Her name is Rahab . . . or Rahab of Jericho. Nothing more. Do you understand?" He gave her his most authoritative look. This was not the way he wanted to repay his sister for the brave and sweet concern she showed for him, but what could he do?

Ada's shoulders drooped at his firm reprimand.

Rahab stooped to Ada's level, whispering as if sharing a secret plan. "Tell people that Rahab of Jericho was saved by the bravest man in Judah. Your brother."

Salmon was momentarily thrown off balance. Pride and embarrassment sloshed like waves pulling him in opposing directions until his eyes fell on Acsah sauntering toward them with a welcoming grin. As always, he found in her a secure mooring. *Just the one I need.*

"She doesn't miss a thing, does she?" Acsah's emerald eyes bored into his as she tousled Ada's hair. "So, Ada, now you have met the woman who saved your brother."

Ada narrowed her eyes, looking from her brother's face back to Acsah's. Then, apparently deciding they were not mocking her, she planted her feet firmly. "Yes, I have," she declared, extending her hand toward Rahab in a grand announcement. "Meet the harlot, Acsah. Her name is Rahab of Jericho."

Salmon sighed.

Rahab

"Welcome . . . Rahab of Jericho." Acsah dipped her head politely.

Rahab's stomach tightened with self-doubt. This was the first woman of Israel to whom she had ever been introduced. Salmon spoke so highly of her and with good reason.

Acsah was simply astonishing. Her face and tall, lithe form were lovely, but there was something more—a rare strength. Although she had the beauty of Lady Asherah's perfectly chiseled features and her divinely regal bearing, there was not a trace of the gilded statue's cruel coldness. Rahab sank at Acsah's sandaled feet in reverent admiration.

"On your feet," Acsah gasped. "Only God is worthy of such obeisance."

"I . . . oh . . . I am not familiar with your customs," Rahab mumbled, slumping down even closer to the earth. "I merely wanted to honor you."

"Say no more, brave woman of Jericho." Acsah extended her hand graciously, but Salmon was faster. He lifted her to her feet with a strong, supportive grip, but his eyes were on Acsah. "Unclean," he said softly, "both of us."

Acsah took a half step back, her face still radiating compassion. "You grew up in a far different world. Our people have no king, no royalty. From Joshua down to our children, we remember that all Israelites were once slaves." She flashed a dazzling smile. "Welcome to a place where identity and dignity are found in covenant with Yahweh."

Rahab pressed back tears and a choking wave of emotion. Her fears of being rejected or marginalized by the people of Israel evaporated. Acsah did not use her inherent majesty to diminish anyone or anything else. "Salmon said you are worth knowing. Now I understand why."

"What is this?" Acsah's eyes crinkled in a feigned attempt to look annoyed. "What else did you say of me, Salmon?"

"I don't remember." Salmon shrugged. "Maybe I said if Israel ever had a queen, it would be you." He winked and flashed his endearing half smile.

The obvious affection between these two stirred an inexplicable ache deep inside Rabab's heart. She tipped her head respectfully in imitation of Acsah's initial greeting. "I am grateful beyond words for the warm welcome my family has received."

"As we are grateful for your courage and kindness to our spies," Acsah replied. She gestured toward the row of lean-tos. "These shelters are not much, but I trust they will serve until you decide where you are going. Our entire camp must seem rather crude compared to the luxuries of your city."

"On the contrary. The cleanliness and order are most impressive." Rahab looked from Acsah to Salmon to Ada, searching for a connection.

"Speaking of clean," Salmon broke in. "We need to wash. Both of us were splattered with the blood of that dying city."

"Dirty as well as unclean?" Acsah's gaze dropped from his face to his smudged garments. "I hadn't noticed."

Every hint of a smile disappeared from Salmon's face. "This is beyond jest, Acsah. I killed a man today. I feel utterly filthy inside and out."

Rahab tilted her head to one side trying to understand. "How is dirty different from unclean?"

Acsah's brows arched in mild surprise.

Salmon adopted the tone he had used when comforting his little sister. "Today we will scrub off the external filth of our ordeal. But even after we wash, we must not touch anything or anyone. One who has been contaminated by death must follow specific rituals of cleansing before walking freely in the camp of the living God. A handful of ashes from a special offering is mixed with living water . . ."

"Living water?"

"Living water is the term we use for the purest water bubbling up from a spring," Salmon explained. "On the third and seventh days of our confinement, a priest will come to splash us with this ash water in a ritual of purification."

"More ash when I am so covered with it already . . ." Rahab tried to make sense of the strange proceedings.

"These are not ordinary ashes. The priests sacrifice a red heifer for the purposes of purification. It is burned along with hyssop, scarlet wool, and pieces of cedar wood. All red objects. The color of blood. The ash, although no longer red, still symbolizes cleansing blood."

"But we need cleansing because we are splattered with blood. How can more blood cleanse us?"

"The blood of the dying in Jericho demonstrates the mortality of human flesh and blood—in contrast to the holiness of an immortal God. Purification reminds us we are not gods."

None of this made sense to Rahab. The offerings of Jericho were simple. You fed the gods, hoping to entice them to respond favorably to requests. The dearer the sacrifice or greater the quantity, the better your chance of capturing their attention.

Salmon took a deep breath then laughed. "It's easier to understand when you have grown up with the concept. Just do it."

"Without cleansing," Ada interjected, standing on tiptoe as if trying to lift herself into the conversation. "We would be slain by Yahweh's glory."

"Slain by his glory. Now *there's* a frightening thought."

Salmon chuckled, but Acsah's piercing eyes studied Rahab's face with great seriousness. "Ada is correct," she said. "Two of our first priests disregarded the procedures for approaching Yahweh and were literally slain by his glory."

Salmon shook his head. "Maybe we should explain this in a way that helps Rahab appreciate the glory of Yahweh, not fear it." His eyes were gentle as he began to explain. "For more than forty years, Rahab, our people have lived with the living God in the heart of our camp. Yahweh not only gave Moses the precise plans for building his tabernacle, he gave him instructions that would keep us safe. Many of his laws teach us how to become just and merciful and good like him. Other laws remind us he is perfect in ways we can never be."

Rahab studied his face as he grew more and more animated while elucidating the mysteries of life in the Israelite camp. She hadn't realized until now how sullied his face and beard were. His teeth shone white in contrast to sooty smudges—a smile all the more precious for what he had gone through to rescue her.

"Any blood from the cycle of life, whether birth or death, is a reminder we are human. When we come in contact with such blood, we are considered unclean. The purification rituals are the way we acknowledge our mortality in contrast to the immortal holiness of Yahweh."

"We . . . I had no idea. Canaanites fear the immortal gods—knowing we can die while they cannot. We are always aware that the gods have the power to slay us—but we never think of them as holy." She paused. The uniqueness of this nation and their God went much deeper than she had thought possible. "The people of Jericho always spoke of you disparagingly as a rude bedouin tribe."

"We are no longer wandering bedouins." Ada's high-pitched excitement burst into the conversation again. "We are here in our Promised Land now. Here to stay. And don't you know, we are not just one tribe? We are the children of Israel—twelve tribes."

"Twelve tribes!" Rahab exclaimed, echoing enthusiasm back to Ada.

"Did you notice our banners?" Ada asked. The child beamed with the pleasure of being included in the conversations of adults.

Rahab had to admit she felt immeasurably more comfortable talking with this child than Acsah. "Your brother pointed out Judah's banner. I am eager to learn more."

Ada became even more animated. "Our twelve tribes are named for the twelve sons of Israel: Reuben, Simeon, Judah, Issachar, Zebulon, Benjamin, Gad, Asher, Dan, and Naphtali. Well, those ten are sons. Ephraim and Manasseh are actually grandsons, the two sons of Joseph. Levi *was* one of the twelve sons, but the Levites are priests and scribes or teachers of the law now and Ephraim takes his place." She took a deep breath, then continued her barrage of information. "So, all our tribes and our priests descend from one man named Israel. That's why we are called the Children of Israel. Sometimes he is called Jacob. Have you heard of him?" She stopped abruptly and took another deep breath.

"Yes . . ." The question took Rahab by surprise. "There are many stories about Jacob." She hesitated as she sorted through her memories for a good one. "My favorite is of *Beth-el*, house of God. The tale of angels on a stairway reaching the gates of heaven."

"I love that story too. Is Bethel far? Could you take me to see the angel stairway?"

Salmon chuckled. "The stairway at Bethel was a dream."

"It's true." Rahab smiled at the child's sweet innocence. "There is nothing to see. Only a shrine close to the city of Luz."

"A shrine?" Salmon looked at her with great curiosity. "So, Canaanites revere the place of Jacob's dream? What else do Canaanites know of our ancestor?"

She blushed. "The darkest stories are the ones most often repeated in Canaan. Everyone knows about the massacre at Shechem. Jacob's name has reeked of that blood-stench ever since."

"What story is that?" Ada asked, looking at her brother.

Rahab was only too happy to let Salmon explain, but he shifted uneasily and shot a silent plea toward Acsah.

Acsah firmly ignored the plea.

"What story *is* that?" Ada repeated.

"Not a good story, little one." Rahab took a deep breath. "Hatred has been brewing for centuries because Jacob's two eldest sons murdered all the men of Shechem. Canaanites believe the gods were punishing Jacob when his family was driven to Egypt by famine."

"I don't know how anyone could believe *that* was the reason our people went to

Egypt," Acsah sputtered.

"That is because you are not Canaanite." Rahab met Acsah's flashing green eyes with steady boldness. *Could she make this woman see she was different from other Canaanites?* "My grandmother heard of your exodus from Egypt while she was trapped like a slave in an abusive marriage. The story awakened a glimmer of hope that there was a god who might help her too, especially when the word coming from the caravan captains was that the tribes of Israel were on the march toward southern Canaan. She began to pray to Yahweh. Not many weeks later, she met your twelve spies and believed her prayers were answered."

Acsah's eyes widened. "My father? Your grandmother met my father?"

Rahab nodded. She had Acsah's attention now. "And Joshua and the others. My mother was a small child then and quite ill with a fever. The twelve prayed for her, and she was immediately better. My grandmother gave the spies food and water in return. Since her husband was away on a business trip, she was free to invite them to rest and hide at her home through the day. She sent them off in the evening, traveling under cover of darkness with those huge samples of fruit from the valley of Eshcol. Then she settled in, eagerly waiting for Israel's army to deliver her, but the Canaanites drove your people back into the wilderness, praising Baal for that deliverance.

"Grandmother Shua panicked. She took my mother in the dark of night and fled to Jericho to live with her brother, the innkeeper. And that is where I was born. We don't understand why it took so long for your people to return, but we believe Yahweh loves and guides you. There is no God anything like him."

"I'm so glad you are going to be an Israelite." Ada's expression was sweetly admiring.

"She isn't going to be an *Israelite*, Ada," Acsah said quietly, "but her home is gone. She may stay with us as long as necessary."

While Rahab floundered for an appropriate response, another of Ada's callow observations gamboled into the stalled conversation. "Rahab is very pretty, is she not? Even with all that black on her face."

"Don't say everything that pops into your head, Ada," Salmon scolded.

Rahab blushed and touched the outer corner of her eye. "It is kohl, Ada. The women of Jericho always line their eyes with it, but I see it is not your custom. I have much to learn."

Acsah exchanged amused smiles with Ada. "Actually, I think she was referring to smudges of ash."

Rahab ran her hand over her cheek and stared at the smear of soot on her palm. It reeked of smoke. Her face must look just like Salmon's. She looked down at her gown, her best gown, chosen so carefully that morning. She brushed at the dust and ash and blood. Unclean did not begin to describe her. "I am not fit to be standing here talking to you. How I must look!"

"You look like a brave woman who passed through streets of mayhem, death, smoke, and fire, escaping a crumbling city." Salmon's tender smile embraced her—filth, shame and all.

"Enough palaver. You both need to wash." Acsah said abruptly. "The soldiers are quarantined down by the river, Salmon. Helek has already gone there since he is corpse contaminated as well. He seemed to understand the importance of obeying the rules of our camp while he is here."

Salmon nodded his understanding. "Ada, find *Ima* and do all you can to be helpful." He squared his shoulders with big-brotherly authority. "And see if you can stay out of trouble." He gave her a wink and left.

Acsah waved a cluster of women back as Salmon walked toward them. "Don't touch him. He is unclean."

She turned her attention to Rahab with a perfunctory smile. "Come. I will show you the tent where you will stay during your week of purification. Apart, but still near your family."

Rahab followed her unquestioningly. Acsah had the presence of a great military commander—with a glimmer of pity softening her eyes. Intimidating, but compassionate at the same time. How would one describe that incongruity? *Graciously magnificent,* she decided.

Acsah began firing off instructions as soon as they reached the site set apart for Rahab. "There is a bathing area screened off for you just beyond that copse of willows. The others have their own bathing place. There is also an elimination trench started for you in the thickest part of the willows. You will find a small shovel there. After using the trench, scoop up the dirt you need for covering from opposite end, extending the trench in one direction as you use it."

Acsah's gaze dropped from Rahab's eyes to her body. "Remove that gown and throw it in the fire pit over there. It is past washing. Inside your shelter, you will find a washbasin and a bathing sheet to wrap up in."

Rahab nodded mutely.

When Acsah's pure green eyes caught hers again, it seemed the filth of her former life was fully open to her penetrating gaze. "You will be quarantined for seven days. Since you are the only woman who needs cleansing, a priest will come here to administer the rite of purification on the third and seventh days. Then on the evening of the seventh day, you will wash again and be clean."

"Let it be as you say," Rahab answered.

Acsah's eyes softened. "I am sorry your first week in our camp will keep you so isolated, but since you are here and are unclean, you must be purified. An unclean person who refuses to complete the ritual will be cut off from our people forever."

Cut off. Acsah's wordless pause gave the words chilling emphasis. Rahab dropped her eyes, not certain what would be appropriate to say.

"I think that covers everything you need to know, but please ask if there is anything you don't understand. I will return with some clean clothes for you."

When Rahab looked up she met a radiantly warm smile. "It was good to meet you at last. Salmon and I have been friends since we were toddlers. Thank you for risking your life to help him."

Before Rahab could think of a response, Acsah was gone.

The entire southern sky was open to Rahab's view from here. Billows of black smoke obscured the expanse of blue over the encampment of these holy people, the judgment on her former home befouling its atmosphere. She could not remember feeling so utterly alone and abandoned. Her faith, so strong on the streets of chaos earlier, crumbled into flakes as fragile as the remnants of Jericho riding the rising smoke toward the heavens. *If only these purification rituals could cleanse her past.* She collapsed inside the tent provided for her.

It wasn't long before she heard an elderly woman's voice outside. If only it were Grandmother Shua . . . but it was the voice of a stranger.

"Rahab of Jericho? Are you sleeping?"

She sat up. A stocky silhouette filled the open door of her shelter. Much as she wished otherwise, there was no hiding.

"No. Not sleeping." she mumbled, embarrassed to be seen still wearing a dress polluted with the filth of Jericho. "I'm still reeling from everything that happened this morning."

"Do you need a drink?" The woman held up a goatskin bag. "My name is Sarah. I feel so honored to serve your brave family."

Rahab shook her head numbly. "Wash . . ." was the only word that came to her lips.

"Oh, my dear girl. I put a basin and large linen sheet inside your tent myself. We set up a privacy screen right over there for you . . . but if you prefer, I could bring the soap and water so you can bathe here."

"That won't be necessary," Rahab mumbled. "I'm sorry. I think Acsah explained it all, but my head is in a fog."

She quickly retrieved the basin and sheet and followed the trail of Sarah's chatter, which only ceased for a moment when Grandmother Shua intercepted them at the bathing area.

"Oh Rahab, my child. I've been watching for you," Grandmother said. "I was bathing in the place set up for the rest of us when you first arrived at the camp. Then we were told not to go near your tent."

Rahab flashed a smile she hoped conveyed her love. She was too weary for conversation, but all too happy to listen to her grandmother and Sarah cluck-clucking back and forth like happy hens as she washed. The sound was wonderfully comforting . . . then gradually, the words of the conversation took on meaning.

"I could not help thinking the worst when Salmon took so long to return to camp with Rahab," Sarah admitted.

"Tut, tut. After all the wonders Yahweh performed today? I *knew* the most precious treasure of Jericho would not be abandoned."

"My harp?" Rahab whispered incredulously. *Did Grandmother realize they had gone back for her harp?*

Shua looked at her sharply. "I am speaking of you, child, and you know it. You are a precious treasure to your family."

"Treasure? More like a broken pot in the rubble," she mumbled.

"If I say you are precious treasure, well then, you are." Shua winked and her eyes crinkled as she smiled. "Only a rude child would contradict the wisdom of her elders. Be glad you are unclean or I might be tempted to swat those lips for speaking nonsense."

Saved by the strict laws of corpse contamination. Rahab's mind matched the quip when her lips could not.

"The sun is dropping close to the western horizon," Sarah pointed out as Rahab tucked the sheet around herself and slid her feet into her sandals. "Let's make sure you have everything you need for Sabbath."

Throughout the walk back to Rahab's lean-to, a stream of kind words flowed as steadily from Sarah's lips as the water had gushed from her goatskin into the basin. "We tried to think of everything. There are several extra skins of water for your family over there under that tree. Yours is here by this oleander. You will find some simple food for Sabbath stored inside the tent beside your bedroll."

Acsah and Ada were waiting at the lean-to with a garment of plain beige cloth hanging over Acsah's arm. She laid it at the door of the tent and gave Sarah a quick, tight hug—water bag and all. "Aunt Sarah, you have taken such good care of everyone that there is little left for the rest of us to do."

"I did no more than any of the others," Sarah answered, flicking her fingers in the air.

Acsah caught Rahab's eyes and gestured toward the clothing. "Here is an under tunic and one of my own gowns for you. I think it will fit nicely."

"Go on, child," Sarah encouraged. "Try on the gown."

As Rahab took the simple gown and dropped the flap of her lean-to, Ada called through the closed doorway, "No more lagging!"

"Ada! You must not talk like that to a grown woman," Sarah admonished.

"Her family said she was lagging all morning."

"That does not mean it is polite for you to say."

"Well, she needs to hurry." Ada whispered loudly enough for Rahab to hear as she pulled on the tunic. "Don't you know Ima is waiting anxiously to meet her? I'll go get her now." Ada's footsteps pattered away.

Sarah filled the silence with chatter as Rahab dressed. "We don't have much time before our day of rest begins. Rest is what we all need most. The people of Israel as well as you Jericho refugees. You will love the Sabbath, Rahab. Our gracious God gave us an entire day of rest every week. Sweet, sweet rest with our families and our God. And it is against our law to do any work or even worry about things that need doing."

When Rahab emerged from her shelter, smoothing the homespun Israelite garment, Sarah clucked her approval. "A wonderful transformation of the refugee girl from Jericho. Cleaner anyway. That is not as fine a gown as the one you were wearing, but it will do for now. You can wash your own clothing after the Sabbath."

"Not that gown," Rahab said emphatically. She peeked quickly at Acsah, hoping her attitude was pleasing. "I already threw it in the fire pit."

"In the fire pit! What a shame. Acsah, do you think it was so badly stained?"

"It is a soiled memory of Jericho," Rahab interjected quickly. "Not something to cling to. I will be glad to watch its ashes blowing on the wind along with the smoke of my city."

"Is this her?" a female voice asked hesitantly.

"What do you think, Ima?" Ada responded impudently. "Of course, it is." She was tugging the woman closer with both hands, bouncing up and down in her excitement. "I told you I would bring you to Rahab."

Ima. Ada's mother would be Salmon's mother. The thought quavered through her in a mix of emotions.

Sarah encouraged her with a fond smile. "You do look lovely, my dear. Quite ready to receive your first guest."

Rahab laughed. "Apparently, Ada has decided I am."

Sarah placed a welcoming hand on the shoulder of the newcomer. "Abijah, I want you to meet the brave woman who rescued your son."

When the woman held out her arms, Rahab hopped back. "Unclean," she gasped breathlessly. *How many times would she have to declare her status?*

"Unclean," Abijah muttered. "I should have known. Salmon too." She regarded Rahab thoughtfully. "Don't look so despondent, my child. We women have to deal with purification quarantine at every turning of the moon. The week will pass quickly enough."

"Salmon did what he promised. He got her out of Jericho." Ada's high-pitched voice always sounded like a little bird. "But he had to fight to save her."

Rahab dipped her head toward Salmon's mother in what seemed the polite Israelite fashion. "I am honored to meet the one who nurtured such a good man. He did indeed save my life and rescue me with his sword. I must confess, however, that I caused the initial delay by searching the inn for my harp." She smiled encouragingly at Ada. "But, yes, your brother managed to get us safely out of the city in spite of all the trouble."

"My nurturing would have been for nothing had you not saved my son's life."

Rahab brushed her hand in the air. "It was nothing. I happened to stumble upon two spies in grave danger and was able to hide them until they could make their escape. Fortunately for them, I have no loyalty to the city of my birth. Salmon and Jathniel saved me and my entire family from a living nightmare. Twelve lives for two. It is we who must be grateful, dear Abijah."

"I lost my husband just a few months ago." A single tear dribbled from the corner of her eye. "Losing my son would have been more than I could bear."

Sarah cleared her throat. "We should let Rahab rest. *Shabbat shalom*, my dear."

"Thank you again, sweet Rahab," Abijah added. "I will always be grateful to you. Shabbat shalom."

"Shabbat shalom," Rahab replied, returning the polite nod.

Abijah took Ada firmly by the arm, joining Sarah on the trail leading back toward Judah.

Acsah

Acsah started to follow, then stopped. She watched Rahab hang the wet sheet over a bushy scrub willow. "I can't imagine what you have endured today. It must be a relief to get cleaned up. Has anyone explained the rules of our Sabbath to you?"

Rahab looked up timidly. "Salmon did explain it a little. Enough for the first one he said."

"Enjoy the time of rest then."

Rahab's shyness struck Acsah as odd. She expected a harlot to wear the brazen look flaunted by the women of Midian. A shiver trembled in her stomach. When marked with the dirt of the city and the remnants of the eye-lining kohl, it was easy to identify Rahab as the harlot. With this fresh-scrubbed face and simple Israelite dress, she looked like any other pretty girl in camp. But she wasn't just any pretty girl. The appearance of innocence made her even more dangerous.

And then there was the harp.

She spotted the instrument propped against a rock near the lean-to. "There was a strict command not to bring treasure from Jericho. Did Salmon permit this?"

Acsah attributed Rahab's startled, blushing expression to guilt until she heard a familiar voice answer the accusing question for her.

"I mentioned it to Joshua already."

Rahab's eyes were fixed with affection and hope on her rescuer, and again Acsah felt the flutter of fear deep inside her. "Salmon! Now I understand why you were selected to go as a spy—so quietly you slip up on a conversation . . . So, did you slip your 'mention' of the harp up on Joshua when he wasn't looking?" The words and her laugh came out with more sarcasm than she intended.

"I mentioned it, and I will make sure he is fully informed. Joshua should be the one to decide if she can keep it, not me."

She fixed his large, compassionate eyes with a steady look. "What decision is there to make? The thing is from Jericho."

"Yes, but I think it will be allowed." He hesitated. "It is not like the Midianites, Acsah. Rahab was renowned in Jericho for her playing, but she intends to use it now only for the praise of Yahweh. In fact, her singing was like a protective shield as we left the city this morning." He tossed a half smile at Rahab and continued his barrage of excuses. "Her extraordinary skill came with her out of Jericho, but there is no instrument like this in Israel. She did not bring any clothing or jewelry or family idols or anything like that. What benefit would her skill be without the instrument? It only makes sense to keep this harp—unless Joshua decrees otherwise."

Acsah shook her head in disbelief as the words gushed from Salmon's lips like a flash flood in the desert, an out-of-control rush obviously springing from doubt. "There is no place for foreign music in the Lord's camp," she answered quietly.

"It is not *foreign* music when it speaks so eloquently of Yahweh. Did not Miriam use the beauty of Egyptian music to lead our people in praise? I have no doubt Rahab's harp will be an equally great blessing to our people—"

"It will soon be Sabbath," Acsah broke in. "Does she know any music appropriate for our holy day?" She left before she said something she might regret.

Salmon

Rahab picked up the harp. "Actually, I do know some appropriate songs," she whispered, but Acsah was already beyond earshot.

Salmon rubbed his short, curly beard slowly. *Jathniel and I shaved to look like Egyptians before we ventured into Jericho as spies, but our beards are growing out quickly. Soon we will look every bit men of Israel again. It will not be so easy for these people to assimilate.*

Rahab retrieved the instrument and collapsed on a cushion near the door, running her fingers over the strings. The sorrow expressed in those mournful notes, along with the deep pain reflected in her eyes, wrung Salmon's heart with an aching desire to shelter her from more hurt.

"Acsah loves music, Rahab," he said slowly, trying to wrap his mind around the irony of sheltering her from someone as true and good as Acsah. "It is just that we had some really bad experiences with the music of foreigners in the past few months."

"The Midianites?" Rahab whispered, her fingers fell limp on the harp strings.

Salmon nodded. "My father was murdered in the rebellion they stirred up."

"Oh Salmon, I'm so sorry." She plucked another lovely rivulet of mournful notes. The melancholy stream moved from a cry of utter grief to an iteration of her powerful song. Salmon could hear the words in his mind.

I will rejoice for Yahweh is my God.
He has saved me by his powerful hand.

He watched courage strengthen Rahab's features as she played. He vowed to do all he could to help her keep that harp. It was, if not part of her soul, necessary to her faith.

She stopped playing and looked at him thoughtfully. "That rebellion explains Acsah's reaction."

"Both to you as a foreign singer as well as to the harp, but Acsah is a wise and wonderful woman. One of my dearest friends. She will soon see you are not like the Midianite women and neither is your music."

"Did Acsah lose her father in the war with the Midianites?"

"Oh, no. Her father Caleb is one of the oldest men in all Israel, one of the spies who met your grandmother. Oh! The name of Caleb reminds me. . ." Salmon waved a hand as if brushing away the previous conversation. "It was the reason I came back."

"I understand her fears." Rahab's eyes seemed focused on some distant place of personal darkness.

"Rahab, listen. I came back with good news." He tried to draw her back with as comforting a smile as he could give. Then, as their eyes met, his breath caught with the power of the connection. *Careful, Salmon. Remember she is Canaanite.* He cleared his throat. "Caleb invited your family to his campfire circle tonight. I just informed them. The stories and singing will continue until late because it is Sabbath and Yahweh has given us a great victory today."

"How wonderful for them."

Salmon watched the shadow possess her face again.

"If only I were not unclean."

"Now do you think I told you about it just to torment you?" He winked conspiratorially. "I know a place up on a little knoll where you and Helek and I can watch and hear most all of it."

He glanced at the untouched plate of food the women had left for her. "Eat something for strength. Helek and I will come by to get you shortly after sundown."

Acsah is right as usual, Salmon told himself sadly as he walked away. *The sooner Rahab and her family move on, the better. Living with our people would undoubtedly bring sorrow upon sorrow to this woman. There will be no way to shield her from all of it.*

He took one last look over his shoulder at the beautiful refugee looking so forlorn by her shabby lean-to.

At least for tonight, I will see that she experiences the Sabbath joy of the people of Yahweh.

It wasn't long before a gloriously red sunset faded to deep purple and the stars blinked into view one by one. The clans of Israel gathered around family campfires, flames crackling with palpable energy, the savory aroma of the evening sacrifice adding its fragrance to the sights and sounds of celebration. Today the people of Israel witnessed the second astounding miracle under Joshua's leadership. The women and children left behind in camp felt the ground shake. They heard the roar and watched the dust rise into the sky. But not until their husbands, fathers, brothers, and sons returned to camp did they learn the details of a victory unlike anything before in history. A city shattered with a victory shout.

Although the men were at a loss for words to describe the abundance and luxury that had gone up in smoke, their families watched designated soldiers carrying an enormous amount of precious metal back to camp for the tabernacle treasury. None begrudged this offering to the God who defeated the glory and pride of Jericho. Unlike the cities east of the river already rebuilt by the tribes of Reuben, Gad, and Manasseh for their families, Jericho was to remain a heap of ashes—a firstfruits offering to the true God of the land of Canaan.

As families settled around blazing fires to hear every heroic detail of the day, the clan leaders repeated Joshua's words of judgment.

> *Cursed before the Lord is the man who undertakes to*
> *rebuild the city of Jericho.*
> *At the cost of his firstborn son,*
> *will he lay its foundations;*
> *At the cost of his youngest,*
> *will he set up its gates.*[10]

No one celebrating around the campfires of Judah noticed the absence of one family from the clan of Carmi that night. No one noticed two figures creeping like shadows along the deserted tent rows of Judah. No one noticed the pair slipping into Achor's dark tent with only starlight illuminating the moonless night. Who would notice when the uproar of joyous singing and dancing from the fire-lit margins of camp had yet to settle into quiet storytelling?

Achor

Fear slammed its fist into Achor's gut at the scuffle of sandals. He threw his sleeping pallet over the spade, the hole, and the small heap of dirt. "Jamin?" he whispered hoarsely.

"Along with Hattil. Were you expecting someone else?"

His son's usual sarcasm was a relief, yet he could not stop the trembling of his hands or the stammer in his speech. "Did . . . did anyone seem . . . to . . . uh . . . notice you?"

"Joshua, perhaps. Maybe Caleb . . ." Jamin replied dryly. "God, of course. It *is* Sabbath, you know."

"Jamin, your father is worried," Hattil reprimanded timidly. "We *were* careful, Father Achor, but in all truth, there was no one around to see us. The whole camp is celebrating."

Mara had been sitting quietly in the darkest corner. Perhaps, it was Hattil's comforting words, perhaps just the familiarity of Jamin's testy retorts, but a scowl replaced her look of fear. Achor knew the look well. The squall preceding the next storm of complaints. He braced for it.

"Hurry up and finish, Achor," she hissed. "How can digging a hole take so long? We're missing the celebration."

"Father, whatever could you be thinking? And choosing this special evening for such a deed?" Jamin wagged his forefinger in front of Achor's face. "There is nothing mother loves more than a victory dance with everyone ogling her finery. Think of your wife for once."

"My dearest boy," Mara crooned. "Listen to him, Achor. Jamin knows I've been waiting ever so long for a proper celebration so I could wear my Midianite scarf again. Can you just imagine the swirl of color floating around me like a cloud at sunset when the women dance?" She waved her arms as if in a dance. "I have not seen another piece so fine in the entire camp. The eyes of every other woman will turn from black to green."

His wife's droning irritated like a buzzing insect. Suppressing the urge to swat her, he seized her arm. "Let's go then, Mara. This will wait." He threw back the tent flap, and moonbeams reflected dimly on two piles of silver coins Mara had been counting out.

"Oooo!" his daughter-in-law breathed.

Achor laughed sarcastically. "We can just leave this all here and go celebrate. Hattil, you can help Mara count coins when we return. But you will have to be careful not to allow them to clink so freely once the neighbors are home."

Hattil squatted down, peering closely at the piles of cold silver. "You were sitting on quite a treasure, Mara." She grinned. "Who needs a campfire? *This* is the place of celebration for me tonight."

Achor caught the furtive glance passing from Hattil to Jamin as she slipped a handful of silver coins into the corner of her tunic and tied it tight when Mara looked away. He didn't care. Hattil deserved a larger portion of the silver simply for her positive attitude.

Mara twisted in his grip. "Let go, you old fool. You are hurting me."

"I just want to take you dancing and singing with the rest of the happy camp." He pointed into the dark night with his thumb. "Come Jamin. Come Hattil. We are missing the celebration."

"We have to stay until we have hidden your stolen treasure," Mara screeched in his face. "I know that."

"Enough, Mother. Enough, Father," Jamin growled. "Keep it down."

"I see my error now, woman. The entire Carmi clan is waiting to watch Mara flaunt her Midianite frippery tonight. Perhaps they would all agree that her husband should find himself a fine robe from Jericho as well."

Mara broke free of his grip. "Don't make fun of me, you selfish man. You brought home the most beautiful robe I have ever seen, but it is for you." She began sobbing hysterically, as she edged back toward Hattil and the silver. "And now you make me miss the fun of dancing."

Achor knew his rage was out of control, but he could not stop. "I guess you didn't notice this?" He picked up the wedge of gold and slammed it hard against her chest. The thudding impact knocked the breath from her and she fell back on the pallet. The blow was greater than he intended, but he simply did not care. "Is this gold and silver nothing at all?"

Mara looked to Hattil for support. "Don't you think it curious . . . *sniff* . . . that the only . . . *sniff* . . . garment . . . Achor found . . . *sniff, sniff* . . . in an entire city . . . is a robe for himself?" She wheezed pitifully.

"Oh forgive me, woman. The quarters for the king's women had caved in. It was impossible to raid their wardrobes, but I should have thought to bring you the king's crown. How could I be so stupid?" Achor smacked his hand against his forehead. "I could have escorted you to the celebration tonight with your Midianite scarf *and* the crown of Jericho's monarch. 'Here she is, Joshua. A woman born to lord it over everyone in camp.'"

"Stem your tongue, Father," Jamin snarled in a hoarse whisper. "Your loud quarreling will bring about the death of all of us."

Achor had the fleeting thought that Jamin would strike him, but his son turned on Mara. "Mother, your sniveling is driving us all crazy. There is enough gold and silver here to outfit us all royally when the time comes. Now, let's get this task done." He flipped his father's sleeping pallet back to reveal the digging and picked up a shovel. "Good. I see you had sense enough to bring in two spades."

"Was there nothing they could have brought for you and me, Hattil?" Mara grumbled under her breath.

Jamin scooped up a shovelful of dirt. Achor could tell he was too angry for more words.

Hattil sighed. "Surely Achor told you the story," she offered timidly. "He didn't go looting. He came upon the body of the king before anyone else did. He brought the crown to Joshua like a good Israelite."

Achor laughed as he shoved his spade into the hole. "And as a good Israelite, I would have burned the robe, but the king himself convinced me to save it. It bestows magical powers on the wearer, he said. Not another like it in all of Canaan. Surely Yahweh intended that such a fine thing be preserved. A gift to me for being such a good Israelite."

"A good Israelite would not be looting Jericho," Mara mumbled.

"Our husbands *are* good Israelites." Hattil stroked Mara's hand soothingly. "Jamin explained it all to me. The robe simply fell into Achor's hands. A gift from God. Joshua's orders about not looting the city were clear and our husbands obeyed him. They did not go looting. They merely kept what was given them."

Jamin grinned at her. "That's my woman."

"Ha! How did you get gold and silver without looting?" Mara demanded.

"Like Hattil said, we took what fell into our hands. Joshua kept the crown to bury with the king's body at sundown and ordered us to carry this silver and gold back to camp. Phinehas saw us and thanked us for carrying such heavy loads back to camp. 'Back to camp,' they both said. Neither one specifically told us that we had to take it to the *tabernacle.*"

"So, you kept only what fell into your hands? Convenient that the king's robe is a perfect fit for Achor, isn't it?"

"Stop whining, Mother. Help Hattil put those coins in the bags now that they are counted out evenly," Jamin snapped. "Ladies, I give you the honor of placing the silver in the bottom of the hole. I will put the gold wedge on it, and, Father, wrap your royal trappings in this blanket and place it on the top. Let's get this job done. After all, it is Sabbath, and like everyone else, we deserve rest."

CHAPTER SEVEN

COLLABORATIONS
AND COLLUSIONS

Caleb

Although it was not yet noon on First Day, lively folds of newly woven fabric lay in heaps all around Acsah and her loom. Caleb had not seen anything like these gloriously gleaming stripes of red and white since he left Egypt. He poured himself a cup of water and settled onto a cushion to rest. "I am impressed with your industry as well as your artistry," he said.

His daughter had been weaving since first light and still the shuttle flew through the loom, the length of cloth growing under her nimble fingers, long and longer still. But Acsah was mysteriously silent about her project.

"I did not know we had so much wool," he said after watching for a while longer. "Even if King Og were still alive and you could possibly be enticed to weave a new robe for him, you have already produced enough to cover his giant frame two times and more."

Acsah smiled slyly as she continued working. "This is a surprise for Abihail and Eliab. Some of the wool was theirs. And Abi helped with the dyeing." She caught his eyes, challenging him with an uncompromising look. "Swear to me that you will not tell, and I will share my secret."

"I would not spoil your surprise," Caleb chuckled, "as long as you promise to save a little wool for our needs."

She stopped at the end of the row, tucking the shuttle into the warp threads, and displayed the full red and white striped glory of the large woven sheet. "I am making a new tent for Eliab and Abihail." Her jaw was tight with determination as she explained. "When they married, Achor gave them the old one they use now, but he hasn't spoken to his son since the crossing. Abihail came to me crying last week—the third day of circling Jericho. Jamin asked Eliab to give the tent back with one week to make other arrangements. He is no longer considered part of the family." Acsah retrieved the shuttle and drove it on another pass through the warp threads.

"That attitude is impossible for me to understand. The young people need a tent. No one else in the family needs that one. Perhaps I need to pay Achor a visit."

"Let them have it." Fire blazed in Acsah's eyes. "And let that greedy-eyed Mara see what the love of good friends will provide."

"Be instructed by the law, dear Acsah. 'Do not bear a grudge against one of your people, but love your neighbor as yourself.'"

"No grudges. And I am loving my neighbor." Acsah did not look up from her weaving. The concentration crinkle in her brow deepened as she passed the shuttle back and forth through the loom. "If Achor's family feel shamed because someone shows kindness to the son and daughter-in-law they rejected, all the better."

"That is a unique way of loving your neighbor as yourself," Caleb mumbled. He sat back and gazed at his daughter thoughtfully. "But it might well be the best way to send Achor and Mara the needed message."

After watching Acsah lay down a span of new fabric, Caleb broke the silence with a noisy clearing of his throat. "Rahab and her family are our new neighbors. We must consider how to love them also."

Acsah's shuttle stopped in the middle of its flying run across the loom. "Have we not shown them a great deal of love already? But they are Canaanites. The sooner they move on, the better for our camp."

Caleb gave her a serious look. "I don't believe they will be moving on. I sense that God has brought them to us to enrich our nation. There is much we can learn from this family."

Acsah frowned. "I was wrong about the Midianite girls. Their tender hearts are becoming more and more devoted to Yahweh each day, but these people . . . Father, there are three generations in that family who have grown to adulthood in that evil culture. Their hearts are tainted with the depravity of a society Yahweh declared to be beyond redemption. You can take a family out of Jericho, but how can you take Jericho out of such a family?"

"You don't think the God who broke down Jericho's walls could accomplish such change?"

"But is that what they seek . . . or just safety?"

"Shua was drawn to the God of Abraham long ago, and I believe she has passed that hope on to her family. You have to admire Rahab—so young and with so little knowledge, yet demonstrating incredible faith."

Caleb watched the frown lines soften as Acsah slipped back into the easy rhythm of her weaving. It would be best to lay this conversation to rest for now.

"Joshua is planning to send out two more spies," he said. "There is a fortress up the road about fifteen miles. He fears they might attack our families when we travel past it on the way to the valley of Shechem for the ceremony."

"Is it Bethel?" Acsah asked hesitantly.

"No. Jokshan does not believe the people there will bother us. The place that concerns him is just a couple of miles southeast of it."

"I didn't know there was another city between us and Bethel."

"It is not really a city. Just a small fortress, but it is important. It guards the pass we must travel through to obey Moses' command to build the covenant monument."

The covenant monument. The law . . .

As sudden and bright as a shaft of sunlight piercing dark clouds, illuminating the landscape on a stormy day, the importance of Moses' clear command lit his understanding. "I think I see now why we must build that stone monument in Shechem. Yahweh's righteous laws will be forever engraved in stone right in the heart of Canaan. When the people of this land read those words, they will know our intention is not to overthrow their kings, but to establish love and justice in the land of Jacob's inheritance."

"Moses said we would destroy seven nations larger and stronger than us."

"But it was a prophecy, I think, more than a command."

"I'm not sure I see a difference."

"We will not set out to destroy them. We will wait to see what Yahweh does. He said *he* would drive out hostile nations before us."

"Will we attack this fort?"

"We will request permission to travel in peace with our women and children, but we must be prepared."

"For a reaction like that of Sihon east of the Jordan?" Acsah did not stop working, but Caleb noticed the tremble in her fingers as she asked the question.

"According to Jokshan, King Birsha is committed to stopping us the moment we try to move up from the Jordan Valley. Yet that is what we must do next."

"I truly hope the people of Bethel never attack us. How sad to fight a battle at the very place where Jacob saw the angel stairway."

"The Canaanite city there is Luz. Jokshan tells me the people know the story and revere Jacob's altar as a sacred shrine."

"You have learned a lot from him, haven't you?" Acsah continued weaving quietly for a few moments, her brow knit in solemn thought. "What is the name of this fort?"

"It is known simply as Ai, The Ruin. The remains of a city, destroyed long ago, are still there, never rebuilt. But a small fortress stands close to the rubble, guarding the pass. The Ruin. Strange name for a fort, eh?"

"Would the people of that fort dare attack us after our victory over Jericho?"

"Not if we stayed in Gilgal. But we are sure to create a panic as soon as we obey the command of Moses to go to Mount Ebal and Mount Gerizim. Joshua plans to lead us there in time for Shavuot."

"We are on day ten of the count now. That doesn't allow much time for spies and battles, grain harvests, and preparations for a trek to the center of Canaan."

"Forty more days. A lot can happen in forty days." Caleb stood up and stretched his back and shoulders. He had tools to sharpen.

Acsah's words were barely audible over the soft swishing of her shuttle sweeping through the loom. "Hopefully, these two spies will not need saving by another incredibly-beautiful singing harlot."

Pallu

Pallu scanned the narrow valley with a practiced eye. Though first and foremost a high elder of the senate, this mission aroused his military instincts. His eyes swept over scores of horizontal ledges on the blocky limestone walls. An occasional shrub or tuft of grass braved the parched slopes, clinging to vertical fissures where rapidly draining water lingered longest. A few scattered trees indicated deeper moisture, important knowledge in this dry region. For the moment, however, his interest was in several shadowed depressions pocking the pale bluff. One of those benign smudges would be the secret entrance to the stronghold of Adoni-Zedek.

Pallu was the youngest of the four elders, but even he welcomed the chance to rest. He threw himself down in the patchy shade beneath a terebinth with his companions. The sun was hot, beginning to move past zenith, and they had begun their journey before dawn. He drank deeply from his water skin, watching their young scouts, Peleth and Irad, tether the donkeys and then make their way up the steep slope in search of the entrance.

He had long known of the cave of Adullam. In more turbulent times, it had been the haunt of raiders and robber bands. That was before Zedek's father used the threat of the first Israelite invasion to unify the kings of southern Canaan. After forming an alliance with the Anakim giants, his armies drove the Israelites back into the desert. He became undisputed leader in the region and seized control of Adullam as a stronghold for the royal city of Jebus.

The cave was a wonder in a land rife with caves. Though talked about by many, its great hall, carved by underground streams in eons past, had actually been seen by very few. According to legend, this ancient cavern had numerous adjoining rooms on several levels, levels successively left high and dry as the water table dropped. It was hard to imagine that amount of water in this place now. A stream at the bottom of the narrow canyon gargled spring rains today, but in another month, it would dry up like every other winter stream. Any remaining trickles would flee the surface, sinking to underground channels. It was said that streams continued to flow in the depths of Adullam throughout the dry season. Yes, this was the consummate redoubt—virtually undetectable, highly defensible, and in possession of a dependable aquifer. What enemy could threaten the great Adoni-Zedek and his forces here?

Pallu snorted at the answer. *One who could flatten the walls of Jericho.*

Ibzan's probing eyes searched Pallu's face. "What is going on in that military mind of yours, my friend?"

"I was just thinking that Zedek feels as secure in this indomitable place as Na . . ."

A long, low whistle arrested his reply. Not far below the jagged line where rimrock met sky, the two Gibeonite soldier-scouts peered down at the elders, signaling with scooping hand motions for their masters to ascend.

White-haired Ibzan rose first and brushed off his robe, surveying his comrades with his usual aristocratic dignity. "Much as we dislike this meeting, it is our duty to be here."

Pallu scuffled reluctantly to his feet and sighed. "Zedek will have to listen to us. We control the passes of southern and central Canaan."

"When our quiet commander speaks, the man who does not listen is a fool." Meshullam's gentle, rasping laugh lightened the heavy mood.

Pallu grunted. He listened. He voted. But there were normally more words than necessary flying back and forth over the senate floor without him adding to the babble. He was the quiet senator because others did so much talking.

"All Canaan has seen the evidence," Ibzan reminded them. "We must press for a treaty with the people of Yahweh." He headed toward a cairn of three stacked stones at the base of a faint trail—the agreed-upon marker. Without this sign, the route up the canyon wall would have been virtually undetectable.

"Zedek is aware of our strength." The portly Meshullam grunted at the effort of getting to his feet. "We may prefer to negotiate by council and covenant, but we can muster the most powerful army in the region when necessary, eh, Commander?"

"Only when necessary," Pallu replied quietly.

"The point is that the southern kings will have to listen to us."

"I can tell you, that flaming firebrand, Adoni-Zedek, will not listen to anyone," Likhi snapped. "Enough talk. We agreed to attend their war counsel. Let's do so." He pushed past Ibzan to lead the way up the near-perpendicular rock face.

Meshullam coughed. "But they need us. Surely, they would not dare attack a formidable enemy without our forces. That will be our best argument."

Pallu tipped his head toward the trailhead. "Go ahead, my friend. I'll follow."

As the elders looped back and forth climbing the steep pathway, Pallu caught glimpses of Peleth and Irad impatiently pacing the narrow ledge at the top. First Likhi, then Ibzan reached the top and conferred quietly with the scouts. Pallu did not like the anxious looks passed between them.

When Meshullam finally wheezed his way to the top and paused to catch his breath, Peleth, the bolder of the two scouts, announced loudly. "The Council of Kings is waiting. The guard said to enter at once, but leave all weapons out here."

As Pallu pressed close to the cave entrance, Irad lowered his voice confidentially, "Treacherous entrance—single-file only. We have been ordered to follow you in. Not lead."

"We cannot protect you," Peleth added in a whisper.

"I'll go first." Pallu ducked into the dark opening ahead of the others. At his first step, the stone floor dropped away, and he found himself charging down a steep grade, fighting for balance, blinking into darkness that was doubly blinding after the glare of full sunlight on the pale canyon walls outside.

The chute was so low-roofed that he needed to bend nearly double, so narrow he could not turn around, and so steep he could not slow down even if he had chosen to. He imagined a gauntlet of a dozen or more soldiers waiting for him at the bottom with spears and was fully aware of the near impossibility of self-defense if that were the case. He clenched his teeth, tensing every nerve and muscle as he ran headlong out of the deadly entrance and lunged into fighting stance on the level floor of a room cloaked in semidarkness.

A derisive laugh echoed through the chamber. "You are not under attack, Gibeonite."

Pallu scowled at the man, a single guard standing in the gray light, casually twirling his long bronze-tipped spear.

"No sense of humor, eh?" the guard asked with a chuckle. "If Zedek had wanted you dead, my spear tip would have greeted you as you shot out of the entry."

Pallu could not see the man's face as he was backlit by light shining through an open doorway, the solid oak doors thrown wide in mocking welcome. The portal to the throne room felt as unfriendly as its laughing guard.

A scuffling clatter announced the coming of the next Gibeonite, and Pallu turned expectantly toward the chute to lend a hand as needed.

"Move on through that door," the guard commanded.

"Do you object to our remaining here?" Pallu asked in a low matter-of-fact tone as Likhi emerged. "The two of us may be needed to steady our more elderly companions as they emerge."

"Just don't try anything stupid, Gibeonite. Adoni-Zedek gave his word that you could come and go in peace, and he intends to keep his word. He would not be happy if I was forced to run you through." The guard caressed the point of his spear. His expression indicated that *he* would not be unhappy at such an outcome.

One by one the remaining two elders and the scouts stumbled from the chute. As soon as their party was complete, the guard gave a mock bow. "Enter the great hall, honored guests." He swept his arms toward the entrance in a dramatic welcoming gesture. "Adoni awaits you."

The Gibeonite delegation pressed close together as they passed through the doors into a naturally-formed stone vestibule with a low ceiling. Pallu led the way, stopping beside a massive stalagmite pillar supporting the ceiling.

Pallu assessed the enormous hall beyond as his comrades lined up beside him. The vault of the ceiling soared upward into dim recesses forty or more feet from the floor—far beyond the reach of the fingers of light from hundreds of torches fastened to the walls. Tracing the line of flames dancing with the shadows along the rippled flowstone walls, Pallu counted five darkened passageways. These, he assumed, led to smaller rooms or to deeper layers of this underground fortress rather than to the outside. Colorful stone draperies curtained the opposite end of the room, dramatically drawing the eye to a hand-carved seat flanked by soaring dripstone wings. A well-worn set of twelve steps cut into the limestone formation led from the floor to this throne where the pompous Adoni-Zedek perched like a vulture. At least a dozen kings of southern Canaan were seated with their retinues on a scattering of colorful cushions and carpets on the stone floor beneath him.

"As one," Pallu whispered. Undaunted by the king's pomp or the size of the room, the elders strode into the room four abreast with their scouts close behind.

Zedek rose to his feet and pounded the limestone ledge where he stood with his staff. He was a man of commanding height, but Pallu wondered if he had any idea how the sheer immensity of such a hall diminished even the greatest of kings.

The king's yad rashi, standing with six armed bodyguards at the base of the stairway, repeated the sound with a smart rap of his own staff. The bodyguards added a final rapping of the stones with their spears, and then the yad's cry for silence echoed to the vaults of the ceiling. The rumbling conversations ceased instantly, all members of the assembly rising to greet the newcomers with silent stares.

"Welcome, elders of Gibeon." Adoni-Zedek peered down imperiously. By moving only two fingers, he signaled a flock of servants waiting in the wings. They scuttled away, the first contingent returning within minutes bearing a carpet large enough for the delegation. Others brought cushions, baskets of parched grain, and platters of raisin cakes along with steaming cups of a fragrant herbal brew.

"Our apologies that we cannot offer you fruit, or milk, or anything fresh—only what can be stored in the silos of Adullam."

"We are most grateful for these fine refreshments after our journey," Ibzan replied with a gracious nod of his head. He and his comrades settled onto the provided carpet woven in vibrant rainbow hues and picked at the paltry provisions. Pallu drew a deep breath as he chewed a mouthful of parched grain, noting how the oily black smoke of the torches was drawn upward on invisible currents. The air was surprisingly fresh. He was impressed yet again by this cave. With such favorable ventilation, an enemy could not easily smoke out its inhabitants.

Adoni-Zedek dropped heavily down on his royal seat to watch his guests eat. A triple set of gold chains jangled against his bronze breastplate, reminding everyone in the room of his presence whenever he moved. The king's eyes, beady and intent, studied the roomful of royals like a bird of prey. One meaty hand still gripped his ornate staff while the other toyed with a jeweled javelin. Pallu had the impression he might wield either weapon against them if they tried his patience by lingering too long over the food.

At last the king signaled with another nearly imperceptible movement of his fingers, and the yad responded with a loud announcement. "Adoni-Zedek—Lord of Righteousness, King of Kings, Renowned Warrior, Defender of the Defenseless, and Arbiter of Justice for all southern Canaan—calls this assembly to order."

The king cleared his throat ceremoniously. "Welcome friends. I do not need to inform you of the evil invader we must face together. This bloodthirsty predator broke through the protective floods of the Jordan, butchered our brothers in Jericho, seized their crops, and crouches now like a lioness flicking her tail, watching for signs of weakness. When she has chosen her next victim, she will roar up from the Jordan Valley, breaking the neck and ripping the flesh of another kingdom of Canaan. It could be any of us."

As the warning hung ominously over the kings, Zedek's eyes swept from man to man, then lingered on the Gibeonites. "Those who dwell in closest proximity live with the most immediate threat. But death threatens every kingdom of Canaan. We know the ancient prophecies—that the children of Jacob would return to take possession of this land. Some say it was the land of their ancestors first, but our great ancestor Canaan took possession of it as a gift from Lord Baal long before the time of Abraham, Isaac, or Jacob. What right do the children of Jacob have to take back an inheritance they could not hold? They intend to bring our civilization to an end. They intend to exterminate us and all memory of Baal. There is but one right course of action. We must obliterate this enemy before it is too late."

Ibzan rose and raised his hands with his fingers steepled beneath his chin in a sign of respect. "As high elder of Kiriath-Baal, the most populous city of Gibeon, I speak for all the people of the Federation. We are pleased that you have called this assembly. We are honored that the kings of southern Canaan value our support and counsel. Most noble Adoni, we trust you will also value our resolution—voted by the senate of Gibeon after numerous meetings debating what we have observed.

"We are resolved not to provoke war with Jacob's descendants, now known as the Children of Israel. We do not believe they are the fierce predator you have described. Our spies tell us that the people took no plunder at all from the wealth of Jericho. They did not attack out of greed, but because their survival depended on it. King Nahari fully intended to obliterate them. He reaped the consequences of that decision."

Adoni-Zedek's eyes narrowed. "I am the Lord of Righteousness in this region. You dare suggest I am wrong? Are you suggesting the alliance I am bringing together is not just, or righteous, or wise? Wisdom demands taking this threat seriously. Righteousness demands protecting our way of life. Justice demands avenging our brothers in Jericho."

With calm resolute speech, Ibzan answered Zedek's growling threats. "You must know that we Hivites, of all peoples, would want revenge. It was our people mercilessly slaughtered in Shechem by the Sons of Jacob centuries ago, but wars of vengeance only bring more death and pain. And we are not so shortsighted as to look back merely to the fall of Jericho. Jacob's conquests of larger and more formidable foes have aroused the fear of all Canaanites, to be sure. But consider those regimes. Sihon, Og, the Midianite Five, and to a lesser extent, Nahari. Each was a destabilizing power within our region. Each one a threat to our peace."

Zedek broke into a sneering laugh. "No kingdom has been as destabilizing in our region as these invaders."

Pallu rose to his feet beside his revered friend. "Listen to the wisdom of Ibzan, most noble Adoni. Sihon and the royal city of Heshbon fell, but we can learn from the remaining Amorite cities east of the Jordan. They settled into an unspoken truce with the tribes who settled there and survived. Learn from King Balak of Moab. He discovered that the machinations of Balaam the Seer could not touch these people. He watched the obliteration of the black-robed hordes of Midian and the realm of the Five burned to the ground. The kingdoms of Moab and Ammon wisely agreed to terms of peace with the Children of Israel.

"This is also the unanimous decision of our Federation. We will cut a formal covenant if possible. If not, we will assume the same state of unspoken truce as the nations east of the Jordan. Let the Israelites have the valley of the Jordan. War with Israel would not end well for any of us. Be certain of that."

"And you think waiting for Israel to attack will produce a better end?" King Piram of Jarmuth growled. "She will attack our cities one by one as she did Jericho until our civilization is lost forever."

Likhi stood up in solidarity beside Ibzan and Pallu. "As elder of the Gibeonite city of Beeroth, I remind you of our years of peace and friendship. The Federation would do anything to help you in time of need. Do we not provide you with timber for your homes? With firewood, food, and wine—always at reasonable prices because you are our brothers? The many wells of Beeroth supply water, freely and generously, to any and all of the kingdoms of Canaan in times of drought. If your cities were truly threatened, we would not hesitate to send our army to your aid. But let us not provoke such an attack by striking first."

Ibzan nodded. "A preemptive strike was the undoing of King Sihon and then Og. And rumor had it that King Nahari of Jericho was planning an attack as well. Each of those kingdoms are gone. I propose sending a delegation of peace without further delay."

"Women talk," King Hoham of Kiriath-Arba growled. His lips twisted in a contemptuous smirk. "Men fight."

Snarls of agreement ringed the room.

Ibzan maintained a calming voice. "A declaration of war against these people is neither safe nor sane."

King Japhia of Lachish sprang to his feet across the circle from Ibzan and Likhi, cat-like eyes squinting in hate. "They declared war on us the minute they crossed the Jordan."

Pallu tensed to defend Ibzan if this leopard should attack. He shouted over the mutterings of agreement with Japhia. "*If* Israel will not cut covenant with us, and *if* she moves up out of the valley to attack any one of us, *then*—and only then—will Gibeon join forces with you to stop them."

"Nahari may have been mentally deranged, but he was a Canaanite king," someone else shouted.

"Hear, hear! Jericho defended our eastern border."

"War on the vermin attacking our cities!"

"War!" another chimed in.

Another and another joined in until a solid chant of "War! War! War!" pulsed around the great hall. The fear reflected earlier in the eyes of the kings morphed to hatred.

Meshullam leaped to his feet beside Pallu, the voices of the four elders united in a simultaneous "No-o-o-o-o!" The elders of the Federation now stood shoulder to shoulder in opposition to the kings.

"War! Join forces. War! War! War!"

The normally gentle Meshullam bellowed back like a challenged bull. "Join forces, yes. But press for alliance before war."

"Cowards," someone roared over the continued chanting for war.

"You know we are not." Ibzan's voice trumpeted firmly over the uproar. "But we are not foolish enough to precipitate our own death and destruction."

"War! Join forces."

"War! Join forces. Destroy the invaders."

"War! War! War!" The roaring chant made further rational arguments impossible.

With a loud crack, Adoni-Zedek slammed the butt of his staff on the stone step between his feet. "Enough! I have called an assembly, not a mob."

A tense silence fell over the room. The circle of kings glared at the Gibeonites while the four elders raised their chins in defiance of ignorance.

Lord Zedek continued, "The alliance of the southern kings has already pledged to expel or exterminate the foreigners. Like it or not, Gibeonites, there will be war. The only question is will the Federation join the alliance or not?"

Ibzan pressed his palms together in a submissive gesture, tilting his head in a respectful bow as he spoke. "Most honorable Adoni, the four cities of the Federation watch the movements of Israel, as you do, with alarm. Our combined army is on high alert, but for now, the settled decision of the senate is to watch and wait." Ibzan did not flinch despite the snarling growl of protest rising from the other kings.

"Watch and wait. That is our settled decision," Meshullam agreed. The power of the raspy voice belied Meshullam's gentle countenance. "We must attempt treaty before war. As you have pointed out, just and righteous Adoni, if Israel moves out to conquer more territory, Gibeon is likely to be the next target . . . unless Israel chooses to turn north. Would it not, therefore, be reasonable to give us the opportunity to negotiate for peace? We alone would bear the consequences if we prove to be wrong."

Adoni-Zedek leaned forward on his throne. "Ah, the wisdom of Gibeon. Just as I have heard, you are so learned . . . so wise . . . for *mortals!*"

A triumphant grin spread over his face. "The high priest of Jebus has been in council with the *shaddayim* along with your own priests at Kiriath-Baal. Koz, come forth! Declare to us the will and wisdom of the immortals."

A booming explosion and dazzling light detonated beside the throne and the priest materialized in the smoke. His white garments glimmered with golden embroidery and glittered with jeweled chains. The impression was that he had just arrived from regions far beyond earth, but Pallu suspected that the distraction of the blinding flash allowed him to step out from a hiding place behind the wing-like formation to the right of the throne.

As the smoke of his appearing spiraled toward the ceiling, the priest announced in a loud voice, "Our fight is not merely against this invading desert people, but against Yahweh, their God."

Koz swept the room with piercing, inscrutable eyes, imposing a moment of dramatic silence. "Who is this Yahweh? He is not of the shaddayim. Which other god leads his followers to victory—then demands that all local gods be entirely eliminated? But that is exactly what Yahweh demands. Behold the land east of the river. Israel not only exterminated the inhabitants of Heshbon but destroyed all traces of their worship. The houses, the weapons, the clothing they plundered, but every image of Baal or Asherah, every altar, every sacred phallic stone was smashed and ground to powder. The sacred groves were hewn down. The high places razed. The gods of the shaddayim have shown me that this is Yahweh's intention for all of Canaan."

Trapping the eyes of the Gibeonite elders one by one, the priest held them until he had wordlessly communicated the will of the shaddayim. *Reassess the settled decision of your senate. Cease watching and waiting.*

"We must do to Yahweh and his followers as he intends to do to us," he finished with a roar. "We must act. No more watching and waiting. Victory will be ours, for—Who . . . is . . . like . . . Ba-a-a-a-a-a-al?"

As the name of Baal thundered through the cavernous room, great pounding footsteps sounded from deep beneath the stony floor, the sound reverberating from the walls, vibrating the floor in every direction so it was impossible to locate the focal point until a huge figure emerged from one of the darkened doorways. He crouch-walked from the passageway, seeming to grow larger and larger as he unfolded his bent frame, unfurling the long pale arms folded close to his body. When at last he shook himself free of the confining space and pulled himself up to full stature, he was three times the height of the largest man in the room.

This was the first time Pallu had laid eyes on Libni, king of the Anakim giants, but he did not have to be told who he was. Everyone in Canaan had heard stories of the ogre with face and hair the yellow-white of creatures who dwell under rocks. The cruel lines of evil etched in the giant's face raked Pallu's innards with talons of terror.

The bored disdain on the faces of most of the kings when the priest of Jebus exploded into view was not lost on Pallu. He guessed that their own priests provided such dramatic entrances when necessary to impress the populace. The appearance of this Anakim monster was something else—as if Lord Baal himself had entered their midst. King Libni shook his huge spear high in the air, eyes flashing like coals of fire. "I heard the counsel of the so-called wise men of Gibeon." His glittering red eyes narrowed contemptuously. "Go home, spineless Hivites. We will defeat Yahweh and his army—as well as your cowardly Federation."

"Baal confirms that truth," Koz intoned, reminding the room not to forget their god. "Victory is sure."

"Victory!" King Hiram bellowed in agreement. "Go home, Gibeonites. We do not need your army. We have the Anakim on our side."

"Victory! Victory!" The southern kings took up the chant.

"Are you blind and deaf, my brothers?" Pallu cried out over the uproar. "Do you really believe that with this son of Anak on your side, you will defeat Yahweh? Did the armies of Israel not destroy Og and his renowned Rephaim warriors?"

"Traitor." The giant's lips curled in disgust as he hurled the epithet again. "Death to every cowardly traitor."

"Traitor! Traitor!" the southern kings chanted. "Death to traitors!"

"Enough!" Adoni-Zedek cried, leaping from his throne and rapping his rod against the stone pavement. "I am Lord of Righteousness. I guaranteed safe passage for the elders of Gibeon, and I do not go back on my word. Take this prophetic word back to your senate, men of Gibeon: Traitors to Canaan *will* die but not by the hand of Adoni-Zedek or his allies." He pointed a bejeweled index finger at Ibzan. "Israel will swarm up from the valley to conquer you, and no one will come to your aid."

Libni sneered at the Gibeonite delegation. "Who do you think will rule the Hivite highlands when you are gone? Who will reap the treasures of your fields, your vineyards, your fine forests, and pools of water?"

Pallu watched the question ignite a greedy fire in Zedek's eyes. *He assumes Jebus will expand its territory while Libni means to make himself the answer to those questions.*

"See to your own thrones, you southern kings," he called out. "Do not think the sons of Anak would hesitate to feed your carcasses to the vultures when you have served their purposes."

A sense of doom choked the vociferous royals. Fear-filled eyes fell on King Libni in a cavernous void of silence.

"Guards." Adoni-Zedek commanded in a hushed voice. "Escort the elders of the Federation out."

The row of statue-like guards lined up below the throne immediately came to life, rushing forward, surrounding, threatening, herding the Gibeonite delegation out of the king's presence. In the confusion Libni rushed Pallu, drawing back his massive spear, eyes blazing with fury. "Prepare to die, traitor!"

Pallu dodged instinctively to one side. The grim-faced guard prodding him toward the exit lurched, stumbling awkwardly into the midst of the Gibeonite huddle. The gleaming bronze point of Libni's spear sprouted from his chest as a comrade caught him and held him up. The man's rasping scream echoed from the dark vaults of the ceiling drowning Libni's angry mutterings about the miss. The giant seized the spear shaft with both hands, lifting the squealing guard above his head, brandishing him like a spitted pig. "Look and tremble, Pallu," he cried "I will skewer you and your comrades and roast you alive on the fires of Baal's altar."

"*Not* in my stronghold," Zedek countered, rapping his rod on his stony platform once more. "The honor of my good name is at stake here. Pallu is right. You Anakim need this alliance with me—if you wish to fare better than Og."

Pallu watched the giant falter, restraining his rage in the face of the king's unwavering calm. The giant dropped the body onto the stony pavement pushing with his foot as he focused on freeing his weapon. The screams of the dying guard morphed to a rush of bright blood as the giant yanked the spear free.

When Libni finished extricating the weapon, Zedek continued in an unruffled voice. "The insult to your name by Pallu of Gibeon will be redressed—but not here, not today. The elders of the Federation came in good faith under my promise of protection."

Pallu found himself admiring the way Zedek stood up to the Anakim king, maintaining at least a semblance of right, but the scowls on the faces of the guards prodding their little group into the low-ceilinged vestibule and the spear tips pressing sharp into their backs were far from reassuring. Promises of safe conduct often were conditional. Pallu's mind raced in search of a plan to protect the group.

The sentry who originally greeted the elders grinned at him foolishly. "Didn't go so well, eh Gibeonite?"

Pallu saw that the guard's grip on the spear was loose. Too low on the shaft to hang on if Pallu surprised him. One spear would not be much defense against the prodding escort, now numbering but five, but it was something. He remained tense, every muscle coiled for whatever action was needed. But, once in the antechamber, the king's bodyguards backed away, returning to the throne room.

Still grinning menacingly, the entrance guard nudged Peleth and Irad toward the dark chute with a loose touch of his spear tip. "Out you go!"

"Our scouts will leave last," Pallu informed him calmly. He peered into the black orifice wondering how it was physically possible to manage an exit. To his relief he could see well-worn handholds cut in the rock. "Meshullam, you must go first. Use these holds. Likhi follow behind, prepared to block a fall."

"I have allowed myself to grow fat, spending far too much time lying on my couch enjoying good food while pondering new philosophies." Meshullam patted his well-rounded abdomen. "I pray my feet will not slip, Likhi, my friend."

Pallu released a short, congenial laugh and tipped his head toward the guard. "That is why I insisted on reserving Peleth and Irad to the end—strong, young back-ups—to prevent our entire troupe from cascading down onto that eager spear tip."

Over the scrabbling and grunting of Meshullam starting up the tunnel, Pallu caught the boasting words of the pale giant. "Canaan will once again know the ancient power of the Anakim." His gut twisted. A lone giant showing up here and there as warrior-hero of an enemy army was frightening enough. But the thought of the sons of Anak gathered as primary players in the machinations of Canaan was intolerable. He tried to listen for hints of the giant's next moves and thought he heard Libni mention *Ai* and perhaps *Luz,* but Likhi had begun following Meshullam up the steep shaft now, doubling the scratching and scuffing. More than that, the look on the face of the guard dissuaded him from any appearance of straining to overhear discussions that no longer pertained to Gibeon.

"You are next, Ibzan," Pallu said quietly. "I will follow close behind, blocking a fall should you falter. Our scouts will provide back up to me." As he spoke, he thought he heard the giant say the word *tonight,* but he couldn't be sure. *That is the problem with speaking,* Pallu grumbled to himself as he ducked into the black chute. *One cannot listen at the same time.*

Pallu could not shake a sense of foreboding as the Gibeonite party hurried down the cliff trail from Adullam and headed up the ridge route north, each man guiding his donkey along the trail in dead silence. He wondered whether his companions feared leaving a trail of words for an enemy or were struck dumb by thoughts of impending war and the gathering of the Anakim. Such thoughts had been looping through his head for hours with no distracting conversations to latch onto.

The sun sank into the western sea as they climbed the ridge trail to Gibeon. The last dim glimmer of twilight faded. Still their troop rode silently on. Not until the blackness of the night totally obscured the path, did Ibzan rein in his donkey and signal the others to come close. The six little beasts nuzzled cheek-to-cheek, nickering reassurances to each other, seemingly comforted as the group formed a closely woven formation.

"We would be foolish to travel further tonight," Ibzan whispered. "Wild beasts, robbers, a misplaced hoof in the darkness . . ."

"King Libni might be abroad on this very road tonight," Pallu added. "I heard him say something about Ai along with the word tonight."

Ibzan groaned softly. "But we must not travel further until first light."

"Where will we find shelter?" Meshullam's voice was stretched, high, and tense.

"I have spotted lions in the forests near Beeroth recently." Likhi's face was a grim mask. "Normally, I would welcome a fire to ward off wild beasts, but if Libni travels this road tonight, I am more inclined to climb into the fork of some large tree."

"Well, I am not inclined to sleep on such a perch," Meshullam grumbled.

"I wonder," Ibzan mused with a low voice. "Do Libni's red eyes give him the night vision of an animal predator?"

"Speculation about the power of the enemy only clouds our judgment." Pallu slid smoothly off his donkey. "Peleth, Irad, come with me. The rest of you wait here. Occupy your minds with the best arguments for persuading the senate to send a peacemaking delegation to Israel immediately."

Pallu was gone only minutes, but returned to find his three companions dismounted and backed up shoulder to shoulder against a boulder, swords drawn and ready. He held his hand up in mock surrender as he emerged out of the shadows. "I hope you recognize a friend."

"What brought you back so quickly?" Meshullam's question was tentative, rising to a high-pitched finish.

"A protected shelter." Pallu announced reassuringly. "Just off the road to our right. Very well hidden. Peleth and Irad are preparing a small fire there for us."

As the Gibeonites ate from their meager provisions, the crackling fire drove the demons from their minds. "For the first time since we left Adullam, I can think clearly," Ibzan said. "Despite the bravado of the southern kings or the rantings of Libni—the kingdoms of Canaan cannot possibly stand against Yahweh and his people. We must persuade the senate of that."

"I would like to know if Koz was correct in saying that Israel intends to annihilate all the kingdoms of Canaan regardless of our stance toward them," Meshullam said, chewing thoughtfully on a strip of dried venison. "Before we approach them with a treaty, I propose we send Peleth and Irad to learn more."

"I would welcome that," Irad responded immediately. "I do not trust the words of Koz. It should not be difficult to prove his allegations true or false."

"Hear. Hear," Meshullam said, with a fond glance at the two young men. "You two have proved to be excellent scouts—fleet as deer and silent as serpents, with an uncanny knowledge of the length and breadth of the land. If any men could creep close to these people and learn their intentions, it would be the two of you."

"I pray the gods that an alliance is possible," Ibzan added in a whisper. "Sundered as we now are from the kingdoms of southern Canaan, we must throw in our lot with Israel. The sooner, the better."

"It is humiliating to cut covenant with invaders out of fear." Likhi's expression was dismal. "The people of Gibeon make treaties only with kingdoms of moral superiority. We know nothing of Israel's laws, only that their God is unstoppable."

"And there you have declared the very reason we cannot form an alliance with Adoni-Zedek," Pallu stated adamantly. He spat on the ground in disgust. "Canaan's Lord of Righteousness is the very opposite of what his name declares."

Ibzan nodded solemnly. "That most unrighteous, greedy, grasping king seeks only what he believes right for himself. And to that end, he allies himself with the vilest of all—the Anakim. Without knowing more, I can honestly declare that a covenant with Israel would be a much more honorable choice."

"Provided they be willing to cut covenant with us," Pallu replied.

Joshua[11]

The twilight glow, red as blood, was quickly fading, but not the disquiet it kindled in Joshua's heart. Jada and Zabad waited expectantly for instructions, but he needed a moment to clear his head. He did not believe in omens, but the gory crimson filtering through the open doorway warned of danger. Not vaguely defined danger, but specifically the danger of spying. Here, with these two young Israelite boys eagerly awaiting their exact assignment, a jumble of troubling memories bombarded his mind—the perils of spies and spying . . . his own exploration with Caleb . . . the terror of Anakim giants . . . the rebellion of the faithless ten. All that forty years ago, but more recently . . . Salmon and Jathniel. He would have lost those two good men but for the courageous faith of a Canaanite girl.

Joshua suppressed the apprehension, methodically refilling his lamp with oil. *Portents from the sky would not control his decisions.*

"Excitement for our trek to Shechem builds throughout the tribes as we count the days to *Shavuo*t," he said, beginning with a statement obvious to the dullest mind. "Moses described the exact spot for the ceremony of blessings and curses, and the timing works out to celebrate the Feast of Weeks while we are there. But there is also tension building at the thought of marching blindly into the highlands of Canaan. After the miracles at the Jordan and Jericho, the people do not doubt that Yahweh will be with us, but they want to know exactly what they are facing. At the urging of the elders, I chose the two of you to scout out the road from the fortress of Ai to the Vale of Shechem—much as our spies explored Jericho and its valley before we crossed the river."

With an unhurried pace, Joshua touched the oil-soaked wick with a burning coal. So far, he had told the boys nothing they didn't already know. He smiled at his own reluctance to get to the point as he set the lamp on an elevated stand. Its flickering light fell over the faces of his scouts. "Two spies again," he mused. He inspected the pair for a few moments, searching first one face and then the other. He was pleased with the character and enthusiasm he read in these young faces. "Only this time, of course, you come from Benjamin and Manasseh. According to the brigade commanders of each of your tribes, you demonstrated great courage in the face of danger at the battle of Jericho."

"Thank you, sir," Jada of Benjamin interjected quickly. "We did our best."

Joshua nodded approvingly, then knelt, rolling back the carpets to expose the bare earth as he continued. "The task before us is quite different than conquering a city, however. Your task is to survey the land. I want a good map of the terrain between here and Shechem. Your commanders believe you have the requisite skills."

"You can't fight a proper battle if you go in blind," Zabad asserted. The two spies looked at one another and grinned.

Joshua cleared his throat. "The task of our nation at this time is not conquest, but the planting of the terms of Yahweh's covenant in the heart of the land. This next step could precipitate a fatal attack when our people travel to the twin peaks of Mount Ebal and Mount Gerizim as commanded by Moses. You can help us avoid that."

He paused and studied the young faces. How could he make his own people understand the importance of this next step in their journey? He could at least start with these two. "The life-changing covenant words of Yahweh came to us at Mount Sinai like the roar of a lion. He birthed a new kind of nation founded on justice and mercy, not power and greed. In his faithfulness he brought the descendants of Abraham back to the land of our inheritance. The monument we build on these mountains in the heart of Canaan will echo the Lion's mighty roar until it resounds through all the earth, a new way of life not for Israel alone, but every nation, tribe, and people in generations to come."

"Now let's get practical," he said as he began to trace a map in the earth with the point of his dagger. "Here is the Jordan River, and here is our camp at Gilgal. These are the hills rising up from this valley toward the west. Our people will travel up to the highlands following the road through this ravine. Here. At the top, I am told, we will transect the road leading along the spiny backbone of the land toward the north to the twin peaks where we will conduct our ceremony. Those two mountains lie about here. In the center of Canaan." Joshua traced the letters for "LAW" on the map.

"According to Jokshan of Jericho, a small fortress guards the pass about fifteen miles from here. The ruins of a larger city, destroyed long ago, lie beside it. For that reason, the fort is known as Ai, the Ruin. Ai is small, but a solid walled fortress—no ruin at all. After the way our courier was treated by Heshbon when we requested peaceful passage through Sihon's territory, I am reluctant to send one man or even a small group. I will make the request myself with my army standing behind me."

Joshua marked the spot and then tapped the point of his dagger a little to the left of his mark. "The city of Luz is located about two miles to the northwest. Jokshan tells me that a shrine to the God of our father Jacob remains there to this day, still called by the name Jacob gave it: *Beth-el.* The people of Luz believe it to be the gateway to heaven because of Jacob's dream. We can only hope they will be friendly to Jacob's descendants."

Joshua paused. He fixed the eyes of his spies with an intense look. "Jacob's family has history in Shechem, the valley between the mountains where our ceremony will take place. His name is surely remembered there with great bitterness. But we are Israelites, not Jacobites. Jacob the Deceiver became Israel the Overcomer. Planting our law in that valley will make a bold declaration of that transformation.

"Rahab's family insists that the kingdoms of Canaan are paralyzed with fear. Jokshan does not believe we would be attacked as long as we remain in Gilgal. And there is the problem. We cannot. It is at the command of Yahweh that we go to build that monument."

He gestured toward the map again. "Scout out the road all the way to the ancient terebinth tree between the twin mountains. You will find it about twenty miles north of Ai. Here. Discover who lives in the valley of Shechem now. Do not let any citizens of Canaan guess that two Israelites spies are traveling in the heart of their land. Keep off-road whenever possible. On your return trip, survey the terrain surrounding the fort itself."

Both men nodded.

"We will move with the stealth of leopards," Zabad of Manasseh asserted.

"Your map is clear, and we understand our mission," his companion affirmed with a somber smile. "Expect us back within four or five days."

Joshua was pleased with their boyish fervor. He did not have a son of his own, but he counted all the young warriors of Israel as his boys. A flood of fatherly concern for these two surged through him. "Observe the city of Ai from a safe vantage point. Do not be foolish. Do not seek exciting exploits for their own sake. Get a general idea of the population of this ruin, but do not attempt to enter it."

The quick glances between Zabad and Jada seemed to say, "*But we are spies. We have heard the spying stories of Caleb and Joshua all our lives. Will we not have spy adventures to recount at evening campfires like them . . . like Salmon and Jathniel?*"

Joshua hoped to quash such foolish aspirations, if that indeed was what filled their minds just now. "I do not wish for your lives to be in mortal danger as were our spies at Jericho. I want a detailed report of strategic hills and ravines. The terrain is quite different from Jericho. We will need that information if this . . . this ruin . . . chooses war rather than granting us peaceful passage through the pass."

"A city choosing war against Yahweh can expect to become a true ruin—like Jericho."

A hint of a smile played on Joshua's lips. The battle of Jericho may have given his army unrealistic expectations, but it also gave them confidence. He had no doubt they were ready for battle as never before. But they must not be careless. "We cannot expect the walls to simply fall. Should it come to battle, we may have to fight this enemy on treacherously unfavorable ground." Joshua's brow furrowed as he jabbed the point of his dagger on the dirt map. "Luz concerns me. See what you can learn about them. Is there much communication between the cities? Our army must not be caught unawares between two Canaanite forces."

Zabad's eyes glittered. "When do you want us to leave?"

"Tonight. There will be no moon to expose you. Proceed as far as you can, guided by the stars. Keep the River of Milk generally over your right shoulder and do not stop until the Scorpion sinks behind the hills. Rest off-road after daybreak, traveling on as far as Mount Ebal when you awake. When you have put some distance between yourselves and Ai, you can take to the open road. According to Jokshan, there are no fortified cities along the central highway until well beyond our destination. But take note of any potential dangers to travelers between Ai and the Ebal-Gerizim valley. The safety of all our people will depend on the thoroughness of your report."

"We will be on the road within the hour, sir," Zabad blurted as the two young men vaulted from their cushions.

"Sooner!" cried his companion, ducking through the doorway into the evening.

"May Yahweh go with you, my sons."

Joshua watched as the pair trotted out of sight leaving a lingering trail of animated chatter.

"What do you think?"

"A tamer task than I expected."

"Are you disappointed that we won't get to enter a Canaanite city?"

"A little. How about you?"

"I am relieved that I will not need to shave like an Egyptian."

"Sadly, my friend, we will have no chance to be rescued like Salmon and Jathniel by a woman of astonishing beauty."

"Are you another of those Israelites who can't take his eyes off the harlot of Jericho?"

"Don't tell me that you would not risk death for the chance to be saved by a woman like Rahab."

"And death you would find if she were a Canaanite beauty with no love for Yahweh."

"Aha! Fear surpasses sense of adventure."

"I fear the thought of my head spiked and scowling from an enemy gate, don't you?"

"Ha, That I do. Missing the thrill of conquest because we lost our heads over a woman."

Joshua smiled as the boisterous banter faded with the crunch of their footsteps. *May that excitement settle into silence before they proceed very far up the road.*

CHAPTER EIGHT

RUINS

As the camp of Israel waited for the return of their spies, they harvested the barley fields of Jericho and continued counting the weeks to Shavuot. The eleventh day of the Omer . . . the twelfth day of the Omer . . . the thirteenth day of the Omer. Then, just before nightfall on day fourteen, shouts announced that the two spies were returning. Crowds gathered, watching the pair wind their way down the steep trail toward Gilgal. With jaunty pace and jubilant faces, they entered camp, reporting their findings to one and all.

"Good news," they called out to the waiting throng.

"Ai requires but a small force."[12]

"No need to send the whole army."

"Good news," they repeated, marching through camp to present themselves to Joshua.

The next morning, the silver trumpets summoned all men of military age to hear the full report brought back by the spies. Ai was a hornet's nest, ready to swarm out and attack if disturbed. Joshua would take a detachment of soldiers with him and personally request safe passage through the pass to Shechem Valley—with his regiments prepared to counter an attack.

As he explained the military assignments and his proposed battle plan if Ai refused to grant their request, expectation erupted into frenzied zeal. The only impediment to their next objective—the ceremony of the blessings and curses—was a ruin, a little fortress, held only by twelve hundred or so men. Those Canaanites would bend the knee and allow the people of Yahweh to pass by in peace . . . or be demolished. With God on their side, Israel was an unstoppable force.

Eliab

As soon as the men were dismissed from the summons, Eliab hurried home. Joyful stripes of red and white beckoned him back to the happiest place in Judah. He set up that tent just last night and already it felt like home. Abihail was humming as she bent over the porridge pot, her sleek, obsidian hair cascading over her shoulders. *Did any other woman's hair gleam in the sun like hers? Not just black, but shimmering with the iridescence of a raven's wing.* "Beyond beautiful," he breathed.

Abihail lifted her head, her dimpled smile and sparkling eyes welcoming him as warmly as an embrace. "Our tent?"

"You," he said, pulling her into his arms. The swelling of her abdomen firm against his body only increased the intoxicating elixir of adoration and desire she stirred in him. Where there had been but one person in the world he couldn't live without, soon there would be two. "You—you, my love, and the child growing within you. I hope for a son, but the thought of a tiny replica of you brings tears of joy to my eyes."

"Perhaps you will get both. Acsah keeps teasing me about twins. Oh! Did you feel the movement?"

He loosened his embrace and she guided his hand to the little nudge intruding into this intimate conversation. He grinned. "What are you saying, little one? That Acsah is right? There *are* two of you in there? A boy and a girl?"

Abihail laughed lightly. "Well, that would explain why I've suddenly become as awkward as a cow."

"A joyfully radiant cow then. And I the proudest of bulls." He kissed her nose and smiled at the flush of joy on her face. "I have never seen you glow as you do right now."

She laughed again. "You silly. It is the reflections of our new tent, not some mysterious luminescence of motherhood—and this mother-to-be is ravenously hungry." She slipped from his embrace, retrieved bowls, and began scooping barley porridge from the bubbling pot.

"Oh, I nearly forgot to tell you what transpired at the assembly," he said, settling at her side to eat. "Joshua will be leading a small delegation of armed men to a fortress at the top of the ridge. It protects the road to the north. He intends to request permission for all our people to travel to Shechem through the pass but does not feel their king is likely to agree. He fears a response much like Sihon of Heshbon. It would only be wise to have his forces in place behind him in case of attack."

"The terror of Heshbon," Abihail whispered. Eliab felt the shiver pass through her body. "I will never forget being trapped in the gorge behind the army with the other women and children watching the endless ranks of Sihon's army advancing toward you across the field."

"This won't be the *terror* of Heshbon, as you call it. Ai is not nearly as large. Our captains cast lots to choose a few from each clan. Only three thousand will go."

"Three thousand?" Her breath caught. "Not you, Eliab?"

He wrapped his arm around her reassuringly. "Of course not. As a new bridegroom, I'm exempted from war for our entire first year of marriage."

Abihail snuggled her head against his chest. "God often seems so frighteningly holy and remote, but now . . . I like thinking he knows me and added this law just for us. That he understands how even a few days of separation would devastate me."

Eliab thought about her words for a minute. "A God who loves lovers . . . I like that thought too." He grinned. "But I honestly don't think separation will be any easier after a year."

"No, but we must be fair, mustn't we? God could hardly say that only unhappily married men, or moderately happy ones, ever have to go to war, while the truly happy get to stay home with their wives."

"Growing their families . . ."

She giggled. "Well, that would be a way to ensure that the largest families were happy ones."

Eliab face became very serious. "Our home will be vastly different from the bickering, bad-tempered home I grew up in. And when the day comes for me to go off to war, I will be a most unhappy soldier every moment I am away from you." He squeezed her shoulders.

"Oh! Feel it again, Eliab." Abihail sat up straight and pressed his hand against the flutter of life. "Our baby just messaged approval of his abba's words."

"A new life," he murmured. "Created by our love."

"Eliab, let's rid ourselves of the last traces of our old life." She stretched out with her foot and pushed at the bundle of goatskin tarps, the tent belonging to his parents. "Why don't you return that thing right now?"

Jamin

Jamin frowned at the fanatical yammering around him as he made his way to his father's tent. Irritated that he had been selected to go with Joshua's special delegation when it gave him no advantage, he mumbled about the unfairness of equal distribution of spoils. If he was going to risk his life in battle, he should be compensated accordingly.

He had nearly reached Achor's doorway, when a scrawny, wide-eyed boy accosted him. "What do you think, neighbor? We are sure to win. The army of Yahweh is the best in the world!"

Jamin silenced him with an irritated scowl and the boy scurried off in search of a friendlier target. He heard the same annoying voice two places farther down the tent row, "Say neighbor, will anyone in your family get to fight?"

He smoldered at the thought. Joshua had announced that only three thousand men would march on Ai. *Why, of all the men in the clan of Zimri, am I the one who has to go? How could Eleazar claim that the blind chance of casting lots reflected God's will? There was no justice in a lottery.* While these thoughts seethed in his head, he caught sight of his younger brother far down the tent row, lugging a large roll of animal hides and tent poles. His lip curled with contempt. *Eliab is such a mouse. Returning the tent without complaint or argument. He would do anything to avoid conflict.*

Instantly, the two thoughts fused in his astute mind. He would lure his brother into performing the military duty for him. Jamin chuckled aloud at his own cleverness.

"Is that you, my son?" Achor pushed his head out of his tent and blinked in the morning light. "I thought I recognized your laugh. I didn't manage to get dressed in time for the assembly." He yawned. "I am just not sleeping well most nights and can hardly get up in the morning. What happened?"

"Your honorable firstborn will tell you about it later." Jamin nodded his head in Eliab's direction. "Here comes the dishonorable son. Returning the tent."

"Eliab," Achor whispered, glancing down the tent row in the direction Jamin indicated.

"Our little fox must have figured out some other way to provide shelter for his new bride," Jamin muttered.

The hint of a wistful smile softened Achor's face. "He is a good lad. Not clever like you, but good. Perhaps we were too hasty."

"You think you have his loyalty?" Jamin shot a contemptuous glance at his father. "Tell him about your new robe."

Eliab

Eliab squinted into the blinding brilliance of the early morning sun. The familiar silhouettes of his father and brother were starkly outlined, huddled in close conversation beside his parents' backlit tent. Obscuring shadows covered their faces. Surely, they saw him, but neither one called out a greeting. An uneasy feeling rose in his gut that he was the topic of their earnest conversation.

The snatches of Jamin's speech drifting toward him confirmed his fears. "Younger son . . . dishonor . . . crossing with Caleb." He squared his shoulders for the unpleasant encounter.

"I will handle this, Father." Although Jamin clearly addressed their father, he locked eyes with his brother.

Eliab tipped his head respectfully. "Shalom, Father . . . Jamin." He stooped to place the large, awkward bundle at their feet. "I am returning your tent. Thank you for—" His words caught in his throat. Without the slightest sign of recognition, his father retreated through the doorway.

For a brief moment with the door flap lifted high, Eliab glimpsed his mother beyond Achor's large frame. Her face was obscured by the dimness of the interior, but he couldn't miss her eyes. She fixed him with a dead stare. Then the door flap closed, the meaning clear. He was no longer their son. The rejection stung more than his brother's contemptuous smirk.

"My brother," Jamin said, slapping his chest and rolling his eyes upward. His voice cracked with forced emotion.

"The tent—" Eliab began once more, gesturing toward the bundle.

But Jamin pulled him into an embrace, kissing both his cheeks in an unusual display of affection. "Oh, my brother. How can I cut you off?" He sank onto a cushion in the shade of the canopy stretched over the tent entrance and dropped his head dramatically into his hands.

Eliab waited uncertainly. *Should he remain standing here until Jamin concluded this . . . drama? Should he sit down and politely comfort him?* His impulse was to leave, but it seemed rude when his brother was putting so much into this display of grief.

After a lengthy pause, his brother groaned. "I am grieved beyond words, Eliab. We must discuss this terrible situation."

Eliab nudged the bundled tent closer to Jamin with his foot and began to back away. "I merely wanted to return the tent Abihail and I have been using—as you asked. Be sure that Mother and Father know how grateful we are."

The odd expression on Jamin's upturned face defied interpretation. "Don't be in a hurry to leave. I have missed our brotherly conversations." Jamin paused to search Eliab's face, then asked abruptly, "So what do you make of the report brought back by the spies?"

Eliab relaxed a little. The joy of the morning assembly animated him still. "Ever since Heshbon, I expected formidable battles with the Canaanites. Now it seems Ai will be even easier than Jericho."

"I am honored to represent the family of Zimri." The smile Jamin donned was obviously fabricated. "What about you, little brother? Are you disappointed at not being selected to go?"

"You know the law. As a new bridegroom, I am exempt for a year. Perhaps, I would be quite envious otherwise."

"Of course . . . the law. Too bad the law will hold you back."

"Abihail sees it as a gift from God. There will be other opportunities."

"Mmmm. But perhaps too late. This family dispute is not good. You suffer. I suffer. And Father and Mother are inconsolably distraught over it." Jamin seemed to be choosing his words carefully. "Sit down, my brother. A thought just occurred to me. A plan that could well lead us all out of this miserable situation."

Eliab sank warily to a cushion opposite his older brother. He had a bad feeling about any plan Jamin devised.

"You want to be welcomed back into the family. I want you back in the family. God knows how much Mother and Father want you back in the family. But you have not honored them as the law requires."

"I? Not honored?"

"Do you think it went unnoticed by our neighbors when you crossed the river with Caleb's clan. Your things on his wagon. Rejecting the assistance and company of your own family?"

"You told me I couldn't—"

"Your lofty ideals spawned a grievous rending of our family and many observed the rift. Mother and Father had no good answer to give . . . other than that you had rejected them." Jamin clutched dramatically at his heart. "The pain they suffered grieves me to this day."

Eliab's distrust grew deeper, but Jamin continued without a pause. "I have been torn. You are my brother, but I must honor my parents as the law requires. It occurred to me just now that there is a simple way for you to reestablish your . . . um . . . loyalty to the family."

"I have never been anything but loyal to all of you!" Eliab broke in defensively.

Jamin closed his eyes, nodding his head slowly. "So my heart has always told me, but our father has suffered much over this."

"It was never my intention to hurt him or sever relations with the family, but I could not support your ill-gotten acquisition of the Midianite plunder. Particularly when you stole from the Levitical share. Jamin, you know I judged rightly."

"I will not dishonor our father by passing judgment on his decisions. His arguments carry a greater weight of wisdom than yours simply because he is our elder, our father. You made your righteous stand but shattered the family ties. That is the issue at stake now for loyal sons. Hear me now. I have a plan to reunite the family, to bind us tighter than ever. Does your heart not yearn for that as we look forward to claiming our inheritance in this land?"

"What do you want me to do?" Eliab's pulse pounded in his ears. No matter what, he would not break the covenant. He would not get involved in some greedy scheme.

"Take my place in the battle of the ruin. It will be an easy victory and a simple way to prove your family loyalty."

Eliab stared at Jamin in disbelief. "Abihail is with child," he whispered hoarsely.

Jamin paused, looking at him from the corners of narrowed eyes. A muffled intake of breath from the interior of the tent told him his parents were listening. "All the more reason to reunite our family," he said, flicking his eyes toward the tent door. He relaxed with a chuckle. "It is not as if you would be heading off for a three-year war."

"You would disregard the statute clearly stated in the law?"

"You have already left your bride behind to go to war once . . . at God's specific command. You marched around Jericho with every man of fighting age. Consider the intent of the law. That the bonding of a man and his wife not be interrupted by lengthy separation. Our army will be gone but one night or two nights at most. Who knows when such an opportunity will arise again? Following the ceremony of blessings and curses, our people will be tied up in working the summer fields, followed by harvests of grapes and olives. There may not be another battle until next spring. Perhaps never if, as Joshua hopes, the remaining kingdoms of Canaan decide to live by the law of Yahweh rather than risk being annihilated in battle with us. You must seize this opportunity to prove your loyalty to our family while you can."

"My first duty is to my wife."

"Abihail will be fine." Jamin leaned in confidentially. "You should be more concerned about our mother. Ever since I told her I would be going to Ai, she has fallen into fits of weeping. She says she had two sons. Now she has but one, and Joshua is sending him off to war. I think she is the only Israelite in camp who doubts an easy victory. You know Mother. There is no consoling her. Father would be totally grateful if you went for me and gave him a little peace. And when you return, Mother will have two sons again."

After a long pause, a tiny sigh answered, "All right." Eliab hardly recognized the voice as his own.

Jamin clapped a strong hand on his back. "Plan to be welcomed back into the family. I will ask Mother and Hattil to check on Abihail while you are gone." Jamin's eyes flicked to the bundle of hides and stakes and back to Eliab. He wore a patronizing smile. "If you need that tent, keep it."

Eliab blinked as he considered his answer.

Jamin picked up the bundle and held it out. "Take it, my brother. Our family cares for its own."

"Actually, we don't need it anymore." Eliab knew he was mumbling. He forced himself to speak more clearly. "Acsah fashioned a large, beautiful tent for us—woven in bold red and white stripes. She finished it just yesterday." Eliab enjoyed the warmth of belonging that spread through him as he told of Acsah's kindness.

"Come, Jamin. Come see our new home this afternoon. Bring Hattil and the little ones. Bring Mother and Father. If I am accepted as their son again, we must celebrate. Let us share a simple meal together this very day . . . before I go."

Jamin's smile faded as Eliab took control of the conversation. "I'm certain Mother will be quite interested to see Acsah's artistry. Abihail and I have never seen anything like it. It stands out a bit more brightly than I would normally be comfortable with, but it positively shouts of Acsah's love for her friend." He sprang to his feet. "I need to return to Abihail. I have some convincing to do before the army leaves tonight."

As he walked away, Eliab heard his mother sputtering from within the tent, "Abihail, married less than a year, has such a special tent?"

"Quiet, woman," his father growled. "You were the one who insisted we pull Eliab's tent from him to punish him."

"I must see it for myself. I must learn how such a thing was fashioned."

Eliab glanced back over his shoulder just as his mother poked her head out the doorway and called to him. "Please tell Abihail, we accept your invitation."

Joshua

Pearl-gray light began to spill over the landscape, quenching all but the brightest stars. Joshua signaled his troops to slip out of the rocky nooks and thickets where they had hunkered down for a few hours' sleep and take to the road again. As they crept up the steep ascent, the black outline of the fortress frowned down from its perch on the cliff. No more than half a mile above them now. Soon, just as Joshua had been told, the steep walls of the canyon blocked it from view—and more importantly hid his troops from the eyes of Ai.

Joshua was pleased with the thorough reconnaissance provided by his spies. From camp to the quarry where they stopped to sleep, their survey had proved precisely accurate. The road they traveled this morning would wind steeply upward through a tight canyon skirting the rocky roots of Ai. Then, not far from the fortress, the army would exit the channel and move out onto a small upland plain. His scouts declared it good ground for a battle in an otherwise rugged terrain, a nearly flat field stretching northward from the city gates and rising gently to a rock-studded, grassy hillside, the highest point in the vicinity.

Ideally, Ai would wake to find battle lines already formed on that high ground opposite the gates. With his forces poised behind him, Joshua would approach the gates to deliver his request for peaceful passage. He would make it clear that Israel did not want war. Ideally, Ai would grant permission for all the families of Israel to travel safely past Ai in time for Shavuot. Ideally. Rarely does a captain encounter the ideal.

Should Ai detect their arrival as the first regiments began to spill out of the gorge, and should the Canaanites marshal an attack before his army was positioned on the high ground, he could still use that broad field to his advantage. The vanguard under Caleb's command was made up of Judah's fiercest fighters. The plan was for them to slice across the field before the armies of Ai marshaled their lines, creating a three-hundred-man shield distant enough from the city walls to avoid a rain of arrows. Joshua was confident that Caleb's vanguard could engage the enemy long enough to allow the remainder of the army to move up out of the gorge behind them. Joshua would mass the entire force of three thousand behind Caleb's cutting edge, forming a solid half-loop completely surrounding the field. With the enemy thus encircled, the battle would be as good as won.

Othniel

Othniel's eyes swept the confining ridges on both sides of the road. Ai was visible again, crouching ominously on the bluff to their right, its high walls and towers dark against the pale yellow glow heralding an imminent dawn. The army, crawling up-canyon at its base, seemed to him like a line of ants, too small and fragile to pose a threat to that fortress.

He glanced over his shoulder. His men were strung out too far behind him. "Move faster. Double-time," he ordered. "Be like the ants. Have the sense to march in close formation."

"The what?" Eliab slowed his pace and tilted his head with a quizzical look.

"Ant wars," Igor answered, giving Eliab a friendly push. "Ants outwit their enemies by reaching their intended target in cover of darkness—a lot of them, in close ranks." He caught Othniel's eyes with a boyish grin.

Fear rumbled a warning deep inside Othniel. *This is not a game, my friend. The boyhood drills of wilderness days are over. In real war people die.*

He lurched into long, loping strides, leading by example, not words. Within moments his chest was pounding from the unrelenting climb, but, when he checked over his shoulder, his squad had picked up the pace and were pulling closer together. "Move on up, five abreast. Tight formation. Let's create a gap behind us that pulls the whole lagging brigade a bit faster up this hill."

When he scanned the rim of the canyon again, his eyes flicked back to the brightening sky opposite Ai for a second look. There, barely perceptible, but plainly not his imagination, wispy gray tendrils of smoke spiraled up from the dark ridge.

A signal. Fear clutched his chest. *Don't create a panic,* he chided himself. *Maybe a signal. Maybe nothing. Maybe a lookout watching for ants or maybe just cooking an early breakfast.*

"Ethan, take the lead. Not sure what that means, but I want to notify my uncle." He pointed to the smoky signal. "Keep pushing Salmon. Let's be a wolf pack on the heels of antelope."

Othniel left his last words trailing behind as he drove himself up the slope toward Caleb and Joshua. Dodging, twisting, turning, he shouldered his way between soldiers laboring up the steep incline in mindless clumps. He could hear nothing but his own blood pulsing in his ears, pushing energy to his calves and thighs, but Salmon must have heard something. He glanced over his shoulder and moved aside, opening a direct path to the two old war heroes at the front of the line. Othniel offered a quick lift of his chin in a salute of thanks as he moved past.

"Caleb . . . Joshua . . ." he gasped. The sound was as feeble as those wisps of smoke. He sucked in a deep breath, struggling for a steady voice as he called again, "Joshua . . ."

Joshua barely glanced over his shoulder. "Later, Othniel. Day is breaking."

Something more ominous may be breaking. Although his lungs were screaming for air, Othniel didn't ease his uphill sprint. If the enemy was awake, Joshua needed to know now. "Uncle Caleb . . . Smoke signal."

Both men looked back now, but Othniel could only puff out incoherent words between ragged breaths. "Smoke . . . northwest . . . opposite Ai."

With one quick glance toward the ridge to the west, Caleb's face paled. "Luz sees us."

"Keep the men moving," Joshua ordered. "I'm going to get a better look." Without waiting for a response, he vaulted up the steep embankment, scrabbling at any hand and footholds he could find in the irregular vertical fissures and crouch-ran along the ridge toward the summit.

Caleb cried out with a loud voice. "Double-time, my boys. We have been seen." He pointed his sword toward the growing signal.

As Othniel dropped back to his own band, he noted an answering puff of smoke rising over the fortress. "Ai is awake," he announced, pointing with his sword as Caleb had.

"Perhaps . . . this is . . . good." Eliab fought for words between breaths. "Won't have to . . . draw them . . . out of the fortress."

"Not good unless we are first on the field," Othniel muttered.

"First or last . . ." Zohar affirmed between breaths. "We are Yahweh's army."

The pluck exuded by these boyhood friends energized Othniel. "The battle is the

Lord's," he cried. "Run to it, my friends."

There was no more speech as the squad of twenty became one living organism hurtling up the steep slope, gravel flying from hammering feet, faces stony with determination as they hit full stride, white-knuckled hands gripping weapons unsheathed and ready.

Just as Caleb disappeared over the crest, the metallic blaring of an enemy trumpet sounded, and the din of war rumbled down from the ridge. Joshua appeared on the ledge to Othniel's left, shouting above the tumult. "Enemy ranks yet unformed. Drive them back. Slam your units into the thick of it as fast as you can get out of this ravine." As quickly as he had appeared, he bounded down slope and out of sight.

Othniel charged out of the ravine onto a field clogged with confusion. The earth beneath his feet trembled with the pounding of thousands of heavy war sandals. Caleb called desperately for support with shrill blasts from his ram's horn. Joshua's cries, more distant now, rang out over the confusion. "Move on. Move on up out of the ravine. We need every man on the field now."

Salmon drove his squad into the chaos, following on Caleb's heels. "Form that defense shield," Caleb bawled. Despite the heat of exertion, a chill shivered through Othniel's body. He imagined he could hear hearts thudding in the chests of his men along with his own. He sensed fear, but there was valor as well. "To Caleb," he cried.

For a time, Othniel caught glimpses of his white-haired uncle and Salmon's cutting-edge squad. He fought to join them but hit a wall of flashing blades. Then the maw of battle swallowed Caleb's front line and they did not reappear. Othniel's mission was clear. Fight through to wherever his uncle was and lend support. But he had no idea which way to go. Fragments of Joshua's orders occasionally sounded over the din, but his voice was distant and incomprehensible.

Othniel heard one truncated shout in his uncle's familiar voice. "Keep back!" Then trumpets blared, overpowering the voice. Any more commands from Caleb, if any were given, were lost in the clashing of swords, the horns and the harsh, guttural vocalizations of Canaanite fighters. Overhead, blood-red banners waved their proud claim—*This ground belongs to Ai.*

As Othniel wheeled and reeled, thrashing with his sword, a growing apprehension hovered at the edges of his mind. A growing understanding of Caleb's words. The onslaught was driving him and his band closer and closer to the city. The weight of his uncle's final warning pressed heavily on his mind. *Keep back. Keep back. Fight the tide sweeping you toward archers on the city wall.*

"Press back," he cried. "Press back from the walls."

No longer trying to reach Caleb, his men turned and hurled themselves against the enemy, but the battle felt like a bad dream where no amount of effort was enough.

His men fought fiercely, trying to force their way back toward the ravine, but could not make headway. Nor could they reverse the tide pushing them closer to the walls of the fortress. Two enemy soldiers seemed to replace each one that fell, the fallen corpses creating a gruesome new impediment. Enemy bodies piled up like heaps of baggage at their feet, making the push forward more difficult—while the enemy, clambering over their fallen comrades, used the dead with the advantage of high ground to drive Othniel's band back, ever closer to the walls.

Othniel's men were cut off from Caleb, wherever he was, and they could not fight their way to the ravine. Reality slammed its fist sickeningly into his stomach. *Joshua could not send reinforcements into this debacle.* It was up to him alone to find a way off the battlefield. As if in mockery, a ram's horn blared with urgent short blasts, and Joshua's voice howled in the distance, "Pull back! Pull back!"

"Pull back?" Igal, the big bear, snorted beside him. "I say, 'Pull me back then. I cannot pull myself.'"

"Pull back . . ." Othniel repeated with a cynical laugh at the mental picture of anyone trying to pull that big bear of a man anywhere, but in the time it took to repeat those two words a desperate plan formed. A glance over his shoulder made it clear that the warriors of Ai steered clear of the area close to the wall. And just that quickly, hope displaced despair.

"Igal, pass the word. When I say, *Shields up*, fall back quickly—all the way to the wall."

Just as Othniel parried a slash from an enemy blade, Igal dispatched the man with a sword thrust into his side. "Thanks, friend," Othniel panted. "Listen for it. *Shields up.* I think we can exit the field under cover of Ai arrows, but we must move quickly and move as one."

Igal grunted his understanding. On Othniel's other side, Eliab hacked desperately at a sinewy, snarling adversary. Othniel struck the edge of the man's shield full force with his own, sending it flying from his grip. "Teamwork," he shouted as the man fell to Eliab's sword. Othniel repeated his plan to Eliab.

Despite the deadly tumult, each man in his platoon passed the word on. Othniel watched the glimmer of hope follow from face to face along with the message. He could not express how deeply he cared for each these boyhood friends. *Help me, oh God! Help me get every one of them safely off this field.*

He could hardly swallow for the lump in his throat, but he put everything he had into the cry. "Shields up!"

Parrying the slashing swords of his assailants with one hand, lifting his shield with the other, Othniel quickly backed into the archer's territory. Immediately, the air exploded with a deadly rain. The hissing of arrows filled the air. Arrows thudded against the polished leather of their shields. Others clattered harmlessly to the ground. Othniel's beleaguered band backed bravely into the deadly storm, shoulder to shoulder, stumbling and dodging in rapid retreat. Their snarling assailants fell into momentary confusion as his men moved back, then rushed to attack, charging heedlessly into the rain of arrows.

Othniel swallowed the bile of revulsion as the entire assault line fell like hay before mowers. *The gory harvest of war.*

Before the enemy could regroup, Othniel turned, racing parallel to the wall, leading the way toward the ravine and freedom. His desperate plan was working. Every man in his unit ran close behind, shields deflecting the darts of death from above. He could see the mouth of the ravine now—no longer a refuge, but the focal point of the struggle.

With no other Israelites left on the open field, it seemed the entire strength of Ai's army was concentrated against the men trapped in the gorge. But beyond the attackers, through the melee, Othniel glimpsed wild white hair bobbing beside Joshua's silver gray. And beside them, a substantial line of young Israelites fought in a tight line, backed by support three men deep. The sight was doubly welcome. Not only had his uncle escaped the battlefield, but finally formed his defense shield, albeit to prevent a sure and certain bloodbath rather than gain access to the field.

He slowed his pace, assessing what the situation meant for his men. One of them grunted close behind him. He glanced over his shoulder and saw a streak of red on Zebulun's bicep. It was the near-miss of a well-aimed shaft, just a glancing hit, but arrows were still hissing all around. It was not wise to linger in fear or uncertainty. "To Caleb and Joshua," he shouted. *Better to die fighting if die they must.*

Othniel sprinted into the mob of soldiers attacking the ravine, driving his sword through the back of an unsuspecting enemy soldier. A bewildering uproar exploded around him as the warriors of Ai turned their swords against the new threat from behind. Othniel sliced and hacked, chopping a path through the attackers toward his uncle. His band—his brothers—followed, puffing and panting, brandishing their own bright blades in reassuringly tight formation beside and behind. As a unit of flashing bronze swords protecting each other's backs, they faced attack from every side. He only hoped the men of the vanguard would recognize they were not enemy soldiers.

Wheeling at the sound of a Canaanite war cry beside him, Othniel blocked a downward slash intended to cleave his head in two. He drove his sword through the man's belly, bright blood gushing from the wound as the man sank to his knees. When Othniel jerked the blade free, the crimson lifeblood spattered faces all around. Not one of those hardened faces was a friend to come to his aid.

Hard and fast, the enemy swords came at him. Othniel struck back, blocking one after another, bronze ringing against bronze, chips flying from his sturdy oaken shield, a mist of blood filling the air as he faced attacker after attacker, every effort to press toward the ravine blocked by a new assailant, each step forward undone by a blade driving him two steps back. Again, he sidestepped a deadly swing, meeting it with a parry so forceful it sent the enemy blade spinning into the air. He had no idea where his men were now, praying only that the falling sword would not impale a friend.

"Charge." Above screaming war cries and guttural curses all around, he heard the distinctive voice of Joshua, strong and authoritative. "Charge!"

Charge? Othniel nearly laughed at the impossible command. *A one-man charge?* He had lost track of his entire squad. *And which way?* Not only was it impossible to move even a step in any direction, he could no longer see his uncle's white hair.

"Charge!" the command rose over the battlefield again, shrill with alarm. Enemy soldiers turned about in confusion to learn what the command meant for them. Othniel glanced back to the fortress to get his bearings. He was so disoriented by the swords assailing him from every side he no longer knew which direction to go. And when he turned back in the general direction of the ravine, a dearly familiar mop of white hair burst out of the confusion, and there in the midst of the chaos, Caleb with his advance squad formed another wall of swords and shields.

"Behind me," Caleb cried with a sidestep to the right. "To the safety of the ravine."

Othniel dove through the small opening in Caleb's human shield, sprinting across the ground they had cleared. Pounding feet and heavy panting followed hard on his heels. *May they be friend not foe*, he prayed. Without turning to make the determination, he stretched toward Joshua at the mouth of the ravine.

The commander's eyes urged him on. "God is good," he cried in a choked voice as Othniel and then his band vaulted, one after another, into the shelter of the rocky walls. "My missing squad . . . or most of you?" Joshua looked at him questioningly as he sank into the rocky arms of the canyon with his companions, panting and wheezing, drinking in deep gulps of air.

Othniel silently took stock of his squad, greatly relieved when the count was full. "None lost, sir."

"None? Good, good." Joshua massaged his forehead between his thumb and fingers. "Salmon lost one good man. Ahihud."

"Ahihud lost," Eliab gasped. "For what? We gained so little ground."

Othniel affirmed the comment with a nod. "Defeated by a *ruin*," he mumbled.

Joshua appraised him coolly for a moment. "A battle is not lost in one assault, my son."

Abihail

Abihail waited for the light. Waited in the dark, unable to sleep without Eliab beside her. She waited, longing for morning, but when her tent brightened at the approach of dawn, the forebodings of the night distilled into panic. The canopy above her seemed to run with deep crimson rivers of blood.

Don't be silly, she chided herself. *Yes, it's your first night separated from Eliab since the wedding, but there are three thousand other tents out there missing husbands . . . brothers . . . sons . . . or . . . fathers.*

"Fathers." She repeated the word aloud and knew precisely which half-empty tent she needed to visit.

Oddly, as she dressed and rushed through her preparations for the day, a lifetime of manna memories swirled in her head. From toddling out with her mother to pick the sweet white flakes from the ground to the grief-filled days after the death of her parents last year, nearly every day of her life began at first light, gathering the day's supply of food before the sun melted it all away. Even through the horrors unleashed by the evil prophet Balaam, the morning ritual got her out of bed into her sandals to face the day. And always, through giggles or tears, Acsah was there. As a new bride, she hardly noticed the end of manna-fall following Passover. Life was filled with so much newness. Today for the first time, her heart ached for that time of communion beginning the day.

The warbling and trilling of songbirds rose from the thickets of the Jordan filling her heart with song, lightening her lead-like feet. Within minutes the anxiety-filled trudging became an eager, child-like sprint. When she reached the slumbering silence of Acsah's tent, she hesitated. *Should she return to her lonely tent or just wait here for Acsah to awaken? Neither,* she decided with a breathless snicker. *Enough waiting.*

"Acsah! Acsah!" she called softly. "Aren't you ready?"

"What?" The muffled voice was groggy and confused.

"Hurry, Acsah. The sun is breaking over the meadow and the manna will soon melt away."

A noisy thrashing issued from the tent. Then Acsah appeared at the doorway, still blinking sleepily, tunic and sash askew, but sandals on and hair brushed. She stooped down, fumbling through the stacks of pots and utensils close to the tent door and came up with her favorite gathering basket.

"Oh dear!" Abihail touched fingertips to mouth in mock surprise. "I forgot. No more manna. We're making barley porridge these days."

"Alright, you got me out of bed. Now what?"

"Well," Abihail answered with a coy smile, "it appears you are not in the middle of anything more pressing. How about walking and talking with a friend? I need to drive worries for Eliab out of my head."

Acsah dropped the basket by the doorway. "The Gilgal is a perfect destination for that purpose."

Broad swaths of fiery orange clouds blazed above the eastern horizon as they left the tent rows behind. "It is good you got me up and out here for this," Acsah said, her broad smile more brilliant than ever in the rich golden light. "I wouldn't have said that ten minutes ago. But now . . ."

Abihail grinned back. "Doesn't this feel exactly like a normal morning heading out to gather manna?"

"Other than us being the only ones out here and no manna on the ground? Absolutely!"

From the top of the monument-crowned hill, Abihail traced their meandering trail crushed in the mounding clumps of dew-wet grasses all the way back across the meadow to Judah.

"Hey, think about where you are, not the trail getting here." Acsah gave one of the stones a resounding slap. "This is rock-solid evidence that Yahweh our God is with us."

Abihail immediately recognized the unique goatskin-water-bag shape of Judah's stone. She brushed its smooth surface thoughtfully. "It wasn't that long ago that every one of these stones lay beneath a rushing flood."

"And now they proclaim the message—our God will see us through, no matter how deep the flood." Acsah stepped inside the ring and slid down to sitting with her back resting against the stone of Judah and Abihail dropped down on the grass beside her.

"Ouch!" She pulled a fist-sized rock from under her and tossed it.

Acsah laughed, watching the stone land less than ten feet away. "Determined to leave it within the circle, are you?" It rolled another inch or two and came to a rest against a stone on the far side of the gilgal. "You are definitely no competition for Othniel."

"Othniel?"

Acsah laughed. "I may be the only one my shy cousin dared tell his story to." She stared up into the clouds, presumably recalling the details as he related them, but it was a perfect gesture to set the stage for an Othniel story.

"A group of young men from Judah organized a strength contest the day of our victory celebration in the valley of Acacias. They took turns heaving a huge rock from the same starting point, each contestant marking where his throw landed. Othniel watched the competition, but it took much urging to convince him to have a try. When he did, his throw ended the game—not because there was no one left to compete against him, but because he hurled it so far. He lobbed this hefty rock far past all other marks, beyond the edge of the meadow grasses, until it tumbled down the rocky bank and was lost in the river. Othniel, of course, was uncomfortable with all the cheers and attention, but the affirmation of his friends gave him a new sense of confidence in his future."

Acsah's eyes glittered merrily as she continued the tale. "Othniel thought he had seen the last of his victory stone, but the best part of the story was yet to come. When my father was poking around the dry riverbed during the crossing, looking for the perfect rock to represent Judah, this one stood out. Its shape, much like a goatskin stretched tight with water, struck my father as significant. God's provision. He hoisted it onto his shoulder and carried it to Joshua for the monument. Remember, the young men picked a rock they could barely lift to hurl across the meadow. Othniel offered to carry it several times in the long trek up from the Jordan. He had a hunch he knew the rock from its unique shape, but he wasn't certain until my father finally let him carry it the last leg of the trek."

"And he didn't breathe a word to your father?"

"You know my cousin." Acsah laughed and shook her hair back, mimicking Othniel's signature attention-dodging habit. "So here it is: Othniel's victory rock rescued from the flood and endowed with a greater victory message for generations to come."

Othniel

Othniel could not remember feeling so exhausted.

"Why do you think Ai gave up so quickly?" Eliab asked hesitantly.

He did not feel like speculating. "Don't get too comfortable," he advised. "Caleb and Joshua are devising a 'regrouping' plan."

"Waiting is harder than fighting," Nathan said.

Igal drummed his fingers on the hilt of his sword. "It's just too quiet—"

A brass-throated trumpet cut him off and shattered the silence. The faces of his friends paled to deathly white.

"There's your answer, Eliab," Othniel muttered. "They didn't give up."

The peaceful lull immediately devolved into mayhem. Othniel watched men up and down the packed roadway turn from the direction of the sound, searching for a path of escape. They pushed hard against the mass of men behind them, who grasping the situation, turned to push against the men behind them. A few began to climb the walls until their captains ordered them back. Othniel snorted. *So much for regrouping. We are ungrouping.*

"Stand firm," Joshua called. "Take your positions. Let them come to us." He clutched his way up and over the rugged rim. Free of the close-walled constriction of the roadway, he raced down the ridgeline, his ram's horn sounding an alarm with short, harsh blasts while the deep and ominous voices of brass trumpets instructed the enemy.

"Close ranks," Caleb cried as the bone-chilling, blood-curdling war cry of a thousand Canaanite warriors shivered down the ravine. "Support the men in front of you."

Igal stumbled forward, slamming against Othniel's back. "Sorry, sir. Zohar pushed me."

Othniel suppressed his annoyance and fought for balance. "Stand strong," he commanded, eyes fixed on the enemy now visible at the mouth of the ravine. Rank upon rank of Canaanite spearmen rumbled down the close roadway led by a rushing mouth of pointed bronze teeth.

"Wait for them," Salmon urged his front line. "Steady. Strong. They are hungry for blood, but they will have none of ours."

Othniel tightened the grip on his sword as the Canaanite spears slammed against the wooden shields of Salmon's front line. The line held strong.

"Well done," Salmon cried. "To sword!"

His men advanced bravely, a flurry of bronze blades clanging against spear shaft and shield, cleaving through the body armor of spearmen still off balance from the impact of their charge.

"Arise to the hour, my boys. We are more than a match for them." Joshua's voice pierced the tumult. He was on the ledge just above them now. "Spears flying. Shields up."

The spears of the second line spearmen were already whistling overhead like wheat straws driven before the wind. One found its mark, driving through Jeshur's shoulder immediately beside Othniel. For one instant he met Jeshur's eyes and nodded encouragement, but his friend, showed no recognition, no emotion as he bravely hacked at the wooden shaft with his own sword, lopping it off close to his body. Not abandoning his place in the frontline squad, Jeshur transferred his sword to his left hand and fought on. The struggle was desperate, but the men of Judah held their place with uncommon courage.

"Humph." Asriel thrashed forward from his place behind Othniel, followed almost immediately by Zohar. "Hold your ground," Othniel cried, turning just as

Eliab fell against Ethan's sword arm.

Eliab looked up helplessly from his knees. "The squad behind is pushing forward—hard," he said.

Othniel's entire squad was scrambling now for footing, quickly falling into disarray. Looking back down the ravine as far as he could see, the entire division roiled with pressure from below like a pot of stew, each regiment jostled and bumped by the regiments behind them. While the frontlines struggled in mortal combat, the rearguard pushed up the ravine in a closing vice, compressing his men. Othniel's blood ran cold.

"They don't know," Eliab groaned, as he struggled to his feet.

"How could they *not* know?" Igal growled.

"How would they?" Othniel responded flatly "The last three divisions entirely missed the first skirmish. They can't see what we are facing and don't understand the hold up. They are still eager to get to the field to share in the victory." The situation was crystal clear. How to react was not, but the enemy gave them no time to ponder their options. A new wave of spearmen hit hard, splintering against Salmon's line of solid shields for the second time.

"For the Lord and for Joshua," Caleb cried

The front line attacked with renewed courage. They leaped against the foe, wielding their bronze blades with even greater ferocity than before. They struck the phalanx in its teeth and broke the formation.

"Pursue! Pursue," Caleb cried, leading a charge back toward the summit and that level field. One last heavy hail of spears thudded against their shields as the vanguard spilled out onto the field, then Ai's spear brigade melted away.

It was a relief to move out of the pressure in the ravine, even when a savage wave of swordsmen hit as Caleb's vanguard emerged from the ravine. Anything was better than standing tense and waiting in that oppressive gulch behind the action. "Spread out. Spread out!" Othniel called. "Every man find a place to fight the foe."

"Jeshur is hurt," a voice wailed as his men struck back at the fighters on the field.

The bright bronze spear tip winked wickedly from the center of the blood-soaked fabric covering Jeshur's shoulder. "But I can still fight," Jeshur shouted.

Othniel grunted his approval.

"Retreat. Jeshur is wounded," Sharar shrieked. "There are too many of them."

"Find your courage, man," Othniel admonished. "You aren't even scratched." *Where did this fear come from? Sharar had been the best swordsmen in all Judah when they trained in the wilderness.*

"Rally to the field," Joshua called to the troops still in the ravine. "Fight alongside your brothers. You are the sword of the Lord." His ram's horn echoed the command, but the sound was drowned by swelling cries of fear. One after another, Caleb's handpicked fighters turned wildly away from the enemy. There at the mouth of the ravine, the vanguard disintegrated. No longer warriors, the men threw themselves like frightened children against the regiments packing the road below them. Despite Joshua's direct orders from the ridge above, despite Caleb's calls of reassurance, despite the bravery of captains and squad leaders here and there, the panic multiplied beyond reason. Israel's warriors no longer fought the enemy. They fought to flee—but flight was futile. Within minutes, a seething, white-eyed mob choked the tight confines of the roadway.

"Face them. Pull back as an army," Caleb called, but there was no turning this into an orderly retreat, no reasoning with witless men.

The enemy smelled the fear and attacked with greater boldness and demonic screams. Like beasts with the taste of blood on their tongues, they tore into the disarray with savage fury. Othniel, Asriel, and Igal took a stand beside Caleb and Salmon. A few others found courage and formed a second line. But their bravery did little to calm the panic behind them.

Asriel was fully engaged with one assailant when a second lunged toward him.

"Asriel!" Igal bellowed in warning.

Othniel reacted quickly, parrying the sword thrust with a two-handed downswing, forcing it away from Asriel's chest, but it pierced a new mark. Asriel staggered and sank to his knees as if in prayer while blood gushed from his thigh. Ethan's face blanched in revulsion, and he lowered his sword.

"Mind the enemy if you don't want to see more blood," Othniel cried, slashing with all his strength against the assailant. The man snarled, dodging Othniel's sword as he ripped his own weapon from Asriel's thigh. He sprang at Othniel as three more swordsmen hurtled downslope against him like a pack of hungry wolves.

As others recoiled, Igal and Caleb lunged to either side of Othniel, swords clanging, sparks flashing as they pushed the enemy back. On the blurred edges of his vision, Othniel noticed Ethan ripping a length of cloth from his tunic to staunch the flow of Asriel's blood. His shield hung uselessly over his back as he pulled Asriel to his feet, supporting him with one arm while guarding him with his sword. *Still able to stand,* Othniel noted with relief, *but neither man is using his shield.* "Protect yourselves," he barked.

"Shields up," Joshua bellowed from somewhere above the ravine. "Prepare for another assault."

The eerie Canaanite war cry pierced the air once more and a swarm of spears whistled overhead. The ensuing panic heaved Zohar cross canyon against Ethan's blade, a bloody slash-line glistening crimson from his scalp to his chin. His eyes wild with terror, he whimpered, "I am not ready to die."

Othniel looked at him with disgust. "It is merely a surface wound. If you won't fight, help Ethan with Asriel."

Just then Ethan flew sideways. His head cracked against the rock wall on the left while Asriel, torn from his hands, lurched to the right.

Othniel grabbed for Asriel before he could be trampled underfoot. "Stand firm," he cried out to the fragmenting lines under his command. "You are not stampeding cattle. Fight this wolf pack like men."

"This is not a fight. It is a slaughter," someone wailed.

"Get a grip, men. You struggle now against your own brothers." Uncle Caleb's voice rang hoarsely over a fermenting brew of enemy war whoops and the terrified shrieks of his men. For a split second in the senseless chaos, Othniel met the desperate look in his uncle's eyes. He could not count the number of times he had heard the story of the panic on the border of Canaan forty years earlier—and that panic was caused by the mere report of enemy strength. Caleb knew the impossibility of turning the tide of fear once the current ran deep as this.

The line protecting the "retreat" was too thin now. Othniel looked around searching frantically for a few good men to replace Asriel and Ethan, men still in control of their wits. He was relieved when Caleb chose for him.

"Eliab! Nathan!" he howled. "Help us hold this line as we drop back to better terrain. Let's set an example of an orderly retreat."

Joshua

As the hours rolled on, Joshua raced back and forth, up and down the rim of the gorge, commanding the rear to retreat as rapidly as possible, calling for the defense line at the head to stand strong, and challenging the muddled middle to find order. So much for regrouping and perhaps saving the day. He bounded down the ridge once more, emotion unchecked, tears streaming down his face. *The frontline could defend an orderly retreat. Why was the ravine still clogged?*

"Retreat," he cried again as he had a hundred times. "Do not push forward."

The division of Simeon understood. Their commanders had turned their troops back down the hill, but movement was at a standstill.

"Keep your men calm," Joshua encouraged their commanders. "Move down as you are able."

With renewed energy, he raced past the division of Ephraim, blasting the signal for retreat on his horn, repeating his commands again and again to men still mindlessly pushing against the impediment ahead. "Retreat! Retreat! The vanguard never reached the field. They are under attack at the top of the ravine. Do not push forward." One by one, he sought out brigade and company captains, informing each one of the gravity of the situation at the front, repeating the grim instruction over and over until he was hoarse. "Retreat! Our vanguard will be lost if you do not draw back."

At last the banner of Ephraim turned, and the standard bearer attempted to move back down the hill. Joshua's entire third division was now in orderly retreat—or would be were the way not blocked. Joshua raced farther down the road where he could see the eagle banner of Dan flapping fiercely. The final company of Ephraimites faced the wrath of Jared, the division commander of Dan. "Prod those cowardly bulls of Ephraim forward," he bellowed. He pulled his sword and touched it to the belly of the closest Ephraimite. "Move on up or move out of our way."

"Noooooo," Joshua howled over the mayhem. "Ephraim is obeying my orders. Cease your advance."

"Advance!" Jared called.

"Stop," Joshua bellowed into the scuffle. "The vanguard is under attack."

Jared echoed the last word. "Attack! Can't you hear Joshua?"

"Attack!" Jasher passed on the command and drove the front lines of Dan even harder against the troops clogging the road.

"Pull back!" Joshua roared. "*We* are under attack. *We* must retreat."

The idea of retreat must have been incomprehensible to his army after the victory at Jericho. Louder and more shrill than before, he heard Jared's distortion of his orders. "Under attack! Must not retreat!"

Joshua groaned. *Too much confusion.*

He moved farther down the packed roadway, blasting the command to reverse direction on his horn as he went. When he came to Palal, commander of the last brigade, Joshua crouched on the rim and called Palal to him.

"I'm sorry, sir." The man said looking up apologetically. "We simply can't move."

"Listen to me, Palal," Joshua said, summoning all the calming authority he could muster. "The situation is deadly at the front. Judah never made it onto the field. They are under fierce attack and are still trapped in the ravine. Reverse your brigade and retreat. Clear the road so our entire army can fall back."

"Fall back?" All color blanched from Palal's face.

"Pull back to the rock quarry where we slept last night as quickly as possible. We can take our stand there if necessary. Pass the word to your company and squad commanders and get your brigade moving quickly."

With the tail of the army finally moving in the right direction, Joshua sprinted back up to the frontline commanders of Dan. Knots of disorderly troops, jostling and fuming at a roadblock impossible to comprehend, were close to pulling swords on one another. "How am I supposed to do my job?" Jared growled as soon as Joshua reappeared. His face was as fierce as the eagle on Dan's banner.

Unruffled, Joshua stooped down and motioned for Jared to come to him. A calm face-to-face explanation worked with Palal. It would work with Jared. "I appreciate your determination, but Judah never made it onto the field. We need to clear the road for their retreat or our vanguard will be decimated."

"Clear the road? You *want* us to retreat?"

"Yes." Joshua smiled grimly. "We're in retreat, but not defeat. Pull back to the rock quarry as quickly as possible. Perhaps we can still regroup there."

Jared responded immediately. "Pull back!" he cried. There was an edge of panic in his voice now that he understood the gravity of the situation. "Return to the quarry."

His commands echoed up and down the line.

"Fall back."

"Return to the quarry."

"Judah is in retreat."

Joshua closed his eyes and sighed as if to drive those words from the air. *The army of Yahweh should not be in retreat.*

He loped up the slope again—for the last time today, he hoped. Even with the rearguard moving toward the quarry, this was a rout, not a retreat.

The time for commands was past. He took a bounding leap down the steep embankment, landing in the thick of the fight beside Caleb. Everything depended on this one thin defense line, inching backward in retreat even as they fought.

Caleb welcomed Joshua's sword with a grunt. All at once at a series of quick metallic trumpet commands, the attackers dropped back and a strange quiet ensued. Then out of the silence a deadly whoosh whispered close to Joshua's ear. One look at the ridge confirmed the sickening truth.

While he was racing up and down the western rim of the ravine, focused on stemming the panic, enemy archers had been creeping along the foundations of Ai, silently slipping out onto the dark rocks of the eastern rim like an invasion of scorpions. Already, the first string of these bowmen knelt above his trapped army, nocking their arrows, drawing the bowstrings tight. Already, the creeping scorpions were loosing their deadly sting against his men.

"Shields up," Joshua roared. "Shields up. Bowmen on the ridge."

Othniel

Othniel sheathed his sword and raised his shield. It felt good to have even a moment's respite for his aching sword arm. For the second time that day, he shrank beneath his shield, the rushing sound of his breath mingling as one with the swooshing storm of arrows. Then somewhere behind him, a sickeningly different sound, a dull, heavy *thunk* distinguished itself from the clattering of arrows against rock or the woody thumping on shields. He turned in time to see Zohar clutch a feathered shaft protruding from his throat. Helplessly, he watched his friend stagger backward, wide-eyed, mouth contorted in a gurgling scream.

"Help your brother," Othniel cried as Zohar slumped in the midst of a clump of horrified men. He shoved through the congestion, pushing the stunned and gawking aside, fighting his way to Zohar. Eliab reached the spot at the same time, and both men dropped to the ground to help.

"This can't be real," Ethan whispered behind him. "Zohar came to help me. He was just taking one of Asriel's arms when it hit."

Othniel looked up with alarm. Asriel still leaned heavily on Ethan's shoulder. "Can you manage Asriel alone and still hold your own shield? The arrow storm seems to be lessening, but it's not over."

Ethan managed a minimal nod. "I believe I can."

"You'd better *know* you can. You are no good to Asriel dead."

"I know I can, Othniel."

"Keep on moving then and mind those shields. He watched Ethan and Asriel take their first trundling steps downslope then returned his attention to the whimpering and gurgling Zohar.

"We are with you, Zohar. You are not alone." Eliab continued whispering a soothing stream of comfort as he attempted to staunch the spurts of blood with his fingers.

It was not enough. Zohar's legs quivered, and wild eyes begged pitifully for help, but he was beyond saving, too much blood lost with no way to stop it. All they could do was carry him home to his family. Ever watchful of his surroundings, Othniel knelt beside his dying friend to lift him to his shoulder. That is when he noticed Eliab's shield on the ground beside his cast-off sword. He felt the hair raise on the back of his neck.

"Eliab! Your shield!"

The warning froze on his tongue as an arrow whirred past his ear, driving deep into one of the few remaining targets. Eliab toppled over Zohar, the deadly shaft protruding from his back. Neither man twitched or stirred.

Time instantly slowed. Panicked shrieks grew fainter. The scuffling of retreating feet faded with the flood of fleeing men rushing down the canyon. Somber stillness descended over the ravine, broken only by the occasional moans of a handful of fallen soldiers littering the roadway like debris following a storm. They, along with the brave soldiers attending the wounded, must have seemed unworthy targets. The swooshing storm of enemy arrows ceased at last.

Othniel had no idea how long he had been kneeling there when, out of the gray cloud of his grief, a towering dark form appeared beside him.

Igal.

"Dead? Both of them?" he asked. Always the largest of the children who grew up in the wilderness, Igal was a huge bear of a man, but he was not ashamed of the tears streaming down his cheeks.

Othniel could not bring himself to say the words or even nod a yes. Igal had the good sense to wait quietly. Finally, Othniel wiped the dust, sweat, and tears off his face with his sleeve and stood. "Let's take them home."

He pulled gently on the leather bands of Eliab's breastplate to lift him off Zohar and heard a wheezing whisper. One word—"Abihail."

Though Eliab's face was pale as death and his eyes rolled, searching blankly, Othniel's heart nearly burst with hope. "We're here, Eliab. We're here. We'll get you home."

As Othniel hoisted Eliab's limp weight smoothly up onto his shoulders, Igal lifted the other man. "Zohar's gone for sure," he said soberly. He raised the massive fist clenching his sword and shook the weapon in a gesture of rage up the hill toward Ai. "I'll watch your back while I follow with Zohar. Go on. Go on. Make haste. Perhaps Eliab can be saved."

"He *will* be saved," Othniel grunted affirmatively. "Stay with me, Eliab. I'll get you home to your Abihail."

Othniel moved down the rocky ravine at a fast lope. Such a short time before it had been a clogged scene of bedlam. Now it was transformed to a desolate scene of heartbreak, as brave men crab-walked awkwardly down the steep roadway carrying the dead and severely injured home. Oblivious to the passage of time, he dismissed exhaustion, ignoring the stiff aching of his shoulders and back as he trekked down the steep road. For the first time he could mull over what he had seen in the thick of battle at Ai.

What *had* he seen? Just as his unit followed Caleb onto the battlefield, he caught a brief glimpse of something . . . or someone. Someone huge and pale. Like the terrifying dream that woke him the night of the Passover festival. It was but a fleeting glimpse, then the heat of battle completely engaged his mind. Now the image chilled his blood. *Did he actually see his nightmare creature in the flesh? The giant so defiant of Yahweh . . . And where was Yahweh today?*

Consumed by these thoughts and questions, Othniel was surprised at how quickly he came to the broadening of the road at the rock quarry. This quarry, according to old Canaanite legends reported by Jokshan of Jericho, was the site of one of Abraham's altars, the spot where God promised this land would belong to his descendants. That seemed completely improbable at the moment.

"Here we are, Eliab. The quarry already . . . where we rested last night." There was no response from his friend, but Othniel felt a hope-inspired surge of energy. *If only I could hear the voice of Yahweh as Abraham did, to hear God himself assure his people they would conquer this land. I may not have a direct promise, but Joshua does. And Uncle Caleb does.* He repeated the promise boldly. "All the land on which you walk will be your inheritance. "

"Do you hear that Eliab? The land on which your feet have walked will be your inheritance. Your inheritance and Abihail's and the inheritance of your little one and all the little ones to follow."

The road was wider now with a gentler grade, and Othniel stopped to readjust Eliab's weight for the remainder of the trek. "The descent goes more quickly than the ascent," he encouraged. "I will have you home to Abihail soon."

"Abihail," his friend mumbled.

On and on Othniel trudged, murmuring encouraging thoughts to his friend. As repugnant as continual chatter was to him, if it would inspire Eliab to hang on to life, he would struggle to find every last encouraging word. At last, the confining roadway opened to a comforting view of the Gilgal campsite. There amid the dull browns and blacks of animal-hide dwellings, a magnificent tent of woven-wool canvas, gaily striped in red and white, bloomed like a flower in the sand.

"Home," he whispered. "Hang on, Eliab. I can see your tent . . . the most beautiful tent . . . created for you and your beautiful Abihail by . . . beautiful hands."

As he trudged down the row of tents to the bright dwelling, he heard shrieks of welcome and shrieks of grief from far and near around camp as other warriors found their families. He didn't see Abihail.

He eased the wounded man onto a sheepskin at the open doorway. "Home," he whispered.

Eliab's eyes flickered at the word.

"Let's take a look at that wound." He braced Eliab on his side with his knees and carefully began unfastening the bloodied breastplate.

"Eliab, is that you? Finally home?" Abihail came around from the back of the tent, wiping her hands on a towel. Then she saw them. Saw the blood. Saw the brass arrow tip protruding from Eliab's bloodstained chest. She flew to him, her lips shaped in a silent scream.

Othniel caught her arm. "Be strong. Your warrior is home." He held her eyes with calming authority and did not release her until he could see the initial shock resolve.

Abihail crumpled limply to the ground beside him. "Oh Eliab, my love . . . It is I. You are home."

When there was no response, she looked up at Othniel imploringly. *Why?* Her eyes asked. *Who would hurt my gentle Eliab?*

Othniel wanted to say, *"We must trust the Lord."* He believed it to his very core, but the words seemed woefully inadequate just now. He placed a comforting hand on her head. "Here is your Abihail, Eliab. You are home."

Abihail gulped as if her throat refused to utter another word, as if doing so might unleash a flood of grief inside her that would never stop. She began stroking Eliab's curly hair and beard, her tears falling onto his dust-smeared face—tragically beautiful, glistening jewels of love. Little by little, an expression of inner peace softened Abihail's anguished features and she found her voice again.

"Eliab . . . Eliab, my love," she whispered. "Your Abihail is here with your child." She took Eliab's hand and placed it on her abdomen. The look of adoration lighting her face seemed to come from heaven itself.

Perhaps it was the sweet sound of Abihail's voice, or perhaps it was the solid reality of his first child beneath his fingers that called to the fading spirit within Eliab. His eyelids fluttered. Feeble fingers explored the swelling protecting his unborn child. He searched for his wife's face as if it were obscured by a deepening fog. "My wife . . ." he breathed. His voice was weak but filled with emotion. "Our son . . ."

At last his eyes found hers, and he breathed a sigh as soft as a dove taking wing. "My Abihail."

"You must live for us . . ." Abihail murmured, her eyes shimmering with the liquid treasure of her love. "For your Abihail . . . for your son."

Eliab closed his eyes as if slipping into the most pleasant of dreams and the smile remained, chiseled forever on his beautiful lips.

Abihail bent close and brushed his cheek with hers—then sat up sharply. She looked up at Othniel. "There is no longer any breath," she said.

Othniel's search for words was jarred by a breathy shuffling. Achor and Mara had slipped up silently and stood now behind Abihail, staring at their son.

"We just received the news." Achor's voice broke. "We . . ."

"Is he . . .?" Mara's face twisted grotesquely.

"Gone," whispered Othniel.

"Oh, my son," Achor beat his fist against his chest. "Rightly was I named *Trouble*." His shoulders shook with deep, heaving sobs while Mara stared blankly.

When Achor gained some composure at last, his voice was hoarse with despair. "It was I, Eliab. It was I. The guilt lies with the father, not the son. I should have been the one to die."

Mara shushed him. "Do not be ridiculous, Achor. Eliab went in Jamin's place not yours, but this is certainly not Jamin's fault. If blame should fall anywhere, it should fall on Joshua."

The idea of blame of any kind at this moment was startling to Othniel. "The arrow was shot by a Canaanite bow. Let the blame fall on our enemy," he replied.

"There you have it," Mara said defensively. "You are in no way to blame, Achor. Don't be stupid." Then her eyes widened, and a crafty smile spread over her lips. "Abihail, my child. You should not be alone. Your parents are gone—buried in the wilderness. Now our son is dead. You have no husband to care for you. Let me hear no protests. Achor and I will move into this tent with you. It is the least we can do."

Abihail rose heavily to her feet. She balled her fists, lifted her chin, and faced Mara with uncharacteristic strength. "Thank you, Mother, but for now I *do* wish to be alone—alone with every precious memory of the son you rejected."

"Achor, reason with her . . ." Mara whined. "How could we remain in *our* tent at such a time and do nothing?"

Othniel interposed himself between Abihail and the parents of his dead friend. His large frame towered over them. "Respect the wishes of a grieving widow, Mara. If you truly desire to be helpful, go get spices and wrappings to prepare the body for burial. Achor, summon Jamin. Take your shovels and dig a burial spot outside of camp. Jamin's children can gather stones for the cairn. When you have finished, you can help carry Eliab's body there."

CHAPTER NINE

THE VALLEY OF ACHOR

Joshua[13]

Joshua threw himself down before the tabernacle, desperately seeking answers. Behind the curtain in the Most Holy Place—the inner sanctum of Yahweh's sanctuary—the holy law of the covenant remained unchanging, eternal, encased in its gilded chest. Joshua's faith assured him that the light of the Presence hovered over it just as this suffocating darkness enveloped his heart and mind. God had never seemed more remote. There was no voice. No guidance. No light. The smell of Canaan-earth filled his nostrils. The gravelly Soil of Promise pressed into his forehead while the wailing of thirty-six families hung over him like a sodden raincloud. A single thought rumbled like pealing thunder through that cloud of lament. *I was the one. I was the one who sent those good men to their deaths. I was the one. If I failed you, you should have punished me!*

His fist closed around a handful of earth. *This is what I am before you, Yahweh— dirt.* He tossed it on his head and cried aloud with deep choking sobs, "Why did you choose me to lead these people? I cannot do it."

Again and again, Joshua lifted his face toward the silent tabernacle, but the leaden cloud pressed down on him all the more. He could not move. He could barely breathe. *O Sovereign Lord . . . why did you insist on bringing us across the Jordan? To make us victims of Canaanite arrows and blades? What can I say after this disaster? After Israel has been defeated by a ruin? When the wind bears this news to the Canaanites—to the seven nations living in this land in rebellion against you—they will band together against us. They will destroy the Children of Abraham, Isaac, and Jacob forever. Then who will proclaim your great name?*

As Joshua lay prostrate on the ground, worn out with weeping, he gradually became aware that several of the elders had gathered around him. Their presence should have been a comfort, but on this bleak day, it magnified his unworthiness. He was not fit to lead the tribes of Israel. He withdrew into a single silent prayer. *O great and mighty God of our fathers, choose a new leader for your people while there is still time to save them.*

The elders took turns laying hands on him and praying aloud. *Meaningless prayers.* He pulled back from their futile encouragement, but the last elder would not let him withdraw. He grasped Joshua's shoulder with a firm hand. "How long this groveling, my friend? You are pathetic."

It was Caleb.

Joshua sat up. The challenge in Caleb's piercing eyes cut through the blur of dust and tears as sharply as his words. "I understand your distress over our defeat. It was the first place we attacked on our own and a so-called ruin. But, Joshua, this is not a disaster. We lost thirty-six men. Not our whole army. You act as if the Land of Promise was lost to us as well. It is time for the commander of Israel to get up. Eat. You have fasted all day. You need your strength."

Joshua could feel the round of flatbread pressed into his hand, but his stomach roiled at the thought of food. "Caleb," he whispered, "I did not ask for this. The people deserve a better leader."

"Stop, Joshua. Stop and remember. Yahweh used you to open a pathway through the Jordan. He used you to defeat Jericho. Remember those miracles and the miraculous victories on the east side of the river. Remember and wait for him. Ask him to show us what went wrong. Ask him what to do next."

"That is precisely what I have been asking him," Joshua whimpered. "But there is no answer."

"No? Perhaps it is the way you are asking. You have been questioning the guidance of Yahweh. You question his right to choose you. You question the authority of Moses his servant who ordained you to be his successor. You are correct in saying you did not ask for this job, but the wisdom of the eternal God called you to it."

Joshua was surprised that he had spoken any of those doubts aloud. He stared at the bread in his hand as he listened to Caleb's counsel. Even in this benumbed state of mind, he recognized wisdom when he heard it. "You must not give in to the spirit of darkness, Joshua. Evil forces strive to defeat our people. I am here to support you, and a vast army awaits your command. All Israel has faith in you and in Yahweh, almighty God."

A sheen of tears spread over Caleb's eyes. "We were all shocked and grieved, Joshua. Not you alone. Every clan and tribe mourns alongside the families of our fallen warriors, but there is something in this tragedy for which to praise God. I have not heard one word of rebellion. I have not heard one word of blame. Or even words of self-pity—apart from you. That is a remarkable victory."

Joshua ripped off a bite of bread, chewing slowly and thoughtfully, soaking in encouragement from the presence of Caleb and the other elders. No one said any more. He was not sure when they slipped away, for they left as quietly as they had come, but the black weight of despair disappeared along with them and a new prayer filled his thoughts. *O Sovereign Yahweh, this is not about me. This is not about the people of Israel. How will you restore your own great name? Show us what to do next.*

No blinding light flashed from the tabernacle. But Joshua heard the voice in his head, growing in volume and clarity—*Stand up! Off your face! My army must be completely loyal or I cannot go with you. You led them against Ai with good intentions, but you went without my command. You went without me.*

"But why, Lord? If I failed you by not waiting for your command, why did you punish these thirty-six for *my* sin?"

It is not your mistake alone. My people were too eager for another glorious victory. They are sworn to covenant allegiance, yet they trampled my command in the dirt.

"But how? What command did they trample in the dirt?"

They robbed me by taking from the forbidden things. I commanded no spoils be taken from Jericho, yet the people coveted what was mine. Even now they hide devoted items among their own possessions. I could not go with you, but you did not notice that I stayed behind. Without me Israel cannot stand against her enemies. One man turned his back on me. Therefore, all his comrades turned their backs and ran. One man lied about the plunder and all Israel became plunder.

The sin of this one man is like a straw cast on the water, an indicator of the prevailing current running throughout camp. There are many who would choose to violate my express commands when they tell themselves there is little or no harm in it. They do not understand that any deliberate breach of the covenant destroys love and trust. No covenant remains. I cannot go with you until you destroy the cursed things.

Joshua staggered to his feet. Hope should have seeped into his bones because now he knew. The withdrawal of God's help had a cause. But he felt as if he had been kicked in the stomach. He stepped closer to the tabernacle and whispered the question that had to be answered. "Who would have done this?"

I will show you. Go. Tell the people this:
The Lord God of Israel says—

Consecrate yourselves, my people. Prepare for a day of judgment. Cursed things are hidden in my camp. My army cannot stand against its enemies until this spirit of rebellion and these things are removed.

At the break of day, Eleazar will call the people of Israel up tribe by tribe.

The tribe that the Lord indicts shall come forward clan by clan.

The clan that the Lord indicts shall come forward family by family.

And the family that the Lord indicts shall come forward man by man.

Thus you will learn who violated my covenant and brought this disaster on all Israel. The hidden will be uncovered. And the person hiding the devoted things shall be stoned and burned, along with all that belongs to him.

Achor

Through the evening and into the night, the horror of the procedure that would begin shortly after dawn consumed Achor. Would it not be better to throw himself willingly on the mercy of God beforehand? Once he nearly bolted from the tent to go confess to Joshua, but Jamin somehow guessed and ordered his children to bar the entrance. "A confession would mean death for all of us," Jamin argued.

Lifetime roles were suddenly reversed. His wife, his daughter-in-law, even the grandchildren supported his son. "There may be others who took plunder from Jericho. Should the lot actually fall on you tomorrow, Father, we will deny any wrongdoing. Offer a search of the tents. It is unlikely that anyone would discover the stolen items, but in the event they do, we have an answer. The whole family must plead shock and ignorance. Let the blame fall on Eliab."

"How can we add lies to what we already did?" Achor moaned. "How can we let Eliab bear our guilt?"

"Why not?" his granddaughter Shelomith snapped. "They can't kill him. Eliab is already dead."

What made a ten year old so heartless? What of her uncle's reputation? What of Abihail and their unborn child?

Jamin rearranged the cushions and sleeping mats, placing the tent returned by Eliab over the buried items and a sleeping mat over that. Achor crouched in a corner, watching, everything a surreal swirl. When Jamin was satisfied with the arrangement, Achor collapsed on his own sleeping mat, listening to Jamin rehearsing the alibi with the family. "Listen, everyone. If the stolen things are discovered, we must all tell the same story. Eliab must have returned this tent when no one was here and buried the stolen plunder in the ground beneath it. We are appalled and grieved that he could be the one who brought this trouble on Israel. But it must be the truth. Our own Eliab must be the guilty one."

Fourteen-year-old Eliada gave Achor a wink. "Watch us wail, Grandfather. Oh, oh, oh! How could our own uncle Eliab do such a thing?"

Shelomith dramatically touched the back of her hand to her forehead. "I simply can't believe it. But who else could have buried those things in our grandfather's tent?"

This was a living nightmare and Achor feared there was no awakening. In his heart he knew with certainty that hidden things would be revealed. The forbidden robe and all the rest would be utterly destroyed. If he tried to cling to them, he would suffer the same fate—but if he and the family confessed, perhaps they could yet find mercy. But Jamin was in control. Jamin was determined to hide their actions. The agony burst from within him as a deep shuddering groan.

Jamin threw him a look of utter contempt, then his eyes narrowed with cruel intent. "Hattil, go to Abihail's tent with the message that Achor is distraught to the point of insanity. Tell her that we fear for his very life. He grieves for Eliab and in the torment of his sorrow, rambles madly that he has lost his beloved Abihail as well as his son's child along with Eliab. She must come to comfort him."

In her haste to obey, Hattil fumbled with the laces on her sandals and her hands could not seem to find the sleeves of her cloak. Jamin pulled it around her roughly and seized her by the shoulders, pushing his face close to hers with a menacing grimace. "Do not mess this up, woman. Do not return until you have convinced Abihail that Father's reason will not return without her help. Sweet-talk her. Tell her we understand. As a grieving widow, she already bears a heavy burden, but families must stick together in hard times. Convince her to come here. It will lend credence to the accusation against Eliab—if such becomes necessary."

Achor cringed. Jamin's cruel manner disturbed him for the first time. His own lifelong choices fathered this son and these irreverent and deceitful grandchildren. He was sorry for Hattil as she left, visibly shaken by his son's threats. But he was even more sorry for Abihail. The sweet, pure girl should know what darkness had stolen her husband from her. A fire burned within him to confess his crime.

After a while, Hattil slunk silently into the tent, eyes downcast, shoulders drooping. Achor had no idea how long she had been gone. But it was long enough to indicate she put effort into the task.

Jamin's eyes smoldered with rage. "Well? Where is she?"

"Abihail will not allow it," she stammered.

"Leave her be," Achor said weakly. "We should all be sleeping."

"Quiet, Father. What do you mean she would not allow it, Hattil?" Jamin raised his hand as if he would strike his wife.

Achor wanted to intervene, but what could he say?

"She drove me away," Hattil whimpered. "'Leave me alone in my sorrow,' she said. 'I even sent Acsah away,' she said, 'and if I do not need my best friend, I do not need the family that rejected my husband.'"

Mara's frown was vicious. "Can't you do anything, you stupid girl?"

Achor rolled his head on his pillow, muttering faintly. "I have sinned against my son Eliab."

Jamin lunged from Hattil to Achor's bed, seizing a heavy bronze urn and swinging it over his head. "More words like that, Father, and your time of judgment will come tonight."

Mara dove between them. "He is out of his mind with grief, Jamin. Are you out of your mind with anger? Just how would you explain his battered condition?"

"She is right." Eliada pulled the urn from Jamin's hands and gave it to his sister.

Hattil peered down at Achor with pity. "No one deserves bludgeoning judgments from you, Jamin."

"I deserve whatever judgment the Lord metes out on me," Achor whispered. He struggled to rise. "I must go to Joshua and confess."

"You made your choices as did I, old man, but I refuse to perish due to your troubled conscience. Listen to me. Eliab is dead. There are six live persons remaining in the house of Achan. As head of that household it is your duty to protect the living."

Hattil gently pushed Achor back on his pallet. "There is no way out of this, Father Achor," she said sadly, restraining him until he fell into silent compliance.

In the next moment, Jamin's expression softened. He stooped beside Achor's bed, his words flowing like soothing water from a spring. "It would be best, Father, if neighbors could see you under the close and affectionate care of Eliab's wife. Sharing your mutual grief."

Achor was barely aware of what was happening when Jamin pulled him to his feet. Hattil's gentle hands slipped a blanket around him, and together they guided him out into the night. Then out of the darkness of his miserable dream, the doorway of a large tent loomed before him flaunting bold dark stripes on white. *Was this the tent of his dead son? Where were the brilliant crimson stripes? Had this darkness robbed the color of lifeblood from Eliab's tent?* He recoiled from the foreboding omen.

"Achor needs you, Abihail." Jamin's voice cut through the murkiness in Achor's head, but there was no response. No one lifted the tent flap. No curious eyes peeked out.

"We beg you, come look, dear sister-in-law. Behold your husband's father."

Abihail's whisper passed through the canvas walls, soft but emphatic. "Be gone. You are not welcome here."

In a stupor, Achor watched Jamin push the tent flap aside. "You must help him," Jamin demanded. Then Achor was stumbling and falling. He slumped to the floor, peering up at his daughter-in-law, wishing his shroud of guilt and shame would shield him from her anger.

He tried to ask for forgiveness but could only manage incoherent mumbling.

Abihail stamped her foot. "Leave this tent. You are drunk."

"'Drunk with grief,' he heard Jamin say before the crunching of his steps faded away.

No. Drunk on the wine of God's wrath. I have to tell her.

"Son . . . sin," he mumbled. "Ay . . . mi . . ."

He pushed himself up to his feet there in the doorway, trying again to explain. "Ay . . ." but Abihail pushed him back toward the night. Without the support of Jamin and Hattil, Achor's knees buckled.

He heard a gasp as everything went black.

Through the final watches of the night, in intermittent moments of lucidity, he was aware of Abihail's soft hands bathing his fevered brow with cool water. Her touch was far too tender for one whose sin had killed her husband. For a father who had killed his son.

Early the following morning, the ominous summons of the silver trumpets wailed over the camp. Achor awoke surprisingly clearheaded. His strength had returned. While he was hanging his sweat-drenched bedding outside to dry in the sun, Mara appeared with a clean robe for him to wear.

She looked warily at Abihail but did not even thank the girl for caring for him through the night. "I brought your best. You must stand proudly as the eldest son of the Carmi family."

"Thank you, Mara." Achor said. A flood of tender feelings for his wife flooded over him. His hands lingered over hers as he took the bundle. "You have managed our household and cared for me well all these years. Go now, dear wife. Summon Jamin, Hattil, and the children while I dress. We will go as a united family."

Mara opened her mouth to protest. "Jamin is in a foul mood. He can find us at the tabernacle."

"Woman, do not argue. Go. Now." His tone was respectful, but commanding.

Mara skittered away, muttering. "Why me? I just brought my husband clean clothes. Am I well enough for all this trotting to and fro? Abihail could go fetch Jamin's family."

When Mara and her grumbling disappeared, Achor dressed and then found his daughter-in-law waiting outside in a warm pool of sunlight. "Abihail, I did not deserve the compassionate care you gave me last night." He held up his hand to silence her. "No, no. Do not protest." Time was short. She needed to know the truth. "Eliab should not have died," he said softly. "I, only I, bear the blame."

Abihail threw her arms around him with a look more warming than the morning sun. "Oh dear Abba, do not blame yourself. My grief, your misery through this long night has forged a bond between us as never before."

Achor pulled back. *I deserve to be struck in anger, not embraced.* He looked at her earnestly. "If I could undo the past, I would not allow Eliab to go to Ai. I should have gone. I never meant to hurt you like this, Abihail."

"Of course, you didn't. You are my Eliab's abba. My baby's grandfather." Her look melted the icy fear of death.

Achor closed his eyes wishing he could confess all. *I cannot bear to tell you the whole truth now, my dear. You must learn in the cruel revelations of the trial by lot.*

Abihail reached out to wipe away a tear gathering at the corner of his eye. "How could you have known? No one expected anything but an easy victory. You wanted to restore the family. That is why we all agreed to send Eliab in Jamin's place. That is what Eliab wanted."

Footsteps approached and Achor straightened his shoulders. "Your child will gain the inheritance belonging to the family of Achor in the Land of Promise. I will not allow more harm to come to either of you."

"I . . . I don't under—"

Mara's voice interrupted. "We're waiting, Achor. You kept us up half the night. Don't make us late now."

Achor winked conspiratorially. "Do not worry about Mara and me moving into your tent, Abihail. I can promise you; it will never happen."

Abihail

The mood of the tribes surrounding the tabernacle was bleak. No happy chatter. Only the swishing robes and crunching sandals of more and more people wordlessly swelling the crowds. Only an occasional cough. Only a mother here and there clucking to calm an unhappy infant. Then the trumpets wailed again, ushering in an even deeper, more ominous silence, a silence so heavy, Eleazar seemed to sag beneath its weight as he invoked the presence of the Lord.

O Great and Merciful Lord,
Beautiful in holiness,
   Magnificent in wisdom and love,
   Perfect in righteousness and justice,
Your people have sinned in your sight.
We have been unfaithful to your covenant.

Abihail cringed at the word "unfaithful." It was irrational, but the old terror gripped her. It was the terror she experienced at Moses' farewell address, the bombardment of guilt as she listened to the litany of curses in the final hour of Moses' farewell speeches. But Eliab was not here today to comfort her. *I was guilty then, Yahweh God. I coveted those beautiful Midianite gifts and closed my eyes to the danger. My choices led to Eliab's unfaithfulness. But we sacrificed our ram, our only ram.* She clenched her jaw, choosing to believe their sacrifice had done its work, and returned her attention to the high priest's prayer.

We waged war with Ai,
   yet we did not inquire of you.
We went forth to battle,
   led only by our flawed understanding.
We did not know that one of our own robbed you,
   that we stood guilty in your sight,
   that we had broken covenant.[14]

A great snorting and bellowing nearly drowned the words, "broken covenant," and Eleazar paused. The twelve princes of Israel, six on each side, pulled a balking, bawling bull into the courtyard. Four ropes and four men secured its head and forelegs. The remaining princes secured its hind legs with eight more ropes. The bull's eyes glittered with fear and rage, rolling wildly in search of a target or way of escape. When the group finally reached the great bronze altar, he lowered his muzzle and pawed the earth with his hoof, horns ready. No one doubted this enormous animal would seize any opportunity for a deadly charge to freedom. Then Salmon, prince of Judah, laid one firm hand on its head, whispering softly. The bull snorted once and lifted his horns to look at Salmon with his right eye. The calming effect was instantaneous. One by one, the other princes reached out to lay a hand on the heaving flanks.

Abihail noticed how each one gripped the restraining cords even more tightly with the other hand, planting their feet in a more solid stance. Just how much help did those tense eleven hands provide? She placed a hand on her abdomen. *What do you feel at my touch, child? My fear? My sorrow? You have no idea what is happening in the world out here, but touching you brings me comfort. Feeling your kick brings me hope.*

The bull remained still, and Eleazar continued his prayer.

> *Accept the blood of this bull in place of our guilt.*
> *Cleanse our camp.*
> *Lead us through this hour of judgment*
> *and restore us once more as your holy people.*
> *Hear O Israel . . .*

Thousands of voices repeated the words, the sound roaring from all sides of the tabernacle like the sound of a mighty waterfall.

> *Hear O Israel. The Lord your God is One.*
> *Love the Lord—*

"Love the Lord . . ." Abihail repeated the words fervently, then caught up to the rhythm of the recitation.

> *O, love the Lord your God*
> *with ALL your heart*
> *with ALL your mind,*
> *with ALL your strength,*
> *and with ALL your soul.*[15]

When the words were finished, Abihail caressed the fullness of life growing within her. Only God and the prospect of raising Eliab's child could hold back the despair of her empty tent, her empty bed, and her own empty heart.

The covenant is like a marriage, Little One. I will teach you to keep your heart pure before the Lord, to love him and his righteousness more than anything else. I loved your father more than life itself. He loved me, and yet his choices on the mountaintop of Baal-Peor inflicted the greatest pain my heart has ever known. The pain of unfaithfulness hurt more than the pain of his death for he did not choose that. Oh my child, may you never be the source of jealousy-pain to our God, and may you never know the terror of standing guilty before him.

She felt a nudge under her fingers and smiled. "You perfect, innocent little life, you heard my thoughts," she whispered. "You will bring honor to your father's name."

Abihail felt, more than saw, Achor turn toward her whisper. She reached for his hand and placed it over the movement, sharing the moment of wonder and joy with Eliab's father.

Achor's hand trembled under hers.

"Your grandson," she whispered.

But the bull's truncated bellow blasted the tender moment.

Phinehas

Keeping one calming hand on the huge sacrificial animal, Salmon took the bronze knife from Eleazar. The razor-sharp blade flashed briefly in the sunlight, then disappeared as he slid it across the bull's throat. Phinehas tensed, pressing a golden bowl below the gushing slash. *Let none of this precious lifeblood be lost,* he kept repeating to himself. The bull's eyes rolled back and the ponderous beast slumped to the ground, but Phinehas managed to drop to one knee, keeping the bowl in place until the flow slackened and stopped. Only then could he relax and exhale.

He wiped away the one small smear of red marring the gleaming exterior of the bowl with his fingers and handed it to his father. Eleazar's garments were designed to give the high priest an aura of the eternal, but today as Phinehas watched his father cradle the bowl in both hands and trudge slowly toward the tabernacle entrance, he seemed bent and stooped and old. He watched until Eleazar pushed through the heavy curtain of red, purple, and blue linen and disappeared into the beauty of holiness.

Beauty of holiness. That is what his father and his grandfather Aaron always called the unearthly splendor of the interior. As Phinehas crouched beside the carcass helping his uncle Ithamar and cousins flay the beast, his thoughts followed his father into the holy place.

A lamp stand stood like a seven-branched tree of solid gold on the left side as one entered. Its lamps burned day and night, sending ethereal light shimmering across the golden walls, reflecting off the golden altar, gleaming from the gilt crown and legs of the bread table, and glittering on the shapes of angels embroidered in gold on a second heavy curtain of scarlet, purple, and blue brilliance. Whether Phinehas was taking his turn trimming wicks and refilling the lamps with oil, or offering the sacred incense, or gathering around the Lord's table with the priestly family to eat the bread of the presence each Sabbath morning, that holy room never failed to engender a sense of awe and wonder—and dread.

Phinehas remembered the story of his grandfather Aaron's two eldest sons, Nadab and Abihu, every time he entered that room to offer incense. Every time he clutched his censer, he remembered how they staggered riotously drunk into this holy place carrying common fire. How could they forget that radiance spilling through every space above and below the curtain had no earthly source? The glorious light of the presence hovering between the cherubim on the ark of the covenant became the deadly flash of fire that incinerated his uncles. He had not yet been born when it happened, but Moses purposefully planted the story in the middle of the priestly instruction manual, the only story in the book of the Levites.

Over the years, Phinehas developed the habit of pulling in a deep breath as he walked through the door to counteract the dread. The air he took in, fragrant with spicy incense and the life-giving aroma of the bread of the presence, helped calm the fear of approaching that immortal consuming fire. Every furnishing, every color, every ritual in that sanctuary communicated that Yahweh God wanted nothing more than to bridge the chasm between himself and mortal man. But the smells did not require thought; they simply calmed him.

The ritual drama today would take place along the dividing curtain with its shining angel guards. He pictured his father stooping down at the southern end of the curtain in the bright pool of light from the lamp stand. He would dip one finger in the blood, sprinkle a little on the ground and advance along that woven wall of protection, as close to the white-light holiness of the presence as a man could be in this chamber. Seven times, in seven stops along the curtain, Eleazar would sprinkle the cleansing blood. After the seventh sprinkling, he would rise and move to the altar of incense where he would press one bloody thumbprint on each of the four horns of the altar. There, where the sweet smoldering spices reflected fire-red on the rim of the altar, the ritual concluded. Somehow that blood of cleansing was the means of restoration. Once again, the sweet mercy of God would cover the stench of human imperfection.

Phinehas was arranging the fat, the kidneys, and the liver of the bull on a large brass platter when a shining flare seemed to brighten the tabernacle courtyard. He wasn't certain if it was his imagination or an actual response from the heavenly presence, but his father emerged from the tabernacle just then. He marched across the courtyard and poured the remainder of the blood at the foot of the great brazen altar. As Phinehas watched the pale sand swallow the dark, scarlet pool, all the world seemed right again.

He rose and held the brass platter while his father took up the bronze tongs to arrange the fat and the organs of the bull around the smoldering lamb of the morning sacrifice. As Phinehas placed the platter, bowls, and utensils in a large basin of water to be cleansed later in the day, the slumbering flames awoke, accepting the offering with crackling and much smoke.

Abihail

The offering ceremony was finished—at last. Abihail's energy was flagging, her back beginning to ache. There was a palpable restlessness all around as Ithamar and his sons loaded the remains of the bloody carcass on a cart to be rolled to the burning place outside camp, but still the people waited. Abihail could barely see Phinehas and Eleazar, father and son, deep in the courtyard dipping water from the laver on each other's bloodstained hands. *Phinehas.* It was hard to remember the tall, serious boy of childhood days. Awkward at games, always on the fringes of the children's play, but courageous to ensure justice for the smaller, weaker children, Phinehas understood even then what his life's work would be.

A sharp intake of breath all around Abihail broke her brief reverie. She looked up to see the priestly pair standing at the courtyard gates clad in glory and beauty like beings from heavenly realms. She gasped along with the crowds at the pair. The brilliant colors of Eleazar's ephod and jeweled breastplate reflected blazing heavenly beauty. But even the simpler garments of the future high priest, the gleaming white tunic bound with a sash of royal colors, dazzled in the sunlight.

Glory and doom. The mysterious work of atonement within the tabernacle was finished. The people could only follow the priestly rituals in their minds, but the pending day of judgment would be all too real. She stared at the Jar of Decision Phinehas held in his hands.

Joshua joined them, the three standing abreast, billows of smoke rising from the atonement offering on the altar behind them. Not a rustle troubled the air as Phinehas passed the narrow-necked clay jar to his father. Eleazar lifted it high above his head. He invoked a brief blessing over the proceedings, then passed the vessel to Joshua. The movements of the priests were formal and unwavering. But Joshua's hands trembled as he took the lot jar from Eleazar. He clutched it to his chest as if to halt the march of time, then yielded to duty before anyone could complete a breath.

"Tribal princes," he cried in a loud voice, "bring your stones."

Stones. The word echoed in Abihail's head. *How often have I piled up stones or kicked them or tossed them in childish play? After this day, all happy memories of stones will be buried under a cold, hard memorial of judgment. Stones of decision. Stones of death.*

The twelve princes of Israel marched into place, each clutching a small, rounded river stone in his fist. Each lot stone would be etched with the name of the tribe. Abihail shuddered. *Not Judah,* she prayed silently. The tramping of the men's feet sounded in her ears like an ominous drumroll. The princes took their places before the triumvirate of judgment and twelve times she heard the clattering of a lot tumbling down the narrow neck of the jar. When the twelve stones had been deposited in the jar, Phinehas formally handed Eleazar a pitcher of water. Joshua held the Jar of Decision while Eleazar filled it with water. The moment of judgment.

"Man pours the lot onto the ground," Joshua intoned, "but the Lord chooses the stone." He wobbled the jar to stir its contents, then turned it neck down. The Levitical lot jar was crafted so only one pebble could fall at a time.

Abihail had witnessed its use many times to settle minor disputes, but never for anything remotely like this. *The Lord chooses the stone,* she reminded herself as one pale pebble plopped on the ground in a wash of water. *Please, Lord, not Judah.*

Phinehas picked up the lot stone, stared at it briefly, then handed it to his father.

"The tribe of Judah has been chosen," Eleazar announced in a loud voice. "Let the elders of Judah bring their lots."

As Joshua shook out the remaining stones to make way for the next set, the eleven men from the exonerated tribes slipped back to their places, audible ripples of relief following in their wake. Salmon, prince of Judah, remained alone etching a new lot with the mark of Perez as the stony-faced elders of Judah formed a line beside him. Even deeper furrows etched their faces as they dropped their lot stones one by one down the narrow throat of the lot jar. As before, Joshua rolled a single stone onto the ground. Phinehas picked it up, and Eleazar called out the name. "Zerah. The Zerahite clan has been chosen. Make way for the chiefs of the clan of Zerah."

Phinehas placed the stone of Zerah beside that of Judah on the ground behind Joshua while the elders returned to their places. Now the clan chiefs of Zerah came forward and scratched the names of their families on fresh lot stones. And when the lot was cast, it bore the name of Zimri. Then all the sons of Zimri came with their stones, and the lot bore the name of Carmi. Phinehas placed the stone in a line with the others. Judah, Zerah, Zimri, Carmi.

Carmi. Achor's father.

Revulsion and shock raked Abihail. Suddenly, she knew. She knew without doubt which name would appear on the final lot. Achan—the formal name of the man standing beside her marking his lot stone. The torment written on his face told the story. Eliab's own father brought all this trouble on Israel.

Through the night she had soothed this horrible man's guilt and ministered to his dread of judgment. Today his sin would fall on the entire family. It would fall on her. *O Eliab, my Eliab. How I need you, but I would not wish you here to witness this. You were too noble to be part of this vile family.*

Abihail recoiled from a light brushing touch on her hand. She knew it was Achor, but she could not look at him. *Would that he had died during the night.*

"Yahweh is both merciful and just," he whispered.

The words disarmed her, and she yielded to his hands lifting her chin, turning her head until he could look into her eyes. The oddly serene look she found there stood in stark contrast to her own dark horror. He said the words again with conviction. "Yahweh is both merciful and just." One by one he repeated the same words to each member of his family. By the time he finished, Achor's three younger brothers were already in their places before Joshua, their stones deposited in the jar.

As the lot stone bearing the name of Achan clattered down the narrow-necked jug, Mara's face paled to the color of morning manna. Abihail was surprised to hear her own voice whisper, "We must all be strong. Be calm like Achor. Yahweh *is* merciful."

Jamin pulled his mother to his side, glaring as if Abihail had just insulted Mara. "No need for fear, Mother. We can be calm because we know the truth."

The stones rattled against the sides of the jar as Joshua sloshed them about, stretching out the process longer than he had the previous times. He waited while the scraping of the stones slowed and came to a stop. It seemed as if the entire congregation held its breath as slowly, reluctantly, Joshua poured the last lot out on the ground. Phinehas picked it up but did not look at it before passing it to his father.

"Achan," Eleazar announced clearly.

"Achan, son of Carmi, son of Zimri, of the clan of Zerah, of the tribe of Judah." He placed the final stone at the end of the line of five.

Slump-shouldered, head bowed, Achor remained in his place as his brothers slunk away. Joshua placed a kindly hand on his head. "My son, give glory to Yahweh. Make your confession to him. Tell us what you did. Do not hold anything back."

"The lot fell true," Achan cried out. "I sinned against Yahweh, our God. In the chaos at Jericho, I saw a Babylonian robe of purple worn by the king himself. It was wondrously beautiful, and King Nahari himself told me it would impart wisdom and power to the wearer. Fearing I would never see another like it in all the land, I hid it beneath my own robe. I also coveted Jericho's silver and gold, and plotted with my son, Jamin, to keep two bags of silver coins and a large wedge of gold for ourselves."

He crumpled at Joshua's feet like a limp garment. "I have sinned."

"My father is demented," Jamin shrieked. "It is his grief over losing Eliab. He doesn't know what he is saying."

Achor lifted his head and shoulders with dignity. "My son, do not add to our sin."

He scrambled to his feet and declared loudly. "I *was* demented in my decision, but my statement now is true. The forbidden items are buried in the ground within my tent—the robe and the gold with the silver underneath."

"If my father speaks truth," Jamin avowed, "I knew nothing of his treason."

"Silence!" Joshua commanded. He called for three young men from the clans of Zimri. "Go to Achor's tent. Look for the stolen plunder. Bring it to me if you find it as Achor has said."

Jamin addressed the gawking crowds with an unhinged wildness. "I know nothing of stolen goods. Ask my wife Hattil. Ask my children. Ask my mother. Achor must have plotted this evil with my brother, Eliab."

Joshua assessed the young man sorrowfully. "What do you say to this charge, Achan?"

"My dead son Eliab is the only innocent one. We banished him from our family long before Jericho, before we crossed the Jordan. Jamin and I illicitly acquired more than our share of the Midianite plunder and Eliab refused to be part of it. Therefore, at Jamin's insistence, we cut him off. Caleb can verify this. Eliab and his wife had to use Caleb's wagon to transport their things across the Jordan."

"That is a lie." Jamin's ranting rebuttal reached a higher pitch. "Eliab tried to entice *us* with the Midianite plunder. He had to cross the Jordan with Caleb because we were angry with him for his dishonesty and wanted no part of it."

Abihail stared at him, aghast. "Your brother loved you."

Jamin's eyes took on the cold look of a snake. "Love includes loyalty."

"Oh, dear brother, have you no idea how Eliab grieved over the separation from your family? How can you accuse him of this evil?"

"Eliab always took what he could get. He took from our family. He took from the Midianite plunder. And I have no doubt he took from the forbidden wealth of Jericho for himself. Apparently, he did not even tell you about it."

Caleb spoke up in the dead boy's defense. "I do not believe any of that to be true. I have never known Eliab to be greedy. In fact, he would have given up all his rightful possessions to reunite his family. He told me so."

Jamin snarled. "Then why was he so eager to go to battle again if not to gain the spoils of war? He wasn't chosen to go up against Ai. He urged me to trade places with him."

Abihail gasped. *Would Jamin twist every true fact in his wild attempt to free himself?* "That is a lie. It was Jamin who convinced Eliab to take his place in the battle of Ai. Eliab did it in order to restore the family."

"All that the young woman says is true," Achor cried out. His voice cracked with passion. "The name of Eliab is unsullied—along with that of his wife and unborn child."

Before Jamin or Mara could protest, the crunching footsteps of the Zimri cousins announced the arrival of the prohibited plunder. "It is just as he said," Azariah panted, casting the bags of silver coins to the ground between Achor and Joshua. The second cousin flung the magnificent purple robe over the silver like a man disposing of a bundle of used menstrual cloths. He stooped to rub his hands on the ground, then shake off the dust. The third cousin, a brawny young man carrying the ponderous weight of the golden wedge on his shoulder, lagged behind the others. When he reached Joshua, he sucked in enough air to gasp out his verdict, "Achor is guilty." With one heave, the gleaming wedge landed at Joshua's feet with a portentous thud.

"Are these items truly from Jericho?" the silver-haired commander asked sternly. Achor nodded but did not look up.

The crowds backed away from the family of Achan as if the earth might open up and swallow them. For the first time since the lot selected Achor, Abihail felt a stab of compassion for him. How pitifully insignificant that pile of plunder seemed in comparison with all Achan risked and lost, but she understood the coveting of beautiful things. More than that, she realized as never before how close she had come to abandoning the covenant herself, choosing Eliab's love over commitment to the God who gave him to her. She knew the shame and terror of guilt in the face of judgment.

"Did you and your family understand the Lord's command concerning Jericho—that the city and all its contents were to be a burnt offering to the Lord?"

Achor lifted his chin and looked directly into Joshua's eyes. "Completely, sir. I and my son, Jamin, our wives, and the grandchildren. We broke our covenant vows and somehow convinced ourselves it wouldn't matter."

Hattil shrieked and collapsed on the ground. Her children huddled around sobbing hysterically, while Jamin lunged at his father's throat. "We had a plan, you old fool." Taking advantage of the confusion, Mara darted away.

"Seize that woman," Joshua shouted.

Two of Achor's nephews blocked her escape and dragged her back.

"Bind them all," Joshua commanded. "Now let representatives from each of the thirty-five other grieving families go collect Achor's possessions and all his livestock. As you buried your dead, so we will bury everything connected to the treason that caused your loss. Salmon, organize that group and meet us on the road to Ai."

While the tent and all Achor's possessions were being collected, Achor followed Joshua up the road to the overlook of a steep, uncultivated valley. Guarded closely by the sons of Zimri, Jamin skulked behind his father. Hattil clung pitifully to her son while Mara walked beside Jamin, grumbling and wailing alternately. "I only wanted the inheritance we were promised," she sniveled. "Why is that so wrong?" Abihail trailed behind with Jamin's daughter, Shelomith, and all the people followed.

In the march up the mountain road, an unexplainable peace enveloped Abihail. She would die with Achor although she had no part in his sin, but strangely she no longer abhorred him for his treason against Yahweh. *The Lord was gracious to me in my sin. Perhaps even yet we will know the mercy of Yahweh.*

When they reached the edge of the precipice, Shelomith hissed at her grandfather. "I hate you!" She began to sob. "Why didn't you follow my father's plan?"

Abihail laid a calming hand on her head. "Hush, hush, child. Don't make our situation worse by rebelling." She pulled the girl into her arms, and they watched the proceedings together.

Joshua summoned Azariah, the eldest male in the family of Zimri, to his side. There on the brink of the valley, the silver-haired warrior knelt beside the devoted items to wrap the Babylonian garment around the gold and the bags of silver. He stood, and his voice echoed across the valley. "This is the Lord's devoted plunder. It, and all attached to it, are devoted to destruction as Yahweh commanded." He turned to Azariah. "Hurl down the stolen items. Cast them away from the covenant people."

Azariah bent part way, then hesitated as if by touching these things, the contamination would pass to him and his family.

"Do it." Joshua said gently. "Your clan bears the brunt of all this trouble."

The young man nodded. He dropped to one knee, his biceps bulging as he pushed himself to his feet and lifted the ponderous bundle over his head, hurling it into the deep valley. It tumbled down the cliff, crashing over brambles, rebounding from jagged rocks, and finally breaking apart in a dizzying flash of brilliant purple, gleaming gold, and a shower of silver coins.

The commander next called for the chiefs and representatives from the thirty-five grieving families to bring all Achan's possessions to the rim of the valley. Abihail wobbled. She shuffled into a more stable stance, clinging even tighter to Shelomith as a battalion of burly, strong-armed men began breaking the necks of the oxen, donkeys, sheep, and goats, then heaved the carcasses into the valley. Abihail swallowed back a wave of nausea and grief at the sight of the familiar tent, Eliab's childhood home, flapping wildly like a distraught mother bird over the furnishings, clothing, and tools as they plummeted into the abyss.

Achor's large, well-crafted wagon was the last of his possessions pushed over the cliff. It cracked and splintered in protest—as Joshua's voice cracked and splintered with grief. "Thus the treachery of the house of Achan dashed the lives of thirty-six families to pieces. Oh Achan, my son, do you have any final words?"

The condemned man closed his eyes.

"If you have nothing to say, let the people lift their stones. Salmon, as prince of Judah, you will cast the first stone."

"Wait." Achor held up a hand and faced the crowds with his chin held high. "All glory to the name of the Lord. Well named is the man you call Achor for no one has brought such trouble on Israel. My greed dishonored the holy name of our God and caused all the destruction you witness today. I put the whole nation in danger. I caused the deaths of thirty-six good men, including my own son. I rest my soul in the justice and mercy of Yahweh. Glorious is his name. Aching is the legacy of Achan."

"Oh, my people," Joshua groaned. "Remember this doxology of death."

"You fool," Jamin snarled. "What did we do that was worthy of death? Just a robe. Just some silver and gold."

"We were going to give Yahweh his devoted plunder from another city," Mara whimpered. "Remember? We said that."

"Jamin, my son . . . Mara, my wife . . . all my family, we broke our covenant vows. Throw yourselves on the mercy of God."

"I am not weak like you." Jamin spat on the ground.

Achor laughed at the irony. "For the first time in my life, I am strong." With an expression of joyous freedom, he turned his face resolutely toward the abyss and leaped into the air. "Hear O Israel . . ." he shouted. "The Lord our God is one . . ." A cry of pain interrupted the recitation only once when his head cracked against the rocky slope. "Love the Lord your God with all—" He thudded against the valley floor. For a moment he appeared dead, then those closest to the valley rim could hear his miserable straining to repeat the familiar words. "With . . . all . . . your . . . heart . . ."

As prince of Judah, Salmon hurled his melon-sized missile with a well-placed shot that silenced the troubler of Israel forever. "And with all your soul and with all your strength," he croaked, tears cascading down his cheeks.

"Why? Oh why?" Joshua's voice rose like the mournful cry of a wolf. "Oh, my son Achan, what aching you heaped on our people!"

At Salmon's command, the clans of Zerah pressed to the edge of the narrow valley and buried the body of Achor beneath a clattering heap.

"Yahweh is cruel," Mara hissed. Her face contorted in hatred. "Plunder is plunder. How can God say, 'You may take what you like from any other city, but if you take this, you will die.'"

"He is God. His commands are righteous and just," Joshua answered, seizing her by the arms. "Cast yourself on his mercy while you can."

"Just like the Garden of Eden," Mara shrieked, "destroyed for a bite of fruit." She twisted and broke from Joshua's grip, stumbling and tumbling over the edge of the cliff. "To such a God I will not—" The bottom of the ravine and a hail of stones swallowed her final bitter words.

Jamin, Hattil, and their children were cast down after her, and the heads of every household in Israel began covering all with a mountain of stones.

Abihail watched numbly. *They have not been kind to me, but they are all the family I had.* Her hand found its way to the roundness of her unborn child. *O my love, my little one, I wish you could know the joy you have brought me. Though you will never see the light of day, your brief life has been a blessing, but the house of Achan must be cut off forever for this great sin.*

Tribe by tribe, clan by clan, the men of every family hurled their stones of judgment, returned to their wives and children, and led them back to camp in somber silence. Abihail waited anxiously, head bowed, the thudding of rocks and the heavy tread of retreating feet pounding in her ears. When she could stand the suspense no longer, she looked up. The crowds around the rim of the valley had noticeably diminished. Joshua stood apart on the brink of the precipice.

She approached him timidly. "Sir, I cannot jump like Achor."

He stared at her blankly.

A shudder shook her body. *Should a condemned woman have to verbalize such a request?* Clearing her throat and clenching her fists for courage, she clarified. "You will have to throw me down."

"What?" Joshua seemed momentarily confused. Then understanding filled his eyes. "They cut you off," he replied. The words were curt, but kindly said. "The name of Eliab was cut off from the family of Achan. Go home, child."

He turned from her abruptly with a command. "Phinehas, bring the censer."

Abihail watched as Joshua led the twelve elders down a steep path into the valley. She lingered while they gathered brush and piled it high over the stone heap and Phinehas ignited it with holy fire from the altar. As the flames began to crackle and spread, the elders left the valley and Abihail turned, following the last of the families home to camp.

Home? She mused bitterly. *My tent is not home. Caring for Achor through the night gave me the barest spider filament of connection to my husband. Now even that is gone.* She took one last look over her shoulder at the smoke and flames licking at the valley of aching, the Valley of Achor. Nothing beneath the rubble of that terrible burning memorial could ever be salvaged, including the pieces of her broken heart.

Feeling chilled, shaky, and desperately alone, she staggered down the road toward camp. It seemed a lifetime ago that her lips had brushed Eliab's cold-as-marble cheeks and lips for the last time. Moving like a sleepwalker, she had washed and wrapped his body. Detached, sometimes feeling like a vapor floating above the scene, she watched Jamin and Achor shovel dirt over the death pallet and build a cairn of stones to mark the grave. Numbness shrouded the day of her husband's burial.

Today, she witnessed Eliab's family buried beneath a cairn of shame, but there was no blessed numbness. Never had she felt so lost, so unprotected. She paused to stroke the unborn child within her and imagined she could feel the tiny heartbeat. *I will never bring you to view this mound of stones and tell you that your abba's family is here . . .*

Her stomach churned. She rushed over to a shrubby stand of willows at the side of the steep road and threw up. When the retching subsided, she stood quickly and wiped the bitter drops from her lips with the back of her hand. Black spots formed before her eyes and a rush of maternal protectiveness flowed through her veins. "Oh, my precious," she whispered. "*Trouble* is not your grandfather. We have been cut off from that family and the horrors of the Valley of Achor."

She took a step toward home, but the dark spots increased, floating, dancing, growing, and merging into a solid black night. Her knees crumpled, and she fell heavily, tumbling down the hill, crashing over rocks, scraping through brush. Faint and far away, she thought she heard Acsah's voice calling, "Othniel, Othniel, help me. Abihail has fallen."

CHAPTER TEN

REAPING

Acsah

Acsah stumbled back to the red-and-white striped tent. The dull pounding in her head deadened her ability to formulate any plan beyond her next footstep. It had been a long night, sleeping fitfully at Abihail's side, repeatedly roused by her friend's every moan or stirring. The freshness and life of the early morning mocked her exhaustion. The bird songs taunted her woe. As she approached the brilliant stripes of Abihail's doorway, she caught the timbre of dissonant notes mingled with the avian melodies of morning. The strains of a foreign tune. Two female voices woven in intricate harmony. And the haunting melody issued from within Abihail's tent.

Acsah flew through the entrance and froze, barely able to believe what she saw. Rahab of Jericho and her grandmother hovered over Abihail's bed, already in the process of a foreign incantation. She opened her mouth but could not force words from her throat. What audacity brought that idol-worshiping harlot and her grandmother into the tent of an Israelite girl when she was helpless to resist? The harlot was poised at Abihail's head, rhythmically tracing circles on her brow in time to her song while the old woman, surrounded by bundles of weeds and bark shavings, squatted beside Rahab, grinding a mysteriously pungent potion in a small stone mortar. Her lower-pitched voice intertwined with Rahab's as she pounded a slow beat in time to the song. Neither woman reacted to her entrance.

At last Acsah found her voice. "In the name of Yahweh, stop what you are doing."

Rahab threw a fleeting glance her direction, but she did not alter her hypnotic song even when the grandmother dropped her harmony and laid the pestle down. "We heard the pregnant girl had taken a bad fall," she said, "so we got up before dawn to gather these." She held up a basket of dew-fresh herbs. "This ancient remedy may well save the baby and should get our young friend back on her feet within a day or two."

Rahab stopped singing then. "My grandmother has much experience in midwifery, and we can see that this girl's condition is serious."

"Leave this tent now," Acsah commanded. "I am caring for my friend, and I will not allow your witchcraft here."

"Trust me, dear child. This is not witchcraft. I am also a believer in Yahweh, your God."

"We do not need your help," Acsah answered firmly. She refused to be swayed by Canaanite deceit. "The initial bleeding has stopped. Abihail is sleeping. The healing rest of the Lord will restore her."

The two women of Jericho looked at one another helplessly.

"I asked you to leave." Acsah signaled her desire with a wave of her hand toward the tent door. "Will you respect my request, or must I summon help?"

"I would be happy to leave the herbs for a healing tea," the old one offered as she scooped her things into a shoulder bag. Acsah waved her hand to signal no and followed the Canaanites as they left the tent. She watched the foreign healers head toward their own marginal place outside of camp. When they disappeared, she exhaled a deep breath ridding herself of the loathsome toxins of Jericho's perverted culture.

Joshua [16]

Joshua woke with a start. *Did someone call my name?* He listened into the silent darkness. Misty shreds of tortured dreams—death, defeat, despair—lingered like fog in his head. *Where am I? What day is it?*

And then he sensed the voice again. Not an audible voice. Only words. Intense, insistent in his head. *Joshua. Go up to Ai again.*

Joshua shrank from it. The thought was demonic . . . too much bloodshed already.

Joshua. You know my voice. When I call, you need not be afraid. Take the entire army with you and go up to that ruin once more. I will be with you.

"How can my boys face that road again?"

Tell them the breach in the covenant is repaired. Tell them I will deliver the ruin into your hands. I have judged King Birsha and his people and found them wanting. Treat Ai and its king as you did Jericho and its king—except you may carry off the plunder and livestock for yourselves.

Joshua dropped his head in submission. "I will go, Lord, if you go with us . . . but I don't want to make the same mistakes. Will more men really make a difference? The men of Luz detected our ascent. They sent up a signal and came to the aid of Ai."

He sensed a smile in the voice. *Whose battle is this, Joshua? Yours or mine?*

Shortly after dawn, Joshua called for Jokshan of Jericho to join the war council. As soon as he sent the summons, he was filled with a sense of rightness regarding the decision. *Exactly what we need. A local man, familiar with the terrain surrounding Ai and Luz.* For the first time since the defeat, Joshua felt confident, almost jubilant.

When the door flap rustled and his sentry escorted Jokshan in, Joshua leaped to his feet, but the foreigner remained at the entrance as if uncertain. "Jokshan, my good man, come in," he urged, tipping his head in a warm welcome.

Jokshan bent in a respectful but hesitant bow without taking a step forward.

"Come. Come sit down." Any lingering uncertainty about the loyalty of this Canaanite had long since melted away—but the lines in Jokshan's face spoke of his own doubts. Or at least his confusion.

"You must be wondering why I summoned you." Joshua gestured toward the Israelite commanders already circled around a crude map etched in the dirt floor. "You know my division commanders, yes? Caleb leads the troops under the standard of the Lion of Judah. Heled commands Reuben's Son of Man. Ira commands Ephraim's Ox. And Jared commands the fourth division, the Eagle of Dan." Each man dipped his head by way of greeting as his name and standard was given.

Joshua squatted beside a roll of carpet bundled back to expose the ground. He grinned at Jokshan. "Yahweh came to me in the night with the command to return to Ai taking our entire army. The idea to invite you here came as part of his battle plan."

Jokshan's eyes widened in horrified confusion. "I . . . I know nothing of war."

"But you know the land and the people. Yahweh expressly indicated that I was to include you as advisor."

"Here, toward the rising sun, is our camp in the Jordan valley." He pointed to Gilgal and then swung the blade tip to the names already carved to the left. "Here are Ai and Bethel, which the Canaanites call Luz." He made a small slashing mark between them. "The plan is to lay an ambush north of Ai to prevent an attack from Luz. Then we are to place a second ambush, lying in wait to swarm onto the field when we have drawn all reserves out of the fortress. A third, smaller ambush will hold back, waiting to enter Ai to plunder and burn when all its soldiers are engaged on the field." He circled the blade above the map but did not make more marks as he explained the second and third ambushes.

"I will command the main divisions as last time. But, God willing, we will arrive while Ai sleeps, forming our lines undetected on the sloping hillside opposite the gates. Yahweh informs me that Ai will attack, not parley. They will send their troops out to meet us on the field, confident of victory as before. We will engage the enemy bravely at first, then in a pretense of confusion and fear, one squad after another will abandon the field, slipping into the rough terrain to the southeast as if fleeing back to Gilgal."

"Brilliant plan!" Jokshan's eyes lit up with enthusiasm. "King Birsha has been paranoid since you crossed the river. He has fortified every inch of that fortress. Your extremely large army would most likely win a street-to-street, door-to-door fight, but only at the cost of many lives. May I . . .?"

Jokshan took the dagger from Joshua and began marking the map with the best places to set the ambushes. He marked a numeral one at Joshua's slash mark between Ai and Luz. "There is enough rocky ground here to hide the units assigned to stop Luz from lending aid. They should access that location, not by continuing up the main road, but this way, through a small, rough gully that curves up around the east of Ai."

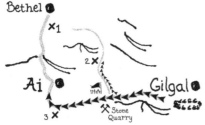

He carved a numeral two on the map. "The principal ambush contingent should take that same road and hide here, to the north of the battlefield. Have your 'deserters' flee toward Gilgal to the south of the ambush keeping those men undetected until needed. The men of the third ambush should follow the main force up the primary road as you did for the first battle, the ambush waiting far enough down to remain out of view."

He marked the best place for the third ambush. "When they hear their signal, they can easily rush up the ravine, entering the unprotected city while the battle rages on the field."

Jokshan sat back and grinned at the commanders. "This ruse reveals the wisdom of Yahweh. I know Birsha. He is driven by pride. I predict overconfidence in his own strength if he sniffs any weakness at all. Never mind that your army is dreaded by all Canaan, he will empty the city of all reserves, certain his superior strength and strategy will prevail.

By midmorning the silver trumpets blared with a call mustering every warrior in Israel. While women and children watched in curiosity, they formed the neat blocks of their divisions, brigades, and companies—but they were not an army. Joshua could feel the dark shadow of fear.

"The Lord sends us up to Ai again," he shouted, pacing back and forth. "We must do it, not despite our defeat, but because of it. How long do you think we would survive in this land once the kings of Canaan learn that Israel was defeated by the smallest walled city?"

He continued striding back and forth before the ranks of the army, challenging his demoralized warriors with bold words. "Do not fear. We failed in the first battle of Ai because we went ahead of the Lord. This time, we will be victorious—for Yahweh our God will go with us." Joshua stopped in his tracks. The Lord had given him an ingenious battle plan, but there was no denying the undisguised throat-clutching terror in every glance toward the western hills. He could not inspire these men that Yahweh's battle strategy would succeed when that dark shroud of hopelessness hung over every man on the field. Even those who did not fight in that first confrontation, men who never laid eyes on the fortress of Ai, were overcome with despair. This battle must first be won here in Gilgal.

Joshua marched his troops to the shattered walls of Jericho. "Who toppled these walls?" he asked. "Not our power, but God's." He marched his army on a complete circuit of the ruins. He had every man touch the rubble. There, with firm-set jaw, he confessed his error in going up against Ai without express direction from God.

He marched his army to the Gilgal. "Look at these stones," Joshua commanded. "We did not cross the Jordan on rafts of our own making. We did not build a dam to stop the water. The Lord commanded our priests to carry the ark of the covenant into the flood. We trusted him. We obeyed. His mighty hand stopped the rushing river and our people crossed on dry ground."

Joshua proclaimed God's promise of victory. He explained the tactical plan. Little by little, he sensed it. A flicker of faith here, another there, until a thrill of hope raced from man to man like a flame through a dry field and every warrior stood to arms, knowing they would prevail—for the mouth of the Lord had spoken it.

"Now return to your tents to reassure your families. Meet me on the road to Ai when the sun drops to two degrees above the western hills. Commanders, form your divisions and units just above the Valley of Achor."

A half-round moon glimmered pale just above the eastern horizon as Joshua watched his army assemble. From the battalions under the lion banner to the rearguard under the eagle, they were a formidable host, thronging the road all the way back to camp. "Impressive, but strength does not lie in numbers," he said under his breath.

"What was that . . .?" Caleb asked, leaning in to hear better.

Joshua gave him a brotherly clap on the back. "Just reminding myself we don't trust in our visible forces, no matter how impressive."

Calling his four division commanders close and gesturing at the moon climbing the sky, Joshua gave final instructions. "We should reach the stone quarry long before the end of the second watch. This bright moon will set about that time. If we arrive before it sets, we will rest there to await the cloak of darkness. We must form our lines and ambushes around the fortress undetected both by Ai and her deadly ally."

Joshua raised his javelin to the sky. "March! Make haste while we have light to guide us. In the morning Ai will learn that *El Elohe Israel*—God, the mighty God of Israel—reigns supreme."

El Elohe Israel! The cheer resounded long and loud from his men.

El Elohe Israel! The echo rang back from the wives and children gathered at the base of the road.

His commanders were grinning. The army of Yahweh had found courage again—and their families had regained faith. "We march for the Lord and for Joshua," the divisions chanted as they began to move. "We march for the Lord and for Joshua."

Over the refrain of their warriors, the crowds answered. "May El Elohe Israel grant you victory."

"We march for the Lord and for Joshua."

"Then go with God. Go with El Elohe Israel."

Long after distance and the tramping of thousands of feet muffled the sweet sound, the chanted prayers of the wives and children rang in Joshua's memory . . . "Then go with God. Go with El Elohe Israel."

Othniel

The silver brilliance of the half-moon increased as twilight fire faded to deep purple and illuminated the craggy ravine leading to Ai. Othniel followed a long line of troops up the road. The same road as before.

Perhaps it should have felt the same. But the differences were astonishing. First, the numbers. Rather than the original three thousand, every man of every battalion, plus all the reserves in Israel, trekked up this road tonight. His own command reflected that difference. Rather than a squad of twenty, he led an entire section of six hundred.

Another notable difference lay in the strategic expectations. On the first march, Joshua hoped the king of Ai would negotiate. And if it came to battle, every soldier expected a new miracle similar to the collapse of Jericho's walls. This time, they had a very precise battle plan—precisely a God-given plan. Beyond that, Joshua brought the Canaanite, Jokshan of Jericho, into his coterie of advisors, adding invaluable geographical information to the reports of the spies. There was no guessing where to plant the ambushes or how to get there.

Othniel snorted. They were definitely not traveling the same road. They had learned two important lessons. *Never take Yahweh for granted. Never underestimate the enemy.*

Halfway up the mountain, close to the stone quarry where they spent the night before the first attack, they came upon a fork in the road. Not exactly a fork. In the muted light of the moon, the prong to the right seemed a mere wadi, a channel deep-cloven by the water rush of many rainy seasons. But for Jokshan, they would not have recognized this gully as a footpath the ambush detachments could take. Othniel was assigned to that ambush contingent under the direction of Uncle Caleb.

Accordingly, there was a halt and some minimal disorder as the first sections of the ambush detail broke from the main body. They pushed into the narrow trail toward Luz with Jokshan and his eldest son, Helek, accompanying Caleb as advisors. As he waited, Othniel watched the main body pass on, tramping up the track of their former defeat. He clearly remembered the road from this juncture upward—the way the road narrowed, sheer rock walls pressing in from either side, imprisoning them all. How could anyone forget the deadly canyon where Eliab, Zohar, and the others were killed? But Joshua's army followed him onward, upward without hesitation.

Leaving the main road behind, Caleb's regiments followed the new trail, swinging up into the highlands to the east of the ruin. The trek dragged on for hours, with no moon now to keep them from stumbling. Like the others, they traveled a narrow ravine with only a restricted view of the movement of the star patterns overhead to mark the passage of time. At last, they halted and divided the troops once more. Othniel hunkered down in the rocky gorge with the main ambush while Helek guided a smaller detachment closer to Luz. The primary ambush needed to be large for the shock value of large numbers swarming the field from behind; but the smaller contingent—led by a group of the finest Benjaminite slingers, also highly skilled with the sword—was no less formidable. Othniel reckoned they were well into the final watch of the night as the ambushes settled in to wait for dawn.

Joshua

Joshua led his forces boldly up the canyon road to the gates of Ai. When he emerged from the narrow draw in the darkness and saw the starlit field—broad, empty, and still bathed in darkness—he felt tears gather in his eyes. Few of his men even saw this battlefield on the first attack. He led his divisions across the grassy expanse and positioned them on the slope opposite the gates of the fortress. There they waited silent and watchful as he returned to the field, throwing himself down a bow shot away from the gates of Ai where he prayed until the first brightening of the eastern sky.

A chill breeze blew as he returned to his command position. The troops looked to him for a command, but he waited. One by one, the pale predawn light extinguished the stars. Still Joshua waited, increasingly aware of the restlessness in the ranks behind him. Phinehas caught his eyes, silently questioning whether it was time to blow the trumpet.

"Not yet," Joshua breathed. His reply, though softly spoken, seemed out of place in the predawn stillness. He did not verbalize the rest of his thought—*Daybreak will announce our presence soon enough.* He did not need to.

Within moments, the first dazzling beams of sunlight broke over the hills, igniting helmets, breastplates, and every bronze weapon with fiery light. The effect was magnificent beyond belief. *Warriors of the Holy One.* Oh yes! His army, standing silent and stern in perfect formation, drenched with the glory of the morning sun, would soon arrest the attention of someone in the guard tower.

And it did. Like the screech of an eagle, a cry rang out, followed by shouts of chaos and confusion. Trumpet blasts from every quadrant jangled conflicting alarms. As the tumultuous scrambling to arms continued, a smoke plume puffed into the sky, soon met with an answering signal from Luz. And then with a long rolling of drums, the sentries flung wide the heavy gates, and the warriors of Ai marched out to meet the army of Yahweh.

Phinehas stood poised and ready at Joshua's left hand, the trumpet of the Lord in his hands. Joshua waited, javelin upraised until the first lines of the enemy reached the middle of the field. Then in rapid succession, Joshua pointed his weapon toward the city, Phinehas blew a long blast on the trumpet followed by three short ones, and the forces of Israel hurtled down the slope to meet the enemy. Banners unfurled as they charged, and the ground shook with hundreds of heavily shod feet racing into the fray.

The enemy wavered, but Ai's war horns wailed a rallying cry. Hundreds of desperately-drawn arrows whistled into the air, and the enemy resumed their charge under the protection of that deadly barrage. War cries mingled in a deafening roar as the two armies met. Joshua pointed his javelin back toward the young priest standing alone on the hilltop holding the gleaming silver trumpet to his lips. *Let the ruse begin.*

The short, rapid trumpet blasts momentarily startled and confused the enemy, but his men knew the signal. A score of Israelite soldiers on the right flank foundered. They broke ranks and fled, slipping, stumbling down the hill in their haste to escape into the wilds between Ai and Gilgal. A squad of enemy soldiers noted the defectors and pursued. Meanwhile, in the heart of the field, where swords slashed desperately in hand-to-hand combat, more and more Israelites feigned panic.

With every breath, Joshua prayed for the success of Yahweh's outrageous plan. As more bands of deserters fled into the rough terrain beyond the battlefield, he howled loud commands for an orderly retreat much as he had during the first battle. He formed desperate new battle lines at the base of the hill, but even as the new lines were set, a third of those men followed their fleeing comrades away from the field. The ruse was executed so perfectly, he would have believed it himself had he not known the plan.

Othniel

Throughout the early morning hours, Othniel observed the battle from a craggy shelter, a well-concealed spot furnishing a clear view of both the field and the ravine leading toward Luz—an observation post Caleb never would have found were it not for Jokshan of Jericho.

"You learn many helpful things serving food and beer to travelers," Jokshan remarked. "They traverse every inch of these roads and talk about it in surprising detail."

Othniel was happy to act as lookout. He would far rather watch and give occasional reports to Caleb's messengers than remain tightly crowded in a gorge with men who did not value silence as he did. It was not yet midmorning and already the sun beat hot upon his back. Still this post was more to his liking than the shade of the gorge.

Joshua was a joy to watch. Commanding masterfully. Retreating. Regrouping.

Advancing. Retreating again. Looking up the rocky gorge toward the city of Luz, Othniel could see Benjaminite warriors, a brigade of swordsmen lying in wait, hidden from Luz by the bends and twists of the ravine. There was no trace of the famed slingers, but he knew they had settled into hiding while it was yet dark. They awaited their moment just as he did.

Suddenly, without warning, the wailing cry of a trumpet shivered the air. The gates of Luz flew open and with fierce battle cries its army thundered down the narrow draw toward Ai, charging like an enraged bull—straight into the ambush. The swordsmen of Benjamin unsheathed their swords at the sound of the enemy trumpet and held steady. They waited in their lines, coiled and ready, even when the foremost enemy division saw them and loosed a whistling rain of arrows. A few thudded against leather-covered shields, but most glanced off the walls of the rocky ravine, clattering harmlessly to the ground as the enemy continued the charge toward the roadblock of swordsmen.

Only ten paces separated the clash of outstretched swords when Benjaminite slingers exploded from behind every crag and crevice high along both sides of the narrow gully. The heavy hail of stones pounded the front lines and decimated the vanguard. The attack became a maelstrom of confusion. The entire army of Luz broke ranks. Scrambling, stumbling, crushing unsteady comrades underfoot, they fled to the safety of their city walls. But safety did not await them there. Only a single squad of Israelites stayed behind guarding the ravine while the remainder of the ambush stormed the gates of Luz before they could be barred against them. The city was lost before the morning breezes carried away the fading smoke signals between Ai and Luz.

Joshua

The field near Ai seethed with war cries and the clashing of swords. Joshua smiled inwardly each time he spotted quaking defectors making a show of slipping away. He nearly laughed aloud as entire squads of enemy swordsmen followed a single man or two. All at once, a huge, ghost-like figure leaped from the ramparts of the fortress.

His fiendish shriek blasted over the confusion. "Do not be deceived. Stay on the field or you will be defeated." With powerful leaps and bounds, he raced toward the wilderness, his blood-chilling words hanging over the battlefield.

The air reverberated with jeers, curses, and terrifying Canaanite war cries. Enemy warriors infused with fresh resolve ignored any more defectors and attacked with renewed fury, confident of impending victory. Joshua's blood turned to ice as he watched them ignore new defectors, redouble their efforts on the field, and press hard against his reduced forces.

"Stand strong, my boys," he howled. "Every man hold your place. We will prevail." In terror that the feigned panic could become real and his diminished army put to rout once more, he flailed his javelin wildly, capturing the attention of Phinehas at the top of the hill with the trumpet of the Lord. He signaled for a call to arms in the name of Yahweh. Every Israelite warrior knew that herald of hope. It was not a tactic, but a promise-claiming prayer.

> *O God of Israel, hear the sound of your holy trumpet,*
> *remember your promise, and rescue your covenant people.*[17]

At the sound, the pale phantom shrieked in rage, disappearing among the ridges north of the battlefield. Joshua pointed his javelin toward Phinehas a second time, prompting a second long prayer blast. At the sound, electrical energy suffused every nerve, heightening Joshua's understanding of the battle. Now retreating, now making a brief stand, he lured Ai's entire army farther and farther from the city while his fighters engaged the enemy with renewed tenacity and courage.

Othniel

Othniel understood that clarion call to arms very well. It was intended to infuse hope and courage in the Lord. *Whence then these cold fingers of fear clutching his throat?*

The answer came with an ear-splitting scream of rage and hate. Great pounding footsteps came from nowhere. Othniel turned in the direction of the sound and saw a huge pale form leaping boulders and bushes, long white hair streaming behind like a ghostly banner. With a great bound, the creature hurtled over the ravine and the hidden ambush battalions. He raced up the hilly backbone of the land toward Jebus and was gone. Othniel had no doubt this was the giant he had seen in his dream, the specter he glimpsed so briefly at the first battle on this field. With long, deep breaths, Othniel calmed every anxious thought, and by the time the trumpet of the Lord sounded a second time, he knew this battle was the Lord's.

The sun crawled toward zenith as Joshua's ably directed retreat, advance, retreat continued, but no more bands of Israelite soldiers fled the field. No new enemy squads pursued into the wilderness—and no more warriors were visible on the city wall. Othniel was convinced the king had emptied Ai of all reserves.

Just then, he heard the scuffling of another messenger from Caleb behind him. Without turning, he whispered, "Any moment now."

"Any what?"

Othniel recognized the voice without looking.

"Any moment, Zebulun. Our wait will be over."

He grinned as his friend clambered up, crouching close beside him in the rocky lookout. "Tell Caleb the ruse appears to be working perfectly. In response to our perceived cowardice, Ai's king has become more and more reckless. His forces are pretty much split in half."

Zebulun assessed the field with a dubious frown. "I see a lot more Canaanites on that field than Israelites."

Othniel acknowledged that truth with a quick lift of his brows. "But fully half his army is crashing through the wilds following our deserters. The city lies unprotected."

"I would love to see the king's face when our ambush hits the field instead of the support he expects from Luz." Zebulun's irrepressible grin reappeared. "I'll give Caleb your assessment," he said and turned to go.

"Wait! The signal!" Othniel shouted.

Both boys sucked in a gasping breath as Joshua's dramatic flourish froze into a commanding pose with his javelin pointing back to the fortress. The signal Othniel had been watching for. The signal Caleb had been waiting for.

Both boys scuttled down into the ravine as fast as possible. They shouted the news to Caleb with one voice. "The signal!"

Othniel tried to clarify. "The javelin—" he started to say. But Caleb already understood. His shofar was already on his lips. Three short blasts launched the attack and the long wait was over. Othniel's section of six companies swarmed over the lip of the ravine like hornets, leading the charge. The minute Joshua saw Othniel's men on the field, he reversed his uphill retreat. Caleb's ambush battalions slammed against the attackers from the rear while Joshua's men pressed back onto the field with full fury. Ai's army was trapped.

But Caleb also held an entire brigade in reserve to trap the Ai warriors who stumbled through the brushy wilds tracking the deserters. As Caleb's reserves, led by a regiment of Israel's best archers, poured over the eastern rim in pursuit of the pursuers, Caleb blew the signal for those soldiers who had feigned flight to turn back against the enemy. The pursuers in the wild would be encircled and exterminated.

On the field, Othniel parried and thrust, fighting hard against a desperate enemy. Between the ambush and Joshua's divisions, they were closing around the army of Ai like the talons of an eagle, but the enemy was not about to surrender. In the thick of the struggle, Othniel caught sight of Joshua's third ambush rushing up from the ravine into the city itself. Within minutes, the first flames rose from the rooftop of the temple of Baal. It couldn't be missed, the highest point of the city. A pennant of fire blazed around the bronze lightning bolt on the pinnacle.

Othniel pointed with his sword and howled, "Victory in the name of Yahweh."

His comrades looked and took up the jubilant shout. "Victory in the name of Yahweh."

The enemy looked back at their fortress, reading their fate in those flames. Eyes across the field reflected the fire and the fear as the smoke of destruction, foul and black, roiled into the air. Battle cries gagged in tightened throats. Arms fell limp with despair. The ordered ranks lost the will to fight and scattered in every direction. Royal banners fell from the hands of the king's attendants, and the monarch himself, correctly reading the smoky portent, leaped from his horse, his helmet-crown clattering to the ground. He scrambled into the melee and Othniel could not see where he went.

Joshua

Joshua glanced at the sky. The sun had reached twenty degrees past zenith and the battle was all but over. Helek of Jericho explained what he knew of the pale phantom seen fleeing the battle. "I have not actually seen him with my own eyes," Helek was saying, "but I instantly recognized King Libni from stories told at the inn. Rare sightings. Mostly at night."

The report confirmed Joshua's fears. The same fearsome giant, so demoralizing to his fellow spies more than forty years ago, made an appearance here today. Now the Anakim king had a name.

"I don't understand why Libni did not stay to aid King Birsha . . ." Helek squeezed his eyes closed as if to block an unwanted vision. "It occurred to me when I saw him," he said hesitantly, "that the gods of Canaan might have devised a ruse as clever as the one Yahweh gave you. What if Baal and Asherah gathered the Anakim under Libni's command, then lured the entire Israelite army away from the tabernacle and the ark where the giants could utterly destroy them?" He paused as if steeling his nerves. "I faced the fact that I might die here, but my commitment to your people did not waver. I may not have my sister's faith in Yahweh, but I want you to know, Joshua—for better or for worse, I have chosen sides. I could never fight on the side of the depraved Anakim."

Joshua nodded. No words were adequate to express his surprise and thankfulness at Helek's words. He took a deep breath and scanned the field.

A small delegation was scrambling up from the ravine north of the field. Benjaminite slingers. Part of the first ambush. They were dragging a single captive across the littered, but now quiet battlefield. Curiously, the man was clothed in a simple tunic. No weapon, no armor, nor any insignia identifying him as a soldier. The slingers forced the captive to his knees at Joshua's feet.

"Why have you brought this man to me?" he asked sternly "Where is your division commander?"

"The rest of our ambush entered the city of Luz hours ago," one man grumbled, "and the battle passed us by."

The faces of the others in the delegation were as full of complaint as their spokesman. "We had one brief moment of glory this morning when we showered the advancing army of Luz with stones," another added. "We drove them back to their city. But it was over in minutes, and when the swordsmen were commanded to pursue—"

Joshua cut off the mewling report with an abrupt question. "What mission was given you?"

"To continue guarding the road from Luz to Ai."

"A necessary and vital position," Joshua pronounced.

"Yes, sir, but we have been slinging stones against the rocks in boredom half the day, merely listening to the sounds of battle from afar. Then just moments ago, one of our men snared this lone fugitive hiding in the ravine. He rails like a madman, muttering that he is a great warrior-king despite his simple apparel. We could not tell if he meant of Luz or Ai. We rather suspect neither, but we thought we had best bring him to you."

Helek's eyes widened with surprise. With a brushing lift of his hand under the man's chin, he tipped the captive's face up. "Birsha!" he whispered.

The king spat at Joshua's feet.

"Do not be fooled by this man's plain tunic," Helek announced. "This is none other than Birsha, king of Ai." He grinned at the Benjaminites. "The biggest catch of the day fell into your net."

Slavering and mumbling madly, the captive cursed the name of Joshua and his God.

Joshua pushed the king flat with his foot, pinning the man's neck to the ground. "It was not Joshua who defeated you this day, but Yahweh—the God you hold in such contempt." He raised his blade and beheaded the king of Ai with the edge of the sword.

"You have done well, men of Benjamin. This was your captive. Take his body and hang it on a tree near the city gate."

Joshua commanded a large force to return to the city to salvage the livestock along with all usable items from homes and stables before the flames spread from the temple complex to the rest of the city. The remaining battalions dragged enemy casualties from the field and nearby gullies, heaping them high atop the slaughtered inhabitants from the city. The plunder was piled onto wagons, but all relics of Canaanite worship were tossed onto the pile of bodies to be burned. As the sun skimmed the hazy western ridges, Joshua removed the body of the king from the tree and laid it at the gates of his own flaming city. He took a large rock and heaved it onto the king's body and called on his officers to do the same.

As the mound of stones grew, Joshua cried out with a loud voice: "You raised your fist in defiance of Yahweh, O Birsha, king of Ai. We came only to request safe passage through this pass, but you heaped one last act of violence on your reign of terror. We now heap stones of judgment on the deeds of your kingdom. May all who pass this ruin remember that the God of heaven watches over the earth and calls all men to account for what they have done. He sees the evil perpetrated against his children and his long-suffering will not last forever."

Abihail

Abihail thrashed through fevered, dream-torn sleep. Every terror of her eighteen years rose in vivid images. And all the dreadful phantoms of the past whirled around a single vortex—the Valley of Achor. The scenes repeated in endless cycle, increasingly sharp and focused as the days passed.

A leering twelve-year-old Jamin stomped on her childhood joys with a bully's demonic laughter. He kicked those happy days into the depths of the valley. An accusing Acsah wagged a long index finger in her face, condemning her greed for keeping gifts given by the seductive women of Midian. Acsah flung their friendship into the pit along with the exquisitely crafted Midianite necklace and the veil of shimmering purple. In scenes darker yet, hundreds of inky black vipers emerged from the nooks and crevices of the rock pile at the bottom of the valley, slithering up over the ledge, creeping toward her with unblinking yellow eyes and flicking tongues. The serpents drove Abihail back into the deadly days that took her parents. Racing to the family tent where her father lay, writhing in pain as fiery venom coursed through his body, she sank again into the drenching, drowning anguish of his final hours. Before her eyes, her mother began to fade, a grieving wraith slipping into the pit where her father had disappeared along with the serpents. In desperate need of comfort, Abihail reached for Eliab's arms—only to be impaled by the arrow tip protruding from his chest. Joy, light, and life oozed from her soul, dripping in thick, red drops into the pit along with the love of her life.

The end of her dream was the end of everything, including hope itself. The Valley of Achor stretched and gulped like a living thing. Having taken her childhood, her parents, and her husband, it consumed Achor, his family, and all that belonged to them. It devoured her lovely, striped tent, followed by all the tents of Israel, all the people of every tribe, finally consuming even the tabernacle of Almighty Yahweh. All that remained was a wasteland beside a bulging, belching mountain of stones.

From the torment of her dreams, Abihail stirred occasionally to bleary moments of chills and burning fever, foul moments that smelled of blood and fetid waste, shrieking moments filled with cramping pangs of travail and moans of dull, dark despair. At times the familiar comfort of Acsah's voice called to her and cooling hands pulled her toward the light. But always the valley won, and she sank back into the whirlpool of phantom-haunted sleep.

The miserable blur of days and nights slipped into a week and nearly two.

As Abihail struggled toward health, the wounds of the camp began to heal. The people resumed the fifty-day countdown from Passover to Shavuot. This counting of the Omer, this looking forward to celebration, had begun so gloriously with the first cut sheaf of barley and the daily marches around Jericho. The crescendo of anticipation built day by day, peaking on the seventh day when the city fell at the shout of God's army. In highest national joy, the people began harvesting the ripened barley as the countdown continued. Then like the crumbling walls of Jericho, the national joy collapsed with the defeat at Ai on the sixteenth day of the Omer.

Learning of the treachery of Achan and his family added yet more anguish to the sharp grief of losing thirty-six warriors. If any fragments of joy remained, the broom of judgment swept them into the depths of the Valley of Achor. Even the subsequent victory at Ai could not restore the lost sense of glory—the triumph of the crossing and the fall of Jericho. But a formal period of mourning was not to be. The barley must be gathered in or lost, and nothing could postpone the impending wheat harvest. So, the people returned to the fields on the twenty-first day, bringing in the last of the barley.

As they counted the Omer with heavy hearts, the alchemy of God turned lead to gold. Silently, imperceptibly, the green wheat around the ruins of Jericho ripened to gleaming, waving seas of gold, and the warm touch of God gilded hearts of lead, transforming the grief-filled work of reaping into a joyful communal dance. Work songs, praise songs, and joyful shouts replaced tears and sighing. Processions of women in graceful cadence wove back and forth through waves of wheat, cutting and collecting the heavy heads in baskets. Straw-mowers worked in sturdier rhythms behind them, bobbing and bowing with long sweeping strokes, swinging their flint-edged wooden scythes, slashing the harvested stalks close to the ground. Gatherers scooped the cut straw into sheaves, hoisting the bundles onto their shoulders, carrying them to the wagons in lines that converged like rills into streams and the streams into rivers of joy.

Acsah

On the thirty-first day of the countdown, Acsah followed the crowds across the dry stubble of the harvested barley fields for the first time and found her place in that happy choreography, mind and body welcoming an escape from the shadows of Abihail's tent. Hogluh the youngest of the Midianite sisters followed close at her side. Though the child was but seven years old, she was industrious and quick to learn. Soon the two of them were hard at work, singing because they could not refrain from it, and Acsah's heart soared with the conviction that Israel was blessed above all nations on earth.

Even the refugees from Jericho proved a blessing to her manna-spoiled, naive people. Like many others, she had expected eternal spring in the land of milk and honey. Who from her generation would have known to gather the wheat stalks as fodder for the animals? What child of the desert would have known that spring grasses withered under the summer heat even here? Jokshan of Jericho instructed Joshua with unexpected wisdom regarding the seasons of Canaan and the preparations necessary for each one.

Acsah and the child labored hard all morning collecting the heads of ripened grain. Only when the sun was directly overhead did Acsah break rhythm, stop, stretch her back, and wipe away beads of perspiration. A gusty breeze rustled the leaves of the olive trees on the terrace above the fields, signaling its intent to move across the valley. Acsah lifted her hair off her neck to receive its cooling caress, thankful for another simple gift.

"See how much wheat we have!" Hogluh tugged on Acsah's sleeve, hopping and chirping like a little bird. "See how much!" She had been carrying the basket for hours, holding it up to catch the fat ears of wheat as they fell from Acsah's blade, but there was no trace of complaint in her voice.

Acsah felt such love for these girls. The childish joy they found in nearly every task around the home awakened the child within her. "We will finish at the end of this row and then go check on Abihail. That basket is surely getting heavy for your little arms."

"Not so very heavy. Helping with the harvest is fun." Hogluh's huge smile pushed her cheeks into round, red globes below sparkling black eyes.

"I better keep you moving." Acsah smothered a laugh as she tousled the child's glossy curls.

"Why?"

"Everyone is on the lookout for firstfruits. Someone may mistake those red cheeks for unseasonably early pomegranates and carry you off."

Hogluh giggled. "Well then, let's move." She ran to the next stand of uncut grain and held the basket up.

By the time they reached the end of the row, the basket was heaped to overflowing. "Not much waste to thresh out," Acsah said with satisfaction as she inspected the heads of wheat. "An excellent morning's work. Here, let me take it now." She reached for the basket.

"Oh, no," Hogluh insisted. "I carried this all morning. You are not taking it from me now." With a cheeky smile, she balanced the heavy load on her head and started up the road toward the threshing floor.

Acsah followed, twirling her sickle like a child and feeling guilty for the sense of freedom. She set her joy to Miriam's tune and began singing,

> *I will sing unto the Lord*
> *for He has blessed us gloriously.*
> *Praise him for this little Midianite girl.*

Hogluh looked back happily. The flicker of affection in her eyes warmed Acsah's heart. "Will we come back out to work again this afternoon?"

"This afternoon will be your sister's turn, but the harvest will continue for many more days. We will be back, you and I. Perhaps tomorrow if Abihail is doing well."

"Promise?"

"Absolutely promise!" Acsah replied with a last backward glance at the sunlit fields.

Just then a mower in a far field dropped his scythe, broke from the dance, and sprinted across the field toward her. "Acsah!" Salmon called. "Are you leaving already?"

The sweatband tied around his head was dark with perspiration, but his eyes glittered with excitement, a zest for life that drew them together when they were toddlers and bound them still as special friends. Salmon was like a brother, but weeks had passed since the last time they spoke. She missed those conversations.

"It has been a while," she said, drinking in the warmth of his smile. She had been isolated at Abihail's side far too long—but it was not over. "I sorely need some catch-up time with you, dear friend, but it will have to be later. I . . . we have been gone too long already . . ."

Salmon grinned at her as if he had not heard her words. "It is so good to see you out here in the harvest fields. Your first day, right?"

He stooped to address Hogluh eye to eye. "Very impressive load you are carrying there, young lady. Acsah is blessed to have such a hard worker by her side."

Hogluh looked away shyly, but a smile played at the corners of her mouth. "Acsah cuts fast. All I have to do is catch the grain."

Salmon straightened, a solemn look heralding the importance of his question. "Could we talk for a moment? I have a favor to ask of you."

She laughed at his serious demeanor. "I don't know. It sounds like a lengthy request. You need to ask quickly so I can go check on Abihail."

"Of course . . . check on Abihail . . ."

Without more hesitation, he stooped down again eye to eye with Hogluh. "Would you do that for me, Hogluh, so I can have a word with Acsah? Go see how Abihail is doing. Come back immediately if she needs Acsah."

Acsah yielded to Salmon's persistence. "That would be a big help to me, Hogluh. I promise I won't be long."

When the child nodded, the basket wobbled precariously on her head. Acsah reached out a hand to steady it. "Here. It's a long steep climb to the threshing floor after you have worked so hard all morning. I will take the basket up as soon as I find out what is so important to Salmon."

Hogluh backed away. "And miss the chance to show off our hard work?" She flashed another mischievous grin. "Not a chance. I will deliver the wheat and still be home long before you." She scampered off with the basket tottering wildly.

"Walk carefully, Hogluh, or there will be little of all our hard work left to show off."

Hogluh stopped, tossed a last sassy grin over one shoulder, and continued on her way at a slower pace.

Salmon grinned at the sweet interaction. "This is our inheritance. Reaping the blessings of the Promised Land."

Acsah suddenly felt guilty for all the happiness of the morning. "Our blessings, Salmon. But Abihail will awaken to dead dreams."

Acsah could see the shadow of her sorrow reflected in his face. "Is she better? I still cannot comprehend that Eliab is gone."

"The fever broke three days ago. Her sleep is deeper and more restful now. But . . . oh, Salmon . . ." Her voice broke with emotion. "She does not awaken."

Salmon's eyes urged her to continue.

"I—" Acsah closed her eyes and composed her thoughts. "I'm sorry. There is still a very real possibility I could lose my dearest friend. I know I have much to be grateful for, but that one unthinkable fact obliterates all other rational thinking."

"Well, I am thankful she has you. A true friend who will spare nothing to help restore her to health."

Through her tears, Acsah watched Hogluh literally bounce-stepping her way up the long path to the threshing floor, weaving in and out through slower-moving clusters of women. "These Midianite children are so much help. I would have had no opportunity to join the harvest were it not for them," she said

Salmon followed her eyes and broke into one of his lopsided smiles. "God has surprising ways of teaching us to be thankful."

"Well, I was certainly surprised when my father sent the girls to me at Abihail's tent."

"Why should that surprise you? They became quite attached to you once you gave them half a chance. Caleb knows that very well."

"Salmon, you know the only reason I felt comfortable leaving Abba alone was that Hodesh and Hogluh have become so capable."

"Trust your father's usual wisdom. Who needs their help more right now, you or him?"

"But he needs help."

"Not in the same way you need it." His voice took on an authoritative tone he did not normally use with her. "How would you accomplish *anything* without those girls? Would you leave Abihail alone in her tent while you fetch water, go off to gather wood, or tend to the animals? You cannot do everything yourself, Acsah."

She opened her mouth to respond when he added, "and Caleb seems to be doing quite well in your absence."

She wasn't sure if it was the thought that her father did not need her or the cavalier way Salmon said it, but the words stung. "He has more important things to do than prepare his own meals."

"Mmm. Maybe you don't know yet . . ." The hint of a juicy secret glinted in Salmon's eyes. "I have noticed Ephah and Maacah bustling about your father's tent this past week. It seems, he does not need to prepare his own meals. I would say you have been replaced."

Acsah gasped as if splashed with cold water. Salmon's teasing tone was inappropriate for such insinuations. "What are newly grieving widows doing prowling around my father's tent?" she cried when she finally found her voice.

Salmon cocked his head to one side and looked at her with exaggerated curiosity. "You don't want your father to have help?"

"Don't be ridiculous. Such behavior is simply unseemly. One would expect the wives of our fallen warriors to remain in seclusion in their own desolate tents at least until after Shavuot."

"Speaking of desolate tents," he said, adroitly changing the subject. "The favor I spoke of . . ."

She had to smile. Whenever conversations were racing toward a cliff, Salmon was quite skilled at diverting their course. She happily took the new path.

"Everyone is in awe of the tent you made for Eliab and Abihail." His eyes were wide and admiring. "If other families supplied the wool, would you weave another while you sit with Abihail?"

"Whoever for? I have not heard of any impending weddings."

"Not a wedding." He grinned. "As leader of our tribe, I want to erase all reminders of our recent *trouble*. People describe the gaping holes in the tent rows of Judah as missing teeth in the smile of a fair maiden, and I quite agree. How fitting it would be to fill the places of the unfaithful family of Achor . . ." He shifted his weight and bounced on his toes, obviously pleased with his idea. "With the faithful family from Jericho."

"The Canaanites?" she whispered.

"Not all of them. Rahab and Shua would take one tent space and the family of the elder brother Helek would take the other. The parents and younger brother are happy where they are. But honestly, all of them need better tents. For more than three weeks, they have been living in the rough lean-tos we first provided. No one in Jokshan's family has ever lived in a proper tent, much less constructed one. They don't even own livestock to slaughter for hides." Salmon flashed a huge enthusiastic smile. "The woven-wool tent you made for Abihail is the finest in camp."

"I . . ." Acsah choked on her answer.

Salmon laughed at her speechless response. "You look a bit overwhelmed. I don't mean those extravagant stripes. Just a nice tent, worthy of our benefactors." His forehead crinkled as his eyes took on a sweetly pleading look. "And I'm not asking you to make all their tents. Could you make just one more, teaching the family how to construct similar ones themselves?"

Acsah searched for the right words. His intentions were honorable, but incredibly misguided. She took a deep breath and began to reason with him calmly. "Only God knows how grateful all Israel is to Rahab for saving the lives of our spies. I cannot bear the thought that we might have lost you in that violent city, Salmon. And I must confess these Canaanites have taught us much valuable knowledge about harvesting. But Salmon, think about it."

She twisted a lock of her hair as she clinched her arguments. "After Baal-Peor there can be no question. It is neither safe nor sane to form connections with those who are not committed to the covenant. As Canaanites, Rahab and her family must camp with the mixed multitude as long as they choose to remain among us. Don't let your tender heart lead to a soft head."

Salmon leaned toward her confidentially. "Spend some time with her."

"But the law." Acsah pulled back sharply when he reached out, leaving his hand patting the air instead of her shoulder.

He met her eyes warmly. "I want you and Rahab to get to know each other. She loves our law and wants to learn more. She is attracted to our God and our people. Her grandmother is as devout as any mother in Israel."

"Salmon, you are the prince of Judah now. We expect good judgment from you."

"My dear Acsah, you are too hasty in yours." He sighed. "My heart tells me she will be a great blessing to our people."

Acsah's stomach twisted at this foolish counterargument. "Then get for yourself the ultimate blessing. Marry her if she is such a worthy woman."

Salmon's face blanched as if she had slapped him. She instantly regretted the wound she inflicted on his tender soul—but he was so wrong.

Acsah made every effort to speak the plain truth as gently as she could. "My dear, dear friend, you know I am right. Your silence declares it. You would not marry Rahab. She is a harlot, impossibly tarnished by the sin of that city. Your own heart tells you her one act of kindness does not redeem her past. She is not one of our people. She does not belong in Judah."

Salmon drew in his breath slowly, puffing it out through his lips. "Acsah, I can't remember a time when you were not a part of my life, my most beloved companion." His eyes reflected a deep soul sorrow much like the pain she had seen there after his father's murder. He focused on some point far off across the grain fields and his breath hitched.

"Although I have never spoken of it before, Acsah, I love you. Since I was old enough to dream of life in the Promised Land, my every dream has included you. I do not know which grieves me more—to hear you suggest I ask another woman to be my wife or to hear such harsh judgment come from the lips of the girl I admire above all others."

When he looked at her again, his dark, round eyes were bright with tears. "You have cruelly judged an alien whom God himself redeemed from Jericho. You always seemed to know my heart. And I thought I knew yours. It appears that neither is true in this case."

Acsah stared in disbelief as he walked away with heavy steps. *They truly had been of one heart and mind their entire lives. Why could he not see the truth about Rahab? And why was this argument suddenly the platform for a declaration of love?*

A huge gulf had just opened between them. A sharp twinge of pain and guilt urged her to run after him and repair the breach before it was too late, but how could the breach be repaired if he would not admit his error? How much more blood, smoke, and tears would these foreigners cause if allowed to infiltrate Israel permanently? This was a time for action not pity.

Before he had taken twenty paces back toward the field, Salmon stopped and turned around as if he could read her mind. "I'm sorry that we do not agree on this, Acsah. However, I *am* prince of Judah. I must do what I believe to be right."

Acsah did not acknowledge his last statement. She hurried back to camp deeply dismayed, but determined to do the right thing.

CHAPTER ELEVEN

THRESHING

Abihail

Abihail's eyes gradually came to focus on familiar stripes of red and white above her. As she lay enveloped in the warmth of her bed, she smiled at the glowing colors, symbols of the love surrounding her. A vague sense that she had endured a wrenching nightmare lurked in the back of her mind, but no details came to mind. "Eliab . . .?" she called, surprised by the weakness of her voice. "Eliab," she called again with more force.

Childish voices, muffled by the tent wall and the lingering fog of sleep, confused her. "You came just in time," one young voice whispered. "She is waking up."

"Stay here," the other answered. "I know where Acsah is. I'll get her." Light footsteps pattered away. Then all was quiet again.

"Hello?" Abihail waited, but no one answered. "Who is here at my tent?"

"It is Hodesh . . ." a child's voices answered hesitantly. "Caleb and Acsah's girl . . . Are you well now?"

"Yes, thank you," Abihail answered almost inaudibly. *What a curious visitor and what an even more curious question.* "How nice of you to come see me so early this morning. Do you know where my husband is?"

There was no answer.

She cleared her throat and called out a little louder. "Have you seen Eliab around this morning?"

"Morning is past, a lovely morning for recovery. It is nearly noon."

Recovery? Who is sick? Abihail tried to sit up, but her head pounded at the effort and her body resisted the sudden movement. *Apparently, I am the one who has been sick.* As she sank weakly back on the pillow, her mind raced. She gazed at the glad colors above her. The dark tent loaned by Achor in the first months of her marriage was gone. All the guilt-ridden memories of Baal-Peor and the plague had been carried out of her home along with it, but . . . here . . . now . . . something else . . . something even darker . . . lurked just out of reach.

Just then Acsah pushed through the door flap breathlessly. "Oh, my darling! I am so glad you have awakened." She knelt beside Abihail's bed with anxious eyes.

"Why are *you* here?" Abihail whispered, fighting back the growing fear. "Where is Eliab?"

Acsah reached for her hand, ignoring the last question. "You fainted and fell as you left the Valley of Achor."

The Valley of Judgment . . . The defeat at Ai . . . Suddenly, all the horrors lurking in the shadowy edges of her mind rushed back in terrifying clarity. She saw Eliab's wounded body. She saw the earth shoveled over him. She saw Achor's face, pallid and distraught as she tended him through the night. She saw the valley of stoning. The scenes were too vivid, and her mind fled before them. Her body shut down.

Acsah

"I am here, Abihail. I am here with you," Acsah repeated as she stroked her friend's hair, but there was no response. "Come back to me, dear sister," Acsah whispered. "You are not alone."

Without being asked, Hogluh ran for water. When the child returned, she set the water jug beside Acsah and began laying out clean, folded woolens. Acsah shook her head sadly. "It is not the same, sweet one. Wet woolen cloths will not help a broken heart. The body is better. Now she needs to find the courage and will to face her loss."

Hodesh brought barley flat bread, bean paste, and cheese for a simple lunch. With troubled faces, the children nibbled their food and watched Acsah.

She knew they interpreted her mood as concern for her friend. She *was* very concerned, but in truth her troubled thoughts returned again and again to her encounter with Salmon. *The ramifications of his decision could be deadly. Hadn't he noticed the way so many men, even married men, ogled Rahab's beauty? Hadn't he heard the indelicate comments about who and what she was? Always before she had taken her concerns to Abba, but if Salmon's intimations were true . . .*

She wasn't certain she could cope without her citadel of strength. She dropped her head in her hands. She simply could not eat.

"Acsah?" Hodesh asked hesitantly. "Abihail does not seem to be waking up after all. Can Hogluh stay with her while you and I go to the wheat fields this afternoon?"

The wheat fields? Acsah looked at her vaguely. *Could there really be a harvest when the promise of a future in this land was crumbling like the walls of Jericho?*

"Can't we go for just a short time? Hogluh can come for you if Abihail wakes up again. Oh pleeeeeeease. I can hear them singing when I go outside, and I really, really, reeeeeeeally want to go."

Acsah shook her head to clear her thoughts. Gently, she lifted Hodesh's face in her hands and looked into her eyes. "We *will* go, precious child, but not just now. I must deal with things more important than the harvest this afternoon. You both stay here. Help each other, and if you need me . . . Hodesh, the moment Abihail awakes again . . . come find me while your sister stays with Abihail."

Hogluh and Hodesh looked at each other. "Where?" they asked in unison.

"Look for me in camp Levi, the eastern end. I must talk to Eleazar."

Acsah was aware of Hodesh following her through the doorway. The child lingered just outside the tent, leaning wistfully toward the distant calls and songs from the wheat fields. Acsah blocked out the sounds of celebration, but she could not disregard the sad little face. "You will have your turn, Hodesh. Trust me."

Acsah's thoughts were spinning as she rounded the corner at the end of the tent row. The faces of the little ones swirled among images of rebellion in the Valley of Acacias. Stomach-turning visions of death and plague. *Please, Lord, I sometimes feel I am drowning in those memories. I could not endure such a thing again.*

She was entering the tents of Levi surrounding the tabernacle, the protective barrier of tents positioned between the other twelve tribes and their holy God. *If only I can find Eleazar. Or Phinehas . . . God's hero. Judah needs his passion for right and his razor-sharp discernment. Rahab may prove to be as dangerous as Cozbi—and Salmon as foolish as Zimri.* Intent on her mission, Acsah plunged boldly through the tent rows of the priests.

She had avoided this area for months because of Jonathan. She still cringed at the thought of the day he came to her and her father with a marriage proposal following the Midianite war. Her friendship with him would never be the same again. And now Salmon. The memory of the pain in Salmon's eyes stabbed her heart again like a dagger, and his profession of adoration twisted the blade. *How blessed were the uncomplicated relationships of childhood.*

She heaved a deep sigh. *I cannot return home if Abba chooses to take up with young widows. I will learn to be self-reliant. Be a friend to anyone who needs me. Live with Abihail in her tent, if she is willing.* She straightened her shoulders and stood tall. *Right now, I will dedicate myself to stopping Salmon's attempts to move Canaanites into the heart of Judah. The future of my people depends on loyalty to the covenant.* Conviction tingled from her toes to her scalp in powerful waves, giving her a strong sense of purpose—unwavering even when the very man she had been avoiding appeared in the path directly in front of her.

"Acsah . . ." Jonathan stammered. "So good to see you. I was just returning to the fields. The barley is in and we have begun wheat harvest." He stopped abruptly and blinked. "You already know that. I saw you working in the fields earlier today . . . but . . . why aren't you there now? Obviously, you are here . . ."

Acsah smothered a laugh and greeted him with a formal nod. "Shalom, Jonathan." A sharper, more chiseled nose and the leaner planes of a man's cheeks and forehead may have replaced the softer features of the boy she had grown up with, but he had not lost his tendency to babble when he was feeling insecure. "Shalom again," she said. "I think your confusion requires a double blessing of peace."

"That it does," he laughed. "Perhaps your double blessing will restore a bit of my dignity." Jonathan's perfect teeth flashed with brilliant whiteness in his short curly beard. "Why is it that self-confidence eludes me when you are around? Allow me to begin again."

With a stiffly formal bow, he asked, "How can I be of service to the fairest of all the daughters of Israel?"

Acsah rolled her eyes at his ridiculous attempt at dignity. She found it quite easy to keep her tone cool and business-like. "I was hoping to find your cousin. Do you know where he is?"

"Phinehas?" Jonathan's smile drooped.

"I must speak to him regarding the covenant."

Jonathan's cheery demeanor bounced back. His eyes sparkled as he crossed his arms over his chest, held his turbaned head high, and peered down at her with feigned gravity. "You just happen to stand before an expert in the law. Remember? Studying and teaching my grandfather's words is the focus of my life now. I told you that when we chanced to meet right after the crossing."

"The serious new Jonathan!" Acsah threw up her hands in mock surprise. "The concept clearly stunned me beyond remembrance. So . . . you, the boy who would rarely stick with anything, have continued in this study then?"

Jonathan's expression became serious. "Acsah, you do not know how I have changed. I lost the two most important people in my life in one week—one to rejection, one to death. I am not the same man . . . except in my devotion to you and to the memory of my grandfather."

Acsah closed her eyes and exhaled.

"I understand where our friendship stands," he added quickly. "I do not want to make you uncomfortable, but I would be more than honored to help you with any questions you have concerning the law."

Acsah hesitated, then guardedly began outlining her quarrel with Salmon, not allowing her eyes to meet Jonathan's at first, but relaxing her guard as she continued. When she looked fully into his eyes at last, she saw a mirror of her own heart. This wiser, more mature Jonathan understood the danger of Salmon's plan. He shared her passion for the covenant and the purity of Israel.

Jonathan

Jonathan listened, enthralled by Acsah's flashing green eyes and strong, warrior-like features. Out of the embers of dying love, the old stirrings of his heart flared anew with burning intensity. Was there any other woman in Israel so resplendent with life and strength? He would pour himself completely into her cause. He would win her respect and eventually, perhaps, her affections.

He chided himself. He had best begin by focusing on her words rather than her exquisite features and bold piercing eyes. "You are more right than you know," he whispered, his voice husky with emotion. He instinctively knew it might betray his heart and summoned his will to take charge.

Stepping back from her and squaring his shoulders, he donned his most Levitical look. "I understand why you did not return to the wheat fields. This danger touches on the very essence of Shavuot. We celebrate the fiftieth day after Passover in memory of Mount Sinai. The day Yahweh our God spoke the words of his law and our people cut covenant with him. We harvest wheat to ensure bread for our tables, but the law is the bread sustaining our souls. We must protect our covenant vows above all else."

Acsah's approving look emboldened him even more. "Remember how quickly the people abandoned Yahweh while still camped at Sinai. You are right to be alarmed. I will show you every teaching regarding Canaanites from my grandfather's scrolls. Come with me to a quiet place."

He did not miss the shadow of suspicion flickering across her beautiful features and quickly summoned his most disarming, boyish humor. "You hesitate?" he laughed. "The Acsah I knew as a child never backed down from a fight."

The crinkle in her brow betrayed her uncertainty. "I expected to turn the matter over to Phinehas."

"I mean this with all sincerity." Jonathan caught and held her eyes. "Your input is vital. The daughter of Caleb was born to be a warrior for God's covenant, but a warrior cannot fight without weapons. You must be armed with the truth. I can help you."

"I am fully occupied with the care of Abihail. I am a nurse, not a warrior . . ." Her voice trailed off uncertainly.

"So I have heard. Who is with her now?"

"Only the Midianite children. I dare not leave them alone for long."

"Go. Attend to Abihail and make certain the little ones know what to do while you take time to study. I will gather the scrolls. Our study will be brief. The law is on our side."

He turned to walk away and from the corner of his eye could see her step toward him.

"Where . . .?" she asked.

He pointed to a pale formation jutting up from the trees near the river. "See that rocky outcropping? Meet me there. It is visible from anywhere in Judah's camp. The little girls will have no trouble finding you, if necessary."

"Must we go so far?"

Jonathan winked. "That is my secret place for study. From the top of those rocks, I can see the promontory across the Jordan where Grandfather delivered his farewell speeches. He and I climbed to the bluffs above it where I helped him pen those words on parchment. His final scroll. And that mountaintop, of course, is where he died. Just seeing those craggy cliffs makes my grandfather's words come alive for me. I believe it will be the perfect place for the two of us together to find the exact counsel from those scrolls to build a shatterproof case. We *will* block Salmon."

"Block the Canaanites," Acsah clarified.

"Block Rahab . . ." Jonathan echoed her correction immediately and emphatically. "And her brother's family, of course, and the grandmother. The Canaanites Salmon plans to bring into Judah." As he said the name, his lifelong jealousy of her friendship with Salmon resurfaced. If he played this rift in their friendship carefully, perhaps he could sever it completely.

"The law above all," he said confidently.

"Inspiration rock . . . alright." Even as she agreed, Jonathan caught a slight negative shake of her head.

Inner conflict. If I do not move slowly, she will bolt.

Abihail

Abihail awoke again late in the afternoon. Eliab was gone. She knew that immediately, but the edge of her grief was a bit less sharp. She lay without moving, watching sun-glow and shadow move across the red-and-white striped ceiling. She strained to bring the hazy memory of Eliab's eyes into focus and replay the musical lilt of his laugh, but as she stirred her memories, the image of his empty death-stare flared up from the ashes. The burning image seared her heart anew before vanishing into blackness. Better dead ashes than such fiery pain.

"I will never forget you, Eliab," she whispered to the sense of his presence lingering all around. Her beautiful tent was desolate now, but it had been the home of love. She determined to be grateful for what she had. For far too many, love never comes at all.

She heard a rustling and muffled voices outside the tent. "Acsah, are you there?" she called feebly.

There were a few quick steps and the door flap swished softly. "I only just returned," Acsah answered breathlessly. "I was searching Moses' scrolls with Jonathan near the river and ran all the way back hoping you would be awake."

Studying with Jonathan? Acsah said the words as if it were a normal thing for her to do. "What is going on?" she asked cautiously. "What day is it?"

"What day is it, indeed!" Acsah's face bent over her grinning. "It is nearly fifth-day eve. More than two weeks since you fainted and fell. It is the thirty-first day of the Omer in the count toward Shavuot. It is about time you came back to us."

Acsah's hands were cool on Abihail's forehead as she continued with an unusual rush of words. "No fever. Good. Hungry? You have sipped only the smallest mouthfuls of broth . . . when I could rouse you at all. You must be famished. I have barley and leek soup—"

Acsah halted as the covering to the doorway swished open again. Hodesh held it back while her sister entered with a steaming cup.

"This is going to make you better, Abihail," Hogluh said sweetly. "We brewed it hours ago. After you woke up the first time."

"Caleb sent it," Hodesh explained.

"I like the smell," Hogluh chirped, pulling a deep breath into her lungs as she offered Abihail the cup. "It tingles my nose!"

Abihail shook her head in refusal. Her stomach recoiled at the sight of the strange, dark liquid. "What is it, Acsah?"

Taking the cup from the child's hand, Acsah frowned at the unfamiliar fragrance. "I don't know. My father has never spoken of such a concoction before. He gave some bundles of leaves to Hodesh while I was away from the tent."

"He got it from Shua," Hodesh added with enthusiasm.

Acsah felt queasy at the name, but she answered the blank look on her friend's face without criticism. "Shua. Rahab the harlot's grandmother. She claims to be a skilled Canaanite midwife."

Abihail smiled at the children. "So, you girls prepared this tea for me yourselves?"

"It was easy. Uncle Caleb gave us a basket filled with bundles of mixed herbs. He said to make it for you each day for seven days—drop one bundle into a small pot of boiling water, let the mixture steep until the fragrance is strong enough to smell without bending close to the pot, and then serve it hot—as much as you can drink."

Acsah sniffed the drink. "I suppose it will not hurt." She offered the cup to Abihail. "Taste it at least."

Taking the cup in both hands, Abihail held it close to her face. *If a midwife sent it . . . surely, I should try it for the sake of the life growing within me.* "Just breathing the minty fragrance clears my head. The heat feels good to my hands too."

Acsah lifted her eyebrows and smiled indulgently as if at a child. "I believe the instructions are to drink, not just hold the cup."

Abihail sipped tentatively and was surprised by the stimulating goodness. Honeyed mint blended with unfamiliar pungent herbs. "It is delicious," she said and quickly drained the cup. As she drank, she could see Acsah's attentive, almost-maternal expression out of the corner of her eye and relaxed into her friend's approval.

She wiped her mouth and handed the empty cup back to Acsah. "Familiar or not, delicious or not . . ." She said as she dropped her head back on her pillow, relaxed by the warmth of the tea inside her. "I will take whatever is good for my baby."

Acsah's smile gave way to a fleeting look of panic, and Abihail instinctively understood.

Her hands flew to her abdomen. "No-o-o-o-o-o!" she screamed. "No, God! Please, God, no!" But the truth lay undeniably soft . . . flat . . . empty . . . under her fingers. Squeezing her eyes closed to block the unthinkable, she turned her face toward the tent wall.

"I'm so . . . sorry." Acsah offered no more words, just gentle hands stroking Abihail's back as the sorrow flowed in silent, shaking sobs from the depths of her soul. At last, her breath came slow and even again. She had no idea how much time had passed. She felt drained. Empty. Aware only of Acsah close by the bed, not talking, just there.

"The dreams were true," she whispered. "The Valley of Achor swallowed my last hope. I am left desolate."

"My sweet sister," Acsah's voice broke. "Your tiny daughter never drew a breath— but, oh Abihail, we did not lose *you.* I was so worried . . ."

"Better I had died." Abihail's voice was barely audible. "Oh Acsah, what am I to do?"

Acsah sighed. There was no glib answer. "The seasons, the weeks, and months of life roll on. We do what we must as Yahweh gives us strength."

"But there is nothing left. My whole world is . . . gone."

"Then you must build a new one."

Acsah went to the doorway to retrieve their sandals. "The wheat harvest is on. Come, let us walk out that way. See how the work is progressing. The fresh air will do you good."

"If you don't mind . . . show me where you laid her."

Acsah didn't answer.

"I need to see." Abihail sat up and set her jaw firmly. "You can just tell me where. You don't have to go."

"She rests beside her father."

Acsah sat down beside her and the two women laced their sandals, sitting side by side.

It seemed a long walk. A long silence. Each woman engrossed in her own thoughts as they followed the path. Abihail was exhausted before they reached the shady hollow.

Though close to the road that led toward the Valley of Achor, the place was secluded and quiet. The songs and shouts of the harvest were muffled by an encircling grove of oaks. Even the crunch of sandals was silenced by luxuriant grasses, soft, thick, and green beneath their feet while the breeze whispered prayers of sacred awe in the leaf-canopy overhead. Long, golden fingers of late afternoon light reached through the rustling leaves to touch the mound of stones marking Eliab's grave. A much smaller cairn, wrapped in a blanket of shadows, snuggled close beside it.

Abihail clenched Acsah's hand fiercely. "I don't remember much about the day we brought Eliab here," she whispered.

Acsah could not find words to make the reality of those cold, hard graves softer.

After a while, Abihail relaxed her grip and murmured, "I wish I could have seen her. I always imagined a little Eliab." Her throat clamped down before she could say anything more. She collapsed on the grass beside her daughter's grave and wrapped her arms around the little heap of stones. "How could a life be so brief and yet so loved?"

"She would have looked very much like you. A perfect and beautiful little girl." Acsah dropped to her knees, embracing the girl who embraced the stones. "The memory of looking at that stillborn child still knifes through me. I prayed with all my heart and soul when you went into labor, but your waters broke foul and dark. We could not save her. That was the most difficult night of my entire life."

Abihail's fingers traced the shape of a stone. "So hard and cold. I still remember the feel of the little person growing and kicking inside of me. A new life created by my love for Eliab and his love for me." She laid her head on the stones. "I can't express how much I loved her."

"I loved her too. I held her up by her heels and slapped her little buttocks, but she didn't take a single breath. I rubbed her vigorously with salt, but life never stirred. She lay limp in my arms and grew cold. A little Abihail, beautiful and still. There was nothing I could do."

Abihail lifted her head to look at her friend's face. Acsah's eyes closed against the memory, but it leaked through her eyelashes in liquid grief. "Your arms held the daughter I will never hold," Abihail whispered, "and we both loved her." She could not cry, but Acsah's tears dripped onto her forehead and cheeks, tears enough for both women.

The sun set, its golden light replaced by glimmering silver moonlight and still they lingered, drawing healing from each other and from the sacred silence of the burial site.

Jonathan

Jonathan watched the smoke curling up from the great bronze altar behind Eleazar as he waited for his uncle to respond. His arm bumped the arm of the beautiful woman by his side and he felt stronger than ever before in his life. For the first time he was not intimidated by this uncle who became high priest. He was no longer a boy, but a Levite scholar. Before he went to bed the previous evening, Jonathan explained the matter to his older and always serious cousin— the *future* high priest. In an exhilarating reversal of their usual roles, Phinehas expressed amazement at Jonathan's clarity of thought. He promised to help Jonathan any way he could to prevent Judah from slipping into compromise. Phinehas' support was a thrill, but the triumph above all triumphs was Acsah's obvious growing respect for his knowledge of the law. Hope surged hotly through his veins.

Eleazar tilted his head to one side in his kind avuncular way, his warm brown eyes studying Jonathan's face with an expression of deep affection. "My son, you have taken up a weighty matter. I cannot tell you how pleased your grandfather would be to see how diligently you have studied his words."

Jonathan stole a sideways glance at Acsah, and they exchanged brief smiles.

Be humble; don't swagger, he reminded himself. Acsah is not impressed with displays of pride.

"There is nothing more important than the covenant," Eleazar went on. "However, this case is not mine to judge, at least at this point. This is the jurisdiction of Salmon and the elders of Judah."

"But sir," Acsah sputtered, "it is Salmon's thinking that needs to be corrected. He is making a terrible mistake."

"We have spoken to him," Jonathan interjected. "Still he does not see his error."

"We must be very careful that our use of the law does not cause injury. That is the purpose of our system of councils and judges. If you think Salmon has made an improper decision, you must call for the elders of Judah to hear your case."

"But . . ."

"God bless you in your zeal for the covenant, Jonathan." The beneficent smile never left Eleazar's lips. "Only when one has exhausted the system of judges and tribal elders should any case come to the high priest." Before Jonathan could frame another word, Eleazar strode across the courtyard, retrieved the urn of holy oil for the seven-branched lamp stand and disappeared into the holy sanctuary.

Acsah stared after Eleazar, no trace of emotion distorting the perfectly chiseled planes of her face. But for the fiery flashing of her eyes, she could have been a fierce-faced goddess, carved of stone. He had been in love with that look for as long as he could remember. No beginning—and no end.

"He is right," he said guardedly.

Surely Providence was working in his behalf. This setback with Eleazar could only work in his favor. Acsah would have to lean on him as advocate for her cause in the councils of Judah. For the first time in their lives, she *needed* him.

"Joshua is like an uncle to me," she whispered. "Let's go to him."

"You are wise to think of using your connections to our advantage, Acsah." Jonathan tried to capture her eyes. "But, my uncle is right. We must follow the law ourselves. This matter lies clearly within the jurisdiction of the council of Judah. Your father, rather than Joshua, is the one to convince before—."

Acsah looked at him questioningly. "Do you think Eleazar disagreed with us?"

"Not at all," Jonathan answered, calming the palpitations of his heart at that connection with her eyes. "If he felt we were wrong, he would have pointed out our error." He manufactured a confident, encouraging smile. "Our task is clear.

Our purpose sure. We must convince the council. What better place to begin than with your father?"

"I fear . . ." She hesitated.

Jonathan raised one eyebrow.

Confusion darkened the astonishing green of her eyes. "My father . . ."

"It is not like Acsah to fear anything."

Perhaps this was the appropriate time to speak of his wounded heart. "I should be the one afraid of your father, Acsah," he said gently. "Caleb rejected me when I requested your hand in marriage."

Acsah inhaled sharply. This was clearly not a turn she expected or desired in this conversation, but Jonathan plowed ahead. "What father in Israel leaves the choice of a husband in the hands of a headstrong daughter?" He laughed nervously. "But, you see, I am unafraid to . . ."

"I merely said 'I fear.' You did not let me finish." She brushed the air with her hand.

"All right then, what is it you fear? I will fight anyone or anything for you."

Acsah began pouring out her concerns regarding the budding friendships between her father and the widows, Ephah and Maacah. Jonathan was stunned. Her cutting words still echoed painfully in his mind. Her response to his proposal—*Only one man has my heart, and that is my father.* If Caleb were to marry again . . . Jonathan looked deep into her eyes as she described her devastation.

"I went back to the family tent to see for myself if the rumors were true, and there they were—those two widows who should be in mourning. My father laughed when he saw me." She growled an imitation of Caleb's crusty baritone voice. *"Well, my dear, you can see it takes two women to accomplish what you normally do each day."*

Jonathan's knees felt weak, and he shuffled to a wider, sturdier stance, shrewdly masking any evidence of his giddy heart. "I understand your concern," he said gently, "but perhaps the attention of these widows is pure charity." He fought the urge to pull her into his arms, to comfort her. His mind knew better.

"I know of no one with more wisdom and integrity than your father," he added thoughtfully. "His support is essential. He is the only one with more influence in the council of elders than Salmon himself." He countered her somber look with a grin and a wink. "And who has more influence with Caleb than you? That influence is not diminished just because a couple of widows are trying to be helpful." Jonathan held her eyes in an intimate look of pure devotion. "I am confident you will see your fears vaporize. Come. Your father is up at the threshing floor."

Jonathan led Acsah up the well-worn path ascending from the grain fields of Jericho to the ancient threshing floor of Atad. Buckthorn brambles edged the dusty road on either side, but the way before them was wide and clear, a perfect metaphor for his present good fortune. For the first time in his lifelong interactions with Acsah, he walked beside her in a position of strength. Paradoxically, in this position of strength, he felt as if he were floating over the ground. He reached for Acsah's elbow and gripped it solidly with his right hand. More to anchor himself than to steady her.

The road opened to an expansive work area teeming with men, women, and thick-muscled oxen. Work crews from each tribe had leveled and rolled the flat hilltop following the barley harvest, leaving the dirt hard-packed and even for the wheat threshing. This place had been the hub of grain processing for hundreds of spring harvests in Canaan. Perhaps Abraham himself had witnessed the activity here. Now for the first time, the sons of Abraham's sons' sons operated the threshing machines. The daughters of his daughters' daughters marched from the fields, balancing baskets of grain on their heads. They chatted and rested on the perimeter until someone cleared a section of floor for new grain.

Unmuzzled, the oxen strained at their task. Round and round, again and again, they circled the wide threshing floor, heavy hooves plodding over heaps of wheat while drivers rode behind on wooden sledges studded with bits of flint. Jonathan marveled at the cutting, crushing, and tearing of those flint teeth and the effectiveness of the trampling hooves working in harmony to separate the rough husks from the kernels.

Caleb darted in and out between passes of the threshing machines, calling out, "Good job. Steady there, son. Keep her moving." He gave hearty pats to the oxen and offered handfuls of grain, stooping in one area after another to inspect the progress of the threshing. As soon as he deemed a section of wheat finished, he signaled the sweepers to scurry in and sweep it onto the great pile at the center. And as soon as a section of the earth floor was cleared, the waiting clusters of harvesters emptied their baskets on the spot, then chattering and laughing, returned to the fields to fill the baskets again.

A warning lump grew inside Jonathan as solid and real as the wheat mound growing at the center of the floor. Was he correct in his interpretation of the law? Phinehas thought so after reviewing the facts of his case, but . . . there was no way his people would have known how to do this harvesting and threshing without the guidance of the refugees from Jericho. He hesitated for a moment. Then one look at Acsah renewed his resolve, and he laughed to lighten his own mood.

"Well, your father will not be difficult to find. My only question is, how do you stop him long enough to ask a question?"

"You may be too late, cousin." Phinehas was suddenly beside them. His look was not encouraging. "Ephah and Maacah began making goatskin tents for the refugees this morning."

Acsah's eyes opened wide at the names. "Ephah and Maacah?"

Jonathan enjoyed a surge of hope as Acsah squirmed. *Thank you for that, Caleb or Salmon—whoever enlisted their help.* "Not a problem," he said dismissively. "Their kindness will not be wasted. The tents they make will serve just as well in the area designated for foreigners outside of camp."

"It would have been better if you had talked to Caleb yesterday, Jonathan."

"Acsah and I took the time we needed to build a solid line of reasoning. Our arguments are invincible. Enough to ensure Caleb's help in our cause and convince the council of elders."

"A council has not yet been called."

"It will be once we speak with Caleb."

"My father appears to be quite busy," Acsah mumbled. "Perhaps this should wait."

"No better time than now," Phinehas answered curtly. "Your father is long overdue a period of rest. I will find someone to replace him." He stopped with a half turn after only a few steps. "Jonathan, go to the water jars and bring back a cooling drink for him."

Jonathan obeyed the command without hesitation, leaving Acsah waiting alone.

Acsah

Acsah closed her eyes and took in several deep strengthening breaths as she waited. And that was all it took for Phinehas to return with her father in tow.

"So. The little ones have freed you up enough to come watch the threshing?" Caleb kissed her forehead and nuzzled her cheek affectionately with his beard. "It is a wondrous process I have not witnessed since my days in Egypt."

Acsah melted into his embrace, feeling like a small child again. "I miss you, Abba."

"Have I been neglecting you?" He patted her back and cackled, "If it isn't war, it is gathering in the harvest. We must work harder now if we don't wish to starve for lack of manna. What did we expect of the Land of Promise?"

"Water for the busy father?"

"Jonathan." Caleb's brows arched in surprise.

Acsah flinched and pulled away from her father's embrace. She hadn't heard Jonathan return. She sent up a wordless prayer as Jonathan offered the water cup to her father. How she longed for simpler days when she just poured out her concerns and trusted her father's wisdom.

"We have not seen much of you in the past few months," her father was saying.

"Busy in my own world," Jonathan said with a bold, flashing smile. "But nothing like this impressive operation. A hard worker like yourself deserves refreshment." He called attention to the cup again with a quick lifting motion.

"I don't know about deserving it, but I certainly will enjoy it. Most kind of you." Caleb regarded Jonathan steadily out of the corners of his eyes as he drained the cup and returned it with a smack of appreciation. "You have grown up since I saw you last."

"Taller? Or more helpful?" Jonathan's good humor was engaging.

Caleb laughed. "A bit of both, I believe. If your growth in wisdom has kept pace with your increase in stature and the comeliness of your appearance, the tribe of Levi is greatly blessed to call you her son."

Acsah stared at her father, wondering at the purpose of such unusual encouragement. *Use this as an opening for your arguments, Jonathan.*

Jonathan's face was blank, but Phinehas nudged him with his elbow as well as his words. "My cousin studies and teaches the law every day."

"In pursuit of wisdom," Jonathan responded proudly. "Like my grandfather. There is nothing I desire more in the world,"

"May God grant you the desire of your heart," Caleb said, and then turned to Acsah, touching her back lightly. "I saw you and Hogluh briefly in the field yesterday, but you left early. How is our sick one?"

Acsah loved the way her father's gray eyes narrowed with concern. "She is fully awake at last and understands the extent of her loss."

"Is she drinking tea from the herbs I sent?"

"Yes . . ." Acsah answered hesitantly. "The little ones press it on her every hour. Perhaps it has helped. She gets up, but she is quite weak. She insists on helping around the tent, working a few minutes and then resting. It is all I can do to keep from taking tasks right out of her hands."

"I hope you don't. That work strengthens her and helps her feel useful."

Acsah laughed, "Yes, but it is hard to watch. It is a good time for me to be away."

Caleb's eyes widened as they did when he was suddenly stuck with a happy idea. "I'll tell you what," he said. "Go join the harvest again with one of the girls. Work on through to suppertime. No need to cook tonight. I will bring enough stew for all of us. Ephah and Maacah continue to take pity on me. They ply me with food enough for three men every day." He winked. "I think it helps them deal with their grief even more than it helps a father who misses his daughter."

The disturbing mental pictures of the widows crashed into this precious time with her father like a rock slide, but she forced a smile. "Hodesh would enjoy that, and I would be delighted to spend the evening with you."

"Until then." Caleb kissed both of her cheeks again. He nodded to Jonathan and Phinehas. "I should get back to the threshing now."

Phinehas nudged Jonathan again.

"Actually, sir," Jonathan called brightly to Caleb's retreating figure. "We had hoped to get your opinion on a pressing matter of law."

Caleb spun back around, his eyes wide—Acsah suspected mock surprise. "I thought you were the expert on the law."

Jonathan smiled confidently. "I study daily to increase my knowledge, sir, but it takes years of experience to gain true wisdom."

"Well, what is it?"

"What is . . . true wisdom?"

Caleb laughed. "What is your question?"

"Um, can we go somewhere more conducive to a serious discussion?"

"Actually, no. Not unless you wish to wait until evening, but then . . ." He turned abruptly to Acsah. "Does this concern you, my dear? I promised to spend the evening with you."

Phinehas broke in, "We have heard, sir, that Salmon wishes to move some of the Canaanite refugees into the camp of Judah. The law does not allow it, and we need your authority to help us stop it. Jonathan has searched the scrolls and is prepared to present his case before the council of Judah and—"

"The law is meant to guide and protect us." Caleb's eyes blazed, and he held up a hand to silence the young priest. "Never to exclude good. Never to prevent godly love and kindness. I have lived long enough to know my God and his law. Do you understand how much his loving heart must have grieved over the destruction of Jericho? They were all his children. He redeemed the few whose hearts turned toward him."

Acsah knew that look of godly anger. She also knew that her father's wisdom and devotion to Yahweh were above reproach. Her certainty in the righteousness of her cause began to crumble. She was not so stubborn as to cling to an opinion proved wrong. "I would like to discuss this more, Abba. Perhaps as we dine together this evening."

Phinehas opened his mouth as if he would reply and then thought better of it, but Jonathan was undeterred. He motioned with his eyes toward the scrolls in his hands. "But, sir, would you allow me to show you the clear teachings in my grandfather's words?"

"Take your arguments to Salmon. Urge him to assemble the council of elders. I have work to do." Caleb wheeled and plunged back into the middle of the threshing.

As Jonathan sputtered his frustration, Acsah watched her father approach one of the grain sweepers and take his broom. She loved that about her father. He never sought the positions of honor—although they often came to him. She watched while the sweeper sauntered off toward the water jugs and Caleb dodged between the oxen and disappeared.

Acsah gently splashed water over fresh-picked figs. *Figs. How often had Abba spoken of them, and yet, she had never been able to imagine the soft, purple fruit he described. Smooth, tender skin bursting between your teeth. A succulent center delicately textured with tiny seeds. More satisfying than . . . manna. Sweeter than . . . well, manna.* Abba could only compare his description of this strange fruit to food she had known in the wilderness—which was, of course, only the many forms of manna.

After the defeat of Sihon and Og east of the Jordan, her people discovered thousands of bushels of dried figs and jugs of sweet fig wine in the food stores of the defeated Amorites, but Caleb assured her that those items could not compare with figs picked sun-warm and ripe from a tree. This very morning, Abihail and Hodesh had discovered the first ripe figs of the season, and Acsah could hardly wait to present this special gift to Abba. He often said that missing forty fruit seasons was the only major punishment of the Wanderings.

Her jaw tightened at the thought of the forty-year detour from the Promised Land. The lesson was clear, was it not? Trust God. Believe and obey him. *How could she make Salmon understand that?* Prince Nashon died in the aftermath of Baal-Peor because the men of Israel could not think straight around the beautiful faces of Midianite women. Even after the tragic loss of his father, Salmon was allowing a beautiful foreign woman to muddle his thinking.

Acsah checked herself, recognizing the downward spiral of her thoughts from her father's love of figs to Salmon's stupidity. *Who do I talk to, Lord, about this but you? Speak to me. You not only spoke to Abraham and Isaac, but to Sarah and Rebecca as well.*

And Hagar too.

Acsah paused and looked up. *Where had that thought come from?* Ragged cloud-shreds high in the western sky suddenly brightened with colors cast back by the dying sun.

With all due respect, El Elohe Israel—speak clearly. What do you want? Your ways are strange to me, but I desperately need your guidance. I can handle one task at a time, but everything is happening at once. My first duty is to Abihail, but there is the harvest with the little ones begging to be part of it. How can I find time to help Salmon pursue the right path? And then . . . what of my father and these widows?

Cradling a delicate purple globe in her hands as she patted it dry, Acsah's face softened at the memory of Hodesh, bright-eyed with excitement, proudly holding up the basket of figs she had gathered with Abihail. The little ones had proved to be an incomparable blessing. One time after another, when recent difficulties threatened to crush her sense of wonder, the bubbling joy of those two children helped her laugh again.

I did not choose them, God. You gave them to me by the hand of my father—against my will. But you proved me wrong. These children did not destroy the peace and joy of our home as I expected. But the widows . . . Acsah shivered.

Voices and footsteps announced her father's arrival. Ephah and Maacah walked side by side close behind Caleb carrying steaming containers of food—and trampling on Acsah's restoring time of prayer. *They will change everything.*

She concentrated on arranging the platter of fruit, keeping her head bent over her work until she could conjure up the necessary hospitality—or at least the proper face. *O Sovereign of the Universe, this is too much for me. How can I confront my father whom I have loved and admired all my life? How do I, a child and a woman, question his lack of judgment?*

"Shalom. Shalom. We are here as promised, Acsah. Your daily bread—and stew—has arrived." Caleb's hearty laugh accompanied his greeting. "Where is my Abihail?"

Acsah slipped to her feet, attempting to hide the heaping platter of figs on the mat behind her. She forced a smile as she received her father's kiss, but the burst of chatter surrounding her was as annoying as morning crows.

"What wonderful construction!" Maacah's head turned from side to side, birdlike, her eyes darting over the red-and-white striped fabric.

"Your daughter is a gifted craftswoman," Ephah crooned after examining Abihail's tent from pinnacle to ground stakes.

"Truly spoken, Ephah. Beautiful from afar, this tent is beyond fabulous when viewed up close."

"Our decision to minister to dear Caleb . . ." Macaah caught the old man's eyes and Acsah felt nauseous at her father's fond smile in return.

"When we discovered he had no help . . ." Ephah interjected.

"That decision returned to us as the greater blessing," Macaah finished her companion's thought.

Both women bobbed their heads like birds in their enthusiasm.

Abba, Abba, what are you thinking? Even if these women had already completed the traditional year of mourning, they are more suitable to be my sisters than my mothers. Maacah must be close to the age of my older brothers. But Ephah is my age. A young woman obviously great with child.

The entire group turned at a rustling of the tent door. Abihail emerged, eyes sparkling and face aglow with the first full-dimpled smile Acsah had seen since Eliab died. She should have rejoiced at this signal of returning health, but she found herself irritated that Abihail's joy came in response to this particular visit.

"Welcome, Caleb. Welcome, friends." Abihail kissed Caleb and warmly embraced each of his companions.

In contrast, Acsah had barely managed a cordial nod when the women arrived. Grateful for Abihail's enthusiastic greeting in contrast to her own uncharitable thoughts, she gestured toward the door. She could at least invite them in. "Won't you come inside?"

"Oh Abihail," Ephah cried out, "your dwelling is the most beautiful in all of Israel."

"I have a gifted and generous friend."

Acsah blushed. "And I have a friend worthy of better gifts than I can give." She turned to her father again. "We have been waiting expectantly."

Abihail giggled. "Our eating mat is spread and waiting for you—but empty of food." She watched Maacah place her steaming cauldron of stew in the center of the mat. "This is not the normal way of hospitality. But thank you for your generous provisions."

"We are delighted to be a help," the widows crooned in unison as they settled down on the far side of the mat beside Hogluh and Hodesh.

"What is left in life for us but to help others?" Maacah opined as she removed the lid from her stewpot.

Acsah dropped to a cushion beside her father, feeling as if she was watching the scene from another room.

Ephah uncovered a basket heaping with flat rounds of barley bread, smiling pleasantly as she engaged the little ones sitting beside her. "So, you are the precious jewels Caleb rescued. We have heard so much about you."

"Indeed, we have," Maacah said. "Such lovely help was surely never before found in a snake pit."

"Actually, a temple of serpent worship," Caleb corrected. His comment was lost in the shower of pleasantries from the two widows and the children's piping responses, but he beamed a fatherly smile over the room. His household had always been a noisy bunch, and Acsah knew he reveled in the big family gatherings. He threw one arm around Acsah and the other around Abihail. "My daughters," he said, lowering his voice confidentially. "I have missed you both." He regarded Abihail for a moment. "Abihail, my dear, you are a delight to these old eyes tonight. The blush of health has returned to your cheeks and the sight of it brings tears of joy."

Abihail's face lit up, and she aimed an enormous smile toward Acsah. "I am in the hands of a skilled healer who just happens to be my dearest friend."

The room was suddenly quiet as the focus turned on Acsah.

"Truly a friend," Acsah mumbled modestly, "but hardly a skilled healer." She reached for the figs as a distraction and offered the platter to her father. "Something special for you, Abba."

Caleb took the plate and waved it before his nose, inhaling deeply. "Ah, the fragrance of fresh figs. One of the few delights of my boyhood in Egypt." He selected a fat one and held it up. "See how it splits with goodness. I call that a perfect fig. Where did you find ripe ones so early, Acsah?"

She waved a hand, brushing away any credit for the find. "Abihail and Hodesh picked them while I worked in the wheat fields with Hogluh. This is wholly their contribution to our supper. I merely washed them and arranged them on this platter."

Dimples flashing, Abihail leaned out around Caleb to look at her full in the face. "The sunlight beckoned and, thanks to Acsah and her healing arts, my strength had returned enough to follow."

Caleb touched the top of Acsah's head in blessing. "Your mother did well to name you 'Ornament' before she died, my daughter . . . a beautiful blessing to the family."

Acsah looked down at her feet tucked close beside her. The Egyptian anklet her mother had given her along with her name gleamed in silver and turquoise beauty on her ankle. A voice within her whispered that her attitude toward the widows had been neither beautiful nor a blessing. She took a small bowl of stew from Maacah's outstretched hand with an intentionally gracious nod. "The stew smells delicious as does the bread, Ephah. Thank you both for bringing this meal. The fellowship tonight is precious to me."

Caleb

The room quieted to the soft slurping and clattering sounds of happy eating, and Caleb quickly reached the bottom of his second bowl of stew. "I don't know why it took me so long to think of doing this," he muttered contentedly. "I eat as much as I can, but every evening these dear women have much leftover food to give away or throw out." He sent his gratitude to Ephah and Maacah as a broad smile. "And thank you, Abihail, for sharing your home . . ." He noticed the bright sheen of tears in her eyes and knew the pain of loss all too well. Often the loneliness was keenest in happy gatherings like this. He paused to wipe away a tear of his own. "It must seem to you that life is over. Never doubt, my dear. Never doubt. Yahweh yet reigns and continues his faithfulness to his covenant people."

Abihail nodded slowly. "I do believe that," she whispered.

Caleb searched her face. "Did Acsah tell you *how* our Lord was at work for us during your time of delirium? How Israel finally triumphed over Ai?"

"Ai?" Abihail looked at Acsah questioningly.

Acsah shrugged helplessly. "Other things seemed more important, Father."

"Abihail, my child, you must learn the story. Ai is at last truly a ruin and nothing more. The way is clear for us to travel to Shechem for the ceremony of blessings and curses."

"The ceremony? When will that happen? I hope I will be strong enough for the journey."

"Ah, that you will. We must finish the wheat harvest first. Then the timing of the ceremony will coincide perfectly with Shavuot. Our little ones can tell you exactly how many days remain in the countdown any time you want to know." He grinned at Hogluh and Hodesh. "How many stones have you laid out?"

The girls glanced at each other. "Thirty-three!" they called out in perfect unison.

"So, the exact time remaining until our journey is easy to calculate. Forty-nine total days to the end of the seven weeks, take away six for the journey and preparations at Shechem leaves forty-three as the day we set out. There you have it, Abihail. We are on day thirty-three. Ten more days until we depart this valley. Ephah, would you pass me some more of that good bread?"

"Will we be traveling up the same road where Eliab was killed? How could the army face it again?"

Caleb barely heard Abihail's question as he took another fragrant round of flatbread and tore off a corner with his teeth. "Yes. That is the the best route to Shechem." His response was muffled with bread, but he could not wait to answer. He swallowed hastily so the explanation would be clear. "On our own, it would have been impossible to face. But as soon as the breach in the covenant was repaired, Yahweh himself gave Joshua the plan of attack and assured him of victory."

Ephah leaned forward toward Abihail with an understanding smile. "My brother said he could not have marched up that road again except that Joshua took the whole army to Jericho and then to the Gilgal to physically touch the proof of Yahweh's power in those solid stones. It took that to renew his hope."

"Hope rising from the ruins," Abihail whispered.

Caleb looked down at his hands, clenching his fists as he remembered. "The first attack, when Eliab was killed, was repulsed because the Lord was not with us. The city of Luz detected our ascent. They sent up a signal and came to the aid of Ai. This time, the Lord's clear instructions foiled that support system."

Abihail looked at Caleb with an expression of profound sorrow. "Why did we not ask the Lord for his plan the first time?"

"We learned that lesson in the hardest way possible. We simply cannot make our plans and expect God to rescue us. We must wait until we discover *his* plan—then join him in it."

Abihail dipped a chunk of bread in the stew broth. "If only Eliab had lived to see God's faithfulness. I can hardly bear the thought of him taking an arrow in the back while fleeing in terror."

"My dear girl!" Caleb looked at her sharply. "Eliab died a hero, not fleeing the disaster. Didn't anyone tell you?"

"Obviously not, Caleb," Macaah said softly. "You must tell the story."

Caleb stared into the past and felt the horror of that day once more.

"We were too late to gain the high ground. By the time we reached the mouth of the canyon road, Ai's forces were already pouring from their gates. My division was supposedly the vanguard. Van, yes. Guard, no. Before we had fought our way more than fifty feet onto the battlefield, Joshua gave the command to withdraw. Even then, we barely managed to fight our way back to the protection of the canyon. Salmon's company lost one man in the melee on the battlefield, and we came close to losing Othniel's entire squad, including Eliab.

"Those boys, the last to exit the battlefield, became the frontline protection for the retreat. Even though they had been trapped and nearly slaughtered on the battlefield, they never flinched when the van that was never 'vanguard' of an attack became the rearguard of retreat. Those brave boys held back the enemy at the mouth of the ravine long enough to allow the others to fall back, but the retreat was too slow. The division of Dan still pressed upward, not knowing the need to retreat. They clogged the road, stalling all movement. Soon the men at the top began to panic because they could not retreat.

"At that point, archers appeared on the rim above the roadway and our trapped men were caught in a storm of arrows. As soon as the first warriors fell, general panic ensued. Men cowered beneath their shields. Others pushed and shoved, attempting to flee with no regard for their comrades. But not Eliab. That foul dart pierced him square in the back as he laid aside his own shield to tend to a fallen comrade. Abihail, my child, your husband died bravely ministering to Zohar in the midst of terror and panic."

Abihail stared distantly, silently into the story for a time, and no one intruded into her silence. "Noble in life," she whispered after a while. "More noble yet in death . . ."

Acsah

Abihail's words, nearly inaudible, struck with a force rendering everyone speechless. Acsah set her bowl down on the mat. It was impossible to eat with the lump blocking her throat. In her concern for Abihail's recovery, it had not even occurred to her to be sure Abihail heard of Eliab's heroism.

Maacah scraped the ladle in the nearly empty stew pot. "Can anyone finish this?"

Hodesh held up her bowl for more. As Maacah filled it, she caught Caleb's eyes again. "Tell of the second battle," she coaxed.

Acsah felt a warm flush of gratitude for Maacah's encouragement. She needed to hear that story again herself. Perhaps with a need greater than Abihail's.

"The dark shadow of Canaan descended over Gilgal after our defeat at Ai. With every look toward the western hills, the warriors who fled that battle felt anew the talons of fear. A dark sense of hopelessness paralyzed our entire camp, even those who never saw the fortress of Ai. Men and women alike wondered how long we could survive in this land if we could not conquer the smallest walled city."

Acsah's head rested on her father's shoulder, the energy of Caleb's storytelling voice radiating through her as the tale proceeded from despair to victory. God was faithful. Israel was safe for the time being, but the story ended with a dark scene of judgment. The poetic drone of her father's voice, comforting and beautiful as it was, could not brighten the full import of Joshua's words.

You raised your fist in defiance of Yahweh, O Birsha, king of Ai.
We heap these stones of judgment against your rule of violence.
May all who pass this ruin remember that the God of heaven
and earth sees the evil perpetrated on this earth and will call all
men to account for what they have done.

So much judgment. So much blood. So much smoke rising from cleansing fires. Israel barely had a toehold in the Land of Promise, yet every turning of the moon seemed to bring another scene of violence, blood, and smoke—the kingdoms of Sihon and Og, the unfaithful elders of Baal-Peor, the Midianites, Jericho, Achan's family, and now the fortress of Ai. How long would such scenes of death and destruction continue?

Acsah longed for time alone with her father. She tried to catch his eyes, but Ephah broke the silence and directed the conversation.

"We women maintained a constant vigil here at home." She smiled shyly at Caleb. "We never ceased pleading for safety and victory until all our soldiers returned home."

"We remembered the power of Moses' uplifted hands during the battle against the Amalekites," Maacah added. "It was thrilling to stand near the gates of the tabernacle and watch as one or another of the priests—sometimes Eleazar, sometimes Ithamar or one of their sons—stood before the smoking bronze altar with hands uplifted in prayer. We all prayed for our army to trust wholly in Yahweh and not in themselves."

"The children prayed too," Hodesh and Hogluh added, with a glance at Acsah for confirmation. "We prayed, didn't we, Acsah?"

She nodded as her father chuckled and tossed a wink to the children.

"Every prayer played its part in our victory," he said, stretching to his feet abruptly. "I am heartily thankful to all of you for this meal." He gave an unfocused nod to all around the circle. "Nothing would please me more than to remain in your delightful company. However, the council of Judah meets this evening and I must go." The tent flap closed behind him, muffling his last words.

Acsah sighed. More unsettling than the blood, smoke, and fire was the ache of separation from her father as their responsibilities took them in opposite directions.

CHAPTER TWELVE

WINNOWING

Caleb

Caleb took a seat directly opposite Salmon. The handsome and charming young prince of Judah was close to an exact replica of his father, Nashon. The same engaging smile, the same contagious laugh, the same intrinsic goodness—but he was no older than Acsah. Caleb studied the clan leaders of Judah one by one as they entered the circle of firelight. The entire council of elders had changed considerably over the past year. Not one remained who had served with him in the Wanderings. Few of these young men had any memory of Egyptian bondage and the Exodus. Hardly *elders* at all. *These boys played their childish games with my sons, studied Torah with them, learned to read and write, and practiced the arts of war, growing to manhood together in the discipline of the wilderness.* Caleb suddenly felt very old.

Salmon's call for silence had the authority to still the drone of male voices. Then he hesitated. "Caleb . . . I would be honored if you would preside over this council tonight. The question before us requires far more wisdom than I have accrued in my few years."

Caleb coughed. "I suspect you are feeling as young at this moment as I feel old." Their eyes locked. "My time has passed, Salmon. You are prince of Judah. This issue regards *your* future and that of your contemporaries.

"Do not deprive us of your wisdom."

"Have no fear of that. I will listen. I will speak. But I will not vote."

A mixed murmur rose from the group. Some in consternation. Some in concurrence.

"My brothers," Salmon began as the circle quieted down again. "We are finding life in the Promised Land much different than we expected, but each difficulty is really a challenge necessary for our growth and understanding. The Valley of Achor taught us how serious the consequences of our choices can be. Ai taught us that victory follows faithfulness."

Caleb noted the quaver in the young man's voice and nodded encouragingly.

Salmon cleared his throat and sat tall. "The question before us tonight is how to understand the covenant law as it relates to Rahab and her family. As you know, I invited her and her grandmother, and her brother's family to fill the empty places left by the judgment on Achan. Although they are Canaanites, these refugees are fast becoming valuable members of our community. Helek has thrown his energies into teaching our people how to farm this land. Rahab and Shua serve as midwives for the women of Judah, bringing with them considerable knowledge of the healing herbs of this land. They trust in Yahweh. They value our law and are committed to the covenant. Inviting these redeemed ones to live among us seemed to me the right thing to do.

"There are those who disagree with me and believe the writings of Moses support a different conclusion. Jonathan is here to present that opposing argument tonight. Listen to him. The council will discuss the matter after he speaks and decide once and for all what is good and right." He nodded to the young Levite waiting in the shadows.

Jonathan bounded into the circle of firelight gripping a set of parchment scrolls. "Thank you, Salmon. I am honored to present the truths contained in my grandfather's writings."

He laid the smaller scroll on the ground at his feet and nodded respectfully, first to Caleb and then to Salmon as he began unrolling the larger one. "Listen. Listen carefully to the words of the law. There is no question which path is right for our people. The prince of the tribe of Judah had honorable intentions. I am confident of that, but he is wrong. I am equally confident you will do the right thing once you understand the clear teaching of the law. No Canaanites should ever be allowed to live in the midst of our covenant-keeping people."

Jonathan was beginning with the same animation as when he told a fireside story, white teeth gleaming in a broad smile, cheeks flushed, eyes glittering with excitement. The demeanor struck Caleb as odd. It seemed his enthusiasm was out of keeping with the consequential effects of the pending decision. *Was it the Levitical role that so stirred him or was there something else?*

"Salmon, help me hold the book," Jonathan called. "See that I read accurately."

Salmon stood immediately and took the open scroll in both hands, watching Jonathan trace the words with his right forefinger as he read.

"When the Lord brings you into this land and drives out the Canaanite nations before you and you have defeated them totally, you must make no treaty with them and show them no mercy."[18]

Jonathan raised his eyes abruptly from the scroll, scanning the faces circling the fire, his smile incongruous with the words "no mercy."

"We conquered the city of Jericho, and due to peculiar circumstances and the mercy of our God, Yahweh preserved one family out of that depraved people. It is his prerogative to show mercy to whomever he wishes, not ours. The writings clearly state we are to show *no* mercy to the inhabitants of Canaan, yet Salmon proposes bringing this family into the heart of the camp of Judah. He intends to show more mercy than Yahweh himself showed the Egyptians who followed our people out of Egypt and live on the margins of our camp to this day. We are explicitly commanded not to make a treaty with any Canaanites, let alone ask them to live in the midst of us. Is not such intimacy with this family even more dangerous than a treaty?"

Jonathan paced back and forth, eyes flashing. He caught the gaze of one man and then another, his words picking up speed and intensity as he read passage after passage from the scroll. He retrieved the Levitical scroll at his feet and read more, the confident smile never wavering.

"In summary, God never intended that we welcome Canaanites into our camp, and he never intended for them to worship at his holy tabernacle. Egyptians and Edomites are not to enter the assembly of Yahweh until the third generation. [19] Ammonites and Moabites cannot enter until after the tenth generation because of their part in the sin of Baal-Peor. What shall we say then of Canaanites who have filled up their cup of iniquity? Search the writings for yourselves. We have no direct counsel regarding a family such as Rahab's because God never intended for Canaanites to be joined to our people."

Noises of agreement rumbled around the circle of elders. Salmon let his breath out slowly. All color blanched from his face. "The words are clearly penned on parchment," he said in almost a whisper. "Does anyone have anything to add?" His large, sensitive eyes scanned the council as if pleading for a counterargument. The fire crackled, and a cluster of sparks ascended with the smoke, but no one spoke.

"Nothing is more important than the holy law," Jonathan added, lifting both scrolls high. His voice was cool and controlled as he continued. "Consider just one of

God's express commands. *You are not to intermarry with them.*[20] Can you tell me this will not happen if a beautiful woman like Rahab moves into our camp—even though all know of her history as the harlot of Jericho? The temptation would be great, and the consequences greater still. Our success or failure in the Land of Promise hangs in the balance. Choose righteousness. Choose life."

Jonathan fixed his gaze on Salmon. "The counsel written by Moses is clear. If you defile the land, it will vomit you out as it vomited out the nations that were before you.[21] Now do the right thing." He flashed his disarming smile once more and rolled up the scroll with dramatic finality before taking his seat.

Caleb poked the fire with a long stick, sending up a shower of sparks.

"The law seems clear," Salmon conceded, swallowing hard. "Perhaps a vote is not necessary. Rahab and her family did not seem Canaanite to me in their hearts, but the words Jonathan read to us are clear enough." His voice was barely audible above the snapping and popping of the fire. "I can see that I made my decision based on compassion rather than my understanding of the law."

"Misguided compassion," Jonathan added with a self-assured smile.

Caleb studied the faces of the elders. A few shot troubled looks at one another. A few scowled fiercely at Salmon. Most stared at nothing at all, faces fixed and flat. He stood slowly. "On the other hand . . ."

He trapped Jonathan's eyes as he began, his words so soft that the men around the circle had to bend toward him. "One of the curses of disobedience is that the alien among you will rise higher and higher while you become less. God obviously expected aliens to live among us. Who would those aliens be if not Canaanite?"

Jonathan looked at the old man with surprise. "Perhaps hundreds of years from now, some remnant of Canaanites might join Israel if they have forsaken their worship of idols in that time. But not now. Can we ever forget the passion of my grandfather's final speeches? Blasting curses will fall on those who follow after the ways of Canaan, and glorious blessings will fall on those remaining true to the covenant."

"Jonathan, did you not bring your grandfather's fourth book with you tonight?"

"The fourth?"

"*The Book of the Wilderness Wanderings.*"[22]

"No. I did not think any of its stories pertained to this question."

"The book is made up of story *and* law, is it not?"

"Yes."

"Why?"

Jonathan raised his chin confidently. "Because the stories enhance the laws."

Caleb nodded. "And the law helps us understand the stories."

"Yes."

"Tell me, Jonathan, what teaching lies at the heart of the *Book of the Wanderings*?"

"Laws regarding future offerings. Offerings we are to bring once we are established in the Land of Promise."

"Who are those laws for? My generation or yours?"

"For those of us who actually will live in the Promised Land."

"Laws concerning the first offerings your generation will bring the Lord from their own crops. What else?"

"Laws regarding purification from inadvertent sin and instructions about wearing these tassels of blue to remind us to be true to the law." Jonathan brushed the fringed hem of his tunic as he spoke.

"And?"

"Laws regarding defiant, high-handed sins. There is no purification for the man who raises his fist in rebellion against God. He shall be cut off from our people. Is this not the importance of my arguments here tonight? We dare not rebel against the clear commands regarding Canaanites—no treaty, no mercy."

"Your knowledge is impressive, Jonathan. Tell me, what stories precede and follow this section of law?"

"These laws lie between two of the worst cases of rebellion against the Lord. The story preceding this section of law tells of the rebellion at Kadesh-Barnea when our fathers listened to the reports of giants and great walled cities and refused to enter Canaan. Directly after it is the story of Korah, Dathan, and Abiram when they rebelled against the leadership of Moses and Aaron and the earth swallowed them."

"Why did Moses place this passage of law for your generation right here between the worst rebellions of *my* generation?"

"These laws highlight the special sacrifices of thanksgiving my generation, the descendants of the rebels, are to bring when we settle the Promised Land. Our parents didn't have to wonder if their rebellion exceeded God's mercy. They would spend forty years wandering in the wilderness and die there. But these laws assured them their children would receive the promise. The passage in its entirety tells us there is mercy for human failure. Yahweh God will be faithful to his promises, but there is a point of rebellion for the individual, or in this case a complete generation, from which there is no turning back." He gave Salmon a pointed look and finished with a sanctimonious smile.

"Well said, my son. I could not be more pleased with your knowledge and understanding. Your grandfather would be proud. One last question. These laws regarding sacrifices of thanksgiving, rituals for purification, and warning about rebellion, to whom do they apply?"

Jonathan hesitated.

"What is written, my son?"

Jonathan's frame sagged ever so slightly, and the smile vanished. "These laws and regulations apply to Israelites and to the alien living among us."

"'You *and* the alien living among you.' Those are the exact words," Caleb lifted his voice to be certain everyone around the circle heard.

"Our God holds the alien in tender regard—as he does the widow, the orphan, and any poor among us. There are statutes requiring the alien to participate in Passover and the other mandated feasts. There are statutes providing support for aliens as well as widows and orphans, ensuring they will not sink into oppressive poverty. We are commanded to share the bounty of our harvest festivals with aliens who do not have a land inheritance. Our judges are admonished to hear cases concerning aliens with the same impartiality afforded to cases between Israelite parties. We must look at the entire intent of the law. Do we make treaties with the enemies of God? Certainly not. But do we show the same kind of mercy we have received to those who choose to respect Yahweh and obey his covenant requirements? Absolutely."

Jonathan hung his head.

"My son, continue studying your grandfather's writings. They *are* the words of Yahweh and they *are* the words of life. But the sum of wisdom contained in them is vast. We must be certain that we do not isolate and exploit one teaching for our own gain or according to our limited interpretation. Our God is merciful beyond comprehension, but he judges violence against the powerless with severity. It is the defiant and rebellious who cut themselves off from his mercy and have no place among our people."

No one around the circle moved or spoke as Jonathan slipped away from the fire-lit council and disappeared into the darkness.

Abihail

Afternoon shadows lengthened over carpets of stubble. The waving oceans of grain around Jericho were gone. Scythes and sickles were stored away. The oxen were at rest after weeks of plodding round and round the threshing floor, dragging the heavy threshing machines. It was time to winnow the threshed wheat.

The women of Rahab's family were eager to teach the women of Israel how it was done in the Jordan valley. Jerusha and Naarah taught them how to weave palm fronds into winnowing fans. Rahab and Keziah taught them how to make flat-edged basket scoops. Shua explained how the warm air covering the sun-kissed plateaus and ridges of Canaan cooled quickly with the lowering sun and rushed downslope into the Jordan Valley. These breezes were perfect for separating wheat from chaff. Armed with knowledge as new as their winnowing fans, an army of women attacked the mountains of grain on the threshing floor of Atad, tossing a glistening storm into the late afternoon sun above Gilgal.

Abihail stopped to wipe away an eye-stinging trickle of sweat. She was getting stronger by the day, but not yet able to keep up with Acsah. She watched her friend rhythmically bending and stretching, flinging one scoop of grain after another high into the air, forehead jeweled with beads of perspiration, cheeks flushed by the red blood of vigorous labor.

Beauty and bounty. The beauty of the low-slung beams of sunlight blazing through the shower of wheat husks, transforming itching particles to glittering gold as the wind carried them away. The bounty pattering to the ground in a hail of heavy kernels—pattering now on a nearly empty threshing floor. The heap of crushed and trampled wheat in the center had disappeared along with the rest of the winnowers.

"What do you think, Acsah?" She swept her arm in a wide arc to indicate the few thin patches of wheat straw still remaining on the packed earth. "I say the job is finished. We are the last group still winnowing."

She stole a sideways glance to see the reaction of Acsah's Midianite shadows, but the girls continued scooting about the floor, chasing the remnants of threshed wheat with their basket scoops and didn't seem to hear. "Hodesh! Hogluh! Stop. If you girls shovel up any more, we will be tossing dirt not grain."

Hodesh looked around, surprised. It had been the children's job to scoop up the grain with their small flat-edged baskets and load the winnowing fans, filling one fan after another as quickly as Acsah and Abihail emptied them. The child watched carefully as the contents of her final scoop trickled onto the winnowing fan. She scrunched her nose at Abihail. "There was hardly any dirt," she said.

"Can I try tossing this last fan?" Hogluh asked. Her pleading eyes turned from Abihail to Acsah and back.

"Of course," Abihail replied without hesitation. "You helped make this fan. You should have a chance to try it out." She held the handle out toward Hogluh's outstretched hands. "It will be easier to manage since it is not a full load."

Acsah watched the child struggling to manage the unwieldy fan. "Why don't both of you girls lift together? Here Hodesh. Put your hands here . . . and here between Hogluh's. Now, when Abi says *toss,* lift it as fast and high as you can."

At Abihail's signal the grain flew into the air, accompanied by gleeful shrieks at the hail of wheat kernels falling onto their heads from a shimmering cloud of chaff.

"Impressive toss, girls," Abihail exclaimed. "The handle is too long and the frame large and unwieldy for small hands, but you caught that breeze."

Acsah laughed as she took the fan from the girls. "By harvest time next year, Abihail and I will be filling the fans for *you.*" She held the semi-oval tool in front of her face, peering through the tiny openings in the loosely-woven mesh. "We have a problem here, Abihail," she said with mock seriousness. "Look at those dusty little faces and that straw-sprinkled hair. How do we separate girl from chaff? Shall we toss *them* in the air before we leave this hilltop?"

Hodesh shook her hair and brushed at her face with her hands, but Hogluh just giggled, "I wish you were not teasing. That would be fun."

Acsah laid the tool down beside the other, appraising it thoughtfully. "These fans winnowed faster and better than I thought they would."

Abihail looked at her from the corners of her eyes. "You have to admit that Israel's debt to the Jericho refugees is steadily mounting."

"They could never repay what they owe us for saving *them* from destruction."

"Acsah! We don't measure good deeds on a balance. Even if we did, saving that family only balanced the scale for rescuing our spies." Abihail wagged her finger in front of her friend's face. "Admit it. I am right. Those foreigners have been and continue to be a blessing."

"I hate not being right." Acsah threw up her hands in helpless resignation. "Let's gather the last of our wheat and get it into the storage silos before the men cover them for the night."

"And there you are," Abihail grinned. "Another example of good Jericho counsel." In mock imitation of Jokshan's deep voice, she added, "Alert. The wildlife in the Jordan valley are well aware of the harvest process. Store your grain immediately or mice and birds will contaminate it or eat it all up."

Hodesh and Hogluh chattered happily as they heaped the baskets with finished grain, never ceasing their childish prattle as they helped lug the grain baskets and tools down the path to the storage wells.

"When we were still Midianites, we kept our grain in clay jars in our house," Hodesh said.

"What did you do in the wilderness, Abihail? You couldn't pack big clay jars all around."

"They didn't have grain, silly. Remember, all they ate for forty years was manna, right Abihail?"

"Mmm-mm," Abihail answered, only half listening. It didn't matter what the children said. Their happy voices warmed her heart with the joy of childhood, belonging, and family.

They tagged onto the very end of the line waiting to empty their baskets. In ancient times a row of pits had been bored deeply into the solid stone on the rocky shoulder of the hill, just below the threshing floor. These strong underground silos had held the grain produced in this valley since long before the time of Abraham.

Now the great-great grandchildren of Abraham were using them. But would they have known to look for them were it not for the Canaanite family from Jericho?

A thought Abihail hardly dared think, let alone express aloud, suddenly distilled into a concrete question. *I wonder if Rahab and her grandmother would teach me the skills of midwifery?* She suppressed the thought immediately. Acsah would not tolerate such a thing. She treasured her friend too much to make a change that might jeopardize their friendship.

She set the scoops and winnowing fans down. "No point in holding these," she said. Acsah continued balancing her basket on her head, apparently deep in thought, but the girls set theirs down. "It is going to be a long wait," Hogluh said looking at the long line of winnowers ahead of them carrying baskets heaped high with wheat for the silos. "We never had this much wheat in our whole village."

"That's because we lived in the desert. We didn't grow it. We had to trade for it."

As the girls chattered, Abihail wondered at Acsah's silence. *Most likely still brooding over her father arguing in favor of Rahab moving into Judah. Acsah is rarely wrong, but on this, I agree with her father.* Without warning, Hogluh lobbed a question directly into her musings.

"Abihail, why were you crying after Igal spoke to you this morning. Whatever did he say?"

A tiny, startled sound, like that of a wounded animal, escaped Abihail's lips before she could think how to respond.

"What?" Acsah turned so suddenly, she had to reach up and stabilize the basket on her head. "Where was *I?*"

Abihail could not answer. It was an innocent question asked by a child, but it hit her like a deadly stone hurled into a city by an enemy war machine. She was physically stronger each day, but her emotions had not made that same steady improvement. One moment, she was happily settled in a sisterly existence with Acsah and the little ones. The next, she was drowning again in unspeakable despair. That hopeless despondency wasn't logical, but it was real.

She was grateful when Acsah took charge.

"This *is* going to be a long wait, girls," Acsah said brightly. "Why don't you both go on back to the tent. Can you manage the tools? Abihail and I will bring the empty baskets after we store the wheat. Fix a little supper for all of us, but don't wait. Go ahead and eat."

The girls did not have to be told twice. Their words drifted back as they scrambled down the hillside toward camp, long fan handles wobbling up and down awkwardly as they ran. "You shouldn't be asking grownups what makes them cry."

"I didn't mean to make her sad again. I just saw her and wondered."

"But you have to think before you say things."

Abihail shivered. In one instant, the void of pain and loss stole the joy from this beautiful day. She could hardly blame the child. Nor could she blame well-intentioned Igal. Logic could no more control this smothering darkness than it could control the cycles of night and day.

By the time Acsah poured their grain into the silo, Abihail was chilled through. But rather than returning to camp, Acsah nudged her in the opposite direction. They followed a path from the storage pits to the top of the rocky ridge and settled themselves on a broad natural bench. Drawing her knees up to her chest and wrapping her arms tightly around them, Abihail listened to the fading sounds of laughter and banter as the last of the winnowers returned to their tents. Acsah neither spoke nor demanded answers. They sat side by side in soothing silence watching the shadows stretch across the valley and grow together until the warm green-gold of the valley was swallowed by gray.

"Shall we go back down? Or do you want to talk?" Acsah asked at last.

Abihail struggled to answer, but a sucking emptiness stole her words before she could say them.

"Igal is such a clumsy bear," Acsah observed casually. "Clumsy with words too."

Acsah gave her the perfect prompt, but . . . her reaction did not make sense. Igal had simply approached her as she went to fetch water for the day. He was concerned about her, he said. Soon—no one knew how soon—the camp would disband, and families would claim their inheritances all over the hills and valleys of Canaan. He could not bear to think of her, a widow, left destitute with no family, no inheritance. As a friend of her husband's, he felt moved to offer her the protecting hem of his garment, to take her as his wife and care for her.

Igal read the shock in her face and was very sweet about it. "I know I could never replace Eliab," he said, "but I would be honored to spend the rest of my life as your second choice, if you would have me." He did not press for an answer, just asked her to think about it.

Abihail managed to hold back her tears until he turned his back. On one hand, she *was* terrified at the prospect of a lifetime of bleak widowhood. On the other hand, she was completely repulsed by the thought of any other man as her husband. Since childhood, she had dreamed of a beautiful home and gardens in the land of milk and honey, pastures filled with flocks and herds, rooms filled with laughing children. But what did any of it mean to her if those children were not Eliab's? If those beautiful days did not end with nights in the arms of the only man she could ever love.

When she shuddered again, Acsah wrapped her arms around her. "I've known you since childhood. I probably know you better than anyone in Israel now that Eliab is gone." She gave Abihail an affectionate squeeze. "You are my sister. I will love you forever."

"I'll love you . . . forever." Abihail repeated in a whisper. "Eliab and I used to tell each other that."

Constellations of stars brightened the darkening sky while constellations of cook fires lit the camp below. It was beautiful, but different from the camp of her childhood when the pillar of fire hovered over the tabernacle. For forty years, that light illuminated the camp of Israel night after night. It was gone now, but everyone knew the light of God's presence still flamed in the heart of the sanctuary.

Eliab had been her guiding light, but now her pillar of fire was gone—and there was no light in the inner sanctuary of her soul. "I used to think loving each other forever was our destiny. That it was reality."

"It was. As real as human love could be."

"It was real, but not eternal. *Forever* is an illusion, a cruel hoax. There is no forever for humanity. The love shared, the little pleasures given and taken, the bonds deepened through pain faced and overcome together—everything we nurtured and created as a couple since we were children is gone. Even the child of our love. There is nothing left."

Acsah's arms warmed her body. Sisterly affection surrounded her like a blanket. But what could ever warm a heart chilled by death?

"Trust the Eternal One, my sweet sister," Acsah spoke the words into her hair, whispering so close the thought seemed her own. "Yahweh speaks hope and truth even into the dark night of death. Your love is strong evidence that the world, all we see and know around us, is the illusion—that Love is the ultimate reality. God only gives good gifts. If he gives us something so beautiful, so strong, so huge that it cries out to go on eternally, there must be an eternity designed to house it."

Pallu

Pallu stood apart from the crowds, staring into the clouds reflected on the great pool of Gibeon. The still waters kept his thoughts unruffled by the jangling clamor of the forum filling behind him. This would be a vociferous gathering. The heads of virtually every household in Beeroth, Gibeon, Kephirah and Kiriath-Baal, the four cities of the Federation, would be here today—and every one of those men would have an opinion. A gusting breeze ruffled the serene reflection of the sky, shattering it to a watery blur. He took a deep breath and released it as a prayer to the gods. *May it not be so with the clarity of my thought today.*

A glance at the senate floor confirmed that the scouts, Peleth and Irad, had arrived. Their report would launch today's session. In a few quick strides, Pallu crossed the packed pavement, passing wordlessly through knots of senators arguing their views. He bounded onto the dais to take his seat with the Four. Likhi and Meshullam were deep in conversation, heads together, voices low. The white-haired Ibzan stared blankly at the hubbub on the floor. He seemed to awaken as the final member of the Four took his place. Recognizing Pallu with a nod and a grim smile, Ibzan pushed himself up from his high-backed stone chair and called for the senators to find their places.

Ibzan was not highest of the high elders merely because he was the eldest in years, nor because his bearing exuded such regal dignity. The power of his leadership lay in his humility. Everyone knew he would listen and consider the views of the least member of the senate. That spirit of diplomacy would be of inestimable value today.

"Great changes are coming to Canaan whether we like it or not," Ibzan began as the clamor settled down. "The kingdoms south of us have formed an alliance under the banner of Adoni-Zedek. Their only objective is the complete annihilation of the invaders. Even more disconcerting, they are in league with the Anakim. Your elders met with them not long after the battle of Jericho. We urged them to join with us in seeking a covenant of peace with Israel, but the southern alliance would have none of it.

"We cannot remain neutral, my esteemed fellow citizens. But our decisions must issue from a unified body guided by sound, rational thinking. Peleth and Irad have been observing Israel over the past several weeks. They are here to arm us with facts as we consider the wisest path. My good scouts, tell us what you have seen and heard. After we hear the report, every viewpoint, every voice will be heard. Only then will we vote on a plan of action."

The two young scouts immediately sprang to their feet. "Ai is now a ruin beyond restoration. Luz is destroyed. And Jericho is reduced to the haunt of vultures," Peleth announced dramatically. "The Federation alone stands watch over the passes protecting central Canaan."

"We know all this," someone shouted. "We want to know what the invaders will do next."

Peleth's mouth twitched.

"We were coming to that, my friend," Irad replied calmly. "In two days, the Children of Jacob will leave the Jordan valley for a harvest festival required by Yahweh their God. They have already selected animals for the sacrifices. And just yesterday morning, Joshua instructed the people to begin packing measures of wheat for grain offerings as well as provisions for the journey."

Several delegates from Beeroth leaped to their feet. "They reap what they did not plant," one shouted angrily.

"And worse, they thank a strange new god for the harvest wealth of Jericho."

"Hear. Hear. Was it Yahweh who watered those fields?"

"Such an affront to Canaan's gods will surely bring on drought."

Closer at hand, a growling voice threw out a question that was not a question at all. "Do we wait for them to destroy *us* and harvest the wealth of *our* vineyards?"

Pallu waved off the remaining comments as he leaned forward in his chair. "We need information not opinions. Peleth, Irad, have you learned why the Israelites are leaving Gilgal rather than celebrating in the Jordan Valley?"

Pallu's question brought on a hush and all eyes returned to the scouts.

"They are going on this pilgrimage in obedience to a command given them by Moses," Irad answered. "His writings specifically direct them to find the ancient terebinth tree of Moreh and rebuild the altar there. They will execute what Joshua calls the ceremony of blessings and curses from the slopes of Mount Ebal and Mount Gerizim and build a monument of seven stones overlooking the valley of Shechem."

Angry voices called out from the senate floor.

"Shechem? The very name burns in Hivite ears."

"Loyal Hivites will never forget Shechem!"

Pallu sensed the stirring of Likhi's anger beside him. "Why would the Sons of Jacob return to that place if not to celebrate that reprehensible victory?" his friend growled.

"We must stop that pilgrimage," someone cried out amid a chorus of agreement.

Pallu snorted derisively. "Remember what happened to Egypt when Pharaoh refused to allow these people to travel three days into the wilderness to worship Yahweh. Pharaoh defied Moses' warning and his land was destroyed. Let them travel peacefully as planned to Gerizim and Ebal. I believe we should approach them with our peace proposal after they complete their festival at Shechem."

"If they ask that we be circumcised as part of the peace treaty, should we trust them?"

Derisive laughter rumbled over the assembly.

Even the gentle Meshullam reacted to the mention of Shechem. "The long history of our people includes many wars, many enemies, and much gruesome violence—but nothing so unforgivable as the despicable deceit of the Sons of Jacob."

"Peleth and Irad are the only ones who actually know anything about the plans of these people. Hear them out," Ibzan admonished. He nodded encouragement to the scouts. "Tell us what you know about the planned monument."

"Very little, actually," Irad admitted. "It will be inscribed with words from their law, but no one has said what those words will be. The dedication of the monument will coincide with *Shavuot*, the Feast of Weeks, so called because it takes place at the end of seven weeks of harvest. They count forty-nine days from the day they cut the first sheaf of barley to the close of the wheat harvest. The celebration takes place on the fiftieth day."

Ibzan's forehead crinkled in an attempt to understand. "I am a bit perplexed. All nations celebrate their spring and fall harvests. But this monument to the law? What do the grain harvests have to do with law?"

Irad eagerly told what he knew. "They say fifty days transpired from the day they left Egypt to the day they were given the law at Mount Sinai, and they celebrate both dates with festivals. Coincidentally, those festivals coincide with the beginning and end of the grain harvests."

Pallu pulled thoughtfully on his beard. "But why at Shechem?"

"Jacob legally purchased land there hundreds of years ago, and according to our laws, his descendants own it still. They will build the monument on their own land."

"What if they launch a military campaign against the Canaanite nations following this festival?" someone questioned from the senate floor.

Likhi had been drumming his fingers on the arms of his chair with increasing agitation. His doubts finally exploded. "We must learn the purpose of the monument. Do not forget the power of that ark of theirs. When they carried it into the Jordan, it stopped the floods. When they carried it around Jericho seven times, the walls collapsed. What is inside that holy chest? . . . The law of Yahweh. What power will reside in a monument inscribed with those same words? Isn't it wise to prevent this construction now rather than try to destroy it after it is imbued with some invincible mystical force."

Pallu met his eyes boldly. "We cannot assume they will not attack more Canaanite cities as they move up out of Gilgal. At the same time, we must not needlessly provoke Israel and her God."

Irad responded quickly and emphatically. "I believe we can assume that—at this time, sir. Joshua clarified their plan of march. The warriors of three of their tribes will be split into a vanguard and rearguard. These are the tribes that left all their women, children, and livestock on the other side of the river. Their families will join the pilgrimage, but those tribes have made a commitment to serve as special guard. The remainder of the men of war will travel unarmed with their families."

"Then we must attack Israel while they travel unsuspecting on the road," one firebrand shouted.

"Yes! We can defeat their vanguard."

"There will be no more appropriate time or place to avenge Shechem."

"Such an act would begin a war we cannot win," Pallu called out over the incendiary voices. "What then?" he asked the spies. "Will the Israelites return to

Gilgal following this festival?"

"Back to Gilgal, yes. There has not been a word of war."

A cacophony of questions and calls for action broke out. Small groups formed, arguing, questioning, and persuading among themselves. The elders watched and listened as the tide of opinion rushed toward war. The only question seemed to be when and where.

"Hear, hear," Ibzan broke in at last. "Your views are many and varied. This body as a whole must consider our options carefully. Pallu, commander of our combined army will address the military options you have put forth."

Pallu stood, arms akimbo, balled fists on his hips. His stance and stony stare stilled the last grumbling utterance. "Some of you suggest we join the alliance of the southern kings. Others that we join with Hazor and the northern kings, perhaps going up against Israel during this festival. Some of you suggest we swoop down and destroy the Gilgal camp while they prepare for the journey. Others, that we avenge the destruction of King Birsha's fortress by ambushing them in the gorge below Ai as they travel to their ceremony.

"As your military commander, I can tell you with assurance that none of these plans are realistic. This is day forty-three in their count. There is not sufficient time to prepare for an effective campaign coinciding with this festival. A hasty attack would be disastrous."

Pallu paused, listening and watching while whispers and reluctant nods of agreement spread over the group. Commanding his captains so the army operated as one machine was far easier than dealing with this rabble. "Do you think we would prevail if only we had the chariots of Hazor or the terror of the Anakim on our side? The mighty empire of Sihon could not stand before them. Nor could King Og of Bashan and his sons, though the Rephaim were giants as huge and fierce as the sons of Anak. The enchantments of Balaam could not touch Israel. The fleet desert forces of the Midianite Five were utterly defeated."

He paused dramatically to let the gravity of the situation sink in. "Going humbly to Israel with a peace proposal is, in my opinion, our only hope. No one survives who goes up against this people and Yahweh their God."

Pallu slumped back into his chair as the senate floor exploded with voices of agreement and dissent. "I return this bedlam to you, Ibzan," he said.

Rather than addressing the tumult on the floor, Ibzan stood up and extended his arm with forefinger pointing to the scribe chronicling the proceedings.

Curiosity silenced the debate.

"Record the words of Ibzan the Elder in the record of today's assembly," he said.

"I, Ibzan of Kiriath-Baal, high elder of the Federation of Gibeon, see no alternative other

than asking to cut covenant with the Children of Israel. I urge our people to avoid war at all costs." He spoke the words slowly and clearly, pausing dramatically as the scribe's pen flew across the parchment. When finished, he sank to his seat beside Pallu, muttering, "We have no other option."

Opposing voices immediately growled their responses.

"Our ancestors were brutally slain while they were recovering from circumcision, a requirement of their covenant agreement with Jacob. How can we trust these deceivers?"

When Meshullam lifted himself heavily from his chair, even the most vociferous senators stopped to listen. "The smoke of Jericho's destruction spirals into the heavens as a warning to the remaining peoples of Canaan." The portly elder's scholarly intonations hung ominously over the assembly. He was not only the historian. He combined the roles of gentle poet and stern prophet as no other man in the Federation.

"From ancient times, Jericho stood as the protective gateway to Canaan. No longer! If we stand defiantly in the path of Yahweh, our Federation will become a byword like that great city—

Fallen,
Fallen is the Federation.
We considered her wise.
We considered her indestructible.
Now she is gone.

"Our survival depends on making a wise decision. We have but one chance to get it right. I suggest we send our scouts to the valley of Shechem," Meshullam added. "Observe the festival and the building of the monument. Read the words inscribed on it. Ascertain Joshua's plans after they return to the Jericho Valley."

Absolute silence reigned on the senate floor when the portly historian sat down.

"Send Peleth and Irad to Shechem," Pallu agreed. "In the interim, I *will* ready our army for battle."

"I agree," Likhi said quietly. "We must not be reckless—either way."

"Are there any opposing voices? Speak now . . ." Ibzan called out. "No? Then I call for a vote. Let the decision recorded in the *Chronicles of Gibeon* today be unanimous."

CHAPTER THIRTEEN

SHECHEM

Joshua

Joshua trudged in silence at the head of the long line of pilgrims. Every member of the twelve tribes trailed behind, reunited again. The families of Reuben, Gad, and Manasseh, separated from their warriors for two months now by the flooded Jordan, responded to the summons, fording the river the day before the trek began. No longer on a journey *to* the Promised Land. This was a journey *in* the Promised Land, a pilgrimage commanded and described quite precisely in the scrolls of Moses for the entire family of Israel. Together.

This was the fourth day on the march. Joshua had calculated the timing carefully, planning to arrive in the Valley of Shechem on day forty-seven of the Omer. That would give them two days to prepare for the first Feast of Weeks ever, as well as the ceremony of blessings and curses. Leaving the lush plains of Gilgal behind on day forty-three, the people plodded up the steep, rough road westward toward Ai, stopping overnight at the stone quarry and passing the charred ruins of the fortress before noon on day forty-four. The grade eased as they trekked northward following the road along the sunbaked highlands of Canaan, enjoying the gentler grade and cool upland breezes. The fields of spring wildflowers rolling away in every direction were rapidly drying to clusters of seeds atop parched stems. Occasionally, deep green oak and terebinth groves broke up the monotony of the open fields, offering brief periods of cooling comfort beneath their shaded canopies.

By midmorning on the forty-seventh day of the Omer, the procession was laboring up the final arc of a long S curve, turning toward the Jordan Valley in the early morning and now heading toward the west. Children clamored for rest and parents were wondering aloud how much longer they could endure when the final bend in the long steep grade broke to a breath-catching view of an emerald jewel. Mount Ebal and Mount Gerizim rose protectively at the far end of a dazzling green valley.

The gently sloping sides of the twin peaks stretched toward each other until they nearly touched toes. Joshua immediately observed the stark differences—a perfect metaphor for the blessings and curses the people would recite there. Where Ebal was rocky and dry, streams, gleaming like ribbons of silver, rippled down the flanks of Gerizim and streamed through green velvet pastures dotted with grazing livestock. The streams had been skillfully channeled to water terraced fields of grain and nurture gardens, orchards, vineyards, and olive groves. Joshua instantly saw the wisdom of Yahweh in choosing Mount Gerizim to fix the blessings of covenant living in the minds of his people in contrast to the shriveling effect of independence from him.

The beauty beckoned, but Joshua knew this valley must be entered cautiously. The steep road swept down through clusters of houses surrounding a low, smoothly-rounded mound, the telltale mark of long buried ruins—the ancient city of Shechem. According to Jokshan of Jericho, Labayu, a powerful Canaanite warlord, ruled this village and controlled travel through this valley and its passes with his band of four-hundred marauders.

Hoping his saddlebags bulging with gifts would be enough, Joshua kicked his donkey lightly in the sides and headed down into the valley to negotiate a peaceful temporary stay for Israel and permission to establish a permanent monument. Before he reached the valley floor, two stern-faced men emerged from one of the houses, striding boldly toward the road to meet him. Joshua dismounted and greeted the men with a deep bow. He held his hands palms together in front of his chest to show he concealed no weapon as he pronounced his *shalom*, hoping his face conveyed every true sentiment of the word. "We come in peace, asking nothing but permission to camp in this valley for a few days to celebrate a festival to our God and to bury our ancestor Joseph on the land legally purchased here by his family centuries ago."

"You are the Children of Jacob who recently crossed the Jordan and destroyed Jericho," the younger man stated flatly. He stared boldly into Joshua's eyes as he spoke, but his expression was inscrutable.

"We are. Forty-one years ago, our recently deceased leader, a man by the name of Moses, led our people to freedom from Egyptian slavery—"

"I am quite familiar with the stories of your people," the man interrupted. "Only the deaf have not heard of the miraculous triumphs of Moses . . . and now Joshua. Had Pharaoh but granted Israel the right to go and worship their God as Moses requested, would they not have avoided the plagues? Our people will not bother you if you truly come in peace. Do what you have come to do."

Does he trust us? Or is he pragmatically comparing Labayu's band of four hundred to our vanguard of thousands?

"I do not wish for our activities to alarm you in any way. Moses led our people from Egypt to Mount Sinai where Yahweh our God gave us his covenant law. Moses' final command was that we rebuild the altar of our ancestors Abraham and Jacob here by the ancient terebinth of Moreh and build a monument on Mount Ebal detailing the laws guiding our people."

"Justice would demand that you also rebuild the ruins of ancient Shechem," the man said with a sly smile. "This mound is all that is left of the city destroyed by Jacob's sons the last time your forefathers walked this valley."

"We cannot undo the evil perpetrated by our ancestors, but the law that governs us now is a law of love and justice." Joshua opened his saddlebags and pulled out bundles clanking with Egyptian and Midianite jewelry. "We thank you for your kindness and offer these small tokens as recompense for pasturing our sacrificial animals on your land for a few days. We have brought our own supplies of food and will not touch your vineyards and gardens."

This time the older man replied. "My lord Labayu has grown wealthy through trade in grapes, olives, wheat, livestock, and pottery. He has no need of recompense for spring grass that will soon wither and die. However, in eagerness to embrace your offer of good faith between our people, I accept this gift in my master's name." The two men bowed seven times before picking up the bundles and returning to the village. Joshua could not help but wonder if one of the two men was Labayu himself.

Peleth

"Ho, what is this?" Peleth dropped to one knee for a closer look at the huge footprints. They were not fresh, but they were definitely the marks of a band of Anakim giants. Ten or more of them.

Irad knelt beside him. "Maybe two or three days old already. Moving northward at a carelessly fast pace."

"Anakim traveling in packs. Canaan hasn't seen anything like this in years."

"To Hazor? But why? Every king from every region of Canaan declined the invitation to join a coalition with the Anakim. All but Adoni-Zedek and his minions."

"Maybe like our federation, King Libni is sending spies to learn what the Israelites are planning."

"More likely to attack and destroy. The Anakim don't spy."

"They don't normally plot ahead either."

Peleth rose to his feet. "Joshua is riding back up the road to the Israelite caravan. He seems to have negotiated a treaty with Labayu."

"He shouldn't have to negotiate. Everyone knows that Jacob bought the entire western end of this valley from Hamor the Hivite. Joshua is cautious for a man returning to the land of his ancestors."

"More cautious than I would have expected after the victory at Jericho."

Peleth and Irad settled themselves in a craggy fissure on Mount Gerizim where they could watch the people stream into the valley and pitch their tents. The encampment extended westward from the settlement of Labayu, filling most of the valley, clustering thickest at the feet of Gerizim and Ebal like children gathered at the feet of a storyteller.

A small knoll nestled between the knees of the two mountains on which one could still see the remains of a stone altar sheltered by an extraordinarily broad canopy of twisted branches. According to legend, that gnarled old tree, the terebinth of Moreh, marked Abraham's first campsite in the land of Canaan. Peleth was inclined to believe the story was not myth. Nor was the promise that this land would be returned to the descendants of Shem through Abraham and his children.

Throughout the afternoon, the scouts strained to catch fragments of story and song, memories of Israel's history and heritage of faith in this land. Some of the tents surrounded the well dug by Jacob. Others camped on the very pastures Joseph crossed when seeking his brothers. They heard people recounting the story of the older brothers' jealousy and the coat of many colors. They told of Joseph captured, thrown into a pit, and finally sold to slave traders. The road through this valley was the very one traveled by the Ishmaelite caravan that carried Joseph to Egypt. What new drama was about to unfold on this ancient stage? Peleth trembled at the thought.

Joshua

Joshua bristled.

The Levites and elders had just left him. Now this delegation of brigade commanders from Manasseh—another group arguing for cleansing this valley of its Canaanite inhabitants.

"That would be greater pollution, not cleansing," he admonished them.

"But Moses commanded us to make no treaty with them," the spokesman growled. "We are to destroy every vestige of Baal worship in this land."

Joshua made his answer as kind, firm, and final as he knew how. "This place still bears the name of the young Hivite prince Shechem, slaughtered by our forefathers along with all the men of his city. Their blood still cries out from this ground. From that day until now, the memory of Jacob festers like a thorn in the flesh of Canaan whenever the name of Shechem is spoken. We are here to heal the wound."

"But you just made a treaty. We must not disobey the commands of the law." The military men sounded more like Levites than battle commanders.

Joshua didn't flinch. "We will not make permanent treaties with nations standing in rebellion to the true God of this land. But we will not attack unless Yahweh himself commands it."

"But we are surrounded by hostile nations. Do you trust Labayu? What if he gathers a coalition and attacks us? Our worship in this valley could well become a deadly trap."

"Who protected Jacob's family as they fled this valley after their brutal crime against Shechem? Who placed a fear on the surrounding peoples so no avenger followed? We don't put our trust in Labayu or any treaty. We trust Yahweh and he commanded us to celebrate in this valley." Joshua wheeled and walked away.

He found himself heading toward the tents of Judah. *What better solace than his oldest and dearest friend?* His friend was not difficult to spot amid the swirl of activity. Joshua paused on the boundary of Caleb's site, watching his white-haired friend, sinews taut, muscles rippling, the powerful blows of his hammer echoing from the surrounding rocks as he drove the last of the tent stakes of the large family pavilion into the earth. Joshua finished setting up his own site much earlier. One simple tent did not take long.

"Ho there, friend. You are every bit as strong as the day we left Egypt."

Caleb looked up and laughed. "You too. I think it might be the forty years of manna."

"Or perhaps we were included in the promise of things not wearing out during the Wanderings—neither shoes, garments, tents, nor a certain pair of old men."

Smile lines crinkled at the corners of Caleb's gray eyes. "We are a pair, aren't we? The only ones left." Caleb was collecting his tools, stuffing them into a leather storage bag along with extra coils of rope and leather lashings when a bright voice called out. "Shalom, Uncle Joshua."

Acsah's smile and greeting warmed Joshua's heart. In Caleb's daughter he found a rare and deep connection with the next generation. "Shalom indeed," he responded. "A historic time. A historic place."

Her green eyes glittered. "This is the setting of so many of our stories, but I never imagined such beauty."

Acsah's enthusiasm was just what Joshua needed after dealing with so many contentious tribal leaders. He drew in a slow, deep breath fragrant with the scent of fertile earth, water, and growing things. "A perfect place for our festival. I expect we will encounter frequent oases such as this throughout our days in this good land."

"Oases?" Caleb raised one bushy white eyebrow. "We are no longer in the desert. The entire land of Canaan is fertile."

Acsah's eyes flashed. "Abba! Don't you understand? Uncle Joshua is not talking about watered land. He means high occasions of joy and renewal."

Joshua laughed. "Precisely, child. This place will be remembered as another wonderful oasis on our journey with God. You have taught your daughter well, my friend."

"Oh my, my, my!" Ephah emerged from a tent bobbing her head. "The daughter is imbued with her father's wisdom. I too thought Joshua merely referred to all the streams and springs."

Maacah tried to catch Acsah's eye. "She has Caleb's fire and devotion to God as well. How blessed to be connected to both father and daughter."

Acsah stood abruptly, giving Maacah and Ephah's words of praise a minimal nod of acknowledgment. She retrieved two mats and rolled them out in front of the large central tent. "Is your site set up already, Uncle Joshua?"

"All settled an hour ago. One old bachelor does not need much. But the Calebite clan grows larger every time I come by." He winked at Maacah and Ephah.

"Hogluh and Hodesh, run and fetch some water before it gets dark. I'll start the cook fire."

"Oases of life," Caleb muttered to himself. "Good thought. Good thought. Be grateful when you come to an oasis. But don't be afraid to move on. There will be more."

"And trust God to get us through the barren stretches between them," Joshua added. "Lessons of the Wanderings."

Acsah shot a pointed look at her father's new concubines. "Maacah and Ephah, don't you still need to organize your tent." She lowered her voice. "We usually try to give Abba and Joshua time to themselves at moments such as this."

"Ha!" Caleb laughed. "Can you believe this, Joshua? I try to provide my daughter with two new mothers and she becomes the mother, training them instead." He waggled his brows.

Acsah rolled her eyes, but the two women smiled good-naturedly and followed her suggestion.

Ephah lugged two bundles to the women's tent and dropped them inside. Standing by the entrance, she groaned softly, arching her spine and rubbing her lower back.

"Look at you, Ephah. Your belly is big as a boulder," Maacah clucked. "No wonder your back bothers you. And look at those swollen ankles. You should have let me do the unpacking. Now sit down on one of these mats. I will help Acsah get supper while you rest."

"Better yet, Ephah," Acsah said as she unpacked a bundle of firewood from one of the donkey packs, "why don't you lie down in your own tent? I put those mats out for Abba and Uncle Joshua." She began to set stones in a ring for the fire.

Maacah and Ephah looked at each other in surprise, then began rummaging through the food supplies. Soon a friendly disagreement ensued—Ephah insisting she should help, Maacah arguing she should rest.

Joshua chuckled. "Your life is richer in family than mine, but also much more complicated."

"I do not complain about blessings from God," Caleb grunted. "And lovely blessings each of these women are to me. Come. Let us walk up to see the terebinth of Moreh."

From the shelter of the old tree at the top of the rise, the two stopped to catch their breath. "Sometimes I forget how great my age," Joshua puffed, "but a little exertion like this reminds me soon enough."

"Sometimes I forget how great the multitude of Israel," Caleb countered with a quick lift of his brows. "With but a little exertion we have this awe-inspiring view of a valley filled with thousands upon thousands of tents. God's promise to Jacob fulfilled. 'Your descendants will be like the dust of the earth, and you will spread out to the west and to the east, to the north and to the south . . .'"

Joshua added the final line. "'All peoples on earth will be blessed through you and your offspring.'[23] It must have been extremely difficult for Jacob to believe those words the last time he stood on this spot." He crouched down at the foot of the tree and ran his hand reverently over the knee bend of one of its massive roots. "Think of it, Caleb. These roots have had centuries to entwine themselves over and around the collection of household gods Jacob's wives buried beneath this tree. They must still be down there, right? Silver and gold do not decay."

Caleb didn't answer. He settled into a seat-like hollow between roots with his back supported by the trunk.

Joshua could make out the footprint of the ancient altar not far away. "Look over there, Caleb. The very spot where both Abraham and Jacob worshipped, but the images of false gods are trapped forever beneath this soil. The altar of Yahweh may be in ruins, but it is still visible."

"Mmm-hmm." Caleb stared across the valley into the past. "Imagine the jumble of thoughts in Jacob's head as he offered his last sacrifice here. How could God honor promises to a family responsible for such a horrible atrocity? Add to that the fear of a bloody reprisal once word got out. Human justice would have been served if his family was hunted down and blotted from the face of the earth. Surely the evil of his sons had exceeded the mercy of Yahweh."

Joshua found a comfortable seat on a twisted knobbly root. "But Jacob didn't run away from God. He cleansed his camp of everything contaminating the covenant commitment . . ."

"Then fled with his family to the faith rock of his youth at Bethel."

"Bethel . . . the city we just destroyed." Joshua buried his face in his hands, muffling a groan. "What a tangled web! Deceit and destruction."

Caleb wisely let the rustling of the evening breezes speak to Joshua's remorse. Above all else, this spot declared the faithfulness of God in contrast to his people's unfaithfulness.

After a while Joshua looked sideways at his old friend. "We are a lot like the aged peaks of Gerizim and Ebal, you and I, Caleb. Two weathered warriors who have been waiting decades for Yahweh to bring his people back to this place. Now we sit side by side in awestruck silence at the sight of—"

"Uncle Caleb! Joshua!"

"Up here, Othniel. Under the terebinth," Caleb called back.

In moments Othniel was there, panting from his sprint up the hill. "Acsah sends word that you should return now if you want your stew hot."

Caleb grinned. "Come, my friend. You are expected, I'm certain." He shifted his position, preparing to get to his feet, but Joshua didn't move. "My three blessings may squabble a bit, but whatever they finally settled on for dinner will be delicious . . . and best hot."

Joshua shook his head in refusal. "Quiet time in this memorable spot is soul food for me, more satisfying than anything ladled from a cook pot."

"Well, my daughter implied the option of cold stew if we don't go now." Caleb chuckled. "It is definitely more peaceful up here. I can just hear the three of them disagreeing on how long to try keeping it hot for us." He gave a hearty slap on an adjacent root. "Join us, Othniel. This old tree has a most comfortable lap."

Joshua regarded the young man with curiosity as he settled beside his uncle. "Tell me, boy, how did you happen to stumble into Acsah's path just when she needed a messenger?"

Othniel shook his hair back over his shoulders and thought a moment before answering. "I was actually hoping to have some time to talk to my uncle. This entire time of counting the Omer has afforded us little time to stop and think, let alone time to seek the wisdom of elders."

Caleb grinned. "Beneath the bows of the terebinth of Moreh—the 'tree of teaching.' I don't know if the name came about because this was where God began teaching Abraham his plan, or if this is where Abraham began serious instruction of his household. Or maybe he had opportunity to teach some of the local Canaanites here. However the name came about, I have a hunch that hundreds of years later we, the children of Abraham, can sit here meditating on how God has led his people— and learn much. An excellent place to seek wisdom for young and old alike."

"Moreh," Othniel repeated thoughtfully. "I wish I could be instructed by Joseph, the dreamer and interpreter of dreams." He settled back, studying the leaves in the canopy above them. "The night of Passover, I woke with a strange dream. A pale-skinned giant broke from an underground cavern, defiantly challenging Yahweh. That dream shook me as no other before. He was monstrously huge—long white hair flying, eyes glinting red in the moonlight, and an evil scowl beyond anything I have ever seen in my life. He seemed hideously unreal, but the sense of danger lingers."

Joshua caught Caleb's eyes. They both knew the fear.

"If you saw in vision what we saw in reality, you will never forget that face," Caleb said. "Your uncle and I encountered a giant fitting that description in the city of Kiriath-Arba forty years ago, and I think I saw him again at Ai."

Joshua squeezed his eyes closed. "I saw him too, Caleb. I'm certain it was him. Helek knows his name—Libni, king of the Anakim."

"I caught a brief glimpse of him at Ai also," Othniel mumbled. "That is when I knew for sure he was not simply a bad dream. Last night the dream recurred while we were sleeping all strung out along the road. I was wide awake the remainder of the night, wondering what I could do if he showed up in reality. The only weapon I could think of was a tent pole!"

The whispering leaves grew eerily still as Othniel spoke.

"My question is, who sends the dreams and for what purpose?" Caleb said, measuring his words thoughtfully.

"I wondered that too. I was so utterly unnerved following the first dream, it seemed demonic. Last night not so much, but my senses were on high alert the rest of the night. I never heard anything specific after I awoke, but I had the feeling something sinister was lurking in the shadows, watching, waiting to strike. It doesn't seem rational." He grinned. "Probably not from a demonic source if it causes me to pray most of the night!"

Joshua nodded. "My guess is those premonitions are not irrational. Pay attention.

They could save your life."

Othniel pulled away from the conversation and gazed out over the valley. Sundown brilliance faded to dusk and still the three remained under the ancient terebinth, so close in heart and mind that words were not necessary. They watched the procession of stars march toward the weathered peaks of Gerizim and Ebal. Star patterns, silent voices proclaiming the same story—evil might win a few skirmishes, but it would never triumph.

"The last part of the promise to Jacob burns in my heart tonight," Joshua whispered. Then with a loud voice, he repeated the well-known words into the night. "I am with you and will watch over you wherever you go, and I will bring you back to this land. I will not leave you until I have done what I have promised you."[24]

"I need to keep repeating that promise until it burns in my own heart," Othniel affirmed quietly.

Caleb's laugh shattered the contemplative mood. "Acsah, Maacah, and Ephah may all be repeating their own version of that right now. *Bring our Caleb back to this land.*" He pushed himself heavily to his feet. "Enough of being Mount Gerizim or Ebal. I am not a fixed mountain, and I am long overdue in camp."

Othniel joined Caleb, but Joshua remained where he was. He could hear Othniel's half-joking remark as he and Caleb began the trek down the mountain. "*I will bring you back* . . . I'll start repeating that promise while I stumble through Judah trying to find our new tent site by starlight—especially if I feel watched."

Joshua smiled, but did not feel the need to follow. He had no family waiting for him and there was a lot he needed to talk to Yahweh about.

Acsah

A pitiful shriek split the stillness of night. It must have been midnight, but the sound jolted Acsah from her sleep.

"Help!" a voice pleaded pitifully. "Call the midwife. Oh, help! Ephah's time has come."

"Quickly, Abihail," Acsah urged, leaping out of bed. "Get up. Let's go. Maacah's cries will soon stir every person within hearing."

Abihail was up instantly, running her fingers through tangled tresses and pulling her warm cloak around her. "But where do we find a midwife?"

"We've done this with sheep," Acsah answered, pushing through the door flap. "We can help her."

"I feared for this on the journey. Her back ached all morning." Abihail puffed the words between panting breaths as they ran toward the one tent glowing with lamplight. "The long trek called the child from Ephah's womb at least a month early."

Acsah exhaled her frustration. "I warned her, but she refused to ride Caleb's donkey while the rest of us walked. And she would not listen even though everyone urged her to lie down instead of setting up camp."

"Acsah, I don't know if we can do this."

"Who else do we call at this hour of the night? If it does not go well, Ephah can only blame her own stubborn choices."

By the time they pushed through the door flap, a baby's feeble wail had already replaced the screams and moans of childbirth. Maacah was holding a puny male infant up by his feet.

"Oh, praise God, someone came," she said, laying the tiny thing on a folded tunic. He clenched his fists and kicked his thin little legs, screaming in protest as she wiped his pinched red face with a strip of cloth. "You seem to have no problem getting air, little one, but let's get that tiny nose cleared out . . ." Without looking up, she switched tones. "See what you girls can do for the new mother."

Ephah's breathing was quick and shallow. Beads of sweat gleamed on her ashen face. Acsah pushed aside the birthing stool and knelt at her feet. "Get some water for those parched lips," she directed as she swept the pile of blood-soaked straw from between the new mother's splayed legs.

"Thankfully, we brought a basket of wool," Maacah said brightly. "Turning that spindle helps me concentrate while listening to stories." She took a tiny puff of clean wool and twisted it into a roll, then pushed the basket closer to the birthing area with her foot while the infant howled louder. She resumed her motherly clucking. "You don't like this, but your nose will feel better when it is clear."

Acsah could see part of the severed cord still attached high in the birth canal. She tugged gently, but the *womb-bread* remained tightly fixed. "Help me if you can, Ephah," she coaxed gently, laying a hand on the abdomen, feeling for even a slight contraction. "We need to deliver the afterbirth."

Abihail pulled the cup away from the girl's lips, trying to make a verbal connection. "If you feel more cramps, push for Acsah." She caught Acsah's eyes with a sad negative shake of her head. Ephah had not so much as fluttered her eyelids.

Acsah kept up her stream of chatter as she worked. "All right, little mother. You have a fine baby boy, and you may hold him as soon as we deliver the womb-bread." When she reached high into the birth canal, feeling for the flat, squishy organ, Ephah moaned pitifully. "This may hurt a little. It is still attached, but I know we can tease it free. I have done this before."

Acsah carefully began pushing her fingers underneath to separate the flat organ from the lining of the womb, vaguely aware of Maacah bustling in the background tending to the still bawling infant. Murmuring constantly, she cleaned the bloody limbs and abdomen and finally swaddled the irate little man tightly with long strips of soft, clean woolen cloth. Usually that calmed an infant, but this one continued his crying even when she held him close to her. "Hush, hush now. Don't you appreciate that I sacrificed a perfectly good robe to make swaddle strips for you? Hush, Hush."

With a great gushing of blood, Ephah's womb-bread suddenly broke free. Acsah delivered it and began packing wads of clean wool into the birth canal as fast as Abihail could hand them to her. But with horror she watched the torrent of blood find its way past the packing and continue streaming from Ephah's body, pooling on the floor beneath her. "Lord help us," Acsah whispered. "I cannot stop the bleeding."

Abihail looked helplessly at Acsah. Ephah began visibly shivering. Abihail tucked the blanket tightly around the girl's upper body. "She is so cold," she said.

"But the child needs to nurse," Maacah answered, pressing in beside Abihail and flashing a tentative smile at Acsah. "Maybe it will help the mother." She slipped the blanket back far enough to expose one breast and held the squalling infant close to the nipple.

"Ephah, look. Meet your new son," she cooed. "He is a bit disagreeable at the moment, but he's trying to say, 'Where is my ima?'"

Ephah lay listless and still, as unresponsive to the baby as to the attentions of the three women. Icy fear gripped Acsah's chest like a vise. She had done all she knew how to do. Ephah was dying and she was totally helpless. She sat back on her heels, feeling as if she were slipping into a dark underwater dream.

There was a new bustling of activity. Others in the room now. A pure, sweet voice, like the voice of an angel, began singing softly of the tender love of Yahweh.

"Steep this in boiling water," an age-crackled voice said with soft authority.

Abihail took whatever it was the old woman wished to have steeped and left the tent.

Acsah did not need to see the women clearly. She knew the voices. The older was Shua of Jericho. The singer, her granddaughter, Rahab the harlot. Maacah remained at her friend's side coaxing the infant to nurse, but he continued to thrash his head from side to side, mewling continuously. Tears streamed down Acsah's cheeks. The world was out of control.

Like a half-awake child, she watched Shua set a pot of warm olive oil and a second dish filled with a thick paste of herbs and honey down between them. The harlot took Abihail's place at the dying mother's head. As the fragrance of pungent herbs filled the air, Shua nudged herself into place beside Acsah and began removing the blood-soaked wool packing.

Oddly, a childish comfort wrapped around Acsah. It was like drowning helplessly in a little-girl catastrophe and feeling her father's strength take charge. Just so she felt the crisis would turn and everything would be right again. Never mind that the responsible adults in the room were Canaanite foreigners. She retreated into a corner to watch, the only one without a task.

Rahab met Acsah's eyes and seemed to be singing directly to her as she stroked Ephah's pale forehead in time to her song.

> *Where can we turn when foundations crumble?*
> *To whom shall we cry when the mountains shake?*
> *The Lord surrounds us like the everlasting hills,*
> *Yahweh, our help, surrounds us with unfailing love.*

Ephah's quick, shallow breathing became deeper, slower in response to the cadence of Rahab's song. Moving quickly, the old woman removed the blood-soaked packing and then plunged a handful of the thick herbal-honey paste into the birth canal, spreading it as a poultice against the streaming blood. She allowed herself only a brief glance away from her work when Abihail returned.

"The brew is ready? Good. Dip out a big cupful for her to drink, then fill the pot with wads of wool . . . Ah, perfect. Now, my dear, begin dribbling a little tea into her mouth as often as she will take it. That is the same brew that helped bring you back to health." She flashed a smile at Abihail. "When she is alert enough to swallow, encourage her to finish the cup."

Shua turned to Acsah's shadowed corner with the same beautiful smile. "Acsah, you did so well with the first packing. It definitely slowed the bleeding. Would you help me now?" She continued the instructions with hardly a pause to acknowledge Acsah's nod of assent. "Bring the pot over here. Ladle the wool out of the hot brew one wad at a time. Squeeze out the water and dip them in the warm oil for me." Shua took the pieces of oil-soaked wool as Acsah prepared them and began repacking the birth canal. This time the wool did not turn scarlet.

Acsah's heart cried out, *I need to learn these skills or never try to deliver a child again.*

Shua sat up straight, cleaning her hands with the last pieces of tea-soaked wool, and announced, "I think our little mother will make it. Now let's do something about all that wailing."

She supported the infant's head firmly with one hand and pressed the nipple against the side of his tiny mouth with the other. "Here you go, little fellow," she crooned, holding him firmly in place until he stopped thrashing. When he started suckling noisily, Shua drew a long, relieved breath and sat back triumphantly. "We have done what we can. Now Yahweh can be about the business of healing." Her face was aglow with beauty and goodness.

Abihail hugged Rahab and sobbed. Maacah threw her arms around Shua. And no one seemed to notice Acsah as she slipped out the door, a sorrowful shadow out of place in that bright and joyful scene.

Yahweh God, what kind of monster am I? . . . I no longer know what is right and what is wrong. It is written in the law. No treaty with Canaanites . . . a harlot is not fit to live among our holy people. Now this Canaanite harlot and her grandmother are the means of saving Ephah. You blessed their healing hands when mine failed.

She stumbled through the darkness finding her way back to the tent she shared with Abihail. *Could Rahab and Shua have saved Abihail's baby? O my God . . . Did Abi's beautiful little daughter die because I was wrong? I cannot bear to believe that, but . . .*

Throwing off her cloak and sandals, she stretched out on her bed. A black soup of wretchedness, gloom, guilt, and self-doubt churned in her stomach.

I have done my best to drive Rahab from our camp. I have irreparably damaged my precious childhood friendship with Salmon. I wanted to do what was right. How could I be so wrong? Speak to me, God. This is beyond tragic.

Acsah had no idea how long she lay there, shivering in the chill of a dark night, exhausted but unable to sleep.

But what of the thousands of men who died after worshiping at Baal-Peor . . . snared by the enticing women of Midian. What of the innocent people we lost because of those women? I loved Auntie Hannah, Prince Nashon, and dear old Jekamiah and Shemai. They died because we allowed evil women to infiltrate our camp. How can I know what is right? What light guides me if not the law? Explain it to me, Yahweh, God of the covenant.

The fountain of her tears ran dry and her soul shriveled with the dryness. She asked a hundred questions, but Yahweh remained silent.

"Acsah."

She did not realize she had fallen asleep until she heard the whisper of her name through her drowsy haze. She had asked Yahweh countless questions, but this wasn't the Lord. It was Abihail. How could she respond? She injured this dear friend as surely as the abominable arrow that pierced Eliab's heart.

"Acsah, are you awake?"

She didn't move or open her eyes even when she felt a soft touch on her shoulder.

"Acsah, don't pretend to be asleep. I heard your breathing change." The bedclothes rustled as Abihail leaned closer. "Before I left, Ephah regained enough strength to drink that entire cup of tea. She was holding her son, weeping tears of joy.

"Acsah!" Abihail shook her shoulder lightly. "Speak to me. I am so excited and happy. I need to talk with you about it."

"Don't Abihail," Acsah whispered hoarsely. "I am glad for Ephah, but I can't share this joy. I don't deserve to be your friend."

"What are you talking about? I don't deserve you."

Acsah listened to her own breathing, soft and rhythmic in the darkness, while Abihail waited for her to answer. *There was no appropriate answer.*

Abihail finally flopped down on her own pillow. "All right, I'll go first. Acsah, I must confess my guilt to you. I was glad your father took Ephah and Maacah as concubines even though I knew it caused you pain. I could not bear the thought of you returning to your old role of helping him and leaving me alone. I need you, my friend. I don't deserve you, but I need you."

"What you need, my dearest Abihail, is a better friend. You would be better off alone than with me."

"Don't be silly. You are far stronger and wiser than I am. We all learned the words of the law growing up, but so often I don't recognize the subtle guises of evil. I want to be faithful to the covenant, but I can't do it alone. I need you."

Acsah groaned. "Yesterday I would have said, 'You must learn to think and evaluate for yourself. No matter the guise, you will recognize evil when you hold it up to the light of the law.' Today, I don't know what to say."

"Where *is* yesterday's Acsah? Let me be chastened by her anger. Aren't you upset that I was glad about you having to deal with Ephah and Maacah?"

"A trifling offense. It does not compare to my own. Your sweet soul is incapable of imagining the darkness of my depravity." She sat up, steeling herself to make the truth known. "Hear me out, and you will drive me from your presence forever—Abihail, I *murdered* your daughter."

"That is ridiculous. I know you loved her."

"I did love her, but she is dead at my hand."

"Stop." Abihail began weeping. "She was dead when you delivered her. You held her for me."

"O my friend, you do not know the whole truth. On the second day after you fell, Rahab and Shua came to your tent with their strange-smelling potions of leaves and bark and Rahab's foreign song. I drove them away. I cared for you in my own way and delivered a dead baby for you."

"Acsah, you did everything you could have."

"I judged as unfit the very ones who could have saved her."

"We cannot know that . . . and it was you who nursed me back to health."

"Truth be told, your strength increased far more rapidly from the day you began drinking their tea. I only allowed it because it came by the hand of my father. Were it not for that, I might have lost you too." She groaned again. "Oh, my dear Abihail, I do not see how you can ever forgive me. When I saw what those Canaanites did for Ephah . . . how they worked with knowledge . . . and in the fear of Yahweh, I saw clearly what I had done. And I cannot bear the agony of it." *There. She knows my unforgivable offense. She will ask me to leave.*

It was quiet for a long time.

"You did what you thought best," Abihail said at last. "We will never know what other outcome might have been, but of this I am sure. God transforms tears into jewels. He has a new plan for me than the life I imagined. A higher place, and it will be good."

Yes, my precious girl, you will move on to a higher place . . . but what of me? I've lost my father. I've lost Salmon. I've lost you. Jonathan is right. I am a woman and have no inheritance. Do I marry him whom I do not love? Do I devote my life to supporting his study and teaching of the books of the law that failed me? I see no path before me. Only an abyss. She rolled onto her side with her back toward her friend.

"Acsah, I came into this tent overflowing with excitement, and you have done everything you can to spoil it for me. Now, listen! Let me tell you what I wanted to talk to you about in the first place or I will be the angry one."

Acsah could not see the fire in her friend's eyes, but she could hear it in her voice. "Say on," she replied dully.

"Oh Acsah, I can hardly contain my joy. Shua and Rahab have agreed to instruct *us* in midwifery, to teach *us* the healing properties of herb, leaf, and bark of all the trees and field plants of Canaan. I may have lost the privilege of raising my own child, but I can be mother to hundreds, maybe thousands of Israelite children. Is this not the most wonderful prospect?"

"It is wonderful for you."

"It is perfect for you too. You can train with me and serve with me—"

Acsah rolled over to face Abihail. "Could you really accept me as your partner?" A glimmer of hope rose in her heart and spilled out onto her lips as a grin. "The two of us—the midwives of the red-and-white striped tent. I like the thought of that."

Abihail smiled coquettishly. "You interrupted me. I will be most happy for you to train with me and serve with me until you meet the love of your life and leave me to be his wife."

"If you can fully forgive me, we will serve as midwives together for the rest of our lives. I will never marry."

Abihail waved her pointer finger in Acsah's face. "Do not make such promises. Only God knows the path he has for you."

CHAPTER FOURTEEN

COUNTING THE OMER

Omer Forty-Eight

The people woke on the forty-eighth day of the Omer in a valley luminous with golden light. While the sacrificial animals rested and grazed on verdant pastures at the feet of Gerizim and Ebal, the temporary camp exploded into a hive of activity. The men built communal ovens for baking, then left the women and younger children to prepare for the feast. By the hundreds, the men of Israel marched up and down the slopes of Ebal like ants on an anthill, dragging seven massive stones and setting them solidly in a row with their flat faces prominently visible from the road. They would be plastered and inscribed with the covenant law as Moses instructed. [25]

Eleazar found the ruins of Jacob's massive stone altar near the terebinth tree. He called for the sons of Levi to rebuild it as Jacob had rebuilt the one his grandfather Abraham built on that same spot. "There will be no pretense of man's grandeur here," he reminded them. "Moses instructed us to fashion this altar of rough, uncut stones to remind us of the simple but powerful faith of our fathers."

The tribes of Ephraim and Manasseh began excavating a natural cave northeast of Jacob's well, enlarging it enough to house Joseph's ornate Egyptian coffin. For forty years the descendants of Joseph's children, Ephraim and Manasseh, carried his remains through the wilderness. They would lay him to rest at last in the Promised Land on property legally purchased from Hamor, father of Shechem—close to the very place where Joseph's brothers sold him into slavery. [26]

Phinehas

"There must be no mistakes. This monument will endure for generations." Phinehas studied the face of his newly-appointed overseer and was pleased with the earnest energy brightening the man's face.

Zerahiah nodded. "I will see that everything is done exactly as Joshua commanded."

"I am certain you will." Phinehas encouraged him with a smile.

Zerahiah, the chief scribe of the Gershonite clan, was skilled at lettering as well as supervising men. With this appointment, Phinehas completed his assignment—choosing and organizing the Levites responsible for the inscriptions on the seven stones. He had appointed accurate scroll readers, the best inscribers, and meticulous text validators assigned to proof the inscriptions—seven sets of eyes checking each word before the plaster set.

While he was giving his final instructions to Zerahiah, he watched Eleazar making his way across the pasture below, passing through scattered clusters of cattle and sheep with all the stateliness and dignity of his office. The incongruity made him smile. *Only my abba.* Satisfied that his overseer would ensure perfect execution of every detail, Phinehas strode down the hill to greet his father.

"Look!" he called across the backs of the grazing herds. "These stones make an impressive statement, yes?"

"Impressive indeed," Eleazar responded.

In a few swift strides, Phinehas reached his father. Side by side, they surveyed the progress of the work. The monument was even more striking from this broader perspective. "May these words speak truth to every traveler who passes this mountain," Eleazar mused.

A spirit of reverent power tingled through Phinehas. A sense of history. A sense of destiny. The monument would commemorate the first Shavuot celebration ever. The feasts, detailed in the law given to Moses at Mount Sinai, were designed for life in the Promised Land, a life arranged around the seasons of grain, olives, and grapes. Accordingly, the entire cycle of feasts hung suspended during the forty-years of the Wanderings. Now at last the Children of Israel were here, the redeemed people of Yahweh beginning a new cycle of life in a new land of planting and harvest.

Eleazar signaled an important communication with a noisy clearing of his throat. With a quick sideways glance from the corners of his eyes, he began. "When we dedicate this altar tomorrow evening, I want our people to realize its great significance. It is, of course, the place where God first promised this land to Abraham, but we must remember how the story of Jacob and his family is inextricably interwoven with the history of this valley. The blessings and curses of our ancestral story are rooted here as deeply as that old terebinth. We must never forget the hope that brought Jacob here—and perhaps more importantly why he left. A tragic rape. Needless bloodshed. A long exile. Now, at last, Jacob's descendants have returned to the hope and the promises. Following the evening sacrifice tomorrow, I would like for you to tell the story of mercy and redemption required to get us here."

Despite the warm sun, a chill shivered down Phinehas' back.

Eleazar glanced at the thick parchment scroll cradled in his arms and held it out. "The *Book of Beginnings*. Take it and find a quiet place to prepare."

"I will do my best." Phinehas' hand trembled as he reached for the scroll, but his father pulled it back.

"The story must be brief. The festival will start at dawn. We don't want our people to be sleepy or irritable the next morning."

Given the seriousness of this new assignment, Phinehas did not respond in kind to his Father's lighthearted demeanor. "Brief it will be," he answered tersely, reaching for the scroll again. But still his father did not release his hold on it. The twinkle in his warm brown eyes seemed incongruent with the solemnity of the assignment.

"And son, why don't you ask Jonathan to help you prepare?" Eleazar lifted his brows in expectation.

"Even better." Phinehas replied, taking the scroll easily from his father's hands. He was amazed once again at Eleazar's ability to encourage the hurting and disappointed. Phinehas remembered Jonathan as he chose workers for the monument this morning, knowing how crushed Jonathan was when the council of Judah did not go the way he expected. But accurate transcriptions and perfect lettering were not his cousin's strengths. Brilliant insights into the ancient words definitely were. Jonathan would be the perfect help for this next assignment.

Talmai of the Anakim

"Mark my word, Jabin of Hazor," Talmai roared at the glittering king. "The very existence of Canaan hangs in the balance. We can and will defeat the Israelite invaders alone—but a king who refuses to fight with us becomes our enemy."

Before King Jabin could reply, Talmai wheeled about and stormed down the long corridor of the throne room. He felt the pavers crackle beneath the weight of his war sandals and stomped all the harder to leave behind a token of Anakim displeasure.

Talmai dreaded his return to Libni. His king would be furious, but Talmai knew in his heart that no one could have done better. His arguments were flawless. The Israelite hordes moved north—rather than south as expected. Following the total destruction of Jericho, they opened the northward pass with their attack on Ai, and now Joshua's massive army crouched in Shechem, poised to roar from the valley and attack the kingdoms of the north.

But Canaan did not face a mere human army. This strange God, Yahweh, fought for the Children of Israel in unheard of ways. Now hints of Israelite activities were trickling out of the valley of Shechem. A strange monument. Plans for a ceremony they were calling the ceremony of blessings and curses. Who would be blessed and who cursed? Only a fool would ask that. Everyone knew how the power of their covenant law chest split the Jordan and crushed Jericho.

How could Jabin not see the urgency? The invaders must be stopped before a ceremony infused the monument with power. The Children of Jacob had already set up a row of seven stones beside the road. They were now in the process of engraving. On the day after tomorrow, they planned to dedicate the monument. After that all traffic in and out of the valley would fall under the spell of those strange inscriptions.

Why was Jabin so blind? The gathering for the ceremony was the perfect time to attack. Talmai explained in graphic detail how the warriors, the women and children, the priests, and even the sacred golden chest would be out in the open for the incantations. The majority, perhaps all, of the warriors would be unarmed. The Anakim would hurl a storm of boulders down on the gathering—a *giant* storm. He roared with laughter at his little joke. But it was no joke.

When the Anakim launched that deluge of rock and earth, a landslide thundering down both mountains simultaneously, every descendant of Jacob along with their sacred chest would be obliterated in one horrifying moment. The plan was infallible. They only asked that Hazor send sufficient chariots to encircle the valley to prevent escape. The risk to Jabin's forces would be minimal, but their blockade would ensure the complete extermination of every Israelite forever.

But King Jabin refused.

Muttering over this setback, Talmai strode down the narrow street, citizens scuttling out of his way like dogs with tails tucked. Wait until they faced the terror of Anakim reprisals. After they annihilated the invaders, Libni's forces would hack the citizens of Hazor to pieces, grind their city to powder and crush it into the ground. King Jabin had just doomed his city to its worst nightmares. No one thumbs his nose at Anakim.

He sneered at the puny gatehouse of Jabin's city, well aware of the guards staring open-mouthed at the face of a scowling giant. "You call this a fortified city?" he taunted. "Anakim children could flatten this gate."

He lowered his head to pass under the parapet bridging the two guard towers—but not quite low enough. With a resounding clang, his bronze helmet smacked the stones and flew from his head. When a chorus of laughter followed the indignity, Talmai's fury knew no bounds. He ripped the bridge from its substructure and hurled it at the guards, stones clattering and thudding, armed warriors toppling like tenpins. Ripping a beam from a side tower, he clubbed the remaining guards as they scurried away like so many rats. There were shrieks of terror, the moaning of the dying, but no more laughter as Talmai left Hazor.

Jonathan

"Hmm. I never saw this before." Jonathan savored the look of bewilderment on his cousin's face. "How many times have we heard this story? We thought there was no more to learn. Now recent events uncover a new message."

Phinehas stared back. His face was blank.

"Jacob was distraught over his sons' abominable vengeance. Tell me how he described the consequences of their treachery?"

His cousin shrugged, uncertain eyes asking for the answer, but Jonathan wanted him to discover this new thought for himself. He pushed the *Book of Beginnings* closer to Phinehas. "Read this."

As he pointed to the lines recording Jacob's words, the word for *trouble* seemed to flame with heavenly fire.

> *Then Jacob said to Simeon and Levi, "You have brought Achor [trouble] on me by making me obnoxious to the Canaanites and Perizzites, the people living in this land. We are few in number, and if they join forces against me and attack me, I and my household will be destroyed."* [27]

"Achor," Phinehas whispered.

"Yes," Jonathan fairly shouted. "This valley, the Valley of Shechem, was Jacob's Valley of Achor."

Jonathan watched the fire of understanding ignite Phinehas' serious eyes. That one word burned through the story, igniting powerful layers of meaning for their generation. There could not be a better way to launch this Shavuot celebration intended to remind the people of the blessings of the law, than to speak of the trouble brought by lawless rebellion. As the cousins bent their heads together to plot a new telling of the story, energy surged through Jonathan's veins.

For a long time after completing their study, Jonathan sat uncharacteristically quiet beside his cousin, staring through the seven stones of the monument into the encampment filling this emerald valley. The great stones seemed to sprout from the earth. Living stones. Organic to the scene. All across the valley, tents housing the descendants of Abraham, Isaac, and Jacob declared Yahweh's faithfulness to his promises. The ancient altar, newly reconstructed, simple and strong, stood close by. A silent witness to the importance of the words inscribed on the monument.

Gradually, Jonathan became aware of the weight of the scroll on his lap. The scrolls were important. Teaching and copying them would be his life work. But the law was more than rules penned in black letters on parchment; more than a list of things to do—or not do. The scrolls were a glimpse into the heart of Yahweh. They told of his abhorrence of evil—the demonic forces that twisted the souls of his children. They revealed the depths of his grief at the misery caused by human greed and cruelty. His pain at human suffering. His mercy toward human failure. There was power in understanding the restoring love of God. Like the monument, the law changed the look of the landscape.

Peleth

Peleth and Irad observed the activities of the Israelites in the Valley of Shechem through the entire day. The preparations were definitely for a festival, not a war. Except for the sizable vanguard of armed men leading the people into the valley, they had seen no weapons at all. Even those warriors did not stand guard but laid their swords down to dig foundations into the hillside for the huge plastered stones. The look of the monument was most impressive, but the scouts were hunkered down in the shadows of a rugged cleft at the top of Mount Gerizim, overlooking the seven stones and the altar from the opposite side of the pass. There was no way to get close enough to read the inscriptions. With seven voices reading the text to seven scribes at the same time, they could make no sense of any individual words wafting toward them.

Irad's brow crinkled with consternation. "What are those stones really for? We need to know that before we return to Gibeon."

"We may not know until we hear the dedication ceremony."

"If these people have a way of imbuing these rocks with magical powers to stop us from using the pass . . . I shudder to think of it."

"Canaan would effectively be cut in half."

"Each half of Canaan would be left to fight on its own."

"But how can anyone fight the power that flattened the walls of Jericho?"

As evening fell, the pair watched the people congregate in the pasture below the altar. White-robed priests ceremoniously slaughtered a lamb, the bright bronze blade and golden bowls flashing in the fiery glow of the low-slung rays of the sun. Robed in a vibrantly-bright tunic woven in an intricate pattern of scarlet, purple, and blue, the high priest took the golden bowl of blood, sprinkling a little on the cornerstones of the altar and pouring the remainder on the ground at its base. With every slow and deliberate movement, the rainbow of jewels gleamed and glinted from the breastplate of gold over his heart. The dignity of the ceremony and the vibrant colors of those garments lent an aura of otherworldly beauty to the pastoral setting. Peleth was overwhelmed by a sense that he stood in a magnificent open-air temple not made by human hands—in the presence of a God more glorious and good than any of the gods of Canaan.

He tipped his head toward the priest. "How majestically he moves."

"He has to move *majestically*." Irad sniffed. "There is no way he could do anything quickly in those cumbersome ceremonial trappings."

"True, but there *is* majesty in all this."

"Listen—"

"For the first time since Jacob fled this valley, O Yahweh our God," the high priest called out in prayer, "the smoke of a burnt offering rises into this sky from those who love you." He lifted his face and hands, his words ringing boldly from the surrounding rocks as the altar fire burst from the heap of wood, a burning frenzy licking at the slaughtered lamb. "You have been faithful to your promises though we have often been unfaithful to ours. Thank you for bringing your people back to this place. May the smoke of our offering be as fragrant in your nostrils as the faith offerings of our fathers hundreds of years ago."

In the deepening twilight, Eleazar beckoned for Joshua to join him at the altar.

"Hear O Israel," Joshua barked, beginning the recitation.

"Hmm. Those words again," Irad mumbled amid the thundering response.

Hear, O Israel: Yahweh is our God—Yahweh is one. And you
shall love Yahweh your God with ALL your heart and with

ALL your soul and with ALL your might.[28]

"*All your might.* There must be power in those words. They repeat them so frequently . . ." Irad looked perplexed.

Peleth finished his thought. "Yet it hardly seems a spell."

"Then why the daily repetition?"

Peleth didn't give so much as a shrug in response. He did not have an answer. They needed to listen, not talk.

"These commandments that I give you today," Joshua shouted, "are to be on your hearts . . ."

> *Impress them on your children*
> *Talk about them when you sit at home*
> *and when you walk along the road,*
> *and when you lie down*
> *and when you get up.*
> *Tie them as symbols on your hands,*
> *and bind them on your foreheads.*
> *Write them on the door frames of your houses and on your*
> *gates.* [29]

"So if you faithfully obey the commands I am giving you today—to love the Lord your God and to serve him with all your heart and all your soul . . ." Joshua prompted.

> *Then I will send rain to your land in its season, both autumn*
> *and spring rains, so that you may gather in your grain, new*
> *wine and olive oil. I will provide grass in the fields for your*
> *cattle, and you will eat and be satisfied.*
>
> *Be careful, or you will be enticed to turn away and worship*
> *other gods and bow down to them. Then the Lord's anger will*
> *burn against you, and he will shut up the heavens so that it will*
> *not rain, and the ground will yield no produce, and you will*
> *soon perish from the good land that the Lord is giving you.*[30]

"Baal commanded the rains of this land for a thousand years," Peleth whispered. "Now it appears his reign is over."

Irad's response was lost in the recitation roaring over the valley.

> *Remember these commands and cherish them. Then you and*
> *your children will live a long time in the land that Yahweh your*
> *God promised to give your ancestors. You will live there as long*
> *as there is a sky above the earth.* [31]

The recitation ceased. The people dispersed, but the scouts didn't move or speak. The bright altar fire dimmed to smoldering red coals. Not an insect sound or a night bird disturbed the silence. Although the star stories brightly spangled in the night sky told of conflict, a cloak of tranquility covered the slumbering camp. Peleth shivered with bone-chilling dread. *What would possibly motivate these people to agree to any kind of treaty?*

"We ought to get what sleep we can," Irad yawned noisily. "We will want to hear the instructions at dawn."

Omer Forty-Nine

The people rose with the dawn to gather wood, prepare breakfast, and fetch the day's water supply from the abundant streams. An aura of wonder surrounded even the most mundane tasks and familiar routines in this Edenic valley, but this was not merely a luxuriant new location for old routines. They had been counting every day from Passover to Shavuot, the counting an integral part of this festival.

By the time the tribes arrived here, anticipation had been bubbling and growing with the count for nearly seven weeks. This morning, each family laid the forty-ninth and last stone of their Omer counters in place and expectation erupted joyously throughout the twelve tribes. They were the covenant people, chosen to bless the world. They were not wiser or stronger or more numerous than other people groups, but Yahweh God showered them with love and gifts far beyond anything they deserved. That divine love effervesced through camp, building powerful waves of affection for family and friend. And in that love, Acsah found her strength renewed.

Acsah

Hogluh and Hodesh took turns grinding with stone mortar and pestle and soon reduced Caleb's sack of wheat kernels to a basketful of fine flour.

"Well done," Acsah said, lifting the product of their labor for a closer inspection.

"This will be the best bread ever." She transferred a large measure of flour to a clay bowl. She added water, oil, and a sprinkle of salt.

Hodesh watched intently. "Uncle Caleb says we are not only celebrating the wheat harvest. It is the anniversary of Mount Sinai too."

"That is right, sweet child. God led the children of Israel out of Egyptian slavery and brought them to Mount Sinai." Acsah smiled inwardly, feeling a bit like her father as she took advantage of the teachable moment. "The journey took nearly seven weeks. Then on exactly the fiftieth day of their new life as a free people, God spoke the words of his law. He made a covenant oath to care for them, and they promised to obey his law. That is what we are celebrating . . . Abihail, scoop in that yeast-honey mixture now."

Tired of watching others add ingredients and knead them together, Hogluh wandered off and kneeled by the little rows of stones marking the Omer. She pushed the forty-ninth stone gently to make it align perfectly with the other six. Seven perfect rows of seven. "We have been counting for so long and soon it will all be over. I wish the feast lasted more than one day."

Acsah laughed. "I'm just excited about reaching the fiftieth day so we can rest." She felt the soft mound of dough. "Still a little sticky," she said, reaching for the flour basket.

"Can I add it?" Hogluh asked, plunging her hand into the flour ahead of Acsah. Acsah nodded, working in the flour as Hogluh sprinkled it over the dough.

"Uncle Caleb told us the story about God speaking at Mount Sinai," Hodesh stated matter-of-factly. "It would be awesome to hear the actual voice of God."

"More than awesome," Abihail said, casting a fond look at the child. She watched Acsah knead. "I will never forget my father telling how Mount Sinai rumbled. Smoke billowed from the top. Flames and fireballs shot high in the air."

Hodesh's eyes widened. "That would have been terrifying."

"Terrifying and wonderful at the same time," Abihail replied.

"Can I help knead the dough?"

Acsah moved to the side so Hodesh could knead. "Here. Push down with all your weight . . . Now fold over and push again. Perfect." She watched the child work and then sprinkled a little more flour over the top. "Whenever it feels sticky, add a little more."

"May I do that part?" Hogluh asked, reaching for another small handful of flour. "Hodesh, tell me when you need it."

"You are such good helpers," Acsah observed. "Soon there will be no household jobs left for Abihail and me."

Hodesh grinned and kneaded all the harder.

"After Passover, we replaced our daily manna with barley flat bread. Now for the first time here in Canaan, we are making wheat bread. Our two grain harvests line up with two very special things God did for us." Acsah did not want to miss the opportunity to instruct these two in the history of their adoptive people. "God freed us from slavery and made us his chosen people. Passover celebrates that freedom from Egyptian bondage. Shavuot celebrates the covenant that keeps us free." The children were listening. *God, give me the wisdom of my father.*

"The law is like the banks of a river controlling and guiding wayward water. Without banks, a flood of water can destroy things or else run so thin in every direction it becomes useless. The laws, statutes, and decrees of the covenant are intended to keep us a free nation—a blessed people, blessing the world."

Acsah reached into the bowl, feeling the soft mound of dough as she finished. "Perfect. Feel how silky the dough is now. We are ready to shape the loaves."

"Not fair. She did all the kneading and I only got to add flour once."

"But Hogluh, you will begin the best part. Shaping the loaves." Acsah flashed a mysterious smile. "First, pull the dough into two pieces. Two pieces just about the same size for the two loaves."

"Like this?"

"Exactly like that. Now we will shape each piece to look like the stone tablets in the ark of the covenant," Acsah instructed. "Each of you can make one."

"No stone ever felt as silky and soft as this." Hogluh giggled. "I hope it isn't rock-hard after it is baked."

"Trust me. It won't be." Acsah stood and pulled back the tent flap. "Something magical is about to happen. Let's take your loaves inside where it is warmer and see what happens as they rest."

Hodesh bobbed her head in excitement. "Master Caleb told us about it."

"Did he tell you they will grow with *inner power.*" Acsah twiddled her fingers in front of their faces. "Mysterious imparted life."

Hodesh giggled. "Yes, he did. He said that's the way God's law works in us too."

Hogluh simply sniffed the yeasty goodness and sat down to watch the magic happen.

Jonathan

When the sun reached the halfway point between zenith and horizon, the silver trumpets summoned the people. Jonathan quickly found his place with the tribe of Levi and watched the sea of people pour into the open field at the feet of the twin mountains. Not only the bloodline of Israel, but the Canaanite family of Rahab of Jericho plus the thousands of young Midianite girls, orphans adopted into the family.

He felt the exhilaration of new understanding. Caleb took him aside just yesterday for a surprisingly intimate man-to-man discussion on God's love for the alien. Caleb's own family had been adopted into Israel from Edomite stock. Jonathan was the grandson of Moses and his Midianite wife. Then there were the Egyptians who left their homeland to join the Exodus. He would never forget the lesson recently learned, bitterly learned. All were invited to share the feast. It was the very first promise given to Abraham—*and all peoples on earth will be blessed through you.*[32]

At the moment, the crowds faced not the monument or the altar, but the cave prepared for the remains of their ancestor, Joseph. The burial was solemn and grand, befitting the high-ranking status of Joseph in Pharaoh's court. It evoked a satisfying sense of closure. Long overdue closure. But when Jonathan caught a glimpse of Acsah with her father and family, separated from him by a crowd of hundreds, he was struck with the sad irony. He was physically closer and felt more connected to that casket of bones than to the woman he loved. It was pathetic, but true.

His family's story was deeply entangled with that of Joseph. He was a Levite, well aware that Levi had been one of the cruel instigators of the plot against the favored son of Jacob with his coat of many colors. In fact, Levi's intention was to murder the hated brother, but other brothers intervened and sold Joseph to a caravan of Ishmaelite slave traders. In spite of his success in the land of Egypt, Joseph spent the remainder of his life longing to return home. As he lay on his deathbed, knowing he would be embalmed and interred in an Egyptian tomb, he summoned his surviving brothers and their families.

He spoke of his boyhood dreams, visions of his brothers bowing to him. Those dreams proved prophetic, but his naiveté in flaunting them also precipitated his troubles. At the end of his life, his dream was no longer to be the favorite son, the honored one. He just wanted to be part of the family. He just wanted to go home. He instructed them not to take his mummified body to Canaan for burial ahead of the family. He firmly believed God would lead them all back when the time was right, and he made his brothers swear that they or their descendants would carry his remains with them.

Jonathan's own grandfather—Moses, a direct descendant of Levi—ensured that the promise was kept. On the chaotic night of the Exodus, he made certain that Joseph's casket left Egypt. The entire family began the homeward journey together.

As soon as the sealing stone was rolled across the opening of Joseph's tomb, Eleazar called for a brief practice of the ceremony of blessings and curses. Jonathan, along with the rest of the Levites, assisted in separating and organizing the twelve tribes, helping each family find their assigned places on the slopes of the twin mountains. Six tribes on Ebal. Six on Gerizim. The tribes had done this with Moses on the other side of the river before he died. Now they would find their correct positions on-site.

Jonathan took advantage of an opportunity for one face-to-face connection with Acsah before he climbed back downslope to his place between the peaks among the Levites. A brief meeting of the eyes. Smiles exchanged. The encounter was painfully fleeting, but he stood with the Levites closest to her at the foot of Mount Gerizim—the Mount of Blessings.

As the Levites called out the familiar words of the recitation, Jonathan's mind returned again and again to his assigned position. It was all too easy for him to feel overwhelmed by disappointments—to feel as if the blessings he longed for and expected fell on someone else's mountain. His place in this scene, the place of his family, was expressly chosen by Moses. His grandfather never saw this valley, but he knew exactly where his grandson needed to stand. At the foot of the literal Mount of Blessings. A sense of his grandfather's love and wisdom lingered warm and wonderful in his heart. Jonathan missed the old man more than he could say. As the Levites recited the last of the curses in the short practice, he wiped away a tear.

And the people shouted, "Amen."

Ahiman of the Anakim

Ahiman was stealthy. Slipping through the brush and rock on the back side of Mount Gerizim, he paused to listen. The babble coming from the Israelite encampment was understandable now. A strong voice trumpeted:

> With this evening sacrifice, the forty-ninth day of the Omer comes to a close. The holy celebration of Shavuot begins.

Creeping even higher toward the summit, he stumbled over two men concealed in a natural bunker. "Hah! Flushed you out of hiding like a pair of nesting partridges," he sneered.

The scrawny faces blinking up at him did not reach his belt. He challenged them with his most intimidating voice. "You are not Israelites. Who are you? And what are you doing here?"

"We were on this mountain first," the shorter one shot back with surprising courage. "Suppose you tell us who you are and why you disturbed us."

"Aha! Brave little heroes, I see." He took a wide stance and folded his arms across his chest. "All right. I am Ahiman of the Anakim, brother to Talmai and Sheshai. Perhaps you have heard of our exploits. Yes? I have been in the king's service at Beth-Shean for the past twenty years, but my brothers came to call me back. The Anakim are gathering under our king again. We have formed an alliance with Adoni-Zedek of Jebus and the southern kings to destroy the Israelite invaders."

The spokesman for the little pair of spies nodded his understanding. "We are from the Federation of Gibeon. Our senate asked us to spy on the Israelite activities and learn their plans. We have been watching and listening for the past two days."

"Will the Federation be joining Zedek?" Ahiman asked gruffly. "Or do you plan to join Jabin up here in the north?"

"The Federation sent us to gather more information before they decide exactly how Gibeon will respond to Israel."

The response struck Ahiman as evasive. "Anakim have no such uncertainty. Crush wherever, however, we can. Anakim do not send spies."

"It is wise to know your enemy."

Ahiman shoved his huge body into a crouch beside the Gibeonites. "It is wiser to find good cover. With very little work this cramped hiding place would make a fine redoubt for warriors my size. Maybe for Libni himself."

The little man looked him straight in the eyes. "There are many similar nooks all over these mountains."

Did this insolent mouse have no fear?

"I could easily wring your necks and roast you for dinner." *At last. A look of revulsion in the eyes of the scrappy one.* " . . . but perhaps you have gathered useful information, hmmm?" Ahiman grabbed the pair by their beards and pulled their heads close to his ears. "King Libni would be quite pleased to know what the invaders are planning next. Tell me what secrets you have learned."

"One learns by listening."

Following our feast tomorrow, we will assemble here before the ark of the covenant for the ceremony of blessings and curses.

Ahiman snorted his disdain. He already knew about the ceremony, the ark, the time and place of the assembly. Libni had wrung that information from one of Labayu's men within minutes of capturing him. *Could these little mice tell him anything he didn't already know?*

The Gibeonites ignored his grunt and continued listening intently.

Seven weeks ago on the day following Passover, I waved the
first sheaf of cut barley before the Lord of Harvest. Our first
ever Omer offering. Hope for a rich grain harvest. How
Yahweh has blessed! We have harvested both barley and wheat
in abundance. Tomorrow morning bring the loaves you baked
from the first wheat. Wave them before the Lord at this altar to
acknowledge his goodness. The season of the grain harvest began
with one wave sheaf of barley and will end with thousands of
loaves waved before him.

"*That* is their secret to fertility?" Ahiman waved his hands above his head and
chortled his derision. "Wave. Wave. It almost makes me sorry these invaders will not
live long enough to experience a *real* fertility celebration."

Along with your wave offering, bring your rams, your goats, or
bulls here at dawn. The priests will take Yahweh's portions to
burn on the altar. The sweet aroma rising throughout the time
of feasting will remind us that our God has a place at our table.
The priests will also take a small portion of each sacrifice, so they
and the Levite families may join in the feasting. You will keep
the largest portion to roast for your own family and guests.

Ahiman squinted at the Gibeonites suspiciously. *If they really have been spying for*
two days, why did they still find this priest's droning blather interesting? "What are you
really up to here, hmmm? You aren't considering forming an alliance with the enemy,
are you? King Libni would be quite displeased if that were the case. His anger is not
something your senate would want to deal with."

Ahiman's predatory instincts homed in on subtle changes in the spies. Eyes
darting down the mountain. Feet ready to run that direction. The little Gibeonites
wanted to escape. *Well, let them.*

He had no more patience for useless palaver from these two or the Israelite priest.
His task was to find as many well-located nooks and crannies as he could. Libni
wanted alcoves for the eighty-something Anakim expected to show up here tonight.
His job was to excavate those protective bunkers as necessary without drawing the
attention of the Shechem side. He would start with this excellent spot.

"Shoo, you worthless rodents," he snarled. "Get out of here. We Anakim have a surprise planned for the celebration tomorrow. I'm commandeering this spot for me and my comrades. And take this word back to that senate of yours—" he jeered as they grabbed their packs and scrambled away. "Little people should avoid snooping about underfoot when Anakim are abroad in the land."

CHAPTER FIFTEEN

SHAVUOT

Jonathan

The final day in the Omer count blinked past and the sky flamed orange in welcome of Shavuot. So much had happened during these forty-nine days, but it was all history now. In another day the long-awaited festival itself would be only a memory—but the monument would remain.

He knew he should be focused on the ritual of the evening sacrifice, but Jonathan could not keep his eyes from returning to the row of plastered stones, massive monoliths commanding the eye, the enduring strength of rock connecting the solid earthy beauty of grasses and trees to the ethereal sapphire sky. It filled Jonathan with a powerful sense of destiny as if he were a living extension of that monument. The grandson of Moses, a Levite. Born to connect the inhabitants of earth to their God. He pictured his future life teaching the law, perhaps sitting in the shade of that old terebinth, future generations of Israelites, perhaps even people of other nations coming to him for instruction.

Only one thing could make this dream any sweeter—winning the heart of a certain green-eyed girl.

"Our preparations for Shavuot are complete." The altar flames engulfing the sacrificial lamb displaced the beautiful image of her face as the high priest's words broke into Jonathan's reverie.

Eleazar moved slowly to the front of the altar and leaned toward the people. "The

Valley of Shechem has a bold new appearance, intended to send a clear message to the inhabitants of Canaan." He tilted his head slightly to one side, eyes gleaming with warmth and love, embracing all the tribes of Israel as family. "Yahweh chose Israel to be a blessing to the world, but we failed—just as our fathers repeatedly failed before us. Our misdeeds have added to the world's load of death and pain. This restored altar will long remain as a testimony to the faithfulness of Yahweh to restore faulty people to his covenant again."

As he spoke, Eleazar held out his right arm, inviting Phinehas to come to him. "I have asked my son to recount the story of Jacob and his family in this valley."[33]

Glittering and glorious as he was in his priestly attire, Eleazar seemed to fade as Phinehas took his place at the front of the altar, still gripping the silver trumpet. He was tall, fierce in demeanor and awesome in the white holiness of his priestly robe. His first words rang out boldly. "Shechem was Jacob's Valley of Achor."

The abrupt beginning startled the crowds. Jonathan sensed the energy sizzling all around and smiled approvingly. *Phinehas. Mouth of brass indeed. My cousin was well named.* The past two days had been exhausting. The people were tired and had little enthusiasm for a familiar story, particularly when they were standing in a pasture rather than sitting in family circles around evening campfires. But with the word *Achor,* dull senses awoke.

"Jacob loved the God of his fathers," Phinehas continued, "but in his passionate desire to possess the covenant birthright, he deceived his blind father and cheated his brother Esau. Forced to leave the tents of his father and mother, he fled, terrified and alone, reaching Bethel as night fell. Perhaps he was comforted by memories of his grandfather's connection to this spot. Abraham had built one of his earliest altars at Bethel. After his failure of faith in Egypt, Abraham returned to Bethel, and God met him there with new assurances and promises. Perhaps, the stone Jacob used as a pillow was pulled from the ruins of his grandfather's altar. And Yahweh God did not disappoint his fugitive son. In the blackest night of his life, haunted by his brother's murderous threats, a glorious stairway connecting heaven and earth appeared before him and God spoke to Jacob for the first time, promising to be with him and bring him back to the Promised Land.

"Finally, after twenty long years in exile, Jacob found himself a wealthy man with a large, thriving family—two wives, two concubines, a notably beautiful daughter and eleven sons. (Benjamin had not yet been born.) His flocks and herds covered the land as far as eye could see. The time had come for Jacob to return to Canaan, to claim his birthright as patriarch in the line of Shem.

"Jacob was convinced that his own cleverness and hard work had produced his success, but God was about to teach him a most important lesson. As Jacob approached the border of Canaan, he was filled with second thoughts. He began to tremble. What if his brother's seething anger had not cooled in the intervening years? With great foreboding, he sent word to Esau announcing his imminent return. He informed his brother of his great wealth. He explained he was no threat to his brother's holdings. All he had ever wanted was the covenant leadership. He would not claim any of the birthright possessions.

"Word came back of Esau approaching with an army of four hundred warriors. Distress and despair roiled in the depths of his stomach. He hastened to select generous gifts from his flocks and herds, sending them ahead in a gesture of peace. He set up his camp to defend his wives and young children against attack in the best way he could, knowing his brother's revenge would not be limited to himself alone. When he had done all a man could do, he found a solitary place for prayer.

"He threw himself on the ground, wracked by deep remorse for the wrong he had done his brother. He felt the shame of his life of grasping deception. He was the second twin, born clutching his brother's heel as if trying to hold him back. In all honesty, Jacob could never remember a time when he did not covet the rights of the firstborn. That sin placed his wives and little ones in mortal danger. Jacob pressed his forehead against the cold earth and wept. No deceit or cleverness could help him now. His family would not survive without heavenly intervention.

"All of a sudden, a soft footfall whispered close beside him. *Could it be Esau already?* A hand seized his shoulder and Jacob leaped to his feet. As he twisted from the powerful grip, a second hand took hold of him. Jacob struggled to stabilize his stance, and the moonlight illuminated the fierce features of his assailant. *Not his brother. It must be one of Esau's warriors.*

"Despair nearly paralyzed him. He was an old man in a fight to the death against a stronger, younger opponent. But Jacob was a man of great determination. He struggled on and on through the night. More than once, the man's forceful grasp nearly throttled him or forced him to the ground. Then he remembered his wives and children and wrestled all the harder. Finally, on the dim edge of his vision, Jacob noticed the brightening of the sky above the eastern horizon.

"He had been struggling for hours, but his adversary's strength had not slackened. He was suddenly weary to the point of despair. Just as he was about to relax his hold, about to surrender to death, the silent warrior spoke. "I must leave for the day breaks." The man pivoted to break away, and in the twisting movement reached out and touched Jacob's groin.

"It was the merest touch, but the pain was brutal, ripping his hipbone from its socket, crippling Jacob more than a violent kick. His assailant was no mortal man. With everything he had, Jacob now clung to his opponent. His life scrolled before him. His manipulative ways. His lies and deceit. His lack of trust in Yahweh. Oh, how he wanted a new story. Jacob grappled now, not to defeat an enemy warrior, but to hang on to his God. Barely able to stand, breathless with the cramping agony of his injury, Jacob cried out, 'I will not let go until you bless me.'

"This time when the warrior seized him by the shoulders and locked eyes with him, Jacob saw nothing but love reflected there. The next words fell gentle on his ears. 'Tell me your name.'

"'Jacob.'

"'No.' The heavenly warrior looked at him with great affection. 'You are no longer Jacob the Deceiver, but Israel the Overcomer.' With that, he vanished.

"Out of the deep travail of that struggle and Jacob's plea for blessing, a new man was born. A new man with a new name. A covenant name given to him by God himself."

Israel.

God Wrestler.

Overcomer.

"But Jacob did not look like a strong overcomer to his brother. Esau's heart melted as Jacob staggered out to greet him, an old and crippled man. The brothers embraced and were reconciled. The God Wrestler, the Overcomer, walked with a limp ever after that day lest he consider taking his own shortcut rather than follow God's path.

"From there the new Jacob-Israel came seeking this particular valley, the place where God gave Abraham the promise of the land for the first time. As Jacob looked around, he saw land protected by walled Canaanite cities. The populace was ruled by violence. There were hilltop shrines polluted by human sacrifices, temples dedicated to the obscene fertility worship of Baal and Asherah. It took a stretch of faith to believe this was his inheritance, but he bought land right here in the heart of Canaan. He dug a well, rebuilt Abraham's altar, and settled in to see what God would do for his Overcomer.

"Now Israel was a changed man, but his children were not. The rape of his daughter by Prince Shechem was a great evil, but his sons' revenge was a much greater atrocity. The young Canaanite proposed to repair the wrong by marrying Dinah, and Jacob's sons, Simeon and Levi, responded with malicious deceit. They proposed a covenant of peace between their peoples as the precondition for the marriage. The men of Shechem's city agreed to undergo circumcision according to the terms of the covenant. But on the third day, while they were healing and unable to fight, Simeon and Levi slipped into the city and massacred every man, including Prince Shechem. The new Jacob-Israel was determined to follow God's path rather than his own, but he was betrayed by his own family.

"This was his Valley of Achor.

"Jacob himself used the word in speaking to these two sons. 'You have heaped abominable *achor* on me,' he wailed. 'Terrible trouble. We will flee the Valley of the Promise. But even if we escape, the name of Jacob will linger in this land as a foul odor.'"[34]

Phinehas paused dramatically with a sweeping gesture toward the monument.

"We are here to rewrite the ending of that story. The law of love and justice written on these seven megaliths will make an enduring statement to the inhabitants of this land. Here with this celebration, we declare that we are a holy nation, loved by Yahweh God, keeping covenant with him. A people guided by good laws—not a people of selfish ambition or reckless revenge."

Jonathan stood straighter in a burst of pride as Phinehas retreated to his place at the right of the altar. The role of warrior, leading the people into battle like Joshua, was not his destiny. But he could stand by the side of his cousin, the future high priest, as the chief Levite of Israel.

Peleth

The story ended, but Peleth continued staring at the young storyteller. "Strange people," he whispered in wonder.

Irad nodded agreement. "What kind of people remember and recite tales of their failures?" His forehead crinkled in confusion.

"Mmmm. Yet his face shone with triumph."

"It helps to be able to see them, doesn't it? To see their faces."

Peleth coughed up a sarcastic laugh. "We can thank Ahiman for our change of location."

"Listen. The high priest is going to speak again."

"Our efforts toward goodness are simply not good enough. But God is always good. Our burnt offerings remind us of that." The high priest reached out affectionately to the altar, laying his hand on the cornerstone closest to him.

The voice was kind. The face, kinder still. It really was an advantage to have this line of sight.

"We will call this altar by the name our father Jacob gave it—*El Elohe Israel*. Mighty, the God of Israel. When Jacob, newly named Israel, worshipped at this altar, he was simply one man, the patriarch of one family. Now we, the people called by his name, have become a great nation. El Elohe Israel!"

"El Elohe Israel!" the people echoed back.

"Mighty, the God of Israel," Irad whispered. "That is just the problem isn't it?"

A cool breeze swept across the darkening valley, but it was not the wind that raised the hair on Peleth's arms. "Their army is no match for ours, but Baal and Asherah are no match for El Elohe Israel."

Irad looked thoughtful. "I believe the intelligence we have gathered will convince the young firebrands of Gibeon to avoid war at all costs."

"I hope that thought helps me sleep better tonight."

"I do not have that problem." Irad yawned and settled his head into a slight hollow in his rocky pillow and promptly fell asleep.

Peleth woke to soft scrabbling noises and snorting vocalizations.

Wild boars? Where? Prickles of fear shuddered down his back. Every sense was on highest alert. He carefully drew a deep breath, looking to the eastern sky to determine the time. The sign marking the beginning of the third watch was just rising. The sign of the Fishes. Fishes pulling this way and that, much like the forces at odds in Canaan right now.

The moon had already set, but there was enough starlight to see Irad now awake beside him listening intently. His eyes were round with fear. It wasn't a herd of wild pigs surrounding them. It was worse. Much worse. The great scraping and scooping of earth, the clattering and thudding of rock—along with muffled sniggers and snickers told the tale. Anakim. Ahiman's friends were at work, digging out strategic bunkers all over the western slopes of both mountains. Digging and stockpiling boulders.

"They really are going to attack during the ceremony tomorrow." Irad breathed the words close to Peleth's ear in the lightest possible wisp of sound.

More discussion was not needed. Giants were as unpredictable as rooting boars—and far more dangerous, especially when gathered in packs. But where were they? The sounds seemed to come from every side. He strained his eyes into the moonless night trying to separate the dark shapes of the Anakim from rocks and shrubs. He stood paralyzed by the uncertainty when an unconventional plan materialized out of his fear.

The one place the Anakim would not be digging would be on the monument side of the mountain and they were already on the top of the ridge. He touched Irad's shoulder and motioned in the direction of the monument stones and the Israelite camp. His companion understood immediately. Quiet as leopards, they crept from their lair, slipping up and over the ridge. They kept to the shadowy cover of rock and shrub just in case the slumbering Israelite camp had posted a watch.

Peleth had no idea exactly how the confrontation between the Anakim and the Israelites would unfold, but there was no doubt in his mind which side would win. He and Irad had more than enough information to tip the senate toward voting for a covenant of peace. The goal now was simply to get back to Gibeon before war broke out.

Libni

The Anakim king groaned and squinted into the morning light. Dawn came too early and too bright for one who had been a cave dweller for forty years, particularly one whose forays out of the cave were primarily at night. And particularly for one who had just spent most of the past night stockpiling boulders. *Hah! A giant-sized stockpile of boulders.*

The sounds from the enemy camp, muffled by the interposing mountains, were unintelligible—but clearly sounds of excitement and celebration. The noise was intensely irritating, but Libni didn't move. He was sequestered in a bunker with three of his men and definitely did not want to arouse them yet. *Well, my thoughts will not disturb their sleep.* He smirked as his plans for the day gradually came into focus. Plans that included much blood and many broken bodies. The Anakim would end that tumult of joy forever.

"Rejoice!"

The loud voice trumpeting the command could not be ignored. He crept out of the excavated hollow, away from the snoring and snorting of his men, and listened.

> *The grain harvests are gathered in. Yahweh, faithful provider of sunshine and rain, invites us to share this Shavuot meal with him. Bring your sacrifices to the priests and let the roasting begin.*

"Hear that?" a sleepy voice snickered from the shadows of the bunker. "Let the roasting begin!" It was Talmai, Libni's second in command. "Let's answer with fire arrows. That's a roasting I would love to see."

"Don't wake the others," Libni growled, "they will want to carry out your jest. We already have an excellent plan. *My* plan." He slithered a body length closer to the ridge, then jerked his head in a silent command for Talmai to accompany him.

Side by side at the top of the ridge, the two stared down at the bustling camp. The vast array of tents lit by the first streams of golden light was undeniably impressive. Directly below his lookout, the smoke of the morning sacrifice to Yahweh already spiraled into a cloudless sky. But at the far end of the valley, a second plume of smoke—Labayu's offering to Baal—rose over the Hivite settlement. "So it begins," Libni whispered. "Behold, Talmai! Dueling prayers to the gods."

Talmai bumped and jostled clumsily beside him in the tight confines of the lookout, eyeing the valley through a rocky fissure too small for both giants to use at the same time. He grimaced. "Yahweh's altar prays louder."

Libni shoved him aside for a better look. It was true. The smoke just below them billowed thicker and blacker, bold with the burning of fat and organs from the people's offerings. An urgent warning twisted his gut. "Go down to Labayu and tell him to keep fueling Baal's altar. It is the gods at war today."

Talmai disappeared into the buckled folds of the hills encompassing the valley while Libni waited, restless and irritable. He peered through the narrow cleft, watching the high priest continually fuel that fire. The priests of Yahweh collected bowl after bowl of offal as the worshippers slew the animals for the feast. And still the line of Israelites bringing their sacrificial animals grew. That smoke would ascend to the heavens all day. His hatred for the descendants of Jacob seethed in a burning rage.

This encampment infects the soil of Canaan like a festering boil. He was seized by an urge to awaken his men, charge down, and scrape that blight from the earth, but he fought to repress that impulse. His eyes returned again and again to the smoke pluming endlessly from the altar, warning him not to esteem Yahweh's power too lightly. He must wait for the right time to strike—which was the ceremony when the Israelites gathered at the foot of the mountain. Hours from now. When the feasting was done.

Libni sniffed the air. The smoky, savory fragrance of roasting meat from thousands of animals wafted to his nostrils from every corner of camp. "Enjoy the feast, you pathetic creatures. It will be your last." It was good that most of his men remained asleep. It would not be easy to hold back a pack of giants. Bloodlust ran strong in Anakim veins.

At the eastern end of the valley, the women and children of the little settlement of Hivites tended their gardens, watching the activities of the Israelite camp from afar. Libni could not see Labayu's four-hundred marauders, but he knew they would be in place when needed to prevent escape toward the east. He nodded approvingly as thicker, blacker smoke rose from their altar fire. At least Talmai managed to get that task done. He had to admit he had no one better to serve at his right hand, but Talmai's failure to enlist King Jabin still goaded him.

As he scanned the ring of hills for Talmai's return, he noticed a shadow crawling toward the peak of Ebal. Looking up, he nearly whooped for joy at the sign of Baal's power gathering in the sky. Dark storm clouds already blocked the sunlight over Yahweh's altar. A chill wind blew, and the billowing blackness spread rapidly. Soon both Gerizim and Ebal were shrouded in gloom. Yahweh's display of power over the past few months was intolerable. Today Baal would show who ruled this land.

When Libni finally saw Talmai skirting through the hills, he scrambled downslope for a debriefing. Talmai was grinning as he approached. "Labayu has already laid a strong loop around the perimeter of the valley. His marauders will be ready when our avalanche of terror begins. As soon as he sees us charge down over the rubble, he will tighten the noose." He chortled with glee. "No survivors. Not one."

"Not one," Libni agreed.

Talmai's eyes narrowed in a crafty grin. "Labayu requested an opportunity to get in on the action. His men want revenge for the ancient massacre."

"Easy enough. We will drive any Children of Jacob who survive the rockslide against his line. A melee of madness at our feet." Libni's laughter garbled his last words. "How long will it take for Labayu to notice clumsy giants stomping and crushing Hivites as they bash Israelite skulls?"

Talmai cackled with glee. "Labayu's warriors won't be able to think with their brains splattered over the ground."

Just then, snorting and hacking punctuated by loud bursts of stinking gasses erupted from rocky hideouts all over the mountainside. Libni groaned. *An Anakim awakening.* His own outburst of raucous laughter had aroused his men earlier than he wished. He might as well make it official.

"Arise, O sons of Anak," he commanded. "Tend to your elimination needs, but don't stray far from your assigned bunker. Pass the wineskins while we wait. Break your fast. You will need all your strength on this most glorious day of battle."

He snorted a laugh at the hissing sound of eighty-two giants making water all across the slopes, dark yellow rain pattering and steaming on the rocks, forming little frothing streams trickling down the mountain. "Hear the sound of Anakim rain, Lord Baal, and send yours on our enemy today."

The great lumbering Sheshai, squatting behind a rock, lifted his head and blinked in confusion. "You praying for Baal to . . .? You saying rain is the storm god making water?"

Sheshai was the eldest of the three brothers, Libni's best fighters. He was the eldest, but the slowest in wit.

"Sheshai want clear skies." With an awkward tenderness, he stroked the battered wooden cudgel he always carried into battle. The death-dealing weapon was cumbersome, shaped from the trunk of a sizable oak, but Sheshai cradled it like a baby. "My sweet Ets is thirsty for blood."

Ets. A tree. A death-dealing tree. Libni bobbed his head approvingly. One did not have to be smart to be deadly. "Your baby will be well fed today."

"Oh yes, my brother," Talmai laughed. "The Sons of Jacob think they gather to feast and dedicate their monument, but Baal gathers them to a feast of terror."

"A monumental reign of terror," Libni added with a smirk.

Ahiman sniggered, kicking at the boulder he had just watered with urine. "A rocky *rain* of terror."

"Sheshai like that rain. Let it fall now. Ets and me, we go play in the rain." The lumbering giant unfolded his great height and lurched toward the summit. "Ets and me go crush skulls."

A chorus of approving grunts rumbled from the bunkers as others crawled from their lairs to follow.

"Sheshai. Stop now," Libni growled. "So you bash a few and the rest run away?" *How many times must he repeat the plan to these unruly dimwits?* "This battle is bigger than anything we have ever faced. The fate of Canaan is at stake. We will win *if* we follow my plan. I will not tolerate more failure."

Eighty-two pairs of eyes cast dubious glances at each other. *Who failed?* the eyes asked.

Libni impaled his second with a pointed look. "Talmai's sortie to King Jabin of Hazor failed. Perhaps I should have gone myself. A ring of chariots surrounding the entire valley would have been a very nice touch."

Talmai scowled but did not reply.

"No matter. Labayu was easy to convince. His four hundred will be enough."

Sheshai scratched his head. "Four hundred puny men? Look at all those Israelites."

Libni took a deep breath, trying to be patient. "Labayu is there to block the road. We launch the rock slide, sudden and swift. Then we rush down and bash brains to our heart's content."

"Why Labayu only block road?" Why his men not fight?

"Don't be stupid." Talmai cuffed his brother's ear. "You want Labayu to rush in to attack while an avalanche of boulders hurtles down the mountains on his men?"

"Anakim fight. Not block. We ready for blood."

"Hear! Hear!" An undercurrent of agreement rose all around. "We want blood. Attack now."

"Ah . . . the sweet taste of blood." Libni smacked as if devouring a tasty morsel. Then he seized Sheshai's club and twisted it, nearly wrenching the weapon from his hands. "Don't spoil my feast. Wait until I say attack."

The ungainly giant thrashed and fell against his companions. Before he could regain his balance, Libni pulled him so close they nearly touched noses, his voice low and menacing. "Don't start something that can only fail. If you mess this up, I will personally burn this precious Ets of yours."

Sheshai cowered into the shadows whimpering, but guttural wolf-like snarls rose from Anakim all around.

Libni growled his pack back into silence. "Remember who you are. Sons of Anak. This battle will reestablish our power in Canaan only *if* we obliterate the entire camp of Israel. My plan will do that—*if* we wait. We attack when they congregate to dedicate their monument and not before."

Sheshai sat cradling his gargantuan club more like a hurt child, it seemed to Libni, than a chastised warrior. He needed to restore Sheshai's fighting spirit. "Listen, Sheshai, your king is depending on your valor and strength when the hour of battle comes. Choose seven of the bravest men in your command. Your assignment will be to rush down and uproot those monument stones as soon as danger from our avalanche subsides. Pull any standing stones from the earth and use them to crush Joshua, any living priests, and that little golden chest they prize so highly. You will have the most important task of all. Do you understand?"

"I do that. I like playing with rocks." Sheshai laughed until he drooled.

Libni joined in the laughter. "Perfect justice—obliterating Joshua and his priests with the megalith they set up to undo Canaanite power. Stories of this Anakim battle will be the talk of Canaan for centuries, long after Joshua's seven stones are forgotten."

Libni's mood became serious as he turned his attention to motivating the remainder of the men. "Labayu assures us his blockade will be strong. His men will eliminate everyone who manages to escape us." He smirked and gave his brows a conspiratorial upward flick. "When every Israelite is exterminated, we'll turn on Labayu and his marauders, erasing every trace of life in his village. We cannot leave one person to contradict our report—that Israel destroyed Labayu and we destroyed Israel in retaliation. The kingdoms of the north will think they would have been Israel's next victims but for us. They will welcome the Anakim back as protectors of Canaan. And when they learn that King Jabin refused to send one chariot to help us, they will join forces with us in destroying Hazor. Anakim will rule Canaan."

Libni's pulse quickened with exhilarating power. *First the north. Then the south. Adoni-Zedek calls himself "Lord of Righteousness." Hah! Might makes right. Zedek's Southern Alliance is too slow in entering the game.*

Certain every Anakim warrior was now solidly behind his plan, Libni crawled again to the lookout. Swirls of foggy mist prowled around the monument. He smiled at the good omen. Then a crack of thunder drew his eyes to the clouds massed over the duel peaks, a black death shroud blocking the sun. Raising his face to the sky,

King Libni thanked the storm god. Wind whipped his face. Lightning crackled. Thunder rumbled. Baal was awake.

Strangely, there was no rain. Despite that, the Hivite villagers were fleeing into their houses for shelter. The giants hunkered down in the eerie darkness, awaiting their king's command. An unnatural pressure in the air put nerves on edge. Squabbles broke out, but were snarled back into submission by Ahiman, Talmai, and the other commanders.

Curious, Libni mused. *The families of Israel finish their feast undaunted by the storm.* His plan demanded the element of surprise, but he would have preferred a little fear at the prospect of Baal's storm.

All at once the sound of duel trumpets split the air, challenging the roar of the tempest. The milling mass of people began moving toward the open pastures below the altar. Then at a second trumpet blast, they split into two groups opening a broad aisle down the center of the congregation. Libni watched a long cavalcade of priests and Levites form and begin marching through the aisle toward the altar. The two leading the procession continued blowing long blasts on their trumpets.

Libni sneered at the mismatched pair. The older man in heavily embroidered garments was high priest of Yahweh, but Baal afforded him no glory today. The embellishments of gold and gemstones decorating his garments appeared dark and drab in the shadow of Baal's storm. Even the young priest in simple white, proudly holding his trumpet higher than the head of the aging high priest, overshadowed the old man.

Libni laughed aloud. *Foolish priests. All that tooting on your horns is only hastening your own demise.*

Directly behind this pair, four priests marched with a stately, steady tread. They carried a bulky object shrouded in blue linen by golden poles resting on their shoulders. Libni's innards twisted with fear and loathing. This was the very thing that held back the floods of the Jordan. This was the war chest that flattened the walls of Jericho. "O Baal, defend your name," he breathed.

The black cumulus pressed down on the shrouded war chest, the four priests, and the train of white-robed men following behind. Smoke was still ascending thick and black from Yahweh's altar, but Baal protested with increased flashings of lightning. Libni looked to the east end of the valley for the smoke plume from Baal's altar but saw nothing. Whether it had gone out or was merely hidden by the dark storm, he could not tell. But no matter. Baal was awake and present. As the four priests set the ark on the stone foundation prepared for it, the thunder rolled.

Libni recognized the silver-haired commander, Joshua, following behind the ark, leading the long train of white-robed attendants. He took a place in the honor guard, he and the trumpet-bearing duo on the right of the ark, the four ark bearers on the left, all at a safe distance from the blue-draped chest. Ten abreast, the white-clad ranks of Levi continued sweeping through the aisle, forming neat blocks, clan by clan behind the ark and the smoldering altar. When the procession was finished, a sea of white completely filled the hollow between Mount Ebal and Mount Gerizim.

The priests lifted their silver trumpets again in a clarion call renouncing the storm. And the voice of the storm god answered with a crashing roar. Surely, the thunderclap was Baal's signal to take up boulders. Libni gestured to Talmai and watched the order pass to the commanders and on from bunker to bunker to all eighty-two Anakim warriors. They understood the importance of launching a perfect storm, the deadly hail of rock and earth blasting down both peaks simultaneously. Libni watched the giants creep to the ridge by squads. He watched them crouch beside the huge stockpiles of boulders, energized and eager for his command, each one selecting, then shouldering his first projectile.

Then the piercing trumpet blasts ceased. There was a breath-clutching silence. The priests slipped the blue coverings from the ark. Even in the muted light of this dismal day, the thing glinted gloriously, great golden wings of mystical creatures arching protectively over the gilded chest.

Libni smirked. *Not protective enough for a hail of rock.*

As the Anakim king watched, the luminescence of the shimmering gold seemed to distill and rise, a brilliant star shining just above the wingtips of those gilded creatures. Talmai gasped as if strangling hands seized this throat. He caught the eyes of his king and his lips formed words, but whatever he said was rendered incomprehensible by an ominous wailing of the wind.

Libni returned his attention to the valley below. The stage was set for a dignified ceremony, but Baal's crashing thunder continued like the sound of drums in battle. Oddly, there was still no rain.

Joshua raised his hands and cried out, "Come up, all you tribes of Israel. Proclaim the blessings and curses of the covenant. Shout aloud and let the winds of Canaan carry the sound throughout the land." The howling command was louder than Baal's rumbling storm.

As the two groups of Israelite tribes trudged up the slopes of the two mountains and found their places, electrical charges sizzled over the rocks. The air was potent with the power of Yahweh. Rumors flew in Canaanite courts about this recital of the blessings and curses. Many feared a powerful incantation. But more than one spy reported a boring recitals of laws.

The Anakim king did not foresee a boring recital. Even if he had not been planning this attack, the gods were obviously present. The recital must be stopped;

but for the first time Libni questioned which god was going to win the battle. One way or another, this would not be an average day in Canaan.

He gave Talmai a stern look and a nod, clearly communicating the command to prepare to launch. He watched his second in command signal the lines of giants at each summit. He watched as eighty-two Anakim warriors raised the boulders from their shoulders, faces tense, muscles taut in preparation to hurl their missiles. Talmai looked to his king for the verbal command, "Now!" But Libni's throat clutched. He crouched paralyzed in his lookout, unable to force even the twitch of a muscle. The back of his neck tingled. The hair on his arms stood on end as sheets of blue flame raced along the ground from mountain peak to base. The slopes of both mountains shimmered with a living, moving light of sapphire-blue, but the ranks of Israelites massed on the far slopes of the mountains seemed not to notice anything at all. As the high priest invoked the presence of Yahweh, the glory light above the ark increased seven-fold. Fiery flashings sizzled around the giants and the rocks in their stockpiles luminesced fiery red with heat.

Libni's heart raged at Yahweh, but his body remained fixed. He could only watch as his Anakim giants began fumbling and dropping boulders too hot to handle. When Sheshai's club burst into flame, he flung it away crying, "My Ets. My poor Ets." He was the first to break from the line and race down the mountain wailing, "Oooh, my ets! Sheshai cannot save you." The club rolled and tumbled after its master, igniting a trail of flaming brush in its wake. One by one, Libni's entire troop abandoned their positions and followed.

The king lurched as a jolt of tingling power shuddered through his frame, releasing his voice and body, but there was no appropriate command left to give. Sick to his stomach, he watched the first muster of an Anakim army in forty years slipping and sliding in their haste to scuttle away from the presence of Yahweh. Suddenly, as eighty-two formidable giants bolted from the ridge, the fiery-hot stockpiles of boulders dislodged with a great rumble, merged with the very earth of the mountain itself, and began to flow down both mountains in burning rivers of molten rock. With great bounds and staggering leaps, Libni joined his pack, and the flaming avalanche followed the Anakim all the way to the rugged terrain of the northern wilderness.

They did not see how the glory light above the ark winked. They missed the unforgettable moment when the sky cleared and sunlight shimmered on the jeweled breastplate of Yahweh's high priest. They did not notice the atmosphere growing quiet and still as if listening to the combined voices of thousands of Levites reciting the first curse.

The man who carves an image or casts an idol, though he worships in secret, brings down a curse on his own head. Such a god, crafted by the hand of man, is detestable to Yahweh.

They did not see the light of the Presence pulsing in radiant joy as the tribes on the slopes of Ebal responded with a resounding "Amen." The Anakim were far from the valley by then, and the sound at that distance was indistinguishable from thunder.

EPILOGUE

Acsah

Happily exhausted, the Calebite clan gathered in a circle around a bright fire for their evening meal. They divided the remnants of the young bullock left over from the feast. Not a crumb of the Omer loaves remained, but the women served savory bean paste and barley flat bread along with the last of the meat and everyone ate their fill. Afterwards, Acsah passed a platter of honey cakes she had made. "A reminder of the manna that sustained us throughout the wilderness wanderings," she said.

Abihail laughed as she pulled out a large basket. "You share a memory of Yahweh's sweet provision in the past—and I bring a foretaste of his sweet provision going forward. The most perfect of the early figs are stored back at Gilgal as firstfruits for the autumn festival, but the children and I gathered figs aplenty to share tonight."

"My two daughters provide me with the sweetest pleasure." Caleb's broad smile embraced them both.

As Abihail moved around the circle, serving her adopted family, her dimples flashed and her eyes crinkled with happiness. But, watching her, Acsah felt a stab of guilt mingled with pity. How meager these smiles, compared to the happiness Abihail enjoyed when the counting of the Omer began. Memories flooded her mind—the love glances between Abihail and Eliab as they celebrated Passover. The shining admiration as Abihail watched Eliab tell his victory tale around the campfire the night Jericho fell. The shyly joyful expression when Abihail admitted to the child growing within her. *Life. Love. Fragile gifts. Beautiful and brief as meadow flowers. Enjoy them while you have them.*

Almost as if he had heard Acsah's thoughts, Caleb mused, "On this high day in the history of our people, my heart aches for those who should be here, but are not."

Acsah toyed with her anklet of silver and turquoise, her connection to Egypt and the mother she never met. *Celebrations like this strengthened and deepened the bonds of family affection, especially bonds reaching back to loved ones lost.*

She exchanged melancholy smiles with Caleb. "Oh Abba, the sorrows of the past year help me understand the pain you have been living with my whole lifetime. You lost parents, brothers, and wives, one by one in the wilderness. I never knew most of them. But I know how much I miss the dear ones who died in the plague and that horrid rebellion in the Valley of Acacias—and now we must add those who were slain at Ai." She took a deep breath. "I wish I could speak face to face with Yahweh as Moses did. I would question him about all the death. I would like to ask with all respect, 'What are you doing, God? We have a covenant here.'"

Maacah looked at her with misty eyes. "I would give everything I own to have my husband here today, but who are we to question the ways of the Holy One of Israel?"

Ephah wiped away a tear. "I understand why Achor and his family had to die. They basically spat in the face of God. Their greed ripped a hole in the covenant of protection over all our people." She clutched her newborn son to her breast and her voice broke. "But this child will never know his father. I cannot understand God's purpose in letting thirty-six innocent men die at Ai."

Caleb pulled his two concubines close and it felt like an affectionate hug to Acsah as well. For the first time, she did not resent these widows. She could see their love meant much to her father. And he filled a huge void for them. God might not provide answers, but he provided belonging.

The warmth of it all diffused through her body. She slipped an arm around Abihail's shoulder. At the same time she saw Maacah clasp hands with her father. One by one, each member of the circle reached out to touch the ones closest to them. There had been loss, there was a cloud of unanswered questions, but the close circle provided warmth even against the chill of death.

Then a wisp of sound drifted over the family like a smoky tendril of incense. Barely audible, the gentle voice infused the atmosphere with sacred sweetness. "In God's hands, even the vilest evil works for good." No one turned to look, for all recognized the voice of Abihail.

"I do not know what other good will come of our recent troubles," Abihail went on, "but this evening I enjoy a profound peace beyond anything I ever knew before. Following the Baal-Peor rebellion and plague, I saw how my greed for the gifts of the Midianite women added to the undoing of Israel—even for my own beloved Eliab. In the days following that, I was trapped in a terrible fear of God's wrath. I feared I would never be righteous enough to meet the demands of the covenant. Even after Eliab and I burned those things, I could not completely shake that sense of guilt." She paused, searching for words. "Strangely, it was Achor who opened my eyes to God's mercy."

Acsah felt a chilling shiver shake the group. Three women here lost their husbands because of that man, including Abihail herself. One could hardly bear to allow his name to enter the mind, let alone say it aloud. Had any other man brought such trouble on Israel? Yet this precious girl, a victim of his greed, was telling how he helped her.

"Achor was half-mad with guilt the night before the stoning." Abihail's voice trembled as she continued. "Jamin brought him to my tent reeling like a drunken man. His speech was slurred and confused. I did not understand why at the time. At first I thought he was intoxicated, but there was no reek of strong drink on his breath. Then I supposed he was overcome by the death of his son. Little did I guess that Achor had chosen the alluring cup, the intoxicating wine of Jericho's luxuries. He thrashed about on his bed in troubled sleep, mumbling, 'The city . . . the city burns . . . I cannot find my way out . . .'

"I spent the night laying cool, wet cloths on his forehead, believing he was suffering the delirium of raging fever. About dawn, he whispered, 'O Yahweh, God of Israel, show me the way. I want to return to you.' And then he slipped into a peaceful sleep.

"I was caught up in my own grief at the time and did not understand. But I have had much time to reflect on this in the past few weeks. I, too, sipped from the seductive cup of unfaithfulness to the covenant. I would have thrown it all away to keep Eliab.

"I believe Achor truly joined in covenant with God for the first time on the day of his death. Only a good and loving God could bring such peace to a man about to be executed. I have found that same deep, healing peace. This afternoon, the curses, as well as the blessings, ran like fire through my bones. For the first time I had absolutely no fear."

"No fear," Othniel snorted a half laugh.

Acsah sat up, startled. She along with most of the family turned to see if it really was her quiet cousin who spoke. Not only was it out of character for Othniel to call attention to himself, but the words were startlingly incongruous with the sweet sincerity of Abihail's confession of faith.

Othniel held up a hand. "Sorry about the laugh," he said. "Abihail's story is far different from mine. A powerful statement of how God turned her Valley of Achor into a Door of Hope." [35] He paused. He didn't shake back his hair and turn his face to the sky but looked at the faces around the fire one by one before continuing. "Her words describe my experience at the ceremony today more precisely than I ever could have myself.

"I have had . . . uh . . . "

Othniel began stammering for words and Acsah expected the usual blush and hair-flinging habit to take over. Surprisingly, he forged on with new confidence.

"Ever since we crossed the river, I have had dreams . . . troubling dreams . . . always of an odious pale-skinned giant. The dreams often leave me edgy, feeling as if our people are being watched—and not by friendly eyes. Those premonitions . . . uh . . . fears have been stronger than ever here in this valley . . . exceptionally oppressive this morning. I half expected that giant to come leaping over the mountain, knocking down our monument and attacking us." He dropped his head and shook it slowly back and forth. "It sounds crazy doesn't it?"

"Maybe not," Caleb said softly.

Othniel raised his head, thanking Caleb with a lift of his brows, and continued. "As we finished our feast, the need to pray for relief totally swallowed my sense of thankfulness. Then as I stood in my place on the slope of Gerizim and the Levites began reciting the blessings and curses, I felt the words run like fire through my bones, as Abihail expressed it—and there was no more fear." He caught Abihail's eyes and chuckled. "Thanks for the words. That sensation was so . . . uh . . . intense. I could not find a better way to describe it."

The fire dwindled to a heap of coals brightened by an occasional leaping flame. Insects chirped in the rustling grasses, stars multiplied in the sky above the family, and a gentle breeze caressed their faces like the breath of God. Acsah turned her face toward it. Their family might be confused at times, they might be wounded, but they knew they were loved. Undoubtedly, conflict with the evil of Canaan would assault them again, but for this moment, for this brief interlude at Shechem, they breathed the rarified air of heaven.

LIST OF CHARACTERS

Bold print identifies the seven primary characters of the Gilgal series, grouped by families. Hebrew meanings are in (parentheses). Names in regular print are actual biblical characters. Names in *italics* are fictional or unnamed biblical characters whom I have named.

GODS

Yahweh (YHWH)   The Holy Name of God in Hebrew; the
                              exact pronunciation is unknown –
                              some say it is the sound of breath
                              itself, the sound of life
Asherah   Canaan's goddess of fertility and war
Baal (Lord, or master)   The Canaanite storm god, controlling
                              fertility of the land through
                              precipitation and drought

ISRAELITES

The Tribe of Judah, the Royal Tribe

Achor (trouble)   Formal name, Achan; an elder in Judah

<u>Achor/Achan's Family</u>

Mara (bitter)	Achor's wife
Jamin (right hand)	Achor's eldest son
Hattil (doubtful)	Daughter-in-law, Jamin's wife
Shelomith (peaceful)	Jamin's daughter
Eliada (known by God)	Jamin's son
Eliab (God is my father)	Achor's younger son
Abihail (father of strength)	Daughter-in-law, Eliab's wife, Acsah's dearest childhood friend
Acsah (anklet, adorned)	Youngest child and only daughter of Caleb, the legendary hero of Judah

Acsah's Family

Caleb (dog) [1]	Acsah's 80-year-old father, one of the two faithful spies (along with Joshua) forty years earlier
Iru (watch)	Caleb's eldest son (1 Chronicles 4:15)
Naam (pleasant, sweet)	Caleb's third son (1 Chronicles 4:15)
Mushi (yielding)	Naam's son, Acsah's nephew
Rebekah (captivating)	Naam's daughter, Acsah's niece
Ephah (gloom)	Caleb's concubine (1Chronicles 2:46)
Maacah (oppression, or depression)	Caleb's concubine (1 Chronicles 2:48)
Hodesh (new moon)	Midianite captives, sisters rescued by
Hogluh (partridge)	Caleb in the Midianite War
Othniel (lion of God)	Future hero-judge of Israel; Caleb's nephew

Othniel's Family

Sarah (princess)	Othniel's widowed mother
Seraiah (Yahweh is ruler)	Othniel's younger brother

---

[1] Caleb appears in two genealogies which attach him to two different sets of names. But Joshua 15:13-19 ties the two together as one man, telling the story of Caleb, descendant of Jephunneh, who is also father of Acsah. Some commentators believe Caleb was a foreigner, a Kenizzite from the family of Esau. His name, meaning dog, indicates he may have been an outcast. At some point he was adopted into the family of Judah as a full-fledged member of the tribe. It is interesting to note that the tribe of Judah also adopted the Canaanite Rahab, and later the Moabite Ruth. Perhaps the infusion of these immigrants of extraordinary faith is what made Judah a much stronger kingdom spiritually when centuries later the twelve tribes split into two kingdoms, Israel and Judah.

Salmon (garment, to cover or enclose)

Prince of Judah; direct ancestor of King David and Jesus

Salmon's Family

Abijah (my father is Yahweh) Salmon's widowed mother
Ada (beauty) Salmon's young sister

The Tribe of Ephraim

Joshua (savior, or whose help is Yahweh)

75-year-old military commander of Israel

Jathniel (gift of God)

One of the two spies (with Salmon) sent across the river Jordan to scout Jericho

The Tribe of Levi

Eleazar (God has helped) High priest; son of Moses' brother Aaron
Phinehas (mouth of brass) Future high priest; eldest son of Eleazar, grandson of Aaron

Jonathan (gift of Yahweh) Levite scribe; first cousin of Phinehas, grandson of Moses

Zerahiah (Yahweh has risen) Overseer of the inscriptions on the monument at Shechem

CANAANITES

Rahab (wide, or fierce)

The harlot of Jericho who rescued the Israelite spies

Rahab's Family

Shua (prosperity) Rahab's grandmother
Jokshan (fowler) Rahab's father
Keziah (cassia, a spice) Rahab's mother
Helek (portion) Rahab's older brother
Jerusha (possessed) Helek's wife
Azuba (forsaken) Helek's daughter
Zetham (olive) Rahab's younger brother
Naarah (a maiden) Zetham's wife
Jared (descent) Zethem's son
Atarah (a crown) Zethem's daughter

The Kings of Canaan, and Their Royal Courts

Adoni-Zedek (Lord of Righteousness)	King of Jebus/Jerusalem
Birsha (son of godlessness)	King of Ai
Jabin (discerning)	King of Hazor, northern Canaan (Joshua 11)
Nahari (snorter)	King of Jericho
Ahuzzath	King Nahari's former captain, now the decomposing head on Jericho's wall
Shinab (splendor of the father)	Captain of the King's guard, Jericho
Koz (thorn)	High priest of Baal at Jebus
Yad Rashi (right hand)	The second-in-command in a Canaanite court

The Southern Alliance, Under Adoni-Zedek (as listed in Joshua 10:3)

Hoham (whom Jehovah impels)	King of Hebron
Piram (like a wild ass)	King of Jarmuth
Japhia (splendid)	King of Lachish
Debir (a sanctuary)	King of Eglon
Labayu	Leader of marauding Hivites in the Valley of Shechem (not mentioned in the Bible, but found in the Armana letters)

The Federation of Gibeon

Ibzan (illustrious)	Highest of the high elders, of Kiriath-Baal
Pallu (distinguished)	Commander of combined army, of Gibeon
Likhi (learned)	Overseer of commerce, of Beeroth
Meshullam (friend)	Historian, philosopher-poet, of Kephirah
Peleth (swiftness)	A Federation spy/scout
Irad (fleet)	A Federation spy/scout

Anakim—Descendants of the Giant, Anak

Libni (white)	King of the Anakim
Ahiman (brother of the right hand)	Three Anakim brothers, warriors of renown (mentioned in Judges 1:10)
Sheshai (noble)	
Talmai (bold)	

ENDNOTES

[1] Quoted in this section: Exodus 15:11, 17–18, from the song of Moses and Miriam.

[2] Psalm 128:1–2, author paraphrase.

[3] The Passover/Exodus story, Exodus 7–12.

[4] From Joshua 5:13–15, 6:1–5.

[5] Joshua 1:3–4 (NIV).

[6] Joshua 6, the fall of Jericho.

[7] God gave a very specific warning that taking any of the "devoted" spoils would bring trouble on the entire people of Israel, Joshua 6:18. For whatever reason, Achan disobeyed, Joshua 7:1.

[8] Leviticus 17:11.

[9] Laws regarding corpse contamination, Numbers 19.

[10] Joshua 6:26.

[11] Joshua 7:2.

[12] Joshua 7:3.

[13] Chapter 9 is based on Joshua 7.

[14] Leviticus 4:13–21, sacrificial ritual for the sin of the entire congregation.

[15] Deuteronomy 6:4–5.

[16] The second battle of Ai, Joshua 8:1–29.

[17] This prayer is based on the promise given in Numbers 10:9.

[18] Deuteronomy 7:2, author paraphrase.

[19] Deuteronomy 23:3, 7.

[20] Deuteronomy 23:3–4.

21 Leviticus 18:28.

22 Caleb's argument is based on Numbers 14–16.

23 Genesis 28:14 (NIV).

24 Genesis 28:15 (NIV).

25 This ceremony was commanded by Moses in Deuteronomy 11:29–30 and fulfilled in Joshua 8:30–35.

26 That Joseph was buried in Shechem is mentioned in Joshua 24:32. We are not told when it happened.

27 Genesis 34:30 (NIV).

28 Deuteronomy 6:4–5 (WEB).

29 Deuteronomy 6:6–9 (NIV).

30 Deuteronomy 11:13–17 (NIV).

31 Deuteronomy 11:18, 20 (GNT).

32 Genesis 12:3b (NIV).

33 Stealing the birthright, Genesis 27; wrestling with God, Genesis 32–33; the massacre at Shechem, Genesis 34.

34 Genesis 34:30, author paraphrase.

35 Allusion to Hosea 2:15.

THE
STONES OF GILGAL
SAGA

Step into an ancient world and brace yourself for a plunge into the chilling conflict between a good God and the evil forces that hold his creation hostage. As prophets, priests, and kings jostle for power and cultures collide, your heart will be touched by the sorrows and chilled by the fears of one brave Canaanite girl and six young Israelites. As they claim their long-lost inheritance and begin carving out a new life in the Land of Promise, their faith is shaken by challenges beyond anything they could ever have imagined. Their names have all but disappeared, pebbles cast long ago into the pool of history, but the ripples of their lives extend to eternity. *The Stones of Gilgal* saga pulls these seven out of the murky water of ancient Scripture for a second look.

- Book One, *Balaam's Curse*, explores one of many Old Testament tales of terror. The seductive plotting, the bloody civil war, the total annihilation of five Midianite kingdoms, and the impaling of a princess are, indeed, cringe-worthy biblical episodes, but they are part of the war story of the universe, balanced by glimpses of a love greater than the darkness.

- Book Two, *A River to Cross,* is a fresh telling of the crossing of the Jordan, plunging into the raging torrent of the river and the perils of life in the city of Jericho. The powers of darkness are strong, but no contest at all for Yahweh. In an astonishing display of glory, the God of Israel announces to all Canaan that a new day is coming.

- Book Three, *Trouble in the Ruins,* see summary on back of book.

- Book Four, *The Pursuit of Zedek,* contrasts the Federation of Gibeon with the ruthless kingdoms of Adonai-Zedek and his cohorts. Experience a day of battle so stupendous and of such import that it brought the sun to a halt while Joshua finished his mission.

- Book Five, Acsah and Othniel's love story and his emergence as a young hero, defeating the last of the Anakim giants.

- Book Six, Othniel saves the young nation of Israel from oppression as the first of its hero-judges. This last book in the series will unveil the final destiny of each character, shaped through small choices over a lifetime.

The Stones of Gilgal novels take you through some of the goriest tales of Scripture along the path toward some of its most glorious miracles. If those years seem confusing and chaotic for Bible readers, imagine how difficult it must have been to live them. At the crossing of the Jordan, Yahweh told the people to build a *gilgal,* Hebrew for circle. In the midst of the miracle, each of the twelve tribes chose one stone from the dry riverbed for that circle. The ensuing years were fraught with more peril than anyone could have imagined, but the stones of Gilgal remained through it all as a solid reminder that their God was powerful and real.

EXCERPT FROM

THE STONES OF GILGAL
BOOK FOUR

THE PURSUIT OF ZEDEK

Grandmother Shua hailed the day with a rattling of cooking utensils and happy mutterings. The comforting sounds evoking dreams of happy days, of early childhood safe with her parents and her grandmother, gradually broke through Rahab's sleepy haze. Then abruptly, she realized who she was and where she was. Those sounds filtered through the black goatskin walls of a rickety lean-to in the refugee camp. "I'm awake, Grandmother," she called, leaping out of bed and chiding herself for sleeping so long into the morning. "I will be out to help in a moment."

She pushed her bedroll into the corner. Even with it stashed away for the day, the temporary shelter barely afforded room to turn around, but she would not allow herself to complain. She wiggled her toes on the wool rug covering the dirt floor. She would be thankful for that. Although the carpets and bedding did not compare in comfort to the soft linens at the inn, how much better to endure scratchy homespun than fear-filled days swathed in the luxuries of Jericho.

She threw back the door covering as soon as she was dressed. The sun was bright on the meadow, and the currents of morning air blew fresh breath into the stale interior. She closed her eyes, savoring a deep breath. The next gust carried a lilting melody in baritone. The sound was more precious than she cared to admit. She slipped back into the shadows to listen and her heart soared.

Prince Salmon had not been by to check on the refugee camp since Israel returned from Shechem, and for the first time she realized how dreary the days when he didn't come. She missed him as one misses the sun on a gloomy day, not aware of being out of sorts until a bright shaft of sunlight pierces the clouds and all is right again—more than all right. Salmon was singing her song. The song from the day he led her out of Jericho.

Jericho.

The name spoiled this taste of joy and churned in her stomach with bitter reality. The delight of hearing a small bit of herself on Salmon's lips was like a honeyed draft of medicine. Wildly sweet on her tongue, it slid down her throat with an undeniably acerbic aftertaste. She was a foreigner—a defiled foreigner—in a holy camp.

The bitter dose diffused through every part of her and cleared her vision. She could no longer deny that Salmon stirred her heart as no other man before, but his sunshine was in no way hers to enjoy. She was a child of the shadows who could only contaminate the pure light of his soul. Judah's prince made his rounds to see to the needs of refugees he helped save, performing his righteous duty to care for the alien and disadvantaged. She steeled herself against any creeping hope of a special bond. His concern for her sprang from pity.

She pressed farther back into the tent, still as a stone. Grandmother could answer his questions very well. She could not bear to see him right now.

"Greetings Grandmother Shua . . ." The warm, mellow voice was less than a bowshot away from her tent now and it tingled through Rahab delightfully. *Surely this pleasure was not a sin. One need not possess a rose to savor its fragrance.*

"Are you rested and resettled after our pilgrimage?" he was asking.

"We are," Grandmother answered. "Quite easily, I must say. Having so few possessions simplifies our lives immeasurably."

"Unfortunately, my news may complicate your lives." Salmon's laugh was like liquid sunshine. "Is Rahab around? This concerns her as well. I want to announce it to both of you at the same time."

"She's right there. In the tent behind you. She must not have heard you or I'm certain she would have popped out to greet you. Nothing makes her happier than seeing her rescuer. Always a-humming and a-singing after one of your visits. Yes, she is."

Rahab cringed at her grandmother's disclosures, but Salmon chuckled. "And I cannot get her tunes out of—"

"Did I hear someone, Grandmother?" Rahab fought the wave of panic and struggled to control the quaver in her voice. "Who is here so early?"

"Come on out, my dear," Shua answered, her tone overly sweet. "It is Prince Salmon. He has news he wants to share with both of us."

Rahab masked her feelings with a face appropriate for a routine business call. She determined not to look into Salmon's eyes lest hers give away her heart, but when she ducked under the draped doorway flap into the sunshine, Salmon's beautiful eyes were the one thing she could not avoid. She froze, half in, half out of the tent.

She was still squinting into the light, wondering vaguely which was brighter, the morning or the man, when she realized he had already begun explaining the purpose of his visit.

" . . filling the empty places left by the family of Achor." His speech was punctuated with animated gestures. "Tents for your parents and your brothers are still in the construction process, but yesterday, Maacah and Ephah finished making one for you and Shua to share. Caleb set it up this morning." His eyes sparkled like an excited child. "It is long past time to replace these shabby dwellings. I inspected your new home just now and am quite satisfied that it is a fine tent, well worthy of you."

New tent . . .? Rahab struggled to grasp Salmon's meaning as she drowned in his gaze. She took her grandmother's arm lest she float away on a tide of her own emotions.

"Only last night, the elders of Judah voted unanimously to invite you to fill one of the tent spaces left by the families of Achor and Jamin. Helek's family will fill the other. Caleb supported this from the beginning, as did I, but there were several who had reservations based on their interpretation of the law. Prior to last night, they would not budge, but all doubts vaporized when Joshua came to meet with us. Like Caleb, he insisted the legal objections some had raised missed the spirit of the law. So, it is settled. All that remains is for you to pack up your things and move in."

"Move . . . into Judah," the old woman whispered. "This is so much more than we deserve."

"Life in Israel is not about what we deserve, but about who we worship and obey."

Life in Israel . . . who we worship . . . The message penetrated the fog in Rahab's mind, but she could find no words. *Was it possible that Israel's God would not only save her from the pit of Jericho, but welcome her into the fellowship of his holy people?*

Salmon laughed. "Have you nothing to say, Rahab? I thought you would be happy for the move."

"Move into Judah?" she whispered at last. "My family? Me?" The ice of her self-loathing began to crack under the warmth of love and acceptance in Salmon's eyes.

"You will be a blessing to us. Particularly those who live within earshot of your voice—the woman who is always 'a-humming and a-singing' as your grandmother tells it." His eyes were so stunningly luminous Rahab forgot to breathe. "I have never heard anything more beautiful than your singing, Rahab."

Beautiful . . . singing. His words and all rational thought were reduced to a soaring, wordless melody.

Shua coughed. "You said Joshua himself met with your council last night? I am aghast. Why would the council ask Joshua to leave his important duties for the likes of us?"

"Actually, we did not ask him. He asked me. He heard about the conflicting opinions. Most likely from Caleb." The corners of Salmon's eyes crinkled as with a pleasant joke. "He made certain everyone on the council knew that you, Shua, have been a believer for forty years. You wanted to join our people when he first met you. It is not your fault that Israel kept you waiting through all our years of wandering. And Rahab—" A full grin flashed in place of his usual half smile. "You demonstrated faith and courage beyond our most inspiring campfire stories. I predict you will become a legend in Israel."

Salmon's warm-as-sunlight laugh melted more of the shards of ice encasing Rahab's heart. Weak as water, she grabbed her grandmother's arm for stability.

"All the same," Shua declared, "I am beyond humbled to hear that Joshua came to our defense. I am sure he has more important duties."

"He has many important duties, of course, but our covenant law gives highest priority to the alien, the poor, and those without family support." Salmon beamed. "I understand that now as never before—Oh!" his eyes suddenly widened, rounder and even more luminous than before.

"I nearly forgot to tell you the other glad news. The ancient prophecies of blessing the nations of the world are coming true. Joshua would have met with our council three days ago, but no sooner had we returned to Gilgal than a group of travel-worn guests arrived. They told us how the truth of Yahweh shines from Gilgal like beams of the rising sun. News of his mighty power led them here inquiring after our God. Our meeting with that delegation of Hivites will always remain a highlight of my life."

"Hivites? From nearby Gibeon? Or Labayu's village in the valley of Shechem?"

"Not from anywhere nearby at all." Salmon dropped his voice to a warm, confidential tone. "The delegation came from far beyond the northern mountains. They staggered into camp three days ago. The sole object of their quest was to learn more about Yahweh."

"But how would a distant people . . .?" Rahab's senses were fully earthbound now.

"Much like you and your family, Rahab. They heard the story of our deliverance from Egyptian slavery decades ago. More recently they heard of our victories over King Sihon and King Og. They sent this delegation to see if the report was true. When they passed through the territory of King Jabin in the north, they learned that Yahweh stopped the flooded Jordan River for us and flattened the famed walls of Jericho. We elders showed them the *Gilgal*. We showed them the ruins of Jericho. And they were convinced of the superiority of our God and asked to cut covenant with us."

"Do you cut covenant in the same manner we do?" Rahab asked. "*May the gods cut us in pieces if we ever break these vows.* There is no breaking such a covenant. Are you certain you wish to ratify a covenant before learning exactly which Hivites these people are?"

"The covenant is cut and ratified. As representatives of our two peoples, Joshua and their high elder walked between the parts of a sacrificed bullock and made the solemn covenant vows yesterday morning. We roasted the bullock and all twelve of our princes as well as the head elders of our clans ratified the covenant by sharing the meal with them. We filled their packs with provisions, gave them new clothing and sandals to replace those worn out from their long journey, and sent them on their way rejoicing. Our people are bound forever in a treaty of peace."

"I pray that this union proves to be a blessing, not a curse," Shua whispered after a stunned pause.

A feeling of sickness churned miserably in Rahab's stomach while Salmon happily rambled on.

"Oh, they have proved a blessing already—especially to you. When the elders of Judah considered how foreign nations were drawn to learn of our God, much misunderstanding of God's laws and statutes was cleared away. It helped bring about the unanimous decision of our council last night regarding Canaanites moving into Judah. At last, the opposing elders had to concede that Yahweh's deepest desire is for all people to come to him. His covenant is for all except those who stubbornly resist his love. Joshua's arguments applied that blessing specifically to you."

Shua's eyes flicked warily from Salmon to the dim outline of the northern mountains. "We have heard that there are Hivites beyond those mountains, but how do you know these men are not really from the cities of Canaan?"

"If you had seen the state of their clothing, you would not ask. They invited us to taste their bread as another excellent proof of their long journey," Salmon answered confidently. "It came hot from their ovens the day they left but was moldered and dry."

"You ate their moldy bread . . .?"

Salmon laughed. "Actually no. We merely passed a sample from hand to hand. We did not need a taste test to know it was not baked recently in nearby ovens."

"Mmmm." Deepening doubt shadowed grandmother's countenance. "Have you considered the possibility of a trick?"

"This was real. These people read the words on our monument as they passed by. They repeated those words back to us. They begged us to prepare a scroll of the entire law for their people. They will send an envoy to receive it at this same time next year. They truly want to learn more of the ways of Yahweh." Salmon's half grin pulled up the corner of his mouth.

Rahab did not want to be the one to douse that beloved smile.

The author hopes you enjoyed this preview.
To order or for more information go to
www.stonesofgilgal.com or www.amazon.com/author/clsmith

CONTACT INFORMATION

MOUNTAIN VIEW PRESS

To order additional copies of this book, please visit
www.mountainviewpress.com
Also available on Amazon.com and BarnesandNoble.com
Or by calling toll free (855) 946-2555

CPSIA information can be obtained
at www.ICGtesting.com
Printed in the USA
FSHW011829310819
61487FS